Fitz The Filibuster

By

George Manville Fenn

Fitz The Filibuster
by George Manville Fenn

ISBN: 978-93-59955-51-3
Published by

DOUBLE 9 BOOKS

2/13-B, Ansari Road
Daryaganj, New Delhi – 110002
info@double9books.com
www.double9books.com
Tel. 011-40042856

ABOUT THE AUTHOR

George Manville Fenn was a very productive author of novels, a writer, an editor, and an educator from England. He was born on January 3, 1831, in Pimlico, London. He mostly learned on his own; he taught himself Italian, French, and German. During the years 1851–1854, he went to Battersea Training College for Teachers and then became the head of a state school in Alford, Lincolnshire. In the early 1850s, Fenn started to write short stories and pieces for newspapers and magazines. The Old Forest Ranger, his first book, came out in 1856. Afterward, he wrote more than 100 books, many of them for teenagers and young adults. He was one of the most famous writers of his time, and his books were well-liked and read by many people. He also worked as a reporter and writer for Fenn. Among the newspapers and magazines, he worked for was The Boy's Own Paper, which he ran from 1866 to 1874. He worked hard to make children's books better and was a strong supporter of education and reading. The Englishman Fenn passed away on August 26, 1909, in Isleworth.

CONTENTS

Chapter One
Aboard a gunboat

"Well, Mr Burnett, what is it?"

"Beg pardon, sir."

"Now, my good boy, have I not told you always to speak out in a sharp, business-like way? How in the world do you expect to get on in your profession and become a smart officer, one who can give orders promptly to his men, if you begin in that stammering, hesitating style? Here, I'm busy; what do you want?"

"I beg pardon, sir, I—"

"Will—you—speak—out!"

"Yes, sir; Mr Storks is going off to-night with an armed boat's crew—"

"Thank you, Mr Burnett, I am much obliged; but allow me to tell you that your news is very stale, for I was perfectly aware of that fact, and gave the orders to Mr Storks myself."

"Yes, sir; of course, sir; but—"

"My good boy, what do you want?"

"To go with them, sir."

"Oh! Then why didn't you say so at first?"

"I didn't know how you'd take it, sir."

"Then you know now: very badly. No; the boat's going on important business, and I don't want her packed full of useless boys. What good do you expect you could do there?"

"Learn my profession, sir."

"Oh! Ah! H'm! Well—that's smart. Yes, I like that, Mr Burnett, much better. Well, I don't know what to say. There's no danger. Perhaps you will be away all the night and get no sleep."

"Shouldn't mind that, sir. Mr Storks said that he wouldn't mind."

"Doesn't matter whether Mr Storks minds or not. Well—yes; you may go. There, there, no thanks; and—er—and—er—don't take any notice, Mr

Burnett; I am a little irritable this evening—maddening toothache, and that sort of thing. Don't get into mischief. That'll do."

Commander Glossop, R.N., generally known as Captain of H.M. Gunboat *Tonans*, on special duty from the Channel Squadron, went below to his cabin, and Fitzgerald Burnett—Fitz for short—midshipman, seemed suddenly to have grown an inch taller, and comparatively stouter, as he seemed to swell out with satisfaction, while his keen grey eyes literally sparkled as he looked all a boy.

"Thought he was going to snap my head off," he mattered, as he began to walk up and down, noticing sundry little preparations that were in progress in connection with one of the quarter-boats, in which, as she swung from the davits, a couple of the smart, barefooted sailors, whose toes looked very pink in the chill air, were overhauling and re-arranging oars, and the little mast, yard and sail, none of which needed touching, for everything was already in naval apple-pie order.

Fitz Burnett ended his walk by stopping and looking on.

"Going along with us, sir?" said one of the sailors.

"Yes," said the lad shortly, and sharply enough to have satisfied his superior if he had overheard.

"That's right, sir," said the man, so earnestly that the boy looked pleased.

"Know where we are going, sir?" the other man ventured to ask.

"Is it likely?" was the reply; "and if I did know do you suppose that I would tell you?"

"No, sir, of course not. But it's going to be something desperate, sir, because we have got to take all our tools."

"Ah, you'll see soon enough," said the boy, and full of the importance of being one in some expedition that was to break the monotony of the everyday routine, as well as to avoid further questioning, and any approach to familiarity on the part of the men, Fitz continued his walk, to come in contact directly after with another superior officer in the shape of the lieutenant.

"Hullo, Mr Burnett! So you are to go with us to-night, I hear."

"Yes, sir," cried the boy eagerly. "Would you mind telling me what we are going to do?"

"Then you don't know?"

"No, sir."

"Then why did you ask the captain to let you go?"

"I wanted to be there, sir. Armed boat's crew going off! It sounded so exciting."

"I don't think that you will find much excitement, Mr Burnett; but wait and see. If you want more information I must refer you to the captain."

This last was accompanied by a nod and a good-humoured smile, as the officer moved away to look at the boat, but turned his head to add—

"Better put on a warm jacket; I dare say we shall have a cold night's work."

"I don't care," said the boy to himself. "Anything for a change. I do get so tired of this humdrum steaming here and steaming there, and going into port to fill up the coal-bunkers. Being at sea isn't half so jolly as I used to think it was, and it is so cold. Wish we could get orders to sail to one of those beautiful countries in the East Indies, or to South America—anywhere away from these fogs and rains. Why, we haven't seen the sun for a week."

He went forward, to rest his arms on the bulwark and look out to sea. The sight was not tempting. The mouth of the Mersey is not attractive on a misty day, and the nearest land aft showed like a low-down dirty cloud. Away on the horizon there was a long thick trail of smoke being left behind by some outward-bound steamer, and running his eyes along the horizon he caught sight of another being emitted from one of two huge funnels which were all that was visible of some great Atlantic steamer making for the busy port.

Nearer in there were two more vessels, one that he made out to be a brig, and that was all.

"Ugh!" ejaculated the boy. "I wish—I wish—What's the use of wishing? One never gets what one wants. Whatever are we going to do to-night? It must mean smuggling. Well, there will be something in that. Going aboard some small boat and looking at the skipper's papers, and if they are not right putting somebody on board and bringing her into port. But there won't be any excitement like one reads about in books. It's a precious dull life coming to sea."

Fitz Burnett sighed and waited, for the evening was closing in fast, and then he began to brighten in the expectation of the something fresh that was to take place that night. But knowing that it might be hours before they started, he waited—and waited—and waited.

There is an old French proverb which says, *Tout vient à point à qui sait attendre*, and this may be roughly interpreted, "Everything comes to the man who waits." Let's suppose that it comes to the boy.

Chapter Two
Bravo, Boy!

The dim evening gave place to a dark night. The *Tonans* had for some two or three hours been stealing along very slowly not far from land, and that something important was on the way was evident from the captain's movements, and the sharp look-out that was being kept up, and still more so from the fact that no lights were shown.

The gunboat's cutter had been swung out ready for lowering down at a moment's notice, the armed crew stood waiting, and one man was in the stern-sheets whose duty it was to look after the lantern, which was kept carefully shaded.

Fitz, who was the readiest of the ready, had long before noted with intense interest the fact that they showed no lights, and his interest increased when the lieutenant became so far communicative that he stood gazing out through the darkness side by side with his junior, and said softly—

"I am afraid we shall miss her, my lad. She'll steal by us in the darkness, and it will all prove to be labour in vain."

Fitz waited to hear more, but no more came, for the lieutenant moved off to join the captain.

"I wish he wouldn't be so jolly mysterious," said the midshipman to himself. "I am an officer too, and he might have said a little more."

But it was all waiting, and no farther intercourse till close upon eight bells, when Fitz, feeling regularly tired out, said to himself—

"Bother! I wish I hadn't asked leave to go. I should have been comfortably asleep by now."

He had hardly thought this when there was a quick movement behind him, and simultaneously he caught sight of a dim light off the starboard-bow. An order was given in a low tone, and with a silence and method learned on board a man-of-war, the boat's crew, followed by their officers, took their places in the cutter, and in obedience to another command the boat was lowered down, kissed the water, the hooks were withdrawn, she was pushed off, the oars fell on either side, and away they glided over the dancing waters in the direction of the distant light.

"Now we are off, Fitz," said the lieutenant eagerly, speaking almost in a whisper, but without the slightest necessity, for the light was far away.

"Yes, sir, now we are off," replied the boy, almost resentfully, and his tone suggested that he would have liked to say, Why can't you tell me where we are going? Possibly the officer took it in this light, for he continued—

"This ought to be a bit of excitement for you, Burnett. We are after a schooner bound for somewhere south, laden with contraband of war."

"War, sir?" whispered the lad excitedly.

"Well, some petty Central American squabble; and the captain has had instructions that this schooner is going to steal out of port to-night. Some one informed. We got the information yesterday."

"Contraband, sir?"

"Yes; guns and ammunition which ought not to be allowed to be shipped from an English port against a friendly state.—Give way, my men!"

The rowers responded by making their stout ashen blades bend, and the cutter went forward in jerks through the rather choppy sea.

"Then we shall take the schooner, sir?"

"Yes, my lad, if we can."

"Then that means prize-money."

"Why, Burnett, are you as avaricious as that?"

"No, sir; no, sir; I was thinking about the men."

"Oh, that's right. But don't count your chickens before they are hatched."

"No, sir."

"We mayn't be able to board that vessel, and if we do, possibly it isn't the one we want. It's fifty to one it isn't. Or it may be anything—some trading brig or another going down south."

"Of course, sir. There are so many that pass."

"At the same time it may be the one we want."

"Yes, sir."

"And then we shall be in luck."

"Yes, sir."

"They must surrender to our armed boat."

Fitz Burnett had had little experience of the sea, but none as connected with an excursion in a boat on a dark night, to board a vessel whose sailing light could be seen in the distance.

They had not gone far before the lieutenant tabooed all talking.

"Still as you can, my lads," he said. "Sound travels far over the sea, and lights are very deceptive."

The midshipman had already been thinking the same thing. He had often read of Will-o'-the-Wisps, but never seen one, and this light seemed to answer the description exactly, for there it was, dimly-seen for a few moments, then brightening, and slowly going up and down. But the great peculiarity was that now it seemed quite close at hand, now far distant, and for the life of him he could not make out that they got any nearer. He wanted to draw his companion's attention to that fact, but on turning sharply to the lieutenant as if to speak, he was met by a low "Hist!" which silenced him directly, while the men rowed steadily on for quite a quarter of an hour longer, when all at once the lieutenant uttered in an angry whisper—

"What are you doing, you clumsy scoundrel?"

For there was a sudden movement behind where they sat in the stern-sheets, as if the man in charge of the lantern had slipped, with the result that a dull gleam of light shone out for a few moments, before its guardian scuffled the piece of sail-cloth by which it had been covered, back into its place, and all was dark once more.

"Why, what were you about?" whispered the lieutenant angrily.

"Beg pardon, sir. Slipped, sir."

"Slipped! I believe you were asleep."

The man was silent.

"You were nodding off, weren't you?"

"Don't think I was, sir," was the reply.

But the man's officer was right, and the rest of the crew knew it, being ready to a man, as they afterwards did, to declare that "that there Bill Smith would caulk," as they termed taking a surreptitious nap, "even if the gunboat were going down."

"Put your backs into it, my lads," whispered the lieutenant. "Now then, with a will; but quiet, quiet!"

As he spoke the speed of the boat increased and its progress made it more unsteady, necessitating his steadying himself by gripping Fitz by the collar as he stood up, shading his eyes and keeping a sharp look-out ahead.

A low hissing sound suggestive of his vexation now escaped his lips, for to his rage and disgust he saw plainly enough that their light must have been noticed.

Fitz Burnett had come to the same conclusion, for though he strained his eyes with all his power, the Will-o'-the-Wisp-like light that they were chasing had disappeared.

"Gone!" thought the boy, whose heart was now beating heavily. "They must have seen our light and taken alarm. That's bad. No," he added to himself, "it's good—capital, for it must mean that that was the light of the vessel we were after. Any honest skipper wouldn't have taken the alarm."

"Use your eyes, Burnett, my lad," whispered the lieutenant, bending down. "We must have been close up to her when that idiot gave the alarm. See anything?"

"No, sir."

"Oh, tut, tut, tut, tut, tut!" came in a low muttering tone.

"Look, boy, look; we must see her somehow. How are we to go back and face the captain if we fail like this?"

The boy made no reply, but strained his eyes again, to see darkness everywhere that appeared to be growing darker moment by moment, except in one spot, evidently where the land lay, and there a dull yellowish light glared out that seemed to keep on winking at them derisively, now fairly bright, now disappearing all at once, as the lantern revolved.

"Hold hard!" whispered the lieutenant, and the men lay on their oars, with the boat gradually slackening its speed till it rose and fell, rocking slowly on the choppy sea, and the eye-like lantern gave another derisive wink twice, and then seemed to shut itself up tight.

"It's of no use to pull, Burnett," whispered the lieutenant. "We may be going right away. See anything, my lads?"

"No, sir," came in a low murmur, and the culprit who had gone to sleep sat and shivered as he thought of the "wigging," as he termed it, that would be his when he went back on board the gunboat; and as the boat rocked now in regular motion the darkness seemed to grow more profound, while the silence to the midshipman seemed to be awful.

He was miserable too with disappointment, for he felt so mixed up with the expedition that it seemed to him as if he was in fault, and that when they returned he would have to share in the blame that Captain Glossop would, as he termed it, "lay on thick."

"Oh, Mr Bill Smith," he said to himself, "just wait till we get back!"

And then a reaction took place.

"What's the good?" he thought. "Poor fellow! He'll get it hot enough without me saying a word. But how could a fellow go to sleep at a time like this?"

"It's all up, Burnett," came in a whisper, close to his ear. "The milk's spilt, and it's no use crying over it, but after all these preparations who could have expected such a mishap as that?—What's the matter with you?" he added sharply. "You'll have me overboard."

For the midshipman had suddenly sprung up from where he sat, nearly overbalancing his superior officer as he gripped him tightly by the chest with the right hand, and without replying stood rigidly pointing over the side with his left, his arm stretched right across the lieutenant's breast.

"You don't mean—you can see—Bravo, boy!—Pull, my lads, for all you know."

As he spoke he dropped back into his seat, tugging hard with his right hand at one of the rudder-lines, with the result that as the cutter glided once more rapidly over the little waves she made a sharp curve to starboard, and then as the line was once more loosened, glided on straight ahead for something dim and strange that stood out before them like a blur.

As the men bent to their stout ash-blades, pulling with all their might, a great thrill seemed to run through the cutter, which, as it were, participated in the excitement of the crew, boat and men being for the time as it were one, while the dark blur now rapidly assumed form, growing moment by moment more distinct, till the occupants of the stern-sheets gradually made out the form of a two-masted vessel gliding along under a good deal of sail.

She had so much way on, as the cutter was coming up at right angles that instead of beating fast, Fitz Burnett's heart now continued its pulsations in jerks in his excitement lest the schooner should glide by them and leave them behind.

It was a near thing, but the lieutenant had taken his measures correctly. He was standing up once again grasping the rudder-lines till almost the last moment, before dropping them and giving two orders, to the coxswain to hook on, and to the crew to follow—unnecessary orders, for every man was on the *qui vive*, knew his task, and meant to do it in the shortest possible time.

And now a peculiar sense of unreality attacked the young midshipman, for in the darkness everything seemed so dream-like and unnatural. It was as if they were rowing with all their might towards a phantom ship, a misty something dimly-seen in the darkness, a ship-like shape that might at any moment die right away; for all on board was black, and the silence profound. There was nothing alive, as it were, but the schooner itself, careening gently over in their direction, and passing silently before their bows.

One moment this feeling strengthened as Fitz Burnett dimly made out the coxswain standing ready in the bows prepared to seize hold with the boat-hook he wielded, while the men left their oars to swing, while they played another part.

"The boat-hook will go through it," thought the lad, as, following the lieutenant's example, he stood ready to spring up the side. The next moment all was real, for the cutter in response to a jerk as the coxswain hooked on, grated against the side and changed its course, gliding along with the schooner, while, closely following, their officers, who sprang on board, the little crew of stout man-of-war's men sprang up and literally tumbled over the low bulwarks on to the vessel's deck.

For a short period during which you might have counted six, there was nothing heard but the rustle of the men's movements and the *pad, pad, pad* of their bare feet upon the deck.

"Where's the—"

What the lieutenant would have said in continuation was not heard. Surprised by the utter silence on board, he had shared with Fitz the feeling that they must have boarded some derelict whose crew, perhaps in great peril, had deserted their vessel and sought safety in the boats.

But the next moment there was a sudden rush that took every one by surprise, for not a word was uttered by their assailants, the thud, thud, thud of heavy blows, the breathing hard of men scuffling, followed by splash after splash, and then one of the schooner's masts seemed to give way and fall heavily upon Fitz Burnett's head, turning the dimly-seen deck and the struggling men into something so black that he saw no more.

Chapter Three
Waking up

It is a curious sensation to be lying on your back you don't know where, and you can't think of the reason why it should be so, but with your head right off, completely detached from your body, and rolling round and round like an exceedingly heavy big ball, that for some inexplicable reason has been pitched into a vast mill on purpose to be ground, but, probably from its thickness and hardness, does not submit to that process, but is always going on and on between the upper stone and nether stone, suffering horrible pain, but never turning into powder, nor even into bits, but going grinding on always for a time that seems as if it would never end unless the millstones should wear away.

That is what seemed to be the matter with Fitz Burnett, for how long he could not tell. But a change came at last, with the gnawing, grinding pain becoming dull. Later on it did not seem that his head was detached from his body, and he had some undefined idea that his hands were where he could move them, and at last, later on still, he found himself lying in comparative calmness and in no pain, but in a state something between sleeping and waking.

Then came a time when he began to think that it was very dark, that he was very tired, and that he wanted to sleep, and so he slept. Then again that it was very light, very warm, and that something seemed to be the matter with his berth, for he was thinking more clearly now. He knew he was lying on his back in his berth, and curiously enough he knew that it was not his berth, and while he was wondering why this was, something tickled his nose.

Naturally enough as the tickling went on, passing here and there, he attributed it to a fly upon his face, and his instinct suggested to him to knock it off. He made a movement to do this quickly and suddenly, but his hand fell back upon his chest—whop! It was only a light touch, but he heard it distinctly, and as the movement resulted in dislodging the fly, he laughed to himself, perfectly satisfied. He felt very comfortable and went to sleep again.

Hours must have passed, and it was light once more. He turned his head and looked towards that light, to see that it was dancing and flashing upon beautiful blue water all rippled and playing under the influence of a gentle breeze. He could not see much of it, for he was only looking through a round cabin-window. This was puzzling, for there was no such window as that in the gunboat, and the mental question came—where was he?

But it did not seem to matter. He was very comfortable, and that dancing light upon the water was one of the most lovely sights he had ever seen. He thought that it was a beautiful morning and that it was very nice to lie and watch it, but he did not think about anybody else or about whys or wherefores or any other puzzling problems, not even about himself. But he did think it would be pleasant to turn himself a little over on his side with his face close to the edge of the berth, and take in long breaths of that soft, sweet air.

Acting upon this thought, he tried to turn himself, and for the first time began to wonder why it was that he could not stir; and directly after he began to wonder what it was he had been dreaming about; something concerning his head aching horribly and going round and round in a mill.

It was while he was obliged to give this up as something he could not master that he heard a click as of a door opening, and the next moment some one came softly in, and a face was interposed between his and the cabin-window.

It was a rather rough but pleasant-looking face, with dark brown eyes and blackish curly hair, cut short. The face was a good deal sunburnt too. But he did not take much notice of that; it was the eyes that caught his attention, looking searchingly into his, and Fitz waited, expecting the owner of the eyes would speak; and then it seemed to him that he ought to ask something—about something. But about what? He did not quite know, for he felt that though he was wide-awake he could not think as he should. It was as if his apparatus was half asleep.

But the owner of the eyes did not say anything, only drew back and disappeared, and as he did so, Fitz found that he could think, for he was asking himself how it was that the fellow who had been looking at him had disappeared.

He came to the conclusion directly afterwards that it was a dream. Then he knew it was not, for he heard a gruff voice that seemed to come through the boards say—

"All right, Poole. Tumble up directly. What say?"

"He's awake, father, and looks as if he had come to himself."

"Eh? Oh, that's good news. Come and see him directly."

Now Fitz began to think fast, but still not about himself.

"Father, eh?" he thought. "Whose father is he? He said he was coming to see some one directly. Now I wonder who that may be."

That was as much as Fitz Burnett could get through upon this occasion, for thinking had made his eyelids heavy, and the bright flashing water at which he gazed seemed to grow dull and play upon the boards of his berth just over his head and close at hand.

From growing dull, this rippling water grew very dark indeed, and then for some time there was nothing more but sleep—beautiful sleep, Nature's great remedy and cure for a heavy blow upon the head that has been very close upon fracturing the bone, but which in this case fell so far short that Fitz Burnett had only had severe concussion of the brain.

Chapter Four
Another boy

It was either sunrise or sunset, for the cabin was full of a rich warm glow, and Fitz lay upon his back listening to a peculiar sound which sounded to him like *fuzz, whuzz, thrum.*

He did not attempt to turn his head for some moments, though he wanted to know what made those sounds, for during some little time he felt too lazy to stir, and at last he turned his head gently and remembered the eyes that had looked at him once, and recalled the face now bent down over something before him from which came those peculiar sounds.

Fitz felt interested, and watched the busy ringers, the passing and re-passing needle, and the manipulation of a mesh, for some time before he spoke.

"How quick and clever he is!" he thought, and then almost unconsciously a word slipped out.

"Netting?" he said.

Needle, string and mesh were thrown down, and Fitz's fellow-occupier of the cabin started up and came to his side, to bend over and lay a brown cool hand upon his forehead.

"Feel better?" he said.

"Better?" said Fitz peevishly.

"Yes, of course."

"Why—Here, stop a moment. Who are you?"

"No doubt about it," was the reply. "That's the first time you have talked sensibly."

"You be hanged!" said Fitz sharply.

But as he spoke it did not seem like his own voice, but as if somebody else had spoken in a weak, piping tone. He did not trouble himself about that, though, for his mind was beginning to be an inquiring one.

"Why don't you answer?" he said. "Who are you? What's your name?"

"Poole Reed."

"Oh! Then how came you in my cabin?"

"Well," said the lad, with a pleasant laugh, which made his rather plain face light up in the warm sunset glow and look almost handsome; not that that was wonderful, for a healthy, good-tempered boy's face, no matter what his features, always has a pleasant look,—"I think I might say what are you doing in my cabin?"

"Eh?" cried Fitz, looking puzzled. "How came I—your cabin—your cabin? Is it your cabin?"

The lad nodded.

"I don't know," said Fitz. "How did I come here?"

"But it is my cabin—rather."

"Yes, yes; but how did I come here?"

"Why, in the boat."

"In a boat?" said Fitz thoughtfully—"in a boat? I came in a boat? Yes, I suppose so, because we are at sea. But somehow I don't know how it is. I can't recollect. But I say, hasn't it turned *very* warm?"

"Yes. Getting warmer every day."

"But my head—I don't understand."

"Don't you? Well, never mind. How do you feel?"

"Oh, quite well, thank you. But I want to know why I am here—in your cabin."

"Oh, you will know soon enough. Don't worry about it now till you get strong again."

"Till I get strong again? There, now you are beginning to puzzle me once more. I am strong enough now, and—No, I am not," added the lad, rather pitifully, as he raised one hand and let it fall back. "That arm feels half numbed as if it had been hurt, and," he added, rather excitedly, "you asked me how I was. Have I been ill?"

"Yes, very," was the reply. "But don't fret about it. You are coming all right again fast."

Fitz lay back with his brow wrinkled up, gazing at his companion and trying to think hard; but all in vain, and with a weary gesticulation—

"I can't understand," he said. "I try to think, but my head seems to go rolling round again, and I can only remember that mill."

"Then take my advice about it. Don't try to think at all."

"But I must think; I want to know."

"Oh, you'll know soon enough. You can't think, because you are very weak now. I was just the same when I had the fever at Vera Cruz—felt as if my head wouldn't go; but it got better every day, and that's how yours will be."

"Did I catch a fever, then?" said Fitz eagerly.

"No," was the reply. "You caught something else," and the speaker smiled grimly.

"Caught something else? And been very bad?"

The lad nodded.

"Then—then," cried Fitz excitedly, "Captain Glossop had me sent aboard this ship to get me out of the way?"

"Well, not exactly. But don't you bother, I tell you. You are getting right again fast, and father says you'll be all right now you have turned the corner."

"Who's 'father'?" said Fitz.

"That's a rum question. Why, my father, of course—the skipper of this schooner."

"Oh, I see; the skipper of this schooner," said Fitz thoughtfully. "Is it a fast one?"

"Awfully," said the lad eagerly. "You will quite enjoy seeing how we can sail when you are well enough to come on deck. Why, if you go on like this we ought to be able to get you up in a day or two. The weather is splendid now. My father is a capital doctor."

"What!" cried Fitz. "Why, you told me just now that he was the skipper of this schooner."

"Well, so he is. But I say, don't you worry about asking questions. Couldn't you drink a cup of tea?"

"I don't know; I dare say I could. Yes, I should like one. But never mind about that now. I don't quite understand why Captain Glossop should send me on board this schooner. This is not the Liverpool Hospital Ship, is it?"

"Oh no."

"How many sick people have you got on board?"

"None at all," said the lad, "now you are getting well."

Fitz lay looking at the speaker wistfully. There was something about his frank face and manner that he liked.

"I don't understand," he said sadly. "It's all a puzzle, and I suppose it is all as you say through being so ill."

"Yes, of course. That's it, old chap. I say, you don't mind me calling you 'old chap,' do you?"

"Well, no," said Fitz, smiling sadly. "You mean it kindly, I suppose."

"Well, I want to be kind to you, seeing how bad you've been. I thought one day you were going to Davy Jones's locker, as the sailors call it."

"Was I so bad as that?" cried Fitz eagerly.

"Yes, horrid. Father and I felt frightened, because it would have been so serious; but there, I won't say another word. I am going to get you some tea."

The invalid made an effort to stay him, but the lad paid no heed—hurrying out of the cabin and shutting the door quietly after him, leaving Fitz deep in thought.

He lay with his white face wrinkled up, trying hard, in spite of what had been said, to think out what it all meant, but always with his thoughts tending towards his head rolling round in a mill and getting no farther; in fact, it seemed to be going round again for about the nth time, as mathematicians term it, when the cabin-door once more opened, and his attendant bore in a steaming hot cup of tea, to be closely followed by a bluff-looking, middle-aged man, sun-browned, bright-eyed and alert, dressed in semi-naval costume, and looking like a well-to-do yachtsman.

He smiled pleasantly as he gave a searching look at the invalid, and sat down at once upon a chair close to the lad's pillow, leaning over to touch his brow and then feel his pulse.

"Bravo!" he said. "Capital!—Humph! So you are thinking I don't look like a doctor, eh?"

"Yes," replied Fitz sharply. "How did you know that?"

"Because it is written in big letters all over your face. Why, you are getting quite a new man, and we will have you on deck in a day or two."

"Thank you," said Fitz. "It is very good of you to pay so much attention to an invalid. I knew you were not a doctor because your son here said so; but you seem to have done me a great deal of good, and I hope you think I am grateful. I am sure Captain Glossop will be very much obliged."

"Humph!" said the skipper dryly. "I hope he will. But there, try your tea. I dare say it will do you good."

As he spoke the skipper passed one muscular arm gently under the boy's shoulders and raised him up, while his son bent forward with the tea.

"Thank you," said Fitz, "but there was no need for that. I could have— Oh, how ridiculous to be so weak as this!"

"Oh, not at all," said the skipper. "Why, you have been days and days without any food—no coal in your bunkers, my lad. How could you expect your engines to go?"

"What!" cried Fitz. "Days and days! Wasn't I taken ill yesterday?"

"Well, not exactly, my lad," said the skipper dryly; "but don't you bother about that now. Try the tea."

The cup was held to his lips, and the lad sipped and then drank with avidity.

"'Tis good," he muttered.

"That's right," said the skipper. "You were a bit thirsty, I suppose. Why, you will soon be ready to eat, but we mustn't go too fast; mind that, Poole. Gently does it, mind, till he gets a bit stronger.—Come, finish your tea.— That's the way. Now let me lay you down again."

This was done, and the boy's face wrinkled up once more.

"I am so weak," he said querulously.

"To be sure you are, my lad, but that will soon go off now. You've got nothing to do but to lie here and eat and drink and sleep, till you come square again. My boy Poole here will look after you, and to-morrow or next day we will carry you up on deck and let you lie in a cane-chair. You will be able to read soon, and play draughts or chess, and have a fine time of it."

"Thank you; I am very much obliged," said the young midshipman warmly. "I want to get well again, and I will try not to think, but there is one thing I should like to ask."

"Well. So long as it isn't questions, go on, my lad."

"I want you to write a letter home, it doesn't matter how short it is, about my having been ill—so long as you tell my mother that I am getting better from my attack. Your son said when I asked him, that I got it on the head, and I am afraid my mother would not understand that, so you had better say what fever it was, for I am sure she'd like to know. What fever was it, Captain? You might tell me that!"

"Eh, what—what fever?" said the skipper. "Ah, ah," and he gave a peculiar cock of his eye towards his son, "brain-fever, my lad, brain-fever. It made you a bit delirious. But that's all over now."

"And you will write, sir? I'll give you the address."

"Write?" said the captain. "Why not wait till you get into port? You will be able then to write yourself."

"Oh, but I can't wait for that, sir. If you would kindly write the letter and send it ashore by one of the men in your boat, it will be so much better."

"All right, my lad. I'll see to it. But there, now. You've talked too much. Not another word. I am your doctor, and my orders are that you now shut your eyes and go to sleep."

As he spoke the skipper made a sign to his son, and they both left the cabin, the latter bearing the empty cup.

Chapter Five
Aghast

As the cabin-door closed Fitz lay back, trying to think about his position, but he felt too comfortable to trouble much. There had been something so soft and comforting about that tea, which had relieved the parched sensation in his throat and lips. Then the skipper and his son had been so kind and attentive. It was so satisfactory too about getting that letter off, and then that evening glow rapidly changing into a velvety gloom with great stars coming out, was so lovely that he felt that he had never seen anything so exquisite before.

"There, I won't think and worry," he said to himself, and a minute later he had fallen into a sleep which proved so long and restful, that the sun had been long up before he unclosed his eyes again to find his younger attendant once more netting.

"Morning," said the lad cheerily. "You have had a long nap, and no mistake."

"Why, I haven't been asleep since sunset, have I?"

"You have, and it seems to have done you a lot of good. You can eat a good breakfast now, can't you?"

"Yes, and get up first and have a good wash. I long for it."

"You can't. I shall have to do that. Here, wait a minute. I will go and tell the cook to get your breakfast ready, and then come back and put you all a-taunto."

The lad hurried out of the cabin, leaving Fitz wide-awake now in every sense of the word, for that last rest had brought back the power of coherent thought, making him look wonderingly out of the window at the glorious sea, so different from anything he had been accustomed to for months and months, and setting him wondering.

"Why, this can't be the Irish Channel," he thought, "and here, when was it I was taken ill? I seem to have been fast asleep, and only just woke up. Where was I? Was that a dream? No, I remember now; the lieutenant and the cutter's crew. That schooner we were sent to board in the darkness, and—"

Here his young attendant re-entered the cabin with a tin-bowl in one hand, a bucket of freshly dipped sea-water in the other, and a towel thrown over his shoulder.

"Here, hullo, midshipman!" he cried cheerily. "My word, you do look wide-awake! But there's nothing wrong, is there?"

"Yes! No! I don't know," cried Fitz excitedly. "What's the name of this schooner?"

"Oh, it's all right. It's my father's schooner."

"And you sailed from Liverpool?"

"I haven't come here to answer your questions," said the lad, almost sulkily.

"That proves it, then. I remember it all now. We boarded you in the dark, and—and—"

Before the speaker could continue, the cabin-door was thrust open and the bluff-looking skipper entered.

"Hullo!" he said sternly, "what's the matter here?"

"Your son, sir, won't answer my questions," cried Fitz excitedly.

"Quite right, my lad. I told him not to until you get better, so don't ask."

"I am better," cried the boy, trying to spring up, but sinking back with a groan.

"There, you see," said the skipper, "you are not. You are far too weak. Why not take my word for it, my lad, as a bit of a doctor? Now, look here! You want to know how it is you came on board my craft—wait patiently a little while, and when I think you are well enough to bear it I will tell you all."

"But I don't want to be told now," cried the boy passionately—"not that. I boarded with our men, and I can remember I felt a heavy blow. I must have been knocked down and stunned. What has become of our lieutenant, the boat and men?"

"Oh, well, my lad, if the murder must out—"

"Murder!" cried Fitz.

"Murder, no! Nonsense! That's a figure of speech. I mean, if the story must come out, here it is. I was going peacefully down channel when your boat boarded us."

"As she had a right to," cried Fitz, "being from one of the Queen's ships on duty."

"Oh, I am not going to argue that, my lad," said the skipper coolly. "I was sailing down channel, interfering with nobody, when I was boarded by a lot of armed men in the dark, and I did what any skipper would do under the circumstances. The boat's crew meant to capture my craft and my valuable cargo, so after a scuffle I had them all pitched overboard to get back to their boat, and gave them the go-by in the darkness, and I haven't seen anything of them since."

"Oh!" exclaimed Fitz. "Resisting one of Her Majesty's crews! Do you know, sir, what it means?"

"I know what the other means, my lad—losing my craft and valuable cargo, and some kind of punishment, I suppose, for what I have done."

"But you have taken me prisoner, then?" cried Fitz.

"Well, not exactly, my lad," said the skipper, smiling. "I shouldn't have done that if I had known. Nobody knew you were on board till the next morning, for we were all too busy clapping on all sail so as to give your gunboat a clean pair of heels."

"Never mind me," cried Fitz excitedly. "What about the boat's crew?"

"Oh, they'll be all right. They got back to their boat. We could hear plainly enough the shouting one to the other, and your officer hailing till the last man was picked up. They were showing their lantern then without stint, not giving us a mere glimpse like they did when we saw it first."

"Oh!" ejaculated Fitz, drawing his breath between his teeth as he recalled the dropping off to sleep of poor Bill Smith.

"It was not till sunrise, my lad, that I knew you were on board. You had had an unlucky crack on the head which sent you down the companion-ladder, and when my lads brought and laid you up on deck it seemed to me the worst part of the night's business."

"Then why didn't you put me ashore at once?" cried Fitz. "You were keeping me a prisoner here," and he looked from father to son, the former where he had seated himself quietly by the head of the middy's berth, the other standing leaning against the bulkhead folding and unfolding the clean towel, with the bucket of water and tin-bowl at his feet.

"Why didn't I put you ashore at once?" replied the skipper. "Say, why didn't I put myself and men all in prison for what I had done? Well, hardly likely, my lad. I couldn't afford it, between ourselves. There! It was your people's fault. You may call it duty, if you like. Mine was to save my schooner if I could—and I did. So now you know the worst. Come; be a good boy and let Poole there wash your face."

"Oh, this is insufferable," cried Fitz. "You are insulting a Queen's officer, sir."

"I am very sorry, sir," said the skipper coolly, "but I have got another duty to do now, and that is to make you quite well. This is only a fast trading schooner, but in his way a skipper is as big a man as the captain of a Queen's man-of-war. He is master, and you have got to obey—the more so because it is for your own good. Why don't I set you ashore? Because I can't. As soon as I safely can, off you go, but till then just you take it coolly and get well."

"Put me aboard the first ship you see."

"I shall put you where I like, my boy; so once more I tell you that you have got to obey me and get well. If you go on like this, exciting yourself, we shall have the fever back again, and then, mark this, the words of truth, you will be too ill to ask me to write to your mother and tell her how bad you are."

Poor Fitz's lips parted, and he lay back upon his pillow speechless and staring with a strange, wistful look in his eyes, making not the slightest resistance, not even attempting to speak again, as the skipper laid a hand once more upon his forehead, keeping it there a few minutes before he removed it.

"Not so hot," he said, "as I expected to feel it. Go on, Poole, my boy, and get him his breakfast as soon as you can."

The lad took his father's place as he vacated it and moved towards the cabin-door, but only to return directly, step to the side of the berth, and take one of the middy's hands and hold it between his own.

"There, there," he said, "I am sorry to be so hard with you, my lad, for you have spoken very bravely and well. Come! A sailor has to take the ups and downs of his profession. You are all in the downs now, and are, so to speak, my prisoner; but we shan't put you in irons, eh, Poole?"

"No, father," said the lad addressed, smiling; "not quite."

"And I shall be disgraced—disgraced!" groaned the midshipman.

"Disgraced! Nonsense! What for? Why, my lad, your captain when he knows all ought to put a big mark against your name; and I have no doubt he will."

As he spoke he left the cabin without another word, and the silence was just as great within; but it was a busy silence all the same, while Fitz lay back, unable to avoid feeling how cool and pleasant was the touch of the water, and how gentle were his attendant's hands.

He was still miserable, but there was something very satisfying later on in being propped up with a great locker-cushion and a well-stuffed pillow, feeling the deliciously warm morning air float through the open cabin-window, what time, by the help of the skipper's son, he partook of a capital breakfast, at first feeling that every mouthful was choking him, then with eager appetite, Poole smiling pleasantly at him all the while.

It was annoying too, for the middy felt that, to use his own term, he ought to hate this "filibustering young ruffian" with all his heart. As for speaking to him unless it were to give him some imperious order, he mentally vowed he would not do that.

But that coffee was newly roasted, and though they were far at sea, the fresh bread-cakes were nice and warm, and the butter not in the slightest degree too salt. Fitz had been long without any food to signify, returning health was giving him the first instalments of a ravenous appetite, and somehow it seems to be one of Nature's rules that *one* fasting has his temper all on edge, while when he is satisfied it does not take much to make him smile.

So it was that before the breakfast was over, Fitz Burnett had forgotten his mental vow. Curiosity got the better of him.

"How far are we from land?" he said.

"The nearest?"

Fitz nodded.

"Oh, about eight hundred miles."

"And where's that? Somewhere south?"

"No, north by east."

"Do you mean it?"

It was Poole's turn now to nod.

The young midshipman sank back aghast, trying to mentally fill up the blank between that night off the dark waters near Liverpool, and the bright sunny sea before him now.

It was a thorough failure, for before many minutes had passed, his thinking powers seemed to be rendered misty by a sunny glow through which he was wafted back to England, Kent, and his own old pleasant home.

His head had sunk back, and he was sleeping peacefully and well, not in the least disturbed by his attendant as the breakfast-things were removed and the cabin touched up. This done, Poole stood beside him, examining his position.

"Seems comfortable enough," he said, "and I don't think he can roll over. Poor old chap! It does seem a nasty turn, but it was not our fault. I hope he'll soon settle down, because he seems to be the sort of fellow, if he wasn't quite so cocky, that one might come to like."

Chapter Six
On two sides

Fitz Burnett slept on during the greatest part of that day and most of the next; each time that he woke up he seemed better, and ready for the food that he had missed for so long and which was now so carefully prepared for him.

Very little had been said; the skipper's son attended upon him assiduously, and was ready to enter into conversation, but his advances were met so shortly and snappishly, that he soon contented himself with playing the nurse seriously, while the invalid frowned and kept his eyes fixed upon the sea through the open cabin-window, rarely glancing at his attendant at all.

It was on the fourth day after the lad had recovered his senses and learned the truth of his position, that Poole made a remark about this change in their passenger to his father, who had come into the cabin to find the midshipman fast asleep.

"Is it right, father, that he should sleep so much?" said the lad.

"Certainly. He's getting on fast. Let him sleep as much as he can. His wound is growing together again as quickly as it can. Can't you see how much better he is?"

"Well, I thought I could, dad," was the reply; "but every now and then I think he's getting worse."

"Eh? What makes you think that, lad? Does he begin to mope for his liberty?"

"I dare say he does, dad. It's only natural; but that isn't what I meant. What I thought was that though he seemed rather nice at first, he keeps on growing more and more disagreeable. He treats me sometimes just as if I were a dog."

"Well, you always were a precious young puppy, Poole," said the skipper, with a twinkle of the eye.—"Ah! No impudence now! If you dare to say that it's no wonder when I am such a rough old sea-dog, I'll throw something at you."

"Then it won't be thrown," said the lad, laughing. "But really, father, he is so stuck up and consequential sometimes, ordering me about, and satisfied with nothing I do, that it makes me feel peppery and ready to tell him that if he isn't satisfied he'd better do the things himself."

"Bah! Don't take any notice of him, boy. It's all a good sign, and means he's getting well fast."

"Well, it's not a very pleasant way of showing it, father."

"No, my boy, no; but we can't very well alter what is. Fellows who have been ill, and wounded men when they are taking a right turn, are weak, irritable, and dissatisfied. I think you'll find him all right by and by. Take it all calmly. He's got something to suffer, poor fellow, both mentally and from that hurt upon his head. Well, I'll go back on deck. I did come down to examine and dress his sconce again, but I'll leave that till another time."

He had hardly spoken before Fitz opened his eyes with a start, saw who was present, and turned pettishly away.

"Oh, it's you, doctor, is it?" he said. "I wish you wouldn't be always coming in here and bothering and waking me up. What do you want now?"

"I was only coming to bathe and re-plaster your head, squire," replied the bluff skipper good-humouredly.

Fitz gave himself an angry snatch round, and fixed his eyes frowningly upon the speaker.

"Look here," he said, "let's have no more of that, if you please. Have the goodness to keep your place, sir. If you don't know that you have a gentleman on board, please to learn it now, and have the goodness to be off and take that clumsy oaf with you. I want to sleep."

"Certainly," said the skipper quietly, and his son gave him a wondering look. "But as I am here I may as well see to your head. It is quite time it was done again."

"Look here," cried Fitz, "am I to speak again? I told you to go. When I want my head bandaged again I will send you word."

"All right, my lad," said the skipper good-humouredly.

"All right, *what*?" cried Fitz. "Will you have the goodness to keep this familiar way of speaking to people of your own class!"

"Oh, certainly," said the skipper. "Very well, then; send for me when you feel disposed to have it dressed; and I'll tell you what, you can let Poole wait till the cool of the evening, and he can bathe it and do it then."

"Bah!" cried the lad angrily. "Is it likely I am going to trust myself in his clumsy hands? There, stop and do it now, as I am awake. Here, stop, get some fresh cool water and hold the basin. Pish! I mean that nasty tin-bowl."

Poole got what was necessary without a word, and then stood by while the injury was carefully bathed and bandaged, the patient not uttering a single word of thanks, but submitting with the worst of graces, and just giving his doctor a condescending nod when with a word of congratulation the latter left the cabin.

There was profound silence then, saving a click or two and a rustle as Poole put the various things away, Fitz lying back on his pillow and watching him the while, till at last he spoke, in an exacerbating way—

"Here, you sir, was that doctor, skipper, or whatever he calls himself, trained before he came to sea?"

Poole flushed and remained silent.

"Did you hear what I said, boy?" cried Fitz.

"Yes," was the short reply, resentfully given.

"Yes, *sir*. Impudent scoundrel! Do you know whom you are addressing? *Sir* to an officer in Her Majesty's service, whatever his rank."

"Oh, yes, I know whom I am talking to."

"Yes, *sir*, you oaf! Where are your manners? Is that fellow a surgeon?"

"No; he is captain of this ship."

"Ship! Captain!" sneered the boy, in a contemptuous tone which made his listener writhe. "Why, it's a trading schooner, isn't it?"

Poole was about to speak out sharply, when a glance at the helpless condition of the speaker disarmed him, and he said quietly—

"Oh, yes, of course it's a trading schooner, but it was originally a gentleman's yacht, and sails like one."

"Indeed!" said the boy sneeringly. "And pray whose is it?"

Poole looked at him open-eyed as if expecting to see him suffering from a little deliriousness again; but as no sign was visible he merely said quietly—

"My father's."

"And pray who's your father?"

Poole looked at him again, still in doubt.

"That is."

"Oh!"

There was silence for a few moments, before Fitz turned himself wearily and said in a careless, off-hand tone—

"And what's the name of the craft?"

"The *Silver Teal*."

"Silver Eel—eh? What a ridiculously slippery name for a boat!"

"*Silver Teal*," said Poole emphatically.

"Silver Grandmother! A nice set you must be to give your gimcrack craft such a name as that! But you may take my word for it that as soon as ever you are caught in your slippery eel you will all either be hung or go to penal servitude for life—though perhaps you'll be let off, as you are nothing better than a boy."

"Oh yes, I am only a boy," said Poole, rather bitterly; "but the *Silver Teal*, or Silver Eel as you call it, has to be caught yet. Your people did not make a very grand affair of it the other night."

"Pooh! That's only because one of our stupid fellows who had been on the watch the night before dropped to sleep. They'll soon have you. You'll have the *Tonans* thundering on your heels before you know where you are. I am expecting to hear her guns every minute."

"That's quite possible," said Poole quietly; "but our little schooner will take some catching, I can tell you."

"So you think," said Fitz, "but you in your ignorance don't know everything. You only sail, and what's the use of that against steam? Just let our gunboat be after you in a calm, and then where are you going to be?"

"I don't know, and I don't think it's worth while to argue about it when we are out here in mid-ocean, and I suppose your gunboat is hanging about somewhere off the port of Liverpool. But look here, hadn't you better take father's advice and not talk so much? I don't mind what you say to me, and it doesn't hurt a bit, but you are rather weak yet, and after all you have gone through I shouldn't like to see you go back instead of forward. Why not have another nap?"

Fitz gave a contemptuous sniff, held his tongue as if his companion in the cabin were not worthy of notice, and lay perfectly still gazing out to sea, but with his face twitching every now and then as he lay thinking with all his might about some of the last words Poole had said connected with the possibility of the gunboat being so far away, and he alone and helpless among these strangers, his spirits sank. How was it all going to end? he thought. What a position to be in! The skipper had said something about putting him aboard some vessel, or ashore;—but how or when? The position seemed hopeless in the extreme, and the poor weak lad thought and thought till his tired brain began to grow dizzy and ache violently, when kindly Nature led him to the temporary way out of the weary trouble which tortured him, and he fell fast asleep.

Chapter Seven
Getting the worst of it

Another morning passed, and the schooner was once more sailing away through the beautiful calm blue see, heaving in long slow rollers which seemed to be doing their best to rock the injured prisoner back to a state of health.

He had breakfasted and been dressed by his sea-going attendant, and was so much better that he was more irritable than usual, while the skipper's son met all his impatient remarks without the slightest resentment.

The result was that the sick middy in his approach to convalescence was in that state called by Irish folk "spoiling for a fight," and the more patient Poole showed himself, the more the boy began to play the lord.

It was not led up to in any way, but came out in the way of aggravation, and sounded so childish on this particular occasion that Poole turned his head and crossed to the cabin-window to look out, so that Fitz should not see him smile.

"I have been thinking," he said, with his back to the boy's berth, "that while we are sailing along here so gently, I might get some of old Butters' tackle."

"Who's Butters?" said Fitz shortly.

"Our bo'sun."

"But what do you mean by his tackle? You don't suppose that I am going to do any hoisting, or anything of that sort, do you?"

"No, no; fishing-tackle. I'd bait the hooks and throw out the line, and you could fish. You'd feel them tug, and could haul in, and I'd take them off the hook?"

"What fish would they be?" cried the boy, quite eagerly, and with his eyes brightening at the idea.

"Bonito or albicore."

"What are they?"

"Ah, you have never been in the tropics, I suppose?"

"Never mind where I've been," snapped out the boy. "I asked you what fish those were."

"Something like big mackerel," replied Poole quietly, "and wonderfully strong. You would enjoy catching them."

The way in which these words were spoken touched the midshipman's dignity.

"Hang his impudence!" Fitz thought. "Patronising me like that!"

"Shall I go and ask him for some tackle?"

"No," was the snappish reply. "I don't want to fish. I have other things on my mind. I have been thinking about this a good deal, young man, and I am not going to put up with any of your insolence. I am an officer in Her Majesty's service, and when one is placed in a position like this, without a superior officer over one, it is my duty to take the command; and if I did as I should do, I ought to give orders to 'bout ship and make sail at once for the nearest port."

"That's quite right; and why don't you?"

"Well—er—I—er—that is—"

"Here, I say, old chap, don't be so cocky. What's the good of making a windbag of yourself? I've only got to prick you, and where are you then? You don't think you are going to frighten my dad with bluster, do you?"

"Blus-ter, sir?"

"Yes, b-l-u-s-t-e-r. You can't call it anything else. I know how you feel. Humbled like at being caught like this. I'm sorry for you."

"Sorry! Bah!"

"Well, I am, really; but, to tell the truth, I should be more sorry if you could get away. It's rather jolly having you here. But you are a bit grumpy this morning. Your head hurts you, doesn't it?"

"Hurts? Horrid! It is just as if somebody was trying to bore a hole in my skull with a red-hot auger."

Poole sprang up, soaked a handkerchief with water, folded it into a square patch, and laid it on the injured place, dealing as tenderly with his patient as if his fingers were those of a woman, with the result that the pain became dull and Fitz lay back in his bunk with his eyes half-closed.

"Feel well enough to have a game of draughts?" said Poole, after a pause.

"No; and you haven't got a board."

"But I have got a big card that I marked out myself, and blackened some of the squares with ink."

"Where are your men?"

"Hanging up in that bag."

"Let's look."

Poole took a little canvas bag from the hook from which it hung and turned out a very decent set of black and white pieces. "You didn't make those?"

"Yes, I did."

"How did you get them so round?"

"Oh, I didn't do that. Chips lent me his little tenon-saw, and I cut them all off a roller; he helped me to finish them up with sandpaper, and told me what to soak half of them in to make them black."

The invalid began to be more and more interested in the neat set of draughtsmen. "What did you soak them in—ink?" he asked. "No; guess again."

"Oh, I can't guess. Ship's paint, perhaps, or tar."

"No; they wouldn't have looked neat like that. Vitriol—sulphuric acid."

"What, had you got that sort of stuff on board the schooner?"

"The governor has in his big medicine-chest."

"And did that turn them black like this?"

"Yes; you just paint them over with it, and hold them to the galley fire. I suppose it burns them. They all come black like that, and you polish them up with a little beeswax, and there you are."

"Well, it was rather clever for a rough chap like you," said Fitz grudgingly. "Can you play?"

"Oh, just a little—for a rough chap like me. One has so much time out at sea."

"Oh, well, we'll have just one game. How many pieces shall I give you?"

"Oh, I should think you ought to give me half," was the reply.

"Very well," said Fitz cavalierly; "take half. I used to be a pretty good fist at this at school. Where's your board?"

Poole thrust his hand under the cabin-table and turned a couple of buttons, setting free a stiff piece of mill-board upon which a sheet of white paper had been pasted and the squares neatly marked out and blacked.

The pieces were placed, and the game began, with Fitz, after his bandage had been re-moistened, supporting himself upon his left elbow to move his pieces with his right hand, which somehow seemed to have forgotten its cunning, for with double the draughts his cool matter-of-fact adversary beat him easily.

"Yes," said Fitz, rather pettishly; "I'm a bit out of practice, and my head feels thick."

"Sure to," said Poole, "knocked about as you were. Have some more pieces this time."

"Oh no!" said Fitz, "I can beat you easily like this if I take more care."

The pieces were set once more, and Fitz played his best, but he once more lost.

"Have some more pieces this time," said Poole.

"Nonsense!" was snapped out. "I tell you I can beat you this way, and I will."

The third game was played, one which took three times as long as the last, and as he was beaten the middy let himself sink back on his pillow with a gesture full of impatience.

Fitz and Poole playing draughts.

"Yes," he said; "I know where I went wrong there. My head burns so, and I wasn't thinking."

"Yes, I saw where you made that slip. You might as well have given up at once."

"Oh, might I?" was snapped out.

"Here, let me give that handkerchief a good soaking before we begin another."

"Yes, you didn't half wet it last time. Don't wring it out so much."

"All right. Why, it's quite hot. It must have made your head so much the cooler. There, does that feel more comfortable?"

"Yes, that's better. Now make haste and set out the men."

Poole arranged the pieces, and Fitz sat up again.

"Here, what have you been doing?" he cried. "You have given me two more."

"Well," said the skipper's son, smiling, "it'll make us more equal."

"Don't you holloa till you're out of the wood," cried Fitz haughtily, and he flicked the two extra pieces off the board. "Do you think I'm going to let you beat me? My head's clearer now. I think I know how to play a game of draughts."

The sick boy thought so, but again his adversary proved far stronger, winning easily; and the middy dropped back on the pillow.

"It isn't fair," he cried.

"Not fair."

"You didn't tell me you could play as well as that."

"Of course not. I wasn't going to brag about my playing. Let's have another game. I think we're about equal."

"No, I'm tired now. I say," added Fitz, after a pause, as he lay watching the draughtsmen being dropped slowly back into the bag, "don't take any notice of what I said. I don't want you to think me cocky and bragging. My head worries me, and it makes me feel hot and out of temper, and ready to find fault with everything. We'll have another game some day if I'm kept here a prisoner. Perhaps I shall be able to play better then."

"To be sure you will. But it doesn't matter which side wins. It is only meant for a game."

Chapter Eight
A basin of soup

Fitz had just finished his semi-apology when the fastening of the door clicked softly; it was pushed, and a peculiar-looking, shaggy head was thrust in. The hair was of a rusty sandy colour, a shade lighter than the deeply-tanned face, while a perpetual grin parted the owner's lips as if he were proud to show his teeth, though, truth to tell, there was nothing to be proud of unless it was their bad shape and size. But the most striking features were the eyes, which somehow or another possessed a fiery reddish tinge, and added a certain fierceness to a physiognomy which would otherwise have been very weak.

Fitz started at the apparition.

"The impertinence!" he muttered. "Here, I say," he shouted now, "who are you?"

"Who am I, laddie?" came in a harsh voice. "Ye ken I'm the cook."

"And what do you want here, sir? Laddie, indeed! Why didn't you knock?"

"Knock!" said the man, staring, as he came right in.

"I didna come to knock: just to give you the word that it's all hot and ready now."

"What's hot and ready?"

"The few broth I've got for you. Ye didna want to be taking doctor's wash now, but good, strong meaty stuff to build up your flesh and bones."

Fitz stared.

"Look here, you, Poole Reed; what does this man mean by coming into my cabin like this? Is he mad?"

"No, no," said Poole, laughing. "It's all right; I'd forgotten. He asked me if he hadn't better bring you something every day now for a bit of lunch. It's all right, Andy. Mr Burnett's quite ready. Go and fetch it."

The man nodded, grinned, in no wise hurt by his reception, and backed out again.

"Rum-looking fellow, isn't he, Mr Burnett?"

"Disgusting-looking person for a cook. Can anybody eat what he prepares?"

"We do," said Poole quietly. "Oh, he keeps his galley beautifully clean, does Andy Campbell—Cawmell, he calls himself, and the lads always call him the Camel. And he works quite as hard."

He had only just spoken when the man returned on the tips of his bare toes, looking, for all the world, like the ordinary able seaman from a man-of-war. He bore no tray, napkin, and little tureen, but just an ordinary ship's basin in one hand, a spoon in the other, and carefully balanced himself as he entered the cabin, swaying himself with the basin so that a drop should not go over the side.

"There y'are, me puir laddie. Ye'll just soop that up before I come back for the bowl. There's pepper and salt in, and just a wee bit onion to make it taste. All made out of good beef, and joost the pheesic to make you strong."

"Give it to me, Andy," cried Poole, and the man placed it in his hands, smiled and nodded at the prisoner, and then backed out with his knees very much bent.

Poole stood stirring the broth in the basin slowly round and round, and spreading a peculiar vulgar odour which at first filled the invalid with annoyance; but as it pervaded the place it somehow began to have a decided effect upon the boy's olfactory nerves and excited within him a strange yearning which drove away every token of disgust.

"It's too hot to give you yet," said Poole quietly. "You must wait a few minutes."

Fitz's first idea had been that he would not condescend to touch what he was ready to dub "a mess." It looked objectionable, being of a strange colour and the surface dotted with yellowish spots of molten fat, while mingled with them were strange streaky pieces of divided onion. But animal food had for many days been a stranger to the sick lad's lips—and then there was the smell which rapidly became to the boy's nostrils a most fascinating perfume. So that it was in a softened tone that he spoke next, as he watched the slow passage round and round of the big metal spoon.

"It doesn't look nice," he said.

"No. Ship's soup never does," replied Poole, "but the proof of the pudding is in the eating, you know. The Camel's about right, though. This is the best physic you can have. Will you try it now?"

This was an attack that the boy could not stand. He wanted to say No, with a gesture of disgust, but Nature would not let him then.

"I dunno," he said dubiously. "Did he make it?"

"Of course."

"But he looks like a common sailor; not a bit like a cook."

"He is a foremast-man, and takes his turn at everything, like the rest; but he does all the cooking just the same."

"But is he really clean?"

"He made all those bread-cakes you have eaten," was the reply.

"Oh," said Fitz quickly, for the soup smelt aggravatingly nice. "Would you mind tasting it?"

Poole raised the spoon to his lips, and replaced it.

"Splendid," he said. "You try."

He carefully placed the basin in his patient's lap, with the spoon ready to his hand, and drew back, watching the peculiar curl at the corners of the boy's lips as he slowly passed the spoon round and then raised it to his mouth.

A few seconds later the spoon went round the basin again and was followed by an audible sip, on hearing which Poole went to the window, thrust out his head, and began to whistle, keeping up his tune as if he were playing orchestra to a banquet, while he watched the dart and splash of a fish from time to time about the surface, and the shadowy shapes of others deep down below the schooner's stern-post, clearly enough seen in the crystal sunlit water set a-ripple by the gentle gliding through it of the vessel's keel.

After waiting what he considered a sufficient time, Poole said loudly, without turning round—

"There's plenty of fish in sight."

But there was no reply, and he waited again until in due time he heard a sharp click as of metal against crockery which was followed by a deep sigh, and then the lad turned slowly, to see the midshipman leaning back in the berth with his hands behind his head, the empty basin and spoon resting in his lap.

Poole Reed did not say what he would have liked, neither was there any sound of triumph in his voice. He merely removed the empty vessel and asked a question—

"Was it decent?"

And Fitz forgot himself. For the moment all his irritability seemed gone, and the natural boy came to the surface.

"Splendid!" he cried. "I never enjoyed anything so much before in my life."

And all that about a dingy basin of soup with fragments of onion and spots of fat floating therein. But it was the first real meal of returning health.

Chapter Nine
A mon frae the North

Poole looked as solemn and calm as a judge as he raised the soup-basin and listened to his patient's words, while all at once a suspicious thought glanced through Fitz's brain, and he looked at the lad quickly and felt relieved, for no one could have imagined from the grave, stolid face before him that mirth like so much soda-water was bubbling and twinkling as it effervesced all through the being of the skipper's son.

"I couldn't have held it in any longer," said Poole to himself, with a sigh of relief, for just then the door clicked and the Camel's head came slowly in with the red eyes glowing and watchful.

Then seeing that the meal was ended he came right in, and took basin and spoon from Poole as if they were his own special property.

"Feel better, laddie?" he said, with a grin at the patient.

"Oh yes, thank you, cook," was the genial reply. "Capital soup."

"Ay," said the Camel seriously, "and ye'll just take the same dose every morning at twa bells till you feel as if you can eat salt-junk like a mon. Ah weel, ah weel! They make a fine flather about doctors and their stuff, but ye mind me there isn't another as can do a sick mon sae much good as the cook."

"Hear that, Mr Burnett?"

"Oh yes, I hear," said Fitz, smiling, with a look of content upon his features to which they had for many days been strangers.

"I am not going to say a word the noo aboot the skipper, and what he's done. He's a grand mon for a hole or a cut or a bit broken leg. He's got bottles and poothers of a' kinds, but when the bit place is mended it's the cook that has to do the rigging up. You joost stick to Andy Cawmell, and he'll make a man of you in no time."

"Thank you, cook," said Fitz, smiling.

"And ye'll be reet. But if ye'd no' mind, ye'll joost kindly say 'Andy mon,' or 'laddie' when you speak to me. It seems more friendly than 'cook.'

Ye see, cook seems to belang more to a sonsy lassie than a mon. Just let it be 'Andy' noo."

"All right; I'll mind," said the middy, who looked amused.

"Ah, it's a gran' thing, cooking, and stands first of all, for it keeps every one alive and strong. They talk a deal about French cooks and their kickshaws, and about English cooks, and I'm no saying but that some English cooks are very decent bodies; but when you come to Irish, Ould Oireland, as they ca' it, there's only one thing that ever came from there, and that's Irish stew."

"What about taters, Andy?"

"Why, isna that part of it? Who ever heard of an Irish stew without taters? That's Irish taters, my lad, but if you want a real good Irish stew you must ha'e it made of Scotch mutton and Scotch potatoes, same as we've got on board now. And joost you bide a wee, laddies, till we get across the ocean, and if there's a ship to be found there, I'll just show you the truth of what I mean. Do ye mind me, laddie?" continued the cook, fixing Fitz tightly with his red eyes.

"Mind you? Yes," said Fitz; "but what do you want with a ship to make a stew in?"

"What do I want with a ship?" said Andy, looking puzzled. "Why, to cook!"

"Cook a ship?"

"Ah, sure. Won't a bit of mutton be guid after so much salt and tinned beef?"

"Oh, a sheep!" cried Fitz.

"Ay, I said so: a ship. Your leg of mutton, or a shouther are all very good in their way, but a neck makes the best Irish stew. But bide a wee till we do get hold of a ship, and I'll make you a dish such as will make you say you'll never look at an Irish stew again."

"Oh!" cried Poole. "He means one of those—"

"Nay, nay, nay! Let me tell him, laddie. He never ken'd such a thing on board a man-o'-war. D'ye ken the national dish, Mr Burnett, sir?"

"Of course," said Fitz; "the roast beef of old England."

"Pugh!" ejaculated the Scot. "Ye don't know. Then I'll tell ye. Joost gi'e me the liver and a few ither wee bit innards, some oatmeal, pepper, salt, an onion, and the bahg, and I'll make you a dish that ye'll say will be as good as the heathen deities lived on."

"Do you know what that was?" said Fitz.

"Ay, laddie; it was a kind of broth, or brose—ambrose, they called it, but I dinna believe a word of it. Ambrose, they ca'ed it! But how could they get hahm or brose up in the clouds? A'm thinking that the heathen gods didn't eat at all, but sippit and suppit the stuff they got from the top of a mountain somewhere out in those pairts—I've read it all, laddies, in an auld book called *Pantheon*—mixed with dew, mountain-dew."

"Nonsense!" cried Fitz, breaking into a pleasant laugh.

"Nay, it's no nonsense, laddie. I've got it all down, prented in a book. Ambrosia, the chiel ca'ed it, because he didn't know how to spell, and when I came to thenk I see it all as plain as the nose on your face. It was not ambrose at all, but Athol brose."

"And what's that?" cried Fitz.

"Hech, mon! And ye a young laird and officer and dinna ken what Athol brose is!"

"No," said Fitz; "we learnt so much Greek and Latin at my school that we had to leave out the Scotch."

"Hearken to him, young Poole Reed! Not to know that! But it is Greek—about the Greek gods and goddesses. And ye dinna ken what Athol brose is?"

"No," said Fitz; "I never heard of it in my life."

"Weel, then, I'll just tell ye, though it's nae good for boys. It's joost a meexture half honey and half whisky, or mountain-dew; and noo ye ken."

"But you are not going to make a mess like that when you get a sheep."

"Ship, laddie—ship. If ye ca' it like that naebody will think ye mean a mutton that goes on four feet."

"Well, pronounce it your own way," said Fitz. "But what is this wonderful dish you mean to make?"

"He means kidney-broth, made with the liver," said Poole.

"Nay, nay. Dinna you mind him, laddie. He only said that to make you laugh. You bide a wee, and I'll make one fit for a Queen. You've never tasted haggis, but some day you shall."

Andy Cawmell closed one eye and gave the convalescent what was intended for a very mysterious, confidential look, and then stole gravely out of the cabin, closed the door after him, and opened it directly after, to thrust in his head, the basin, and the spoon.

"D'ye mind, laddie," he whispered, tapping the basin, "at twa bells every day the meexture as before."

He closed the door again, and this time did not return, though Fitz waited for a few moments before speaking, his eyes twinkling now with merriment.

"Haggis!" he cried. "Scotch haggis! Of course, I know. It's mincemeat boiled in the bag of the pipes with the pipes themselves chopped up for bones. You've heard of it before?"

"Oh yes, though I never tasted it. Andy makes one for the lads whenever he gets a chance."

"Do they eat it?"

"Oh yes, and laugh at him all the time. I dare say it's very good, but I never felt disposed to try. But he's a good fellow, is Andy, and as fine a sailor as ever stepped. You'll get to like him by and by."

"Get to like him?" said Fitz, pulling himself up short and stiff. "Humph! I dunno so much about that, young fellow. Look here, how long do you expect it's going to be before I am set aboard some ship?"

"Ah, that's more than anybody can say," replied Poole quietly.

Fitz was silent for a few moments, and then said sharply—

"What's the name of the port for which you are making sail?"

"Name of the port?" said Poole.

"Yes; you heard what I said, and I want to know."

"Yes; it's only natural that you would," said Poole. "I say, shall I get the tackle now?"

"No; I want an answer to my question," replied Fitz, firing up again.

"Well, I can't tell you. That's my father's business. We are sailing under what you would call sealed orders on board a Queen's ship."

"That's shuffling," cried Fitz angrily, with the black clouds coming over the little bit of sunshine that lit up his face after his soup. "Now, sir, I order you to tell me, an officer in the Queen's service, where this schooner is bound."

Poole was silent. "Do you hear me, sir?"

"Oh yes, I hear," said Poole, "but I am in a state of mutiny, and I'm going to ask old Butters to lend me his long line and hooks."

He moved towards the door as he spoke, but Fitz shouted to him to stop.

It was all in vain, for the lad closed the door and shut in the midshipman's angry face.

"Gone!" ejaculated Fitz. "He's too much for me now; but only just wait till I get well and strong!"

Chapter Ten
What Fitz wanted

"What do you think of this for weather?" said Poole, one morning. "Isn't it worth sailing right away to get into such seas as this?"

"Yes," said Fitz dreamily, as he lay on one side in his berth with his hand under his cheek, gazing through the cabin-window at the beautiful glancing water; "it is very lovely."

"Doesn't it make you feel as if you were getting quite well?"

"I think it would," said the boy, almost as if speaking to himself; "it would be all right enough if a fellow could feel happy."

"Well," said Poole, "you ought to begin to now. Just see how you've altered. Father says you are to come up this afternoon as soon as the heat of the day has passed."

"Come on deck?" cried Fitz, brightening. "Ah! That's less like being a prisoner."

"A prisoner!" said Poole merrily. "Hark at him! Why, you are only a visitor, having a pleasant cruise. Father's coming directly," he added hastily, for he saw the look of depression coming back into the boy's face. "He says this is the last time he shall examine your head, and that you won't want doctoring any more. Come, isn't that good news enough for one morning?"

Fitz made no reply, but lay with his face contracting, evidently thinking of something else.

"As soon as he's gone," continued Poole, "I am going to bring the lines and some bait. Old Butters said you could have them as much as you liked. Don't turn gruff again this time and say you don't want to try."

Fitz appeared to take no notice, and Poole went on—

"There are shoals of bonito about, and the Camel can dress them fine. You don't know how good they are, freshly caught and fried."

Fitz made an impatient gesture.

"How soon is your father coming below?" he said.

"Oh, he may be down any moment. He and Mr Burgess are taking observations overhead and calculating our course."

"Then he won't be very long," said Fitz.

"Oh no. Want to speak to him?"

"Yes, particularly."

Poole gave the speaker a sharp look, which evidently meant, I wonder what he wants to say.

At that moment the boys' eyes met, and Fitz said, as if to evade a question—

"Don't you learn navigation—take observations, and that sort of thing?"

"Oh yes, lots of it; but I have been having a holiday since you've been on board. So have you. It must be quite a change after your busy life on board a gunboat, drilling and signalling, and all that sort of thing."

Fitz was hearing him speak, but listening intently all the time, so that he gave an eager start and exclaimed—

"Here's your father coming now."

For steps were plainly heard on the companion-ladder, and the next minute the door was thrust open, and the bluff-looking skipper entered the cabin.

"Morning, sir," he cried. "How are we this morning? Oh, it doesn't want any telling. You are getting on grandly. Did Poole tell you I wanted you to come up on deck this afternoon?"

"Yes, sir; thank you. I feel a deal better now, only my legs are very weak when I try to stand up holding on by my berth."

"Yes, I suppose so," said the skipper, sitting down by the boy's head and watching him keenly. "You are weak, of course, but it's more imaginary than real. Any one who lays up for a week or two would feel weak when he got out of bed."

"But my head swims so, sir."

"Exactly. That's only another sign. You are eating well now, and getting quite yourself. But I am going to prescribe you another dose."

"Physic?" said Fitz, with a look of disgust.

"Yes, fresh air physic. I want you to take it very coolly for the next few days, but to keep on deck always except in the hottest times. In another week you won't know yourself."

"Hah!" ejaculated the boy. "Then now, sir—don't think me ungrateful, for nobody could be kinder to me than you and Poole here have shown yourselves since I have been aboard."

"Thank you, my lad, for both of us," said the skipper, smiling good-humouredly. "I am glad you give such ruffians as we are so good a character. But you were going to say something."

"Yes, sir," said the boy excitedly, and he cleared his voice, which had grown husky.

"Go on, then. You are beating about the bush as if you had some favour to ask. What is it?"

"I want," cried Fitz excitedly, and his cheeks flushed and eyes flashed— "I want you, sir," he repeated, "now that you say I'm better and fit to get about—"

"On deck," said the skipper dryly.

"Oh yes, and anywhere as soon as this giddiness has passed off... I want you now, sir, to set me ashore."

"Hah! Yes," said the skipper slowly. "I knew we were coming to that."

"Why, of course, sir. Think of what I must have suffered and felt."

"I thought Poole here had done his best to make you comfortable, my lad."

"Oh yes, and he has, sir," cried the boy, turning to look full in his attendant's eyes. "He has been a splendid fellow, sir. Nobody could have been kinder to me than he has, even at my worst times, when I was so ill and irritable that I behaved to him like a surly brute."

"It's your turn now, Poole," growled the skipper, "to say 'Thank you' for that."

"But you must feel, sir, how anxious and worried I must be—how eager to get back to my ship. In another day or two, Captain Reed, I shall be quite well enough to go. Promise me, sir, that you will set me ashore."

The skipper had pursed up his lips as if he were going to whistle for the wind, and he turned his now frowning face to look steadfastly at his son, who met his eyes with a questioning gaze, while the midshipman looked anxiously from one to the other, as if seeking to catch an encouraging look which failed to come.

At last the boy broke the silence again, trying to speak firmly; but, paradoxically, weakness was too strong, and his voice sounded cracked as he cried, almost pitifully—

"Oh, Captain Reed! Promise me you will now set me ashore!"

The skipper was silent for a few moments, before turning his face slowly to meet the appealing look in the boy's eyes.

"Set you ashore?" he said gruffly.

"Yes, sir, please. Pray do!"

And the answer came—

"Where, my boy? Where?"

Chapter Eleven
Thoughts of home

Fitz Burnett looked wonderingly at the skipper as if he did not comprehend the bearings of the question. "Where?" he faltered. "Yes; you asked me to set you ashore. I say, where?"

"Oh, at any American or English port, sir."

"Do you know how far we are from the nearest?"

"No; I have no idea how far we have come."

"Never mind that," said the skipper gravely. "Let's take it from another way of thinking. Do you know what it means for me to set you ashore at some port?"

"Oh yes, sir: that I shall be able to communicate with any English vessel, and get taken back to Liverpool."

"Well," said the skipper grimly, "you are a young sailor, but I am afraid that you have very small ideas about the size of the world. I dare say, though, that would be possible, sooner or later, for you go to very few ports now-a-days without coming across a ship flying British colours. It would be all right for you; but what about me?"

Fitz looked at him wonderingly again. "What about you, sir?" he stammered. "I was not thinking about you, but about myself."

"That wanted no telling, my lad. It's plain enough. You were not thinking about me, but I was. Look here, my boy. Do you know what my setting you ashore means just now?"

"Yes, sir," said the boy sharply. "Getting rid of a very troublesome passenger."

"Oh, you think so, do you? Well, I'll tell you what I think. It would mean getting rid of one troublesome passenger, as you call yourself, and taking a dozen worse ones on board in the shape of a prize crew. Why, young Burnett, it would mean ruin to me and to my friends, whose money has been invested in this cargo."

"Oh no, *no*, sir. I am alone out here, and my captain's vessel is far away. I couldn't go and betray you, even if I wanted to. You could set me ashore and sail away at once. That's all I want you to do."

"Sweet innocency!" said the skipper mockingly. "But I won't set it down to artfulness. I think you are too much of a gentleman for that. But do you hear him, Poole? Nice ideas he has for a beardless young officer in Her Majesty's Navy. Why, do you mean to tell me, sir, you know nothing about international politics, and a peculiar little way that they have now-a-days of flashing a bit of news all round the world in a few minutes of time? Don't you think that after that bit of a turn up off Liverpool way, a full description of my schooner and her probable destination has been wired across the Atlantic, and that wherever I attempted to land you, it would be for the port officials to step on board and tap me on the shoulder with a kindly request to give an account of myself?"

"I didn't think of that," said Fitz, slowly.

"No," said the skipper. "You thought that I could hail the first ship I saw, or sail up to the side of a quay, pitch you ashore, and sail off again. Why, Fitz Burnett, as soon as I came in sight I should be overhauled, seized, delayed for certain, and in all probability end by losing schooner, cargo, and my liberty."

"Surely it would not be so bad as that, sir?"

"Surely it would be worse. No, my lad; I am sorry for you. I regret the ugly accident by which you were knocked over; but you are thinking, as we said before, about your position, your duty. I have got to think of mine. Now, here's yours; you came on board here, unasked and unseen until the next morning when we had put a good many knots between us and your gunboat. It was impossible to land you, and so we made the best of it and treated you as well as we could. Time is money to me now, and my coming up punctually means something much more valuable than hard cash to the people I have come to see. To be plain, I can't waste, even if I were so disposed, any time for sailing into port to put you ashore."

"Never mind that, then, sir," cried Fitz excitedly. "Speak the first vessel you see, of any country, under any flag, and put me aboard there."

"No, my lad," said the skipper sternly. "And I can't do that. I am going to speak no ships. My work is to sail away and hold communication with no one. I have no need to make all this explanation to you, my boy, but I am doing it because we are sorry for you, and want to make things as easy as we can. Now, look here, you are a sensible lad, and you must learn to see your position. I can do nothing for you beyond treating you well, until

I have made my port, run my cargo of knick-knacks, and cleared for home. By that time I shall have a clean bill of health, and be ready to look all new-comers in the face."

"But how long will that be, sir?" cried Fitz excitedly.

"Dunno, my lad. It depends on what's going on over yonder. If all goes smooth it may be only a month; if all goes rough, perhaps two, or three. I may be dodging about a long while. Worse still, my schooner may be taken, condemned, and my crew and I clapped in irons in some Spanish-American prison, to get free nobody knows when."

"Oh!" groaned Fitz excitedly.

"I am being very plain to you, my lad, now that the cat's out of the bag, and there's nothing to hide. I am playing a dangerous game, one full of risk. It began when I was informed upon by some cowardly, dirty-minded scoundrel, one who no doubt had been taking my pay till he thought he could get no more, and then he split upon me, with the result that your captain was put upon the scent of my enterprise, to play dog and run me down in the dark. But you see I had one eye open, and got away. Now I suppose the telegraph will have been at work, and the folks over yonder will be waiting for me there, so that I shall have to hang about and wait my chance of communicating with my friends. So there, you see, you will have to wait one, two, perhaps three months, before, however good my will, I can do anything for you."

"But by that time," cried Fitz, "I shall be disgraced."

"Bah! Nonsense, my lad! There can be no disgrace for one who boarded a vessel along with his crew, and had the bad luck to be struck down. Now, my boy, you know I'm a father. Let me speak like a father to you. Your real trouble is this, and I say honestly I am sorry, and so's Poole there, not so much for you as for your poor relatives. There, it's best I should speak quite plainly. It's as well to know the worst that can have happened, and then it generally proves to have been not so bad; and that's what clever folks call philosophy. The real trouble in your case is this, that by this time your poor relatives will probably know that your number has been wiped off your mess; in short, you have been reported—dead."

"What!" cried the boy, in a tone full of anguish. "They will have sent word home that I am dead?"

"I am afraid so," said the skipper. "It's very sad, but you have got to bear it like a man."

"Sad!" cried the boy passionately. "It's horrible! It will break her heart!"

"You mean your mother's," said the skipper gravely, and he laid his hand kindly on the boy's shoulder. "But it's not so bad as you think, my lad. I have had a little experience of women in my time—wives and mothers, boy—and there's a little something that generally comes to them in cases like this and whispers in their poor ears. That little something, my boy, is always very kind to us sea-going people, and it's called Hope. And somehow at such times as this it makes women think that matters can't be so bad as they have been described, or that they can't be true. Now I'd be ready to say that in spite of the bad news that's come to your mother about you, she won't believe it's true, and that she's waiting patiently for the better news that will some time come, and that it will be many, many months, perhaps a year, before she will really believe that you are dead."

"Oh, but it's too horrible!" cried the boy wildly.

"No, no, no. Come! Pluck up your spirits and make the best of it. Look here, boy. You must bear it for the sake of the greater pleasure, the joy that will come when she finds that she was right in her belief, and in the surprise to all your friends when they see you come back alive and kicking, and all the better for your voyage. I say, look at the bright side of things, and think how much better it has all been than if you had been knocked overboard to go down in the darkness at a time when it was every one for himself, and no one had a thought for you."

Fitz turned away his head so that neither father nor son could see the workings of his face.

"There, my lad," said the skipper, rising, "I was obliged to speak out plainly. I have hurt you, I know, but it has only been like the surgeon, to do you good. I am wanted on deck now, so take my advice; bear it like a man. Here, Poole, I want you for half-an-hour or so, and I dare say Mr Burnett would like to have a bit of a think to himself."

He gave the boy a warm pressure of his hand, and then strode out of the cabin, his example being followed the next moment by Poole, whose action was almost the same as his father's, the exception being that he quickly caught hold of the middy's hand and held it for a moment before he hurried out.

Then and then only did Fitz's face go down upon his hands, while a low groan of misery escaped his lips.

Chapter Twelve
Making friends

"Well, what is it?" said the skipper gruffly, as his son followed him on deck and touched him on the arm.

"Don't you think it possible, father, that—"

"That I could turn aside from what I have got to do, boy? No, I don't."

"But he's ill and weak, father."

"Of course he is, and he's getting better as fast as he can. What's more, he's a boy—in the depth of despair now, and in half-an-hour's time he'll be himself again, and ready to forget his trouble."

"I don't think he will, father."

"Don't you? Then I do. I have had more experience of boys than you have, and I have learned how Nature in her kindness made them. Look here, Poole, I believe for the time that boys feel trouble more keenly than do men, but Nature won't let it last. The young twig will bend nearly double, and spring up again. The old stick snaps."

The skipper walked away, leaving his son thinking.

"I don't believe father's right," he said. "Fitz doesn't seem like most boys that I have met. Poor chap, it does seem hard! I don't think I ever felt so bad as he must now. I wish I hadn't had to come away, for it was only an excuse on father's part. He doesn't want me. It was only to leave the poor chap alone."

Acting upon these thoughts, Poole tried to think out some excuse for going down to the cabin again as soon as he could. But as no reasonable excuse offered itself, he waited till the half-hour was expired, and then went down without one, opened the cabin-door gently, and gravely stepped in, to stop short, staring in astonishment at the change which had come over his patient, for he was sitting bent down with his hands upon his knees at the edge of his berth, swinging his legs to and fro, with every trace of suffering gone out of the eyes which looked up sharply.

If Poole Reed was surprised at the midshipman's appearance, he was far more so at his tones and words.

"Hallo!" he cried. "Thought you'd gone to fetch those fishing-lines."

"I—I—Oh, yes, I'll get them directly," stammered Poole.

"Look sharp, then. The fish are playing about here like fun. I saw one spring right out of the water just now after a shoal. The little ones look like silver, and the big chap was all blue and gold."

"All right; I won't be long," cried Poole, and he hurried out, letting the door bang behind him.

"Well, I was a fool to worry myself about a chap like that. Why, he doesn't feel it a bit."

But Poole Reed was not a good judge of human nature. He could not see the hard fight that was going on behind that eager face, nor how the well-trained boy had called upon his pride to carry him through this struggle with his fate.

Poole thought no more of his patient's condition, but hurried to the boatswain, who scowled at him fiercely.

"What!" he said. "Fishing-lines? Can't you find nothing else to do, young fellow, on board this 'ere craft, besides fishing?"

"No; there is nothing to do now."

"Wha-a-at!"

"You know I spoke about them before. It is to amuse the sick middy."

"Yah!" came in a deep growl. "Why didn't you say so before? Poor boy! He did get it hot that time."

"Yes," said Poole maliciously, "and I believe it was you who knocked him down."

The grim-looking, red-faced boatswain stared at the speaker with his mouth wide open.

"Me?" he said. "Me? Why, I was alongside the chap at the wheel."

"Were you?" said Poole, grinning to himself at the effect of his words. "Then it couldn't have been you, Butters. Come on and get me the line."

"Gammon!" growled the boatswain. "You knew it warn't all the time. Come on."

He led the way to his locker and took out a couple of square reel-frames with their cord, hooks, and sinkers complete.

"Ketch hold," he said gruffly, and then giving Poole a tin box whic rattled loudly, he growled out, "Plenty of spare hooks in there. But don lose more than you can help. Where are you going to fish? Off the taffrail?"

"No; out of the stern-window."

"What! How are you going to haul in your fish?"

"Oh, I don't know."

"See what a mess you'll make, my lad."

"I'll clean up afterwards," said Poole.

"I don't believe you will get any. If you hook one you'll knock it off in pulling it in. Why don't you bring the poor lad up on deck and let him fish like a human being, not keep him cuddled up below there like a great gal?"

"But he's so weak, he can hardly stand."

"Set him down, then, in a cheer. Do him good, and he'll like it all the more."

"Well, I never thought of that," said Poole eagerly. "I will. But oh, I mustn't forget the bait. I must go and see the Camel."

"Nonsense! Bait with a lask cut off from the first fish you catch."

"Of course," cried Poole; "but how am I to catch that first one first?"

"'M, yes," said the boatswain, with a grim smile. "Tell you what; go and ask the Camel to give you a nice long strip of salt pork, fat and rind."

"Ah, that would do," cried Poole; and he hurried off to the galley, where he was welcomed by the cook with a nod and wink, as he drew a little stew-pan forward on the hot plate, and lifted the lid.

"Joost cast your nose over that, laddie," he whispered mysteriously.

"Eh? What for?"

"It's the middy laddie's soup fresh made, joost luvely."

"Oh yes, splendid," said the lad, and he hurriedly stated his wants, had them supplied, and went back to the cabin ready to prepare for catching the first fish.

"Look here, Burnett," he said, "it'll be very awkward fishing out of this window. How'd it be if I put a cane-chair close up under the rail? Don't you think you could manage if I helped you up there?"

"I don't know. I am afraid I couldn't walk," said the boy dubiously. "I'd try."

"Oh, never mind about your walking! If you'll come I'll run up and put a chair ready, and then come back for you. I could carry you easily enough if I got you on my back."

One moment Fitz had been looking bright and eager; the next a gloomy shade was passing over his face.

"Like a sack," he said bitterly.

"Well, then, shall I make two of the lads carry you in a chair?"

"No," said the boy, brightening up again. "If I put my arm over your shoulder, and you get one round my waist, I think I could manage it if we went slowly."

"To be sure," cried Poole, and he hurried on deck, thrust a long cane reclining chair into the place he thought most suitable, and had just finished when his father came up.

"What are you about, boy?" he said; and Poole explained.

"Well, I don't know. I meant for him to come up this afternoon, but I thought that it was all over after that upset. How does he seem now?"

"Just as if he were going to make the best of it, father."

"Then bring him up."

A minute later the tackle and bait were lying on the deck beside the chair, and Poole hurried down to the cabin to help his patient finish dressing, which task was barely completed when there was a tap at the door and the Camel appeared, bearing his morning "dose," as he termed it.

This was treated as a hindrance, but proved to be a valuable fillip after what the boy had gone through, and the preparation for that which was to come, so that, with the exception of once feeling a little faint, Fitz managed to reach the deck, leaning heavily upon his companion; but not unnoticed, for the mate caught sight of him from where he was on the look-out forward, and hurried up to take the other arm.

"Morning, Mr Burnett," he said eagerly. "Come, this is fine! Coming to sit in the air a bit? Oh, we shall soon have you all right now."

The boy flushed and looked pleased at the kindly way in which he was received, and as he reached the chair there was another welcome for him from the hand at the wheel, who had the look of an old man-of-war's man, and gave him the regular salute due to an officer.

"Feel all right?" said the mate.

"Yes, much better than I thought."

"Fishing, eh?" said the mate. "Well, good luck to you! Come, we shan't look upon you as an invalid now."

"Lie back in the chair a bit," said Poole, who was watching his companion anxiously.

"What for?"

"I thought perhaps you might feel a little faint."

"Oh no, that's all gone off," cried the boy, drawing a deep long breath, as he eagerly looked round the deck and up at the rigging of the smart schooner, whose raking taper masts and white canvas gave her quite the look of a yacht.

There was a look of wonder in the boy's eyes as he noted the trimness and perfection of all round, as well as the smartness of the crew, whose aspect suggested the truth, namely, that they had had their training on board some man-of-war.

From craft and crew the boy's eyes wandered round over the sea, sweeping the horizon, as he revelled in the soft pure air and the glorious light.

"How beautiful it seems," he said, half aloud, "after being shut up so long below."

"Come, that's a good sign," said Poole cheerily.

"What's a good sign?" was the sharp reply.

"That you can enjoy the fresh air so much. It shows that you must be better. Think you can hold the line if I get one ready?"

"Of course," said Fitz, rather contemptuously.

"All right, then."

Poole turned away and knelt upon the deck, laughing to himself the while, as he thought that if a big fish were hooked the invalid would soon find out the difference. And then the boy's fingers moved pretty quickly as he took out his junk-knife and cut a long narrow strip from the piece of fatty pork-rind with which the cook had supplied him.

Through one end of this he passed the point of the hook, and then brought it back to the same side by which it had entered, so that a strip about six inches long and one wide hung down from the barbed hook. The next process was to unwind twenty or thirty yards of the line with its leaden sinker, and then drop lead and bait overboard, running out the line till the bait was left about fifty yards astern, but not to sink far, for there was wind enough to carry the schooner along at a pretty good pace, trailing the bait twirling round and round behind, and bearing no small resemblance to a small, quickly-swimming fish, the white side of the bait alternating with the dull grey of the rind, and giving it a further appearance of life and movement.

"There you are," said Poole, passing the line into the midshipman's hands. "I will unwind some more, have fished like this before, haven't you?"

"Only a little for whiting and codlings," was the reply. "I never got hold of anything big. I suppose we may get a tidy one here?"

"Oh yes; and they are tremendously strong."

"Not so strong but what I can hold them, I dare say," said Fitz confidently.

But his confidence was not shared by his companion, who unwound the line till there was no more upon the frame, and then gave the end two or three turns about one of the belaying-pins, leaving a good many rings of loose line upon deck.

There was need for the foresight, as was soon proved. Fitz was sitting leaning right back with his eyes half-closed, thoroughly enjoying the change; the trouble of the morning was for the moment numbed, and no care assailed him. He was listening as he enjoyed the sensation that thrilled the nerves of his arm as the bait and lead sinker were drawn through the water far astern with a peculiar jigging motion, and questioning Poole about the kind of fish that they were likely to encounter as far south as they then were.

"You have been across here, then, before?" he said.

"Oh yes; four times."

"Ever seen any sharks?"

"Lots; but not out here. I saw most close in shore among the islands."

"What islands?"

"Oh, any of them; Saint Lucia, Nevis, Trinidad. Pretty big too, some of them."

"Ever catch one?"

"No, we never tried. Nasty brutes! I hate them."

"So does everybody, I suppose. But, I say, think we shall catch anything to-day?"

"Oh yes; but you mustn't be disappointed if we don't. Fish swarm one day, and you can see as many as you like; another time—you go all day long and you don't see one."

"I say, this isn't going to be one of those days, is it? I haven't had a bite yet. Think the bait's off?"

"Not it. That tough skin closes up round the hook, and you would almost have to cut it to get it over the barb. It makes a capital bait to stick on, but of course it isn't half so attractive as a bit of a bright silvery fish. I'll change it as soon as I can. I wish we had got one of those big silvered spoons. I think father's got two or three. I will go and ask him if you don't soon get a—"

"Oh! Poole! Here! Help! I—I can't— Oh, he's gone!" panted the middy.

For all at once his right arm received a violent jerk, and as the line was twisted round his hand he was dragged sideways, and but for Poole's ready help would have been pulled off the chair helplessly on to the deck. Fortunately for him the skipper's son was on the *qui vive*, and stopping the convalescent's progress with one hand, he made a snatch at the line with the other.

"He's too much for you," cried Poole. "Here, shake your hand clear of the line. I've got him. That's the way. Has it hurt you?"

"It seemed to cut right into the skin," panted Fitz. "He must be a monster. Oh, whatever you do, don't let him go!"

"No, I won't let him go," was the reply; "not if I can help it. He is a pretty good size. We will make a double job of it. Here, I'll haul him in a few feet, and then you can take hold in front of me, and we will haul him in together. No, he won't come yet. I shall have to let him run a little—I mean, we shall have to let him run a little. Now then, foot by foot. Let's let the line run through our hands."

This was done steadily and slowly, till another fifty yards of line had been given, the fish that had been hooked darting the while here and there, and at a tremendous rate, and displaying enormous strength for a creature of its size.

But it had to contend not only with the drag kept up by the boys, but the motion of the schooner as well, with the result that its strength soon began to fail, till at last it was drawn behind the gliding schooner almost inert.

"There," cried Poole; "now I think we might have him in. I was afraid to haul before for fear of dragging the hook out of its jaws. Look at that now!" he cried impatiently.

"What's the matter? Don't say he has gone!"

"Oh no, he's not gone. Why, he is making a fresh dash for his liberty. But we can't lift him in by the hook, and I never thought about getting a gaff.—Here, hi!" he cried. "Come here, Chips!"

One of the sailors sidled up—a dry-looking, quaint man with a wrinkled face, who broke out into a smile as he saw what was going on.

"Fish, sir?" he said, and his hand made a movement toward his cap. "Want me to fetch my bag of tools?"

"Yes," cried Poole. "I mean, get that long-handled gaff from down below."

"Right, sir," and the man trotted off, leaving the two lads slowly and steadily hauling in yard after yard of the line.

"Still fast on, sir?" cried the man to Fitz, as he stood what looked like a highly-educated boat-hook against the rail.

Fitz made no reply, for his face was flushed and his teeth hard set in the excitement of his task.

"Oh yes, we've got him fast enough, Chips," said Poole. "Be very careful, for he's a heavy one, and Mr Burnett here wouldn't like to lose him now."

"All right, sir," said the man, taking up the long shaft again, and lowering it down over the side. "I don't know, though, whether I shall be able to reach him from up here. It looks like being best to get down to the rudder-chains. No; it's all right. I shall manage him if you get him close up to the side."

"Steady! Steady!" cried Poole. "He's making another flurry. Let him go again. No, it's all right—all over; haul away."

By this time the great drops of perspiration were standing upon Fitz's brow, joining, and beginning to trickle down the sides of his face; but his teeth were still hard set, and intent upon the capture he kept on hauling away as hard as his weakness would allow.

"There," cried Poole, at last. "You caught him; but you had better let me have the line to myself now to get him closer in, so that Chips can make a good stroke with the gaff and pull him right aboard."

"Yes," said Fitz, with a sigh; "I suppose I must," and with his countenance beginning to contract with the disappointment he felt, he resigned the line and sat back in the chair, breathing hard, gently rubbing his aching muscles, and intently watching what was going on. That did not take long, but it was long enough to attract the other men who were on deck, and they came round, to form a semi-circle behind the middy's chair, while Poole hauled the fish closer and closer in beneath the counter, and then stayed his hand.

"Can you do it now?" he cried.

"Not quite. I'll come round the other side," replied the handler of the gaff, who, suiting the action to the word, changed his place, leaned right over the rail, almost doubling himself up, and then uttered a warning—

"Ready?"

"Yes," was the reply.

"Now then, half-a-fathom more."

What followed was almost instantaneous. Poole made two fresh grips at the line, pulled hard, and then with an ejaculation fell backwards on to the deck with the hooks upon his chest.

"Gone!" groaned Fitz; but his exclamation was drowned in a roar of laughter from the men, and a peculiar flapping, splashing noise caused by the fish, in which the gaff had taken a good hold, bending itself into the shape of a half-moon as it was hauled over the side, giving the man saluted as Chips a violent blow with its tail, and then as it flopped down upon the deck slapping the planks with sounding blow after blow.

Following directly upon the laughter there was a loud cheer, and in the midst of his excitement at the triumphant capture, Fitz heard the mate's voice—

"Well done, Mr Burnett! That's about the finest bonito I ever saw. I thought you'd lost him, Chips."

"Nay, sir; I'd got my hook into him too tight; but it was touch and go."

"Yes, that's a fine one," said Poole, taking hold of the detached hook and drawing the captive round in front of Fitz's chair.

"Yes," replied the boy, who sat back wiping his brow; "but it isn't so big as I expected to see."

"Oh, he's pretty big," said the mate—"thick and solid and heavy; and those fellows have got such tremendous strength in those thin half-moon tails. They are like steel. Going to try for any more?"

The mate looked at Fitz as he spoke.

"It's very exciting," he said, rather faintly, "but I am afraid I am too tired now."

"Yes," said the mate kindly. "I wouldn't try to overdo it the first time you are up on deck. Lie back and rest, my lad. Send for the Camel, Poole, lad, when you have done looking at it. Now, my lads, two of you, swabs."

He turned away, and a couple of the men set to work to wash and dry the slimy deck, but waited until the little admiring crowd had looked their fill, the foremost men seeming to take a vast amount of interest in fishology, making several highly intellectual remarks about the configuration of the denizen of the deep. Before long though the real reason of their interest escaped them, for one made a remark or two about what a fine thick cut could be got from "just there," while another opined that a boneeter of that there size ate tenderer boiled than fried.

By that time Fitz's excitement had died down, and he no longer took interest in the beautiful steely and blue tints mingled with silver and gold, that flashed from the creature's scales. In fact, in answer to a whispered query on the part of Poole, he nodded his head and let it lie right back against the chair. This was the signal for the Camel to be fetched to help bear the big fish forward to the galley, ready for cutting up, while the two men with bucket and swab rapidly finished cleaning and drying the deck, so that the damp patches began to turn white again in the hot rays of the sun.

It was all very quickly done, and then Poole began to slowly wind up the long line, giving every turn carefully and methodically so as to spread the stout hempen cord as open and separate for drying purposes as could be.

He took his time, dropping in a word or two now and then, apparently intent upon his task, but keenly watching his companion all the while.

"Hasn't been too much for you, has it?" he said.

"No," replied Fitz; "not too much, for it was very interesting; but it was quite enough. I don't quite know how it is, but I have turned so sleepy."

"Ah, you are tired. Sit quite back, and I will draw the chair over here into the shade. A nap till dinner-time up here in the air will do you no end of good, and give you an appetite for dinner. There; the sun won't be round here for an hour."

It was easily done, the cane legs gliding like rockers over the well-polished deck, and the lad returned to his place to turn the winder where he had stood the line to dry. This process was going on rapidly, and he stopped bending over the apparatus to examine the hook and stout snood, to see that it had not been frayed by the fish's teeth. This done, he turned to speak to Fitz again, and smiled to himself.

"Well," he said, "it doesn't take him long to go to sleep," for the tired midshipman's eyes were tightly closed and he was taking another instalment of that which was to give him back his strength.

Chapter Thirteen
A question of duty

The wind was paradoxical. A succession of calms and light breezes from adverse quarters—in short, as bad as could be for the schooner's expedition.

But, on the other hand, the days grew into weeks in a climate that might be called absolutely perfect, and from his first coming on deck and helping in the capture of the bonito, Fitz Burnett advanced by steps which became long strides on his journey back to health.

With the disappearance of suffering, away went all bad temper with the irritation that had caused it. The boy had lain in his berth and thought every night before going to sleep about his position and his helplessness, and had fully come to the conclusion that though the people among whom he was, skipper, officers and men, were in a way enemies, he could not be held accountable for anything they did, and as they had treated him throughout with the greatest kindness, it would be ungracious on his part to go, as he termed it, stalking about on stilts and making himself as disagreeable to them as he would be to himself.

"Old Reed's quite right, after all," he said, "though I don't like it a bit. I must make the best of my position. But only let me get half a chance, and I shall be off."

The boy then, as he rapidly recovered his strength, went about the deck amongst the men, and became what he termed extremely thick with Poole. There were times when he felt that they were becoming great friends, for Poole was a thoroughly intelligent lad who had had a good deal of experience for one of his years; but in these early stages of his recovery, so sure as there was a little change in the weather, with the damp or wind, twinges of pain and depression of spirits attacked the midshipman; the physical suffering introduced the mental, and for a few hours perhaps Fitz would feel, to use his own words, as disagreeable as could be.

It was during one of these attacks that the idea came back very strongly that he was not doing his duty as an officer. He worked himself up into the feeling that he was behaving in a cowardly way now that he had great opportunities, and that if he did not seize one of these it would be to his disgrace.

"I ought to do it," he said, "and I will. It only wants pluck, for I have got right on my side. It is almost as good as having the gunboat and her crew at my back. It's one of those chances such as we read of in history, where one fellow steps out to the front and carries all before him. I did not see it so clearly before as I do now. That's what I ought to do, and I am going to do it. Poole will think it abominably ungrateful, and his father will be horribly wild; but I have got my duty to do, and it must be done, so here goes."

But "here" did not go, for on second thoughts matters did not seem quite so clear; but a day or two after, when the notion had been steadily simmering in his mind it seemed at last to be quite done, and shutting his eyes to all suggestions regarding impossibility or madness, he made his plunge.

Fitz was not well. The weather had grown intensely hot, and unconsciously he was suffering from a slight touch of fever, which he complained about to Poole, who explained to him what it was, after reference to his father, and came back to him with a tiny packet of white crystals in some blue paper, and instructions that he was to take the powder at once.

"Fever, is it?" said Fitz, rather sourly. "One couldn't be catching fever out here in the open sea. I shall see your father myself. Why didn't he come on deck yesterday?"

"Because he isn't well. He's got a touch of fever too. He had got the bottle out of the medicine-chest, and was taking a dose when I went into his cabin."

"What!" cried Fitz. "Then he's caught the fever too?"

"Oh no; he caught it years ago, on the Mosquito Coast, and now and then when we get in for a change of weather like we have just had, it breaks out again and he's very ill for a few days; but he soon comes round."

"But I was never on the Mosquito Coast," cried Fitz impatiently. "I never caught a fever there, and I couldn't catch one like that of your father."

"No," said Poole; "father was talking about it, and he said yours was a touch due to your being susceptible after being so much hurt. That's how he said it was. Now then, come down to the cabin and take your physic like a good boy."

"I am not going to do anything of the sort," said Fitz shortly. "I took plenty while I was ill and weak, and you could do what you liked with me. But I am strong enough now, and if what I feel is due to the weather, when it changes the trouble will soon go off."

"I dare say it will," said Poole, laughing; "but you needn't make a fuss about swallowing this little scrap of bitter powder. Come on and take it like a man."

"Don't bother," said Fitz shortly, and he walked away right into the bows, climbed out on to the bowsprit, and sat down to think.

"He's a rum chap," said Poole, as he stood watching him, and putting the powder back into his pocket. "He makes me feel as if I liked and could do anything for him sometimes, and then when he turns cocky I begin to want to punch his head."

Poole turned and went down into the cabin, where his father was lying in his berth looking flushed and weary, and evidently suffering a good deal.

"Well, boy," said the skipper; "did he take his dose?"

"No, father. He's ready to kick against everything now."

"Well," said the skipper shortly, "let him kick."

Fitz was already kicking as he sat astride the bowsprit, looking out to sea and talking excitedly to himself.

"Yes," he said, "I like them, and we have got to be very good friends; but I have got my duty to do as a Queen's officer, and do it I will. Why, it's the very chance. Like what people call a fatality. That's right, I think. Just as if it were made on purpose. Of course I know that I am only a boy—well, a good big boy, almost a man; but I am a Queen's officer, and if I speak to the men it is in the Queen's name. And look at them too. They are not like ordinary sailors. I have not been on board this schooner and mixing with them and talking to them all this time for nothing. It was plain enough at first, and I was nearly sure, but I made myself quite. Nearly every one of them has been at some time or other in the Royal Navy—men who have served their time, and then been got hold of by the skipper to sign and serve on board his craft. They are a regular picked crew of good seamen fit to serve on board any man-of-war, and I wonder they haven't been kept. They weren't all trained for nothing. See how well they obey every order, as smart as smart. That means training and recollecting the old discipline. Why, if I talk to them right they won't stop to think that I am only a middy. I shall speak to them as an officer, and it will come natural to them to obey—in the Queen's name. It is my duty too as an officer, and as an officer it means everything— midshipman, lieutenant, captain or admiral—an admiral is only an officer, and at a time like this I am equal to an admiral—well, say captain. I don't care, I'll do it.—All these rough plucky chaps of course wouldn't be afraid of me as a boy; they'd laugh at me. Of course I know that; but it will be the officer speaking—yes, the officer."

The middy's head began metaphorically to swell out until it seemed to grow very big indeed, making him feel quite a man—and more.

"Yes," he said, "I'll do it. I must do it. Now's the time, and I should be an idiot if I neglected such a chance."

Drawing a deep breath, he turned his head slowly, and assuming as careless a manner as he could command, he looked back inboard beneath the swelling sails, to see that several of the men were lying asleep in the shade, while others were smoking and chatting together. The boatswain was not visible, and the mate was apparently below, the after part of the vessel being vacant save that the man at the wheel was standing with outstretched hands resting upon the spokes, moving his lower jaw slowly as he worked at his succulent quid.

Poole was still below with his father in the cabin, so that to the middy's way of thinking he had the deck to himself. He took another deep breath, and with his heart beating heavily, swung himself round, laid hold of a rope, and climbed inboard again, when assuming a nonchalance he did not feel as he dropped upon the deck, he thrust his hands into his pockets, mastered the desire to run, and beginning to whistle, stalked slowly aft till he reached the companion-hatch, and began to descend the steps without a sound.

Now was the critical time, for as he went down he could see that the cabin-door was shut, and hear the dull burr, burr, burr-like murmur of the captain's voice talking to his son.

Half-way down Fitz stopped short, for he heard a movement as if Poole were crossing the cabin, and if he came out now the opportunity was gone.

The middy felt the sensation as of a spasm attacking his chest, and as he paused there, half suffocated, he trembled with anger against himself for losing such a chance; but the sound within the cabin ceased, the captain's voice went murmuring on once more, and the suffocating sensation passed away, leaving the boy ready to seize his opportunity, and quick as thought he descended the last few steps, paused at the cabin-entry, and raising his hand quickly and silently, secured the outer door.

Chapter Fourteen
A bold stroke

Fitz Burnett did not pause to think of the rights or wrongs of his proceedings, but smothered up everything in the belief that he was doing his duty.

He would not even pause to consider whether his ideas were possible or impossible; everything was swallowed up in action, and with feverish energy he hurried back on deck to make the most use of the flying moments while he could.

Hurrying forward to where the men were dozing, smoking, and thinking, he signed to those who noticed his approach, and called to the others.

"Now, my lads!" he cried.

The men sprang up wonderingly, apparently influenced by old traditions, and in no wise surprised to find the young officer about to give them some order.

"Look here, my lads," he said, in a low, quick, excited voice; "a word with you! I know you were all ABs to a man."

"Ay, ay, sir!" said the nearest sailor at whom he looked.

"It is my duty to make you, a crew of good men and true, know exactly how you stand."

"Old men-of-war's men," continued Fitz to another.

"Ay, ay, sir! That's right," said the sailor.

"It is my duty to make you, a crew of good men and true, know exactly how you stand."

The listeners looked wonderingly at the excited boy, and then at one another, as if asking for the meaning of these unusual words.

"Look here," continued Fitz, "you have all been good fellows to me since I have been aboard."

"Ay, ay, sir! Why not?" said one of the men, with his face broadening into a hearty grin.

"And that's why I, an officer in the Navy, feel friendly disposed to a set of smart fellows who used to serve the Queen."

"Ay, ay, sir! We served the Queen," came in a murmur.

"You did it in ignorance, no doubt, but in what you are doing you are offenders against the law, and may at any time be taken, and perhaps be strung up to the yardarm after a short trial. Certainly you will be severely punished."

A low murmur of dissent, almost derision, came from the little knot of men, and one of them laughed.

"You don't believe me," cried Fitz. "It is true. And now listen to what I say, one and all; I call upon you in the Queen's name to obey my orders, for I take possession of this schooner as an officer in Her Majesty's service. In the Queen's name!"

There was a low murmur of mingled surprise and derision at this.

"Silence, there!" cried Fitz. "I know that I am a very young officer to speak to you, but I am in the Queen's Navy, and I order you in Her Majesty's name to obey all my commands. I am going to sail at once for Kingston, where I have no doubt there will be a man-of-war on the station, and if you behave well I shall speak to the captain and get him to make it easy for you, but of course I shall give up the skipper and his son as prisoners."

"Here, say something, Chips," growled one of the men; and the carpenter spoke out.

"Say, squire, won't that be rather hard on them?"

"Silence, sir! How dare you! That is not the way for a common sailor to address an officer."

"Beg pardon, sir, but I am not a common sailor; I am a hartisan. Why, you know—the Chips."

There was a titter here.

"Attention!" roared Fitz. "This is no laughing matter, my lads. Perhaps each man's life, certainly his liberty, is at stake."

"Ay, ay, sir!" came in a growl.

"That's better," said Fitz. "Now, I don't want to be hard on you, my lads."

"Hear, hear! Thank you, sir," cried the carpenter.

"And I should be sorry to be harsh to any man; but once more, as an officer in the Royal Navy, I have got my duty to do, and I mean to do it."

"Ay, ay, sir!" came again, in a low acquiescent growl. "But he needn't keep on a-telling us."

"Those men who stand by me and do their duty in navigating this vessel shall have ample pay and reward."

"What about prize-money, sir?" shouted a voice.

"There'll be no prize-money."

The men groaned.

"But there will be reward in the shape of salvage, my lads. I, single-handed, have taken this schooner as a prize to the gunboat *Tonans*, commanded by Captain Glossop, whose officer I am. She will be condemned and sold, and those who help me loyally will have their reward. Now then, every man stand forward who is ready to do his duty by me."

At that moment there was a sharp tapping heard from below.

"What's that?" cried Fitz sharply, though he perfectly well knew.

"It's the skipper, sir, a-opening his eyes, I think," said the carpenter. "You've woke him up, talking like that, and he's coming on deck with a pair of revolving bulldogs, to begin potting us all round. Here, who's coming below?"

"Silence, sir; and keep your places."

The carpenter stepped back behind the rest, and the next moment there rang out a most perfect imitation of the crow of a bantam cock, which was followed by a roaring outburst of merriment from the men.

Fitz turned scarlet with rage.

"How dare—" he began.

"Ahoy! On deck, there!" came faintly from the cabin, followed by a heavy sound of beating and kicking.

One of the men made a start aft for the companionway, followed by two more, but Fitz stepped before them.

"Stop!" he shouted fiercely.

"On deck, there! Do you hear? Open this door!" came from below.

"Take no notice," shouted Fitz, "until I give orders. Here, you carpenter; where's the arm-chest?"

"Down in the cabin, sir."

"No, no; I mean the other one—the men's."

"Arn't no nother one, sir. We always goes to the captain's tool-chest when we've got anybody as wants killing, or any job of that kind on hand!"

"Ahoy, there!" came from below once more, and then the sharp report of a pistol, a crash, and Poole came bounding up on deck, revolver in hand.

Just as he came into sight the skipper's voice was heard distinctly—

"Lay hold of the first mutineer, Poole, and drag him down here."

"That's meant for you, Mr Fitz, sir," said the carpenter with a chuckle, and the men roared again.

Fitz turned upon him, white as ashes, like an angry dog about to bite.

"Silence, you insolent scoundrel!" he shouted.

"What's the meaning of this, Burnett?" cried Poole.

"This, sir," said the lad haughtily, stepping forward to meet him, laying one hand on his shoulder, and making a desperate snatch at the revolver; "I seize this schooner in the Queen's name. Now, my lads, make this boy your prisoner."

Poole clapped the pistol behind him as he shook himself free.

"Look here, sir," he cried; "have you gone mad?"

"Do you hear, men?" cried Fitz, seizing him again. "Forward! You, Poole, in the Queen's name, surrender!"

Not a man stirred, all standing in a group looking on, some wonderingly, some thoroughly amused, while the carpenter whispered—

"All right, lads; let them fight it out. Of all the cheek!"

"Did you say, You Poole or You fool?" said the skipper's son quietly; "because one of us seems to be behaving very stupidly. Take your hand off my collar. This pistol's loaded in five chambers, and was in six till I blew the lock off the cabin-door.—Quiet, I tell you, before there's an accident. Why, you must have gone off your head."

"Did you hear what I said, men?" shouted Fitz furiously. "In the Queen's name, make this boy your prisoner! Here, you, boatswain, take the lead here and obey my orders." For that individual had just made his appearance on deck.

"What's the row, young gentlemen? Here, you, Squire Poole, put away that six-shooter. If you and Mr Fitz here has fell out, none of that tommy-rot nonsense. Use your fists."

"Boatswain," cried Fitz haughtily, "I, as an officer, seize this schooner in the Queen's name."

"What, has she telled you to, sir? I never heared her come aboard."

"No trifling, man. For your own sake, obey my orders. Seize this lad, and then make sail for the nearest British port."

The boatswain took off his cap and scratched his head, looking at the boys in a puzzled way, while Poole made no further resistance, but resigned himself to being held, as he kept the pistol well behind his back.

"Do you hear me, men?" shouted Fitz, his heart sinking with despair the while, as he noted the smiling looks of every face before him, and felt what a miserable fiasco he had made.

"Oh yes, I can hear you, sir," said the boatswain. "I'd be precious deaf if I didn't; but you're giving rather a large order, taking a lot on yourself now as the skipper's lying in dock. Any one would think as you had got a gunboat's well-manned cutter lying alongside, and I don't see as it is. What was that there shot I heard?"

"I blew the lock off the cabin-door by my father's orders," cried Poole. "We were locked in."

"Ho!" said the boatswain. "Then this 'ere's been what they used to call aboard a ship I was in, a hen-coop *de main*. I don't quite exactly know what it means, but it's something about shutting up prisoners in a cage. But don't you think, young gentleman, you have been making a big mistake? But oh, all right—here's the skipper hisself coming on deck."

Fitz turned sharply towards the companion-hatch, to see the head and shoulders of the skipper as he stood there holding on by the combings, and swaying to and fro, looking very ill and weak. His voice, too, sounded feeble as he said huskily, addressing the boatswain—

"Is there any boat alongside, Butters?"

"I arn't seen one, sir," replied the boatswain.

"Any cruiser within sight?"

"No, sir."

"Where's Mr Burgess?"

"Down below, sir. I'm afraid he's got the fever too."

"Tut-tut-tut!" ejaculated the skipper. "There, I needn't ask any questions. I have heard and seen enough. Mr Burnett, come here. No? Well, stay where you are. My good lad, have you been too much in the sun, to begin playing such a silly prank as this? There, no more nonsense!" he added sternly, and with his voice gathering in force. "It is evident to me that you don't know what stuff my men are made of. But I'm too weak to stand talking here. Come and lend me a hand, Poole. You, my young filibuster, had better come below with me, where you can talk the matter over like a man. Ha, ha, ha!" he added, with a peculiar laugh. "There, I'm not angry with you, my boy. I must say I admire your pluck; but you must see how absurd all this is!"

The midshipman's hands had dropped to his sides, and a strange, hopeless, bitterly despondent look made his face display so many incipient wrinkles, the germs, so to speak, of those which in manhood would some day mark his frank young features.

"It's all over," he groaned to himself; "they are all laughing at me. I wish I were overboard! What an idiot I have been!"

The laugh was there all ready in the eyes of the crew, and ready to burst out in a roar, as, thrusting the revolver into his breast, Poole ran to his father's side, and steadied him as he went back into the cabin; but not a sound was heard till the way was quite clear and Fitz stood alone looking wildly about him like some hunted animal seeking a place of refuge where he might hide. But the lad's choice was limited to the cook's galley, the cable-tier, and the forecastle-hatch, none of which would do.

There were only two courses open, he felt, and one was to end his troubles by going overboard, the other to surrender like a man, obeying the skipper's orders and following him below—anywhere to be out of sight of the jeering crew, whose remarks and mirthful shouts he momentarily expected to hear buzzing about his devoted head. And hence it was that as soon as the companion-hatch was clear he drew himself up to his full height—it did not take much doing, for it is very hard work for a boy to look like a man—and gazing straight before him, walked haughtily to the cabin-hatch and disappeared.

The men seemed to have been holding their breath; their faces relaxed into smiles and grins, and the carpenter exclaimed—

"Chips and shavings! Bantams aren't—"

In another moment there would have been a roar of derisive laughter, but Butters growled out hoarsely and sternly—

"Stand by! D'y' hear? Steady, my lads! None of that 'ere! Grinning like a set of Cheshire cats! What have you got to sneer at? My word! My word! And a boy like that! That's what I call genuine British pluck! What a hofficer he'd make!"

"Ay, ay!" cried the carpenter. "Right you are. All together, lads! He is the right sort! Three cheers!"

They were given, with the boatswain pining in, and Fitz winced as he heard them down by the cabin-door; but he was himself again directly, for there was no jarring note of derision in the sound.

Chapter Fifteen
A miss-fire

Fitz Burnett felt the next moment as if it would be easier to do that which had never fallen to his lot—board with an excited crew an enemy's ship, as he stood there for a few brief moments at the cabin-door listening to the heavy breathing and movements of the skipper, sounds which he knew meant that he was being helped back into his berth. For the cabin-door had swung to, and he could see nothing of that which was passing within.

But the task had to be done, and the men's cheer, rightly interpreted, seemed to have heartened him up, so that feeling more himself, he waited till he heard a heavy sigh of relief which told its own tale, and then giving the door a thrust, he stepped into the little cabin, to face its owner lying extended upon his back.

Seeing Poole standing by his father's head, facing him, he waited motionless for a few moments.

"Hah! That's better!" sighed the skipper. "Get me the quinine-bottle out of the chest, my boy. This fever has made me as weak as a rat."

Poole moved to one of the lockers at once, leaving the way clear for his father to see the young midshipman where he stood; and the boy set his teeth as the skipper's fierce fiery eyes seemed to look him through and through.

"Now for it," thought Fitz, as he held his breath. "What will he say?"

He was not long kept in doubt, for the skipper spoke at once, not with some furious denunciation, not with mocking contempt of the childish effort of which the lad had been the hero, but in a quiet, easy-going tone, strangely contrasted with the fierce look in his eyes.

"Oh, there you are, my lad," he said. "Do you see what work these tropic fevers can make of a strong man? Why, if you had only had me to deal with you would have had it all your own way. There, come and sit down, and let's have a palaver."

"I can stand, sir, thank you," said the boy coldly, "and you needn't exert yourself to talk. I know all that you would say, and I confess at once that

I have failed. But," he added excitedly, "I am not sorry, not a bit. I felt it my was duty under the circumstances, and I feel now that I might have succeeded, and that it would have been right."

"Of course you do," said the skipper quietly. "But there, come and sit down here, all the same. That's right. We can talk more easily now. One moment; just open that window a little wider. This place is like an oven, and I want cool air.—Hah! That's better."

He lay with his head thrown back and his eyelids half-closed.

"Well," he said at last, good-humouredly, and with a smile beginning to play about his rugged face, with the effect of sending a thrill of anger through the boy's frame, as he flashed out furiously—

"Don't laugh at me, sir! Put me in irons; punish me as much as you like; but don't jeer at me. I can't bear that."

"Steady, my boy, steady!" said the skipper quietly. "You must cool down now. Why, Burnett, my lad, you had better furl up all your romantic sails and let's talk like men. I am not going to put you in irons, I am not going to punish you. What nonsense! Why, when I was your age and just as thoughtless, if I had been placed in your position I might likely enough have tried on just such a trick. It will be a lesson for you to follow out the old proverb, 'Look before you leap.' You can't see it now, but some day I have no doubt that you will feel that it was a mad idea, attempted because you didn't know the people among whom you had been cast, nor thought it out so as to see how impossible it all was for a boy like you—a lad like you, single-handed, but with all a man's pluck, and even unarmed, to make yourself master of my little craft. It was rather a big venture to make, my lad; don't you think it was?"

"No, sir," said the lad firmly. "I had something else behind me."

"What, the belief that my lads only wanted a leader to turn against me?"

"No, sir; that I was backed up, as an officer of the Queen, by the whole power of the law."

"Oh, I see," said the skipper. "Yes. Exactly. That's all very big and grand, and it might act sometimes and in some places, and especially when there are men well-armed to back it up as well; but if you had thought it out, my lad, I think you would have seen that it could have had no chance here.—Oh, that my dose, Poole? Half or full?" he continued, as he raised his hand to take a little silver mug which his son had brought.

"Only half, father," replied the lad. "You had a full dose just before you went to sleep."

"To be sure; so I did," said the skipper, whose hand was trembling as he took the cup.—"It's of no use to ask you to drink with me, Mr Burnett?"

Fitz shook his head.

"No, I suppose not," continued the skipper; "but we are going to be good friends, all the same."

Fitz watched the sick man as he drained the cup.

"Ah! Bitter stuff! If you just think of the bitterest thing you ever tasted and multiply it by itself, square it, as we used to call it at school, you would only come near to the taste of this. But it's not a nasty bitter, sickly and nauseous and all that, but a bitter that you can get almost to like in time.— Thank you, Poole," and he handed back the cup. "It makes me feel better at once. Nasty things, these fevers, Squire Burnett, and very wonderful too that a man, a strong man, should be going about hale and hearty in these hot countries, and then breathe in something all at once that turns him up like this. And then more wonderful still that the savage people lower down yonder in South America—higher up, I ought to say, for it was the folk amongst the mountains—should have found out a shrub whose bark would kill the fever poison and make a man himself again. They say—put the cup away, Poole—that wherever a poisonous thing grows there's another plant grows close at hand which will cure the ill it does, bane and antidote, my lad, stinging-nettles and dock at home, you know. I don't know that it holds quite true, but I do know that there are fevers out here, and quinine acts as a cure. But there's one thing I want to know, and it's this, how in the name of all that's wonderful these South American people first found it out."

Fitz looked at him in a puzzled way. "What does he mean," he thought, "by wandering off into a lecture like this?" The skipper smiled at him as if he read his thoughts. "Hah!" he said. "I am beginning to feel better now. The shivers are going off. Not such a bad doctor, am I? You see, one always carries a medicine-chest, but one has to learn how to use it, and I have been obliged to pick up a few things. I shouldn't be at all surprised some day if I have to doctor you for something more than a crack on the head. Look here, Poole," he continued, with a broad, good-humoured smile crossing his features, "come into consultation. What do you think? Our friend here is a bit too hot-blooded. Do you think he need be bled? No, no; don't flush up like that, my lad. It was only my joke. There," he cried, holding out his hand, which had ceased to tremble—"shake. I'll never allude to it again. You did rather a foolish thing, but it is all over now—dead and buried, and we are going to be just as good friends as we were before, for I like you, my lad, none the less for the stuff of which you are made—the pluck you have shown. But take my advice; don't attempt anything of the kind again. Fate has put you into this awkward position. Be a man, and make the best of it. Some day or other you will be able to say good-bye to us and go back to your ship, feeling quite contented as to having done your duty. Come now, let's shake hands and begin again."

He held out his hand once more, and after a moment's hesitation, Fitz, who dared not trust himself to speak, placed his own within it, to have it held in a firm, warm pressure for some moments before it was released.

"There," said the skipper, smiling, "I am coming out in a nice soft perspiration now, and I feel as if that bit of excitement has done me good. Here, Poole, I'm tired, and I think that I can sleep and wake up better. Burnett, my lad, perhaps you would like to stay below the rest of the day.—Poole, mix Mr Burgess a dose. You know how many grains. Tell him I can't come to him myself, and see that he takes it. It's my orders, mind. These attacks are sharp but short. I'm half asleep already. Oh, by the way—"

He stopped short, drawing a heavy breath.

"By the way, I—"

He was silent again.

"I— Poole."

"Yes, father," said the lad softly.

"Are you there?"

"Yes, father."

The boys exchanged glances.

"I—I think—Hah!"

The skipper was fast asleep.

The two lads remained silent for a few moments, watching the sleeper, and then Poole looked full in his companion's eyes and slowly took out the revolver which he had thrust into his breast, before raising the hammer and bringing the cartridge-extractor to bear so that one after another the charges were thrust out, each to fall with a soft tap upon the cabin-table, after which the chambers were carefully wiped out, and the weapon put back into a holster close to the head of the berth, the cartridges being dropped into the little pouch attached to the belt.

When all was done, steadily watched by Fitz the while, Poole raised his eyes to his companion once again.

"Shall we do as you and father did just now?" he asked.

"Yes," said Fitz slowly and sadly, "if you will."

"Will?—Of course!"

The two lads shook hands.

Chapter Sixteen
Land ho!

Two days passed, during which time Fitz kept to his cabin, and towards evening Poole came down, to find the middy seated with his back to the door gazing through the cabin-window at what seemed to be a beautiful blue cloud low-down on the horizon.

"Hullo!" cried Poole cheerily. "You can see it, then?"

"Yes," said Fitz, without looking round. "That's land, I suppose."

"Yes, that's one of the islands; but look here, what's the good of going on like this?"

"If I choose to sit at my prison-window and look out for the islands, I suppose I have a right to do so," said Fitz coldly.

"I say, take care. Recollect you have not quite got your strength up again. Mind you don't fall."

"May I inquire what you mean?" said Fitz haughtily.

"Of course. I mean, take care you don't tumble off the stilts now you have got on to them again."

"Bah!" ejaculated the boy.

"Well, what's the good of going on like that, sulking and pretending you are a prisoner?"

"There's no pretence in that," said Fitz bitterly.

"Yes, there is," retorted Poole quickly. "It's all shammon and gam—I mean, gammon and sham. You are no more a prisoner than I am. Why, even father says you seem to be riding the high horse. I suppose you do feel a bit awkward about coming on deck amongst the men, after going through that—I mean, after what happened."

"Oh, say it!" cried Fitz angrily. "After going through that performance, you meant."

"I am not going to argue and fence. Look here, you have got to face the men, so why not make a plunge and do it? You think the lads will be winking and exchanging glances and whispering to one another, when all the time there's only one body on board the *Teal* who gives all that business a thought, and that's you. Tchah! Sailors have no time to think about what's past. They have always got to keep a sharp look-out for the rocks ahead. You are such a sensitive chap. Come on up, and let's have a turn at fishing."

"Is your father quite well again?" said Fitz, without heeding his companion's proposal.

"Oh yes; that was only one of his fits. They come and go."

"And how's Mr Burgess?"

"Pretty well right again. Come up. Have the glass. You can see another island astern, one of the little ones, and I think we are going to have one of these lovely tropic sunsets, same as we had last night when you wouldn't come and see it."

"How can a fellow situated as I am care for sunsets?"

"Just in the same way as he can care for sunrises if he's awake early enough. Oh, do pitch all that up! It has all gone by. But I see how it is. You think that you made a mistake, and that everybody will be ready to laugh at you."

"And so they will," cried Fitz passionately. "I can never show my face on deck again."

"Ha, ha!" laughed Poole. "Well, you are a rum chap, fancying a thing like that. Why, my father's too much of a gentleman ever to notice it again, and I'm sure old grumpy Burgess wouldn't, from what he said to me when I was telling him all about it afterwards."

"What!" cried Fitz, flashing out. "You went down tale-bearing to the mate like that?"

"There you go again! I didn't go tale-bearing. He'd heard about it from one of the men, and next time I took him his quinine he began questioning me."

"And what did he say?" cried Fitz fiercely.

"Shan't tell you."

"What!" cried Fitz. "And you profess to be my friend!"

"Yes; that's why I won't tell you," said Poole, with his eyes twinkling. "I want to spare your feelings, or else it will make you so wild."

"The insolent piratical old scoundrel!" cried Fitz. "How dare he!"

"Oh, don't ask me. He's a regular rough one with his tongue, as you know by the way in which he deals with the men; gives the dad the raspy side of his palaver sometimes, but dad never seems to mind it. He never takes any notice, because Burgess means right, and he's such a splendid seaman."

"Means right!" cried Fitz angrily. "Is it right to abuse a prisoner behind his back when he's not in a position to defend himself?"

"Yes, it was too bad," said Poole sympathetically.

"What did he say?"

"Oh, you had better not know," replied Poole, winking to himself.

"I insist upon your telling me."

"Oh, well, if you will have it—only don't blame me afterwards for letting it out."

"What did he say?" repeated the boy.

"It was while he had got a very bad fit of the shivers on, and the poor fellow's teeth were all of a chatter with the fever."

"I think your teeth seem to be all of a chatter," snarled the midshipman fiercely.

"Ha, ha! You are a wonderful deal better, Queen's man," cried Poole merrily.

"Have you come down here like the rest to insult and trample on me?" cried Fitz, springing to his feet.

"Ah, now you are getting yourself again."

"I insist upon your telling me what that man Burgess said."

"What he said? Well, he said you were a plucked 'un and no mistake."

"Bah!" ejaculated Fitz, and there was silence for a few moments, during which Poole thrust his head out of the cabin-window to give his companion time to calm down.

"Yes," said the lad, looking round. "Clouds are gathering in the west, and we are going to have a grand show of such colours as I never saw anywhere else. Come on up, there's a good chap."

Fitz remained silent, and the skipper's son winked to himself.

"Where's Mr Burgess now?" said Fitz at last.

"He's in his cabin, writing home to his wife. You would never think how particular such a gruff old fellow as he is about writing home. Writes a long letter every week as regular as clockwork. Doesn't seem like a pirate, does it?"

"Is your father on deck?"

"No. He's in his cabin, busy over the chart. We are getting pretty close to the port now."

"Ah!" cried Fitz eagerly. "What port are we making for?"

"San Cristobal."

"Where's that?"

"In the Armado Republic, Central America."

"Oh," said Fitz. "I never heard of it before. Is there a British Consul there?"

"Oh, I don't know. There generally is one everywhere. I think there used to be before Don Villarayo upset the Government and got himself made President."

"And is it to him that you are taking out field-guns and ammunition?"

"I never said we were taking out field-guns and ammunition," said Poole innocently. "There's nothing of that sort down in the bills of lading—only Birmingham hardware. Oh no, it is not for him. It is for another Don who is opening a new shop there in opposition to Villarayo, and from what I heard he is going to do the best trade."

"What's the good of your talking all this rubbish to me? Of course I know what it all means."

"That's right. I supposed you did know something about it, or else your skipper would not have sent you to try and capture our Birmingham goods."

"Birmingham goods!" cried Fitz. "Fire-arms, you mean."

"To be sure, yes," said Poole. "I forgot them. There are a lot of fireworks ready for a big celebration when the new Don opens his shop!"

"Bah!" cried Fitz contemptuously; and then after a few moments' thought, "Well," he said shortly, "I suppose I shall have to do it. I can't stop always in this stuffy cabin. It will make me ill again; and I may just as well face it out now as at some other time."

"Just," said Poole, "only I am afraid you will be disappointed, for you will find nothing to face."

Fitz turned upon the speaker fiercely, looking as if he were going to make some angry remark; but he found no sneer on the face of the skipper's son, only a frank genial smile, which, being lit up by the warm glow gradually gathering in the west, seemed to glance upon and soften his own features, till he turned sharply away as if feeling ashamed of what he looked upon as weakness, and the incident ended by his saying suddenly—"Let's go on deck."

Chapter Seventeen
"Old Chap"—"Old Fellow"

Days of slow sailing through calm blue waters, with quite an Archipelago of Eden-like islands showing one or another in sight.

Very slow progress was made on account of the wind, which was light and generally adverse.

Fitz passed his time nearly always on deck with the skipper's glass in hand, every now and then close enough in to one of the islands to excite an intense longing to land, partly to end his imprisonment, as he called it, partly from sheer desire to plunge into one or another of the glorious valleys which ran upward from the sea, cut deep into the side of some volcanic mountain.

"Lovely!" was always on the boy's lips. "I never saw anything like this before, Poole. But where's the port we are sailing for? Are we never going to land?"

"Oh, it's only a little farther on," was the reply. "If this wind only gets up a little more towards sundown I expect we shall soon be there."

"That's what you always keep saying," was the impatient retort.

"Yes," said Poole coolly; "but it isn't my fault. It's the wind."

"Oh, hang the wind!"

"You should say, blow it!" said Poole, laughing. "But I say, old chap, I don't want to damp you, but you really had better not indulge in any hope of seeing any consul or English people who will help you to get away. San Cristobal is a very solitary place, where the people are all mongrels, a mixture of native Indians and half-bred Spaniards. Father says they are like the volcano at the back of the city, for when it is not blowing up, they are."

"Well, I shall learn all that for myself," said Fitz coldly.

"You will, old fellow, and before long too."

"What do you mean by that?" said Fitz sharply. "Only that we shall be there for certain to-night." As it happened, the wind freshened a little that evening, while the sunset that Poole had prophesied was glorious in the extreme; a wondrous pile of massive clouds formed up from the horizon almost to the zenith, shutting out the sun, and Fitz watched the resplendent hues until his eyes were ready to ache—purple, scarlet, orange and gold, with flashes in between of the most vivid metallic blue, ever increasing, ever changing, until the eye could bear no more and sought for rest in the sea through which they sailed, a sea that resembled liquid rubies or so much wine.

But the end was coming fast, and like some transformation scene, the clouds were slowly drawn aside, the vivid tints began to pale till they died away into a rich, soft, purple gloom spangled with drops of gold. And a deep sigh escaped from the middy's breast as he stood wondering over the glories of the rapid change from glowing day into the soft, transparent, tropic night.

"I never saw anything like that before," sighed the boy.

"No, I suppose not," was the reply. "It was almost worth coming all this way to see. Doesn't it seem queer to you where all the clouds are gone?"

"Yes," said Fitz; "I was thinking about that. There is only one left, now, over yonder, with the sun glowing on it still."

"That's not the sun," said Poole quietly.

"Yes, it is. I mean there, that soft dull red. Look before it dies out."

"That's the one I was looking at, and it won't die out; if you like to watch you will see it looking dull and red like that all night."

"Oh, I see," cried Fitz mockingly; "you mean that the sun goes down only a little way there, and then comes up again in the same place."

"No, I don't," said Poole quietly. "What you see is the glow from the volcano a few miles back behind the town."

"What!" cried Fitz. "Then we are as close to the port as that?"

"Yes. We are not above a dozen miles away. It's too dark to see now, or you could make out the mountains that surround the bay."

"Then why couldn't we see them before the sun was set?" cried Fitz sceptically.

"Because they were all hidden by the clouds and golden haze that gather round of an evening. Yes, yonder's San Cristobal, and as soon as it is a little darker if you use the glass you will be able to make out which are the twinkling electric lights and which are stars."

"Electric lights!" cried Fitz.

"Oh yes, they've got 'em, and tram-cars too. They are pretty wide-awake in these mushroom Spanish Republic towns."

"Then they will be advanced enough," thought Fitz, "for me to get help to make my way to rejoin my ship. Sooner or later my chance must come."

Within an hour the soft warm wind had dropped, and the captain gave his orders, to be followed by the rattling out of the chain-cable through the hawse-hole. The schooner swung round, and Fitz had to bring the glass to bear from the other side of the deck to make out the twinkling lights of the semi-Spanish town.

Everything was wonderfully still, but it was an exciting time for the lad as he leaned against the bulwarks quite alone, gazing through the soft mysterious darkness at the distant lights.

There were thoughts in his breast connected with the lowering down of one of the boats and rowing ashore, but there was the look-out, and the captain and mate were both on deck, talking together as they walked up and down, while instead of the men going below and seeming disposed to sleep, they were lounging about, smoking and chatting together.

And then it was that the middy began to think about one of the four life-buoys lashed fore and aft, and how it would be if he cut one of them loose and lowered himself down by a rope, to trust to swimming and the help of the current to bear him ashore.

His heart throbbed hard at the idea, and then he turned cold, for he was seaman enough to know the meaning of the tides and currents. Suppose in his ignorance instead of bearing him ashore they swept him out to sea? And then he shuddered at his next thought.

There were the sharks, and only that evening he and Poole had counted no less than ten—that is to say, their little triangular back-fins—gliding through the surface of the water.

"No," he said to himself, "I shall have to wait;" and he started violently, for a voice at his elbow said—

"Did you speak?"

"Eh? No, I don't think so," replied the boy.

"You must have been talking to yourself. I say, what a lovely night! Did you notice that signal that we ran up?"

"No," cried Fitz eagerly.

"It was while you were looking at the sunset. Father made me run up a flag. Don't you remember my asking you to let me have the glass a minute?"

"Yes, of course."

"Well—I don't mind telling you now—that was to the fort, and they answered it just in time before it was too dark to see. I think they hoisted lights afterwards, three in a particular shape, but there were so many others about that father couldn't be sure."

"Then I suppose that means going into port at daylight?"

"Yes, and land our cargo under the guns of the fort. I say, listen."

"What to?"

"That," said Poole, in a whisper.

"Oh yes, that splashing. Fish, I suppose."

"No," whispered Poole. "I believe it's oars."

He had hardly spoken when the skipper's voice was heard giving orders almost in a whisper; but they were loud enough to be heard and understood, for there was a sudden rush and padding of feet about the deck, followed by a soft rattling, and the next minute the middy was aware of the presence of a couple of the sailors armed with capstan-bars standing close at hand.

Then all was silence once more, and the darkness suddenly grew more dense, following upon a dull squeaking sound as of a pulley-wheel in a block.

"They've doused the light," whispered Poole. "It's a boat coming off from the shore," he continued excitedly, with his lips close to the middy's ear. "It's the people we expect, I suppose, but father is always suspicious at a time like this, for you never know who they may be. But if they mean mischief they will get it warm."

Fitz's thoughts went back at a bound to the dark night when he boarded with the cutter's crew, and his heart beat faster and faster still as, leaning outward to try and pierce the soft transparent darkness of the tropic night, he felt his arm tightly gripped by Poole with one hand, while with the other he pointed to a soft pale flashing of the water, which was accompanied by a dull regular *splash, splash*.

"Friends or enemies," whispered Poole, "but they don't see us yet. I wonder which they are."

Just then the lambent flashing of the phosphorescent water and the soft splashing ceased.

It was the reign of darkness far and near.

Chapter Eighteen
Anxious times

As the minutes glided by in the midst of that profound silence, a fresh kind of feverish feeling began to steal over Fitz. There in the distance, apparently beyond the dome of great stars which lit up the blackish purple heavens, was the dull glowing cloud which looked like one that the sunset had left behind; beneath that were the twinkling lights of the town, and between the schooner and that, a broad black plain of darkness, looking like a layer which extended as high as the top of the masts.

But as Fitz looked down, it was to see that the blackness below his feet was transparent and all in motion with tiny glowing specks gliding here and there as if being swept along by a powerful current.

There were moments when he could have fancied that he was gazing into a huge black mirror which reflected the vast dome of stars, but he knew by experience that these moving greenish golden specks were no orbs of light but the tiny phosphorescent medusas gliding in all directions through the transparent water, and every now and then combining to emit a pale green bluish flash of light, as some fish made the current swirl by giving a swoop with its tail.

Moment by moment in the silence all seemed to grow more and more unreal, more dream-like, till he felt ready to declare that all was fancy, that he had heard no splash of a coming boat, and that the next minute he would start into wakefulness and find that it was all imagination.

Then all at once he was listening with every nerve on the strain, wishing that he knew Spanish instead of Latin, for a low clear voice arose out of the darkness, saying, as he afterwards learned —

"Aboard the English vessel there! Where are you? I have lost my way."

The skipper answered directly in Spanish.

There was a quick interchange of words, and then the latter gave an order in English which came as a relief to Fitz and made his heart jump, suggesting as it did that the next minute there was going to be a fight.

"Get the lads all round you, Burgess, and be on the alert. It seems all right, but it may be a bit of Spanish treachery, so look out."

As he was speaking Fitz with straining eyes and ear saw that the pale golden green water was being lifted from the surface of the sea and falling back like dull golden metal in patches, with an interval of darkness between them, the bestirred water looking like so much molten ore as it splashed about.

Then there was the scraping of a boat-hook against the side, close to the gangway, and the dimly-seen figure of a man scrambling on board.

No enemy certainly, for Fitz made out that the newcomer grasped both the captain's hands in his, and began talking to him in a low eager excited tone, the captain's responses, given in the man's own tongue, sounding short and sharp, interspersed too with an angry ejaculation or two. The conversation only lasted about five minutes, and then the visitor turned back to the side, uttered an order in a low tone which caused a little stir in the boat below, and stepped down. Fitz could hear him crossing the thwarts to the stern, and the craft was pushed off. Then the golden splashes in the sea came regularly once more, to grow fainter and fainter, in the direction of the city lights; and then they were alone in the silence and darkness of the night.

It was not Fitz's fault that he heard what followed, for the skipper came close up to where he was standing with Poole, followed by the mate, who had sent the men forward as soon as the boat was gone.

"Well," said the skipper, "it's very unfortunate."

"Is it?" said the mate gruffly.

"Yes. Couldn't you hear?"

"I heard part of what he said, but my Spanish is very bad, especially if it's one of these mongrel half Indian-bred fellows who is talking. You had better tell me plainly how matters stand."

"Very well. Horribly badly. Things have gone wrong since we left England. Our friends were too venturesome, and they were regularly trapped, with the result that they were beaten back out of the town, and the President's men seized the fort, got hold of their passwords and the signalling flags that they had in the place, and answered our signals, so that they took me in. If it had not been for his man's coming to-night with a message from Don Ramon, we should have sailed right into the trap as soon as it was day, and been lying under the enemy's guns."

"Narrow escape, then," said the mate.

"Nearly ruin," was the reply.

"But hold hard a minute. Suppose, after all, this is a bit of a trick, a cooked-up lie to cheat us."

"Not likely," said the skipper. "What good would it do the enemy to send us away when they had all we brought under their hand? Besides, this messenger had a password to give me that must have been right."

"You know best," said the mate gruffly. "Then what next?"

"Up anchor at once, and we sail round the foreland yonder till we can open out the other valley and the river's mouth twenty miles along the coast. Don Ramon and his men are gathering at Velova, and they want our munition badly there."

"Right," said the mate abruptly. "Up anchor at once? Make a big offing, I suppose?"

"No, we must hug the coast. I dare say they will have a gunboat patrolling some distance out—a steamer—and with these varying winds and calms we should be at their mercy. If we are taken, Don Ramon's cause is ruined, poor fellow, and the country will be at the mercy of that half-savage, President Villarayo. Brute! He deserves to be hung!"

"I don't like it," said Burgess gruffly.

"You don't like it!" cried the skipper. "What do you mean?"

"What do I mean? Why, from here to Velova close in it's all rock-shoal and wild current. It's almost madness to try and hug the coast."

"Oh, I see. But it's got to be done, Burgess. You didn't take soundings and bearings miles each way for nothing last year."

"Tchah!" growled the mate. "One wants an apprenticeship to this coast. I'll do what you want, of course, but I won't be answerable for taking the *Teal* safely into that next port."

"Oh yes, you will," said the skipper quietly. "If I didn't think you would I should try to do it myself. Now then, there's no time to waste. Look yonder. There's something coming out of the port now—a steamer, I believe, from the way she moves, and most likely it's in reply to our signals, and they're coming out to give us a surprise." The mate stood for a few moments peering over the black waters in the direction of the indicated lights.

"Yes," he growled, "that's a steamer; one of their gunboats, I should say, and they are coming straight for here."

"How does he know that?" whispered Fitz, as the skipper and the mate now moved away.

"The lights were some distance apart," replied Poole, "and they've swung round till one's close behind the other. Now look, whatever the steamer is she is coming straight for here. Fortunately there is a nice pleasant breeze, but I hope we shall not get upon any of these fang-like rocks."

"Yes, I hope so too," said Fitz excitedly; and then Poole left him, and he stood listening to the clicking of the capstan as the anchor was raised, while some of the crew busily hoisted sail, so that in a few minutes' time the schooner began to heel over from the pressure of the wind and glide away, showing that the anchor was clear of the soft ooze in which it had lain.

Chapter Nineteen
Ticklish

Burgess the mate went forward, to stand for a few minutes looking into the offing, before going back aft to say a word or two to the man at the wheel, as the schooner was now gliding rapidly on, and then walked sharply to where the skipper was giving orders to the men, which resulted in a big gaff sail being run up, to balloon out and increase the schooner's rate of speed through the water.

A short consultation ensued, another man was put on the look-out forward, and the mate went back to take the wheel himself.

"Ah, that's better," said Poole quietly.

"What's better?" asked Fitz.

"Old Burgess taking the wheel himself. It's a bad enough place here in the daylight, but it's awful in the darkness, and we are not quite so likely to be carried by some current crash on to a rock."

"Then why, in the name of common-sense, don't we lay-to till daylight?"

"Because it wouldn't be common-sense to wait till that steamer comes gliding up, and takes possession of the *Teal*. Do you know what that means?"

"Yes; you would all be made prisoners, and I should be free," cried Fitz, laughing. "My word, Master Poole, I don't want you to have a topper first, but I'd let you see then what it is to be a prisoner aboard the *Silver Teal*."

"Oh yes, of course, I know," replied Poole mockingly. "But you don't know everything. When I asked you if you knew what it meant it was this, that our cargo would go into the wrong hands and about ruin Don Ramon's cause."

"Well, what does that matter?"

"Everything. Ramon, who has been striking for freedom and all that's good and right, would be beaten, and the old President Don Villarayo would carry on as before. He is as bad a tyrant as ever was at the head of affairs, and it's to help turn him out of the chair that my father and his Spanish friends are making this venture."

"Well, that's nothing to me," said Fitz. "I am on the side of right."

"Well, that is the side of right."

"Oh no," said Fitz. "According to the rule of these things that's the side of right that has the strongest hold."

"Bah!" said Poole. "That would never do, unless it is when we get the strongest hold, and that we mean to do."

"Well, I hope old Burgess, as you call him, won't run this wretched schooner crash on to a rock. You might as well hand me out a life-belt, in case."

"Oh, there's time enough for that," said Poole coolly.

"I'll take care of you. But I say, look! That gunboat is coming on two knots for our one. Can't you see?"

"I can see her lights, of course, but it doesn't seem to me that she is getting closer."

"She is, though, and she's bound to overtake us, for old Burgess is keeping right along the main channel. Why, if I didn't know who was at the wheel," cried the lad excitedly, "I should be ready to think that the steersman had proved treacherous, and was playing into the enemy's hands. Oh, here's father! I say, dad, do you see how fast that gunboat is overhauling us?"

"Oh yes," said the skipper coolly. "It's all right, my boy; Burgess knows what he's about. He wants to get a little more offing, but it's getting nearly time to lie over on the other tack."

He had hardly spoken when the mate at the wheel called out—

"Now!"

The skipper gave a short, sharp order or two, the men sprang to the sheets, the schooner was turned right up into the wind, the sails began to shiver, and directly after they began to fill on the other tack, were sheeted home, and the *Teal* lay so over to starboard that Fitz made a snatch at a rope so as to steady himself and keep his feet.

"Why, he'll have the sea over her side," whispered Fitz excitedly.

"Very likely," said Poole coolly. "Ah, you don't know how we can sail."

"Sail! Why, you will have her lying flat in the water directly."

"Make the sails more taut," said Poole coolly. "I say, we are going now. I didn't see what he meant. We have just turned the South Rocks. Talk about piloting, old Burgess does know what he's about. We are sailing as fast as the gunboat."

"But she's overhauling us."

"Yes, but she won't try to pass those rocks. She will have to keep to the channel. We are skimming along over the rocky shallows now."

"Yes, with the keel nearly up to the surface," panted Fitz excitedly.

"All the better! Less likely to scrape the rocks."

"Well, you are taking it pretty coolly," continued the midshipman. "This must be risky work."

"Yes, we don't want to be taken. You wait a few minutes and watch the gunboat's lights. You will see that she will be getting more distant as she goes straight on for the open sea. Her captain will make for the next channel, two or three miles south, to catch us there as we come out—and we shan't come out, for we shall go right on in and out among the shallows and get clear off, so as to sail into Velova Bay. We shall be all right if we don't come crash on to one of the shark's fin rocks."

"And if we do?"

"Well, if we do we shan't get off again—only in the boats—but old Villarayo's gang won't get the ammunition, for that will go down to amuse the sharks."

"Well, this is nice," said Fitz. "The schooner was bad enough before; now it's ten times worse."

"Nonsense. See how we are skimming along. This is a new experience for you. You will see more fun with us in a month than you would in your old tea-kettle of a gunboat in twelve."

"Phew!" ejaculated the skipper, coming up, straw hat in one hand, pocket-handkerchief in the other, and mopping his face. "This is rather warm work, Poole, my boy. Well, Mr Burnett, what do you think of blockade running for a change?"

"What do I think of it, sir?" said Fitz, who was still holding on tight to one of the ropes.

"Yes. Good as yachting, isn't it?"

"Well, I don't like it a bit, sir. I don't call it seamanship."

"Indeed, young gentleman! What do you call it, then?"

"Utter recklessness, sir."

"Oh!" said the skipper. "Well, it is running it rather close, but you can't do blockade running without. Not afraid, are you?"

"Oh, I don't know about being afraid, sir, but I think that we shall have to take to the boats."

"Yes, that's quite likely, but the chances are about equal that we shall not. Mr Burgess knows what he is about, and as likely as not we shall be right into Velova Bay soon after sunrise, and the President's gunboat twenty miles away."

Several times over during the rest of the night's run, Fitz observed that there was a little anxious conference between the skipper and the mate, the former speaking very sternly, and on one occasion the latter spoke out loud in a sharp angry voice, the words reaching the middy's ear.

"Of course it is very risky," he said, "but I feel as if I shall get her through, or I shouldn't do it. Shall we take soundings and drop anchor in the best bit we can find?"

"Where we shall be clearly seen as soon as day breaks? No! Go on."

It was a relief then to both the lads when the day broke, showing them a line of breakers about half-a-mile away on the starboard-bow, and clear open water right ahead, while as the dawn lifted more and more, it was to show a high ground jungle and the beautiful curve of another bay formed by a couple of ridges about three miles apart running down into the sea.

"There," cried Poole triumphantly; "we have been running the gauntlet of dangerous rocks all night, and we've won. That's Velova Bay. You will see the city directly, just at the mouth of the valley. Lovely place. It's the next city to San Cristobal."

"Fetch my glass, Poole," said the skipper; and upon its being brought its owner took a long searching sweep of the coast as he stood by the mate's side.

"I can only make out a few small vessels," he said; "nothing that we need mind. Run straight in, and we can land everything before the gunboat can get round, even if she comes, which is doubtful, after all."

"Yes, knowing how we can sail."

The boys were standing near, and heard all that was said, for their elders spoke freely before them.

"What about choice of place for landing?" asked the mate.

"Oh, we will go up as close as we can get. Ramon is sure to have a strong party there to help, and in a very short time he would be able to knock up an earthwork and utilise the guns as we get them ashore. That would keep the gunboat off if she comes round."

"Yes," said the mate quietly, and he handed over the wheel to one of the men, the sea being quite open now between them and the shore a few miles away.

"Well," said the skipper, "what do you make of it?" For the mate was shading his eyes and looking carefully round eastward.

"Have a look yourself," was the gruff reply.

The skipper raised the glass he had lowered to his side, and swept the horizon eastward; knowing full well the keenness of his subordinate's eyes, he fully expected to see some suspicious vessel in sight, but that had not taken the mate's attention, for as soon as the glass had described about the eighth of a circle the skipper lowered it again and gave an angry stamp with his foot.

"Was ever such luck!" he cried.

"No," replied the mate; "it is bad. But there is only one thing to be done."

"Yes, only one thing. We must get out while we can, and I don't know but what we may be too late even now."

For the next few minutes all was busy on board the schooner. It was 'bout ship, and fresh sail was set, their course being due east, while as soon as Fitz could get Poole to answer a question, what had so far been to him a mystery was explained.

"We are in for one of those hurricanes that come on so suddenly here," said the lad, "and we are going right out to sea, to try and get under shelter of one of the isles before it breaks."

"But why not stop here in harbour?" said Fitz sharply.

"Because there is none. When the wind's easterly you can only expect one thing, and that is to be blown ashore."

"But is there time to get under the lee of some island?"

"I don't know. We are going straight into danger now, for as likely as not we shall meet the gunboat coming right across our bows to cut us off."

Chapter Twenty
On two sides

The speed they were able to get out of the schooner, and the admirable seamanship of her commander enabled them to reach the sought-for shelter before the fury of the West Indian hurricane came on. It was rough work, but with two anchors down, the *Teal* managed to ride out the blast, and fortunately for her crew the storm subsided as quickly as it had risen, leaving them free to run in for Velova with a gentle breeze over a heavy swell, which as evening approached began to subside fast.

It still wanted a couple of hours of sunset when the morning's position was reached, and with favourable wind and the signal flying they were running close in, when Fitz suddenly caught Poole by the arm.

"Look yonder," he said.

"What at?—My word!"

The boy rushed aft to where his father was standing watching the distant city through his glass; but that which he was about to impart was already clearly seen. From behind a wooded point about a mile behind them the black trail of smoke rising from a steamer's funnel was slowly ascending into the soft air, and for a few moments the skipper stood with his teeth set and his face contracted with disappointment and rage.

"Think they have seen us, Burgess?" he said at last.

"Yes; they have been lying in hiding there, watching us till we were well inside."

"Can we get outside again?"

"Not a chance of it," was the reply; "the wind will be dead in our teeth, and we can only tack, while they are coming on full speed, and can begin playing long bowls at us with heavy shot whenever they like."

"What's to be done?" said the skipper, and without waiting for an answer he added, "Keep on right in. There is one chance yet."

"There, don't look so precious pleased," Poole whispered to Fitz. "We are not taken yet."

"I—I wasn't looking pleased."

"Yes, you were," said Poole sourly; "but you needn't be, because you would be no better off with them than you are with us. But you are not with them yet. Father seems to be taking things very easily, and that only means that we are going to get away."

It did not seem like it, though, for as the schooner sailed on into the beautiful orange glow of the coming evening, the gunboat neared them swiftly, spreading a golden trail of light far behind her over the sea which her screw churned up into foam, while overhead trailed backward what seemed to be like a triumphant black feather of smoke.

The city before them looked bright and attractive with its gaily-painted houses, green and yellow jalousies, and patches of verdure in the gardens, beyond which the mountains rose in ridge after ridge of green and purple and grey. The bay in front of them was singularly devoid of life. Probably on account of the swell remaining from the hurricane there were no fishing-boats afloat save one, with a long white lateen sail running up into the air like the pointed wing of some sea-bird gliding over the surface of the sea.

No one paid any heed to the boat, which drew nearer and nearer from the fact that it was gliding across the bay right in the schooner's course. In fact, every eye was directed at the gunboat, which came steadily on without hurry, as if her commander felt that he was perfectly certain of his prize, while what went on upon her deck was plainly visible through the glass, the boys noting in turn that her heavy gun was manned and ready to bring them to whensoever the gunboat captain pleased to make her speak.

"Oh, Fitz!" groaned Poole. "It does seem so hard. I did think we were going to do it now."

"Well, I can't help being sorry for you," said the middy. "Yes, it does seem hard, though I suppose I oughtn't to speak like this. I say, though, look at those stupid niggers in that boat! Why don't they get out of the way? We shall run them down."

"Murder! Yes," cried Poole, and pulling out his knife he ran to one of the life-buoys to cut it free; but ere he could reach it there was a sharp crack as the schooner seemed to glide right over the fishing-boat, the tall white lateen sail disappeared, and Fitz ran to the side, expecting to see those who manned the slight craft struggling in the water.

To his surprise, though, he saw that a dark-complexioned man was holding on with a boat-hook, boat and trailing sail were being carried onward by the schooner, and another man was climbing over the port bulwark.

What followed passed very quietly. The man gained the deck and ran aft to where the captain and mate were hurrying to meet him.

There was a quick passing of something white, and then the man almost glided over the bulwarks again into the boat, which fell astern, and those who manned her began to hoist the long lateen sail once more.

"A message from the shore," whispered Poole excitedly, as he saw his father step into the shelter of one of the boats swinging from the davits, to screen himself from any observant glass on the gunboat's deck, and there he rapidly tore open a packet and scanned the message that it contained.

"Oh, I should like to know what it says," whispered Poole, "but I mustn't ask him. It's lucky to be old Burgess," he continued, for the captain walked slowly to his chief officer, who stood sulkily apart as if not paying the slightest heed to what was going on.

The skipper stood speaking to him for about a minute, and the lad saw the heavy-looking mate give a short nod of the head and then turn his eyes upwards towards the white spread sails as they still glided on through the orange glow.

Boom—thud! and Fitz literally jumped; the report, and its echo from the mountain-backed shore, was so sudden and unexpected.

"Blank shot," said Poole, looking at the white smoke curling up from one of the man-of-war's small guns.

"Order to heave-to," said Fitz; "and you will have to, or a ball will come skipping along next."

"Yes, I suppose so," said Poole, "across our bows; and if we didn't stop for that I suppose they would open fire with their big gun. Think they could hit us?"

"I don't know about them," said Fitz, rather pompously, "but I know our old *Tonans* would send you to the bottom with her first shot."

"Then I'm glad it isn't the *Tonans*" said Poole, laughing. "Here, we are not going to be sunk;" for in obedience to the summons the schooner was thrown up into the wind, the big sails shivering in the soft breeze, and gradually turning of a deeper orange glow. Meanwhile there was a bustle going on aboard the gunboat, and an orange cutter manned by orange men glided down into the sea. Then oars began to dip and at every stroke threw up orange and gold. So beautiful was the scene that Fitz turned from it for a moment to look westward for the source of the vivid colouring, and was startled for the moment at the curious effect, for there, balanced as it were on the highest point of the low ridge of mountains at the back of the city, was the huge orange globe that lit up the whole bay right away to sea, and even as he gazed the sun seemed to touch the mountains whose summit marked a great black notch like a cut out of its lower edge.

"Here they come," said Poole, making Fitz start round again. "What swells," he continued bitterly. "The dad ought to go below and put on his best jacket. Look at the golden braid."

"I say," cried Fitz, "he'll see my uniform. What will he say to me?"

"Take you for an English officer helping in a filibustering craft."

"Oh, but I shall explain myself," cried Fitz. "But it would be rather awkward if they didn't believe me. Here, you, Poole, I don't understand a word of Spanish; you will have to stand by me and help me out of a hole."

"And put my father in?" cried Poole. "You are a modest chap!—Why, look there, I am bothered if the dad isn't going to do it!" cried the lad excitedly.

"Do what?"

"Put on his best jacket. Look, he's going to the cabin-hatch. No, he isn't. What's he saying to old Butters?"

The lad had no verbal answer, but he saw for himself. The gunboat's cutter was still a couple of hundred yards away, and coming steadily on, when, as if by accident or from the action of the swell, the spokes of the wheel moved a little, with the consequence that the wind began to fill the schooner's sails, the man at the wheel turned it a little, and the canvas shivered once more.

But the schooner had begun to move, gliding imperceptibly along, and as this manoeuvre was repeated, she moved slowly through the water, keeping the row-boat almost at the same distance astern. A full minute had elapsed before the officer noticed this, and he rose in the stern-sheets and shouted an order in Spanish, to which the mate replied by seeming to repeat it to the man at the wheel, who hurriedly gave the spokes a turn, the sails filled, and the *Teal* glided steadily on.

"Yah!" roared Butters furiously. "Out of the way, you great clumsy lubber!" And he made a rush at the man, who loosed his hold of the spokes and backed away as if to shelter himself from blows, while, swinging free, the rudder yielded to the pressure of the swell and the schooner glided along faster still.

There was a threatening shout from the boat and a hostile movement of weapons, to which Butters responded by roaring out in broad, plain English—

"Ay, ay, sir! All right! Clumsy lubber! Break his head."

As he spoke he moved slowly to the wheel, seized the spokes, rammed them down as if confused, and then hurriedly turned them the other way, with the result that the schooner still kept gliding slowly on, with the cutter at the same distance astern.

"That'll do," said the skipper; "drop it now," and trembling with excitement as he grasped the manoeuvres being played Fitz made a grab at Poole's arm, while Poole made a grab at his, and they stood as one, waiting for the result.

In obedience to his orders, the boatswain now turned and held the schooner well up in the wind, her forward motion gradually ceasing, and the gunboat's cutter now gaining upon them fast.

"Why, the sun's gone down," whispered Fitz excitedly.

"Yes," said Poole, "and the stars are beginning to show."

"In another five minutes," said Fitz, "it will be getting dusk."

"And in another ten," whispered Poole hoarsely, "it will be dark. Oh, dad, now I can see through your game."

"So can I," whispered Fitz, though the words were not addressed to him. "Why, Poole, he means to fight!"

"Does he? For a penny he doesn't mean to let them come on board. Why, look at Butters; he's lying down on the deck."

"Yes," whispered Fitz; "to be in shelter if they fire while he's working the spokes. Look, the sails are filling once again."

"It's too soon," whispered Poole hoarsely. "They'll see from the gunboat and fire, and if they do—"

"They will miss us, my boy," said the skipper, who had approached unseen. "Lie down, my lads—every one on deck."

"And you too, father," whispered Poole. "They may hit you with a bullet."

"Obey orders," said the skipper sternly. "The captain must take his chance."

Crack, crack, crack, and *whizz, whizz, whizz!*

The officer of the cutter saw through the manoeuvre at last, and fired at the retreating schooner's skipper, while a minute later, as the *Silver Teal* was gliding rapidly into a bank of gloom that seemed to come like so much solid blackness down the vale, there was a bright flash as of lightning, a deep boom as of thunder, which shook the very air, and a roar of echoes dying right away, while the great stars overhead now stood out rapidly one by one in the purple velvet arch overhead.

Chapter Twenty One
By the skin of their teeth

"When we have escaped," cried Fitz excitedly, a few minutes later, a very brief time having sufficed to shut out the cutter and gunboat too.

"Escaped!" said Poole, with a little laugh, as he clapped his companion on the shoulder. "Well, *we* have."

"Yes, yes, of course," said Fitz; "I meant you. But what will be done now? We are—you are regularly shut in this bay. The gunboat will keep guard, and her boats will begin patrolling up and down so that you can't get away. It only means waiting till morning."

"Waiting till morning, eh?"

"Of course. And then they'll sink you as sure as you are here."

"Yes," said Poole, laughing merrily; "not a doubt about it."

"Well," said Fitz, "I don't see anything to laugh at."

"Don't you? Then I do. Why, you don't suppose for a moment that we shall be here? The fellows in that fishing-boat brought father some despatch orders for a *rendezvous* somewhere else, I should say. Just you wait a little, my boy, and you will see what the *Teal* can do. She can't dive, but she can dodge."

"Dodge in a little bay like this—dodge a gunboat?"

"Of course. Just wait till it's a little darker. I dare say father has got his plans all ready made, just the same as he had when it seemed all over just now. If he and old Burgess were too much for the Spanish dons in broad daylight, you may depend upon it that they will give them the go-by in the dark. Quiet! Here he is."

"Yes, here I am, my boy," said the skipper quietly. "Look here, you two. Hear—see—as much as you can:—and say nothing. Everything on board now must be quiet, and not a light seen."

"All right, father," replied Poole, "but I can't see anything of the gunboat's lights."

"No, and I don't suppose you will. They will take care not to show any. Well, Mr Burnett, may I trust you not to betray us by shouting a warning when the enemy are near? We are going to play a game of hide-and-seek, you know. We shall do the hiding, and the Spaniards will have to seek. Of course you know," he continued, "it would be very easy for you to shout when we were stealing along through the darkness, and bring the enemy's boats upon us just when they are not wanted."

"Well, yes, sir, I was thinking so a little while ago," replied the middy.

"Well, that's frank," said the skipper; "and is that what I am to expect from your sense of duty?"

Fitz was silent.

"Well, sir," he said at last, "I don't quite know. It's rather awkward for me, seeing how I am placed."

"Yes—very; but I don't believe you would think so if you knew what sort of a character this usurping mongrel Spaniard is. There is more of the treacherous Indian in his blood than of the noble Don. Perhaps under the circumstances I had better make you a prisoner in your cabin with the dead-light in, so that you can't make a signal to the enemy with lamp or match."

"It would be safer, sir," said Fitz.

"But most unpleasant," continued the skipper. "But there, my lad, situated as you are, I don't think you need strain a point. Give me your parole that you will content yourself with looking on, and I won't ask you to go below."

"Oh, he will, father. I'll answer for that," cried Poole.

"Answer for yourself, my boy. That's enough for you to do. Let Mr Burnett give me his own assurance. It would be rather mean, wouldn't it, Mr Burnett, if you did betray us?"

"Yes, sir; horrible," cried Fitz quickly. "But if it were one of our ships I should be obliged."

"Of course," said the skipper; "but as it is you will hold your tongue?"

"Yes, sir; I shall look on."

"That's right. Now then," continued the skipper, "the game's going to begin. There is sure to be some firing, so keep well down under the shelter of the bulwarks. Of course they will never have a chance to take aim, but there is no knowing what a random shot may do."

"Want me to do anything, father?" said Poole eagerly.

"No, my boy. There is nothing you can do. It will all lie with Mr Burgess; Butters, who will be at the wheel; myself, and the men who trim the sails."

"You are going to sail right away then; eh, father?"

"That all depends, my boy—just as the chances come."

"But as the schooner draws so little water, sir," said Fitz eagerly, "won't you sail close in under the shore?"

"No, my lad. That's just what the enemy will expect, and have every boat out on the *qui vive*. I don't mind telling you now what my plans will be."

He was silent for a few minutes, and they dimly made out that he was holding up his left hand as a warning to them not to speak, while he placed his right behind his ear and seemed to be listening, as if he heard some sound.

"Boat," he said, at last, in a whisper, "rowing yonder right across our stern. But they didn't make us out. Oh, I was about to tell you what I meant to do. Run right by the gunboat as closely as I can without touching her, for it strikes me that will be the last thing that they will expect."

He moved away the next moment, leaving the boys together once again, to talk in whispers about the exciting episode that was to come.

"I say, Fitz," whispered Poole excitedly, "isn't this better than being on board your sleepy old *Tonans*?"

"You leave the sleepy old *Tonans* alone," replied the middy. "She's more lively than you think."

"Could be, perhaps; but you never had a set-out like this."

"No," said Fitz stiffly, "because the *Tonans* never runs away."

"That's one for me," said Poole, laughing. "There are times when you must run, my lad, and this is one. Hullo, they're shaking out more canvas. It's going to be yachting now like a race for a cup. It's 'bout ship too."

"Yes, by the way one can feel the wind," replied Fitz; "but I don't believe your people can see which way to steer."

"Nor I neither," said Poole coolly. "Father is going to chance it, I believe. He'll make straight for where he saw the gunboat last, as he thinks, and take it for granted that we can't run on to her. Besides, she is pretty well sure to be on the move."

"Most likely," said Fitz; "but it's terribly risky work."

The rippling of the water under the schooner's bows came very plainly now, as the boys went right forward, where two men were on the look-out. These they joined, to find that they had the sternest instructions, and these were communicated by the men to the two lads.

"Mustn't speak, gentlemen," they said.

"Just one word," whispered Fitz. "What are you going to do if you make out that you are running right on to the enemy?"

"Whistle," said the man addressed, laconically.

"What, for more wind?" asked Fitz.

"No, sir," said the man, with a low chuckle; "for the man at the wheel. One pipe means starboard; two pipes, port. See?"

"No," said Poole, "but he can hear."

As they were whispering, the louder rippling beneath the schooner's cut-water plainly told of the rate at which they were gliding through the dark sea. The stars were clear enough overhead, but all in front seemed to be of a deep transparent black, whose hue tinged even the staysail, jib, and flying-jib, bellying out above their heads and in front. As far as the lads could make out they had been running in towards the city, taken a good sweep round, and then been headed out for the open sea, with the schooner careening over and rushing through the water like a racing yacht.

There are some things in life which seem to be extended over a considerable space of time, apparently hours, but which afterwards during calmer thought prove to have taken up only minutes, and this was one.

Poole had just pointed out in a low whisper that by the stars they were sailing due east, and the man nearest to them, a particularly sharp-eared individual, endorsed his words by whispering laconically—

"Straight for the open sea."

The water was gliding beneath them, divided by the sharp keel, with a hissing rush; otherwise all was still; for all they could make out the gunboat and her satellites, sent out to patrol, might have been miles away. There was darkness before them and on either hand, while in front apparently lay the open ocean, and the exhilaration caused by their rapid motion produced a buoyant feeling suggesting to the lads that the danger was passed and that they were free.

Then in another moment it seemed to Fitz Burnett as if some giant hand had caught him by the throat and stopped his breath.

The sensation was appalling, and consequent upon the suddenly-impressed knowledge that, in spite of the fact that there was about a mile and a half of space of which an infinitesimally small portion was occupied by danger, they were gliding through the black darkness dead on to that little space, for suddenly in front there arose the dull panting, throbbing sound of machinery, the churning up of water to their left, and the hissing ripple caused by a cut-water to their right.

It was horrible.

They were going dead on to the gunboat, which was steaming slowly across their bows, and it seemed to the breathless, expectant group that the next moment they would be cutting into her side, or more likely crumpling up and shivering to pieces upon her protecting armour. But there is something in having a crew of old man-of-war's men, disciplined and trained to obey orders in emergencies, and thinking of nothing else. The skipper had given his commands to his two look-out men, and in the imminence of the danger they were obeyed, for as Fitz Burnett gripped his companion's arm, involuntarily drawing him sideways in the direction of the bulwark, to make a leap for life, a sharp clear pipe, like the cry of some sea-bird, rang out twice, while the panting and quivering of the machinery and the churning rush of the gunboat's crew seemed right upon them.

Suddenly there was a loud shout, followed by a yell, the report of a revolver, succeeded by the deep booming roar of a fog-syren which had been set going by the funnel, and then as Fitz Burnett felt that the crash was upon them, the roar of the fog-horn was behind, for the *Teal* had as nearly as possible scraped past the gunboat's stern, and was flying onward towards the open sea.

For a few moments no one spoke, and then it was one of the look-out men.

"About as near as a toucher, that, messmate."

"Ay, and I seemed to have no wind when I wanted to blow. Once is quite enough for a job like that."

"Is it true, Poole?" whispered Fitz, and his voice sounded hoarse and strange.

"I don't quite know yet," was the reply as the lad walked aft. "It seemed so impossible and queer—but it is, and, my word, how close!"

Chapter Twenty Two
In the dark

"Silence there!" came in a stern, deep voice. "Sound travels in a night like this."

It was the speaker's ultra caution spoken in a moment of intense excitement in which he hardly realised how far they had left the gunboat behind. But his orders were obeyed, utter stillness ruling on board the schooner till they had visual proof that there was no necessity for such care.

"What's that? Look!" whispered Fitz, as there was a faint lambent glare far astern, one which gradually increased, and Poole whispered back—

"They are burning a blue light."

"Yes," said the skipper, who was still close at hand. "Know what that means, my boy?"

"Well, I suppose it's to try if they can see us, father."

"Not it," said the skipper sharply. "You know, Mr Burnett?"

"I should say it's a signal, sir, to recall their boats."

"Right, my lad; that's it; and that will take some little time, for I dare say they are spread all over the bay. She's not likely to have a consort; eh, Burgess?"

"I should think not," was the reply. "No, I don't think we need trouble ourselves about that."

"Right, then. Get well out into the offing, and then sail for south-east by south."

The mate grunted, gave an order or two, with the result that a gaff-topsail was run up, and the schooner heeled over more and more, while now the dim light that had been thrown down on the binnacle was increased a little, and the skipper took his place beside the steersman.

"That means that he is not afraid of our being seen," said Poole quietly. "I say, what an escape we had! Don't you call this exciting?"

"Yes," said Fitz; "rather more so than I like. Let's go right forward again to where the look-out men are."

"To help them keep a sharp look-out for rocks? There are none out here, or we shouldn't be going at this rate."

"Think that they will come after us?"

"Sure to," said Poole. "Full steam ahead."

"Then they'll see us again at daylight."

"Think so? Why, we have got all the night before us, and the gunboat's captain isn't likely to follow in our wake."

"I suppose not. It would be a great chance if he did. How beautiful the water is to-night!"

"Yes! One had no chance to admire it before. 'Tis fine. Just as if two rockets were going off from our bows, so that we seem to be leaving a trail of sparks behind."

"Yes, where the water's disturbed," said Fitz. "It's just as if the sea was covered with golden oil ready to flash out into light as soon as it was touched."

"Why, you seem quite cheery," said Poole.

"Of course. Isn't it natural after such a narrow escape?"

"Yes, for me," replied Poole banteringly; "but I should have thought that you would have been in horribly low spirits because you were not captured and taken on board the gunboat."

"No, you wouldn't," said Fitz shortly. "I know better than that. I say, you will stop on deck all night, won't you?"

"Of course. Shan't you?"

"Oh yes. I couldn't go to sleep after this. Besides, who can tell what's to come?"

"To be sure," said Poole quietly. "Who can tell what's to come? In spite of what old Burgess says, the gunboat may have a consort, and perhaps we are running out of one danger straight into another."

Perhaps due to the reaction after the excitement, the lads ceased to chat together, and leaned over the bows, alternately watching the phosphorescent sea and the horizon above which the stars appeared dim and few.

Fitz looked more thoughtful as the time went on, his own words seeming to repeat themselves in the question—Who knows what might happen?

Once they turned aft, to look right astern at where they caught sight once or twice of the gunboat's light. Then it faded out and they went forward again, the schooner gliding swiftly on, till at last the mate's harsh, deep voice was heard giving his orders for an alteration of their course.

It was very dark inboard, and it was not until afterwards that the two lads knew exactly what had taken place. It was all in a moment, and how it happened even the sufferer hardly knew, but it was all due to a man having stepped in the darkness where he had no business to be; for just after the giving of the order, and while the spokes were swinging through the steersman's hands, one of the booms swung round, there was a dull thud, a half-uttered shout, and then a yell from one of the foremost men.

"Man overboard!" was roared, and as the skipper ran forward, after shouting to the steersman to throw the schooner up into the wind, another man answered his eager question with—

"It's Bob Jackson, sir. I saw him go."

The captain's excited voice rang out mingled with the shrill whistle of the boatswain's pipe, and then to be half-drowned by his hoarse roar as the men's feet pattered over the deck, now rapidly growing level as the pressure was taken off the sails.

"Now then, half-a-dozen of you!" came hoarsely. "Don't stand staring there! Are you going to be all night lowering down that boat? Sharp's the word! I am going to show you the way."

As he spoke, Fitz had a dim vision of the big bluff fellow's action, as, pulling out his knife, he opened it with his teeth.

"Sharks below there!" he roared. "'Ware my knife!" and running right astern he sprang on to the rail, looked round for a moment, fixed his eyes upon a luminous splash of light that had just taken Fitz's attention, and then sprang overboard into the black water, which splashed up like a fountain of fire, and the bluff sailor's figure, looking as if clad in garments of lambent gold, could be seen gliding diagonally down, forming a curve as it gradually rose to the surface, which began to emit little plashes of luminosity as the man commenced to swim.

"Well done! Bravo!" panted Fitz, and then he rushed to the spot where the men were lowering down, sprang on to the bulwark, caught at the falls, and slipped down into the boat just as it kissed the water.

"You here!" cried a familiar voice.

"Yes," panted Fitz, "and you too!"

"Why, of course! Pull away, my lads. I'll stand up and tell you which way to go."

The falls were already unhooked and the oars over the side, the men pulling with all their might in the direction where the regular splashes made by the motion of the boatswain's arm could be seen as he scooped away at the water with a powerful side stroke.

"Pull, lads—pull!" roared the skipper's son, while in his excitement Fitz scrambled over the oars to get right in the bows, where he strained his eyes to try and make out the man who had gone over first, and a terrible catching of the breath assailed him as he realised the distance he had been left behind by the swiftly-gliding schooner.

Even the boatswain was far away, swimming hard and giving out a heavy puff like some grampus just rising to breathe.

"This way, boys!" he shouted. "Come along! Cheer up, my hearty! I am coming fast."

He ceased speaking now, as the boat followed in his track, and Fitz as he knelt in the bows reached behind him to begin fumbling for the boat-hook, finding it and thrusting it out like a little bowsprit, ready to make a snatch when the time should come. But his effort seemed as if it would be vain, for after what seemed in the excitement to be a terribly long row, the boat was brought abreast of the swimming boatswain.

"Can't you see him, Butters?" shouted Poole, who had now joined Fitz.

"No, my lad," came in a hoarse gasping tone. "Can't you?"

"No. I saw the water splash not a minute ago. It was just beyond where you were swimming."

"No; more to the left," cried Fitz. "Ah, there! There! There!" and he pointed out in the direction he had described.

"Yes, that's it," roared the boatswain, who seemed suddenly to have recovered his breath, and throwing himself away from the boat, whose side he had grasped, he splashed through the water for a few yards towards where a ring of gold seemed to have been formed, and as the boat followed, and nearly touched his back, he seemed to be wallowing in an agitated pool of pale greenish fire, which went down and down for quite a couple of fathoms, the boat passing right above it with the men backing water at a shout from Poole, so that they passed the disappearing swimmer again.

"Now," shouted Fitz, as the golden light began to rise, and thrusting down the boat-hook he felt it catch against the swimmer's side.

The next moment the boatswain was up with a rush, to throw one arm over the bows.

"Got him!" he gasped.

There was a quick scramble, the water almost lapped over the side as the starboard-bow went down, and then, partly with the hauling of the boys, partly by the big sturdy boatswain's own efforts, the unfortunate Bob Jackson was dragged aboard, the boatswain rolling in after him with his messmates' help, and subsiding between two of the thwarts with a hoarse, half-strangled groan.

"Hooroar!" came from the men, the boys' voices dominating the shout with a better pronunciation of the word.

"Hooroar it is!" gasped the boatswain. "Bravo, Butters! Well done! Well done!" cried Poole.

"Well done? I am done, you mean. I thought I'd let him go. Keep back, some on you—give a fellow room to breathe. That's better," came with more freedom. "Now then, give your orders, Mr Poole," panted the man; "I've lost my wind. Get him on his back and pump his into him. That's your sort!" he continued, as in obedience to the young skipper's commands two men began to row while the others set to work upon the first aid necessary in the case of a half-drowned man.

"Ah!" sighed the boatswain, now sitting up in the bottom of the boat and shuffling himself aft a little so as to give more room. "I am as weak as a babby. Well done! Pump away, my lads. That's your sort! Pore chap, he's all water and no wind now! I dunno what he'd been about. Had he been soaping his feet?—Think he's coming round, Mr Poole?"

"I hope so," was the reply. "I am afraid, poor fellow, he must have been half-stunned. Come and look, Butters; I want you to feel his chest." The boatswain came and leaned over. "Keep it up, my lads. It will be all right soon. Oh yes, his own pump's going on inside. His kit won't be for sale. But I don't believe he'd have taken his trick at the wheel again if I hadn't gone down and fetched him up."

"No; you saved his life, Mr Butters," cried Fitz excitedly. "I never saw anything so brave before. Would you mind—"

"Eh!—What, sir?—Shake hands?—Certainly, sir, hearty, and same to you!"

"Oh!" ejaculated Fitz involuntarily. "I am very sorry, sir. Did I squeege too hard?"

"Why, it was a scrunch," said the boy petulantly. "But it's all right now. Your fingers, though, are as hard as wood."

"Well, they arn't soft, sir. But hallo! I never shut up my knife." He closed the keen blade with a sharp snap. "There! Now you see the vally of a lanyard," he continued, as he thrust the great clasp-knife into the waistband of his trousers.—"Keep it up, my lads. I'll take a turn as soon as I've got my own wind again. Ah, there's nothing like a lanyard. If it hadn't been for that my snickersee would have gone zigger-zagging down through the dark black water disturbing the little jellyfish and lighting the way for a snip, snap, swallow, all's fish that comes to their net style, to go inside some shark. But I've got it safe. It's a fine bit of Sheffield stuff, and I'll be bound to say it would have disagreed with him as had swallowed it. Here, somebody—who's got a match? Mine'll be all wet. Strike a light, will you; I want to see if he's beginning to wink yet."

A match was struck, and as it burned steadily in the still air a faint light was shown from the schooner far, far away.

"See there, my lads? He's winking his eyes like fun; but go on pumping slow and steady to keep him breathing—mustn't let him slip through your fingers now. Pull away there, my lads; put your backs into it. My word, there's a stiff current running here!"

"Yes," said Poole; "we are much farther away than I thought."

"But what an escape!" cried Fitz.

"Eh? What do you mean?"

"Look yonder; that streak of light gliding along and making the water flash. You can just make out now and then something dark cutting through it."

"Ah, that's plain enough," said the boatswain; "a jack shark's back fin, and a big un too."

"Lucky for you both," said Poole, "that you are safe on board."

"Lucky for him, you mean," said the boatswain. "That knife of mine's as sharp as hands can make it. If I had let him have it he'd have shown white at daylight, floating wrong side up."

"If you had hit him," said Fitz.

"If I'd hit him, sir! A man couldn't miss a thing like that. But of course there wouldn't have been time to pick my spot."

"Oh!" ejaculated Fitz, in a long-drawn sigh. "Seems to turn me quite over! That's about the most horrible cry I know—Man overboard! It's bad enough in the daylight, but on a night like this—"

"Ah, it would make you feel a bit unked, my lad," said the boatswain, "if you had time to think; but it was a fine night for the job. I have been out in a boat after one of these silly chaps as didn't mind where he was going, when you couldn't make out his bearings at all. To-night the sea brimed so that you could tell where he was at every move. Splendid night for the job!"

"And it was a very brave act, Butters," said Poole warmly.

"What was, sir?"

"Why, to jump overboard on a dark night, not knowing whether you would ever reach the schooner again."

"Tchah! Nonsense, sir! You shouldn't talk stuff like that to a wet man! It was all charnsh, of course; but a sailor's life is all charnsh from the moment he steps aboard. We are charnshing now whether they'll pick us up again, for they can't see us, and we don't seem to be making no headway at all in this current. Here, you, Sam Boulter, get right in the stem and stand by there with that there box of matches. Keep on lighting one and holding it up to let it shine out. Be careful and don't burn your ringers."

A low chuckle rose from the oarsmen, followed the next moment by a deep groan and a low muttering from the reviving man.

"Hah!" said the boatswain. "He's coming round now, and no mistake."

Just then there was a sharp scratch, a pale light of the splint of wood stood out in the darkness, and mingled with a spluttering husky cough came the voice of the half-drowned foremast-man.

"Here, easy there! What are you doing? Hah! Boat! Boat! Help!"

This was consequent on the gleaming match shining out before the poor fellow's eyes.

"Steady there!" roared out the boatswain. "What are you singing out like that for? Can't you see you are safe aboard?"

"Eh? Eh? Oh, thank goodness! I thought it was the schooner's lights. That you, Mr Butters?"

"Me it is, my lad! All right now, aren't you?"

"Yes, yes; all right. But I thought it was all over with me that time."

"So it ought to have been! Why, what were you about? Did you walk overboard in your sleep?"

"I—no—I—I dunno how it was. I suppose I slipped."

"Not much suppose about it," said the boatswain, as the man sat up. "Here, I'll give you a dose that'll do you good. Take one of them oars and pull."

"Oh no!" cried Poole. "The poor fellow's weak."

"'Course he is, sir, and that'll warm him up and put life into him. Tit for tat. We've saved him from what the old folks at home calls a watery grave, and now it's his turn to do a bit of something to save us."

"To save us, Mr Butters?" whispered Fitz, laying his hand on the boatswain's arm. "Why, you don't think—"

"Yes, I do, sir. I'm thinking all the time, as hard as a man can. Here, you'd better not handle me; I'm as wet as wet."

"But we shall soon get alongside the schooner, shan't we?"

"Well, it don't seem like it, sir. Wish we could! I should just like a good old jorum of something warm, if it was only a basin of old Andy's broth as he makes so slimy with them little round wet barley knobs. I'm all of a shiver. Here, you number one, get up and I'll take your oar. I don't like catching cold when I'm at sea."

"But surely they'll tack round, or something, so as to pick us up."

"Here, hi! You look alive there with another of those matches. You don't half keep them going, so that they can see where we are."

"Aren't any more," said the man in the stem. "I held that one till it did burn my fingers, and it was the last."

"Humph!" grunted the boatswain. "Well, they can't see us, of course, and the sea's a bit big and wide out here; let's try if we can't make them hear."

He had scarcely spoken when there was a soft bellowing roar; but the sound took form and they made out—"Ahoy-y-y-y! Where away there?" breathed, it almost seemed, so distant and strange was the hail, through a speaking-trumpet.

"Cease pulling!" shouted the boatswain. "Now then, all together. Take your time from me. One, two, three—Ahoy-y-y-y!"

Every lusty throat on board the boat sent forth the cry at once, and a strange chill ran through Fitz's breast as he noted not only how feeble the cry sounded in the immensity of space, but how it seemed thrown back upon them from something it could not penetrate—something soft and impervious which shut them in all round.

Chapter Twenty Three
Boating

"Well, Mr Poole, sir, we seem to have got ourselves into a pretty jolly sort of mess. I feel quite damp. You are skipper, sir; what's to be done?"

"Shout again," cried Poole; "all together,"—and another lusty yell was given.

"There, 'tarn't no use, sir," said the boatswain, "if so be as I may speak."

"Speak? Of course! I am only too glad of your advice. What were you going to say?"

"Only this 'ere, sir—that it aren't no use to shout. I am wet and cold, and hollering like this is giving me a sore throat, and the rest of the lads too. There's Dick Boulter is as husky as my old uncle Tom's Cochin fowl. Here, I want to know why the skipper don't show a blue light."

"He dare not," said Poole hastily. "It would be showing the gunboat where the schooner is."

There was a sharp slap heard in the darkness, caused by the boatswain bringing his hand smartly down upon his sturdy thigh.

"Right you are, my lad. I never thought of that. I oughter, but it didn't come. 'Cause I was so wet, I suppose. Well, sir, what do you think?"

"Try, every one of you," said Poole, "whether you can make out a light. The *Teal* oughtn't to be very far away."

"Nay, sir, she oughtn't to be, but she is. Off shore here in these seas you get currents running you don't know where. We don't know, but I expect we are in one of them, and it's carrying us along nobody knows how fast; and like as not another current's carrying on the same game with the *Teal*."

"Well, we must row, and row hard," said Poole.

"But that may be making worse of it," put in Fitz, who had been listening and longing to speak.

"Well done," said the boatswain. "Spoke like a young man-o'-war officer! He's right, Mr Poole, sir. I am longing to take an oar so as to get warm and dry; but it's no use to try and make what's as bad as ever it can be, ever so much worse."

"That would puzzle you, Mr Butters," said Fitz, laughing.

"Oh, I don't know, sir," said the boatswain seriously, and perfectly unconscious of the bull he had made. "We might, you know. What's to be done, Mr Poole?"

"I can only see one thing to be done," said the skipper's son, "and that seems so horrible and wanting in spirit."

"What's that?" said Fitz sharply.

"Wait for daylight."

"Oh!" cried Fitz impatiently. "Impossible! We can't do that."

"Well, I don't know, Mr Burnett, sir," growled the boatswain, gazing round. "Seems to me as if we must. Look here, you Bob Jackson," he almost roared now, as he turned sharply on the shivering foremast-man who had just been brought back to life, "what have you got to say for yourself for getting us all into such a mess as this? I always thought you were a bit of a swab, and now I knows it."

"Don't bully the poor fellow," cried Poole hotly. "It was an accident."

"Of course it was, sir," cried the boatswain, in an ill-used tone, as he drew off his jacket and began to wring it as tightly as he could; "and accidents, as I have heared say, will happen in the best-manned vessels. One expects them, and has to put up with them when they comes; but people ought to have accidents at proper times and places, not just when we've escaped running ourselves down, and the Spanish gunboat's arter us. Now then, Bob, don't sit there hutched up like a wet monkey. Speak out like a man."

"I haven't got nothing to say, Mr Butters, sir, only as I am very sorry, and much obliged to you for saving my life."

"Much obliged! Sorry! Wuss and wuss! Yah! Look at that now! Wuss and wuss. It never rains but it pours."

"What's the matter?" cried Fitz, for the boatswain had made a sudden dash with one hand as if striving to catch something that had eluded his grasp.

"Matter, sir? Why, I squeeged my brass 'bacca-box out of my jacket-pocket. It was chock-full, and it would go down like lead. Here, I give up now. Give your orders, Mr Poole, and I'll row or do anything else, for I'm quite out of heart."

"Never mind your tobacco-box," said Fitz. "I'll give you a good new one the first time I get the chance."

"Thankye kindly, sir," replied the man, "but what's the good of that? It aren't the box I mind. It's the 'bacca. Can you give me a mossel now?"

"I am sorry to say I can't," said Fitz.

"I've got plenty of that, Mr Butters, sir," said his wet companion, dragging out a box with some difficulty, for his wet hand would hardly go into his tight breeches-pocket, and when he had forced it in, declined to come out.

"You've got plenty, Bob, my lad?" cried the boatswain. "Then you are a better man than I thought. There, I'll forgive you for going overboard. It were an accident, I suppose.—Hah! That's better," he continued, opening his knife and helping himself to a quid, which completely altered the tone of his voice. "There you are, my lad; put that there box back, and take care on it, for who knows but what that may be all our water and biscuit and other stores as will have to last us till we get picked up again? Now, Mr Poole, sir, what's it to be? I am at your sarvice if you will give the word."

"I think we had better keep pulling gently, Butters, and go by the stars westward towards the land. It will be far better, and the feeling that we are doing something will keep us all from losing heart."

"Right, my lad. Your father the skipper couldn't have spoken wiser words than them. Here, you Bob Jackson, get out of that jacket and shirt, and two of you lads hold the things over the side and one twist one way and t'other t'other, like the old women does with the sheets on washing-day. I am going to do just the same with mine. And then we two will do what bit of rowing's wanted till we gets quite dry. Say, Mr Fitz, sir, you couldn't get better advice than that, if you had been half-drowned, if you went to the best physic doctor in Liverpool."

Shortly after, steering by the stars, the boat was headed pretty well due west, and a couple of oars were kept dipping with a monotonous splash, raising up the golden water, which dripped in lambent globules from the blades. All above was one grand dome of light, but below and around it was as if a thick stratum of intense blackness floated on the surface of the sea.

So strangely dark this seemed that it impressed the boat's crew with a sense of dread that they could not master. It was a condensation of dread and despair, that knowledge of being alone in a frail craft at the mercy of the sea, without water or supplies of any kind, and off a coast which the currents might never let them reach, while at any hour a tempestuous wind might spring up and lash the sea into waves, in which it would be impossible for the boat to live.

"Don't sit silent like that, Burnett," whispered Poole. "Say something, there's a good fellow."

"Say? What can I say?" was whispered back. "Anything. Sing a song, or tell a story. I want to keep the lads in good heart. If we show the white feather they'll show it too."

"That's right enough," said Fitz gloomily; "but I don't feel as if I could do anything but think. I couldn't sing a song or tell a story to save my life."

"But you must. It *is* to save your life."

"I tell you I can't," cried Fitz angrily.

"Then whistle."

The middy could not even whistle, but the suggestion and the manner in which it was said did have a good effect, for it made him laugh.

"Ah! That's better," cried Poole. "I say, Butters, do you think if we had a fishing-line overboard we should catch anything?"

"Like enough, lad, if we had a good bait on. Fish is generally on the feed in the night, and there's no end of no-one-knows-whats off these 'Merican coasts. Might get hold of something big as would tow us right ashore."

"Yes, or right out to sea," said Fitz.

"Ay, my lad; but we should have to chance that."

"But there's not likely to be a line in the locker," said Poole.

"And if there was," said Fitz, "you have no bait."

"'Cept 'bacca," said the boatswain, "and they wouldn't take that. And even if they would, we couldn't afford to waste it on fish as most likely wouldn't be good to eat. You catches fishes off these coasts as is painted up like parrots—red, and green, and yaller, and blue; but they are about as bad as pison.—Getting warmer, Bob?"

"Bit," said the man addressed.

"So'm I.—Tell the lads to keep their ears open, Mr Poole, for breakers. There may be shoal water anywhere, and we don't want to run into them."

"You think it's likely, then," said Fitz, "that we may reach the shore?"

"Oh yes, sir; we might, you know; and if we did I dare say you young gents would find it an uninhabited island where you could play at Robinson Crusoe till a ship come and took us off. What do you say to that?"

"Nothing," said Fitz. "I want the daylight to come, and a sight of the *Silver Teal*."

"Same here, sir. My word, I'm beginning to feel like wishing we had got the Camel here, though he would be no good without the galley and his tools. Not a bad chap to have, though, Mr Poole, if we was to land in a sort of Robinson Crusoe island. There's worse messmates at a time like that than a chap as can knock up decent wittles out of nothing; make a good pot of soup out of a flannel-shirt and an old shoe, and roast meat out of them knobs and things like cork-blocks as you find growing on trees. Some of them cookie chaps too, like the Camel, are precious keen about the nose, long-headed and knowing. Old Andy is an out-and-out clever chap at picking out things as is good to eat. I had a ramble with him once up country in Trinidad. He was a regular wunner at finding out different kinds of plants. 'Look 'ere,' he says, 'if you pull this up it's got a root something like a parsnep whose grandfather had been a beet.' And then he showed me some more things creeping up the trees like them flowers at home in the gardens, wonvuluses, as they call them, only he called them yams, and he poked one out with his stick, and yam it was—a great, big, black, thick, rooty thing, like a big tater as had been stretched. Andy said as no fellow as had brains in his head ought to starve out in a foreign land; and that's useful to know, Mr Poole and Mr Burnett, sir. Come in handy if we have to do the Robinson Crusoe for a spell.—Keep it up, young gents," he whispered; "the lads like to hear us talk.—'That's all very fine, Andy,' I says," he continued, aloud, "'but what about water? Whether you are aboard your ship or whether you are in a strange land, you must have plenty of water in your casks!' 'Find a river,' he says. 'But suppose you can't,' says I. 'Open your snickersee,' says he, 'and dig a hole right down till you come to it. And if there aren't none, then use your eyes.' 'Why, you can't drink your eyes,' I says, 'and I'd rather have sea-water any day than tears.' 'Use them,' he says; 'I didn't say drink 'em. Look about. Why, in these 'ere foreign countries there's prickly plants with long spikes to them to keep the wild beasts from meddling with them, so as they shall be ready for human beings; and then all you have got to do is to rub or singe the spikes off and they're chock-full of water—juice, if you like to call it so—only it's got no taste. Then there's plahnts with a spunful of water in their jyntes where the leaves come out, and orkard plahnts like young pitchers or sorter shucks with lids to keep the birds off, and a lot of water in the bottom of them, besides fruits and pumpkin things. Oh, a fellow can rub along right enough if he likes to try. I could manage; I know that.' And I believe he could, gentlemen, and that's what makes me say as the Camel would be just the right sort of fellow to have with us now, him and old Chips, so long as old Chips had got his basket of traps; not as he would stand still if he hadn't, for he's just the fellow, if he has no tools, as would set to and make some."

And the night gradually wore on, with the men taking their turns at rowing. The boatswain and Bob Jackson both declared themselves to be as dry as a bone, and what with talking and setting despair at defiance, they went on and on through the great silence and darkness that hovered together over the mighty deep, till all at once the boatswain startled Fitz by turning quite suddenly and saying to him—

Fitz was the first to make it out.

"There aren't no farmyard and a stable handy, sir, to give us what we want. Could you make shift to do it?"

"To do what?" said Fitz wonderingly. "Crow like a cock, sir. It's just the right time now."

"You don't mean to say it's morning, Butters?"

"No, sir; it's Natur' as is a-doing that. You've got your back to it. Turn round and look behind you. That's the east."

Both lads wrenched themselves round upon the thwart where they sat, to gaze back over the sea and catch the first glimpse of the faint dawn with its promises of hope and life, and the end of the terrible night through which they had passed.

And after the manner of the tropics, the broad daylight was not long in coming, followed by the first glint of the sun, which, as it sent a long line of ruddy gold over the surface of the sea, lit up one little speck of light miles upon miles to the north of where they lay.

Fitz Burnett was the first to make it out, but before he could speak the boatswain had seen it too, and broke out with—

"Three cheers, my lads. Put all you know into it, hearty. There lies the *Teal*. Can you see the skipper, Mr Poole, sir?"

"See my father?" cried the lad. "No! What do you mean?"

"Ah, you want practice, sir. You ought to see him with your young eyes. He's there on deck somewhere with that double-barrelled spyglass of his, on the look-out for this 'ere boat."

"Perhaps so," said Poole quietly, "and I suppose that's one of the *Teal's* sails; but it's only half as big as a pocket-handkerchief folded into twenty-four."

Two hours later they were on board, for it had not been long before the double-barrelled spyglass had picked them out.

Chapter Twenty Four
On the wrong side

An anxious look-out had been kept up all through those early hours on board both schooner and boat, for during the long delay caused by the accident, it seemed highly probable that as the gunboat did not come in sight she must have passed them in the darkness, gone on, and hence might at any moment come into view.

A man was sent up to the cross-trees, and a sharp look-out was kept up as well from the deck for the missing crew who were got safely on board, and the schooner sailed away towards the south and west, and still with no danger in sight.

"You've given me a bad night, young fellows," said the skipper, as he stood looking on at the lads enjoying their morning meal, one over which the Camel seemed to have taken extra pains, showing his large front teeth with a smile of satisfaction as he brought it in relays of newly-made hot cakes, before retiring to slip fresh slices of bacon in the pan.

"Yes, father," said Poole; "but see what a night we had!"

"Ah, but yours was merely physical, my boy; mine was mental."

"I thought ours was both; eh, Burnett?" said Poole, laughing.

"Oh, yes, it was," cried the middy. "You don't know what a night we had, Captain Reed."

"Well, I suppose you did not have a very pleasant time, my lads.—Oh, here's Mr Burgess. Well, they don't seem much the worse for it, do they? Nothing in sight?"

"No, nothing. I don't think she could have followed us out. Have you any more to say to me about the course?"

"No," said the skipper. "I think we pretty well understand about the bearings as given in the letter. The Don put it all down pretty clearly, and in very decent English too."

Fitz looked up sharply, for the mention of the letter brought to mind the light fishing-boat with the bird-wing-like lateen sail and the rapidity with which the bearer of the despatch delivered it to the skipper and went overboard again.

Captain Reed noticed the boy's inquiring look, and said quietly—

"Perhaps we had better say no more about that with an enemy present."

Fitz was in the act of helping himself to some more of the hot bread, but at the skipper's words he flushed warmly, put down the cake without taking out of it a semi-circular bite, and rose from his seat.

"I don't wish to play the spy, sir," he said haughtily. "I will go on deck till you have finished your business."

"Sit down!" cried the skipper. "Sit down! What a young pepper-castor you are! Mayn't a man think what he likes in his own cabin?"

"Certainly, sir; but of course I cannot help feeling that I am an intruder."

"That's just what I feel, my boy, for coming in and disturbing you at your meal. Sit down, I say. If anybody is going to leave the room, I am that person; but I am not going to leave my cabin, so I tell you."

The skipper gave his son a peculiar look, his eyes twinkling the while.

"Think we can trust Mr Burnett here?" he said.

Fitz gave a start.

"Oh yes, father. He won't go and tell tales. He won't have a chance. What was in that letter?"

"Just a few lines, my boy, to say that everything was going very wrong at present, and begging me whatever I did to keep the schooner's cargo out of Villarayo's hands, and to join Ramon as soon as I possibly can."

"But where, father? Both the towns are in the enemy's hands."

"At his hacienda at the mouth of the Oltec River."

"Hacienda?" said Poole. "That means a sort of farm, doesn't it, father?"

"Yes, my boy, and of course that's just the sort of place to deliver a cargo of such agricultural implements as we have brought on board. What do you say, Mr Burnett?"

"Agricultural implements, sir? Why, Captain Glossop had notice that you had taken in guns and ammunition."

"Oh yes; people do gossip so," said the skipper dryly. "I didn't examine them much myself, but I know there were things with wheels."

"But there was a lot of powder, sir—kegs of it, I heard."

"Chemical manure perhaps, my lad; potash and charcoal and sulphur perhaps to kill the blight. Must be innocent stuff, or else my old friend Don Ramon would not want it at his farm."

"I don't understand," said the middy.

"Well, it doesn't matter," cried Poole, laughing. "Go on, father."

"That's what we are doing, my boy. But you go on with your breakfast, Mr Burnett, and make a good one while you have a chance. We may be getting news any minute that the gunboat is in sight; and if it is, there's no knowing when we shall get a square meal again."

"But whereabouts is this Oltec River, father?"

"Well, as near as I can tell you, my boy, it's on the coast about thirty miles by sea from Velova, though only about half the distance through one of the mountain-passes by land. We ought to have been there now, and I dare say we should have been if Mr Burgess had not run us on to a rock. But that fellow going overboard quite upset my plans. It was a great nuisance, and I seemed to be obliged to heave-to, and wait to see if you people would come back on board."

"Yes, father, I suppose so," said Poole coolly.

"Done eating, you two?"

The lads both rose, and the whole party went on deck to scan their position, the lads finding the schooner gliding along southward before a pleasant breeze, while miles away on the starboard-bow a dim line marked the coast, which seemed rugged and broken up into mountain and vale; but there was no sign of gunboat nor a sail of any kind, and Poole breathed more freely.

"One's so helpless," he said to his companion, "on a coast like this, where one time you have a nice sailing wind, and the next hour it has dropped into a calm, so that a steamer has you quite at its mercy."

"Yes," said Fitz dryly; "but I don't see that it matters when you have nothing on board but agricultural implements and chemical manures. What business is it of the gunboat?"

"Ah, what indeed?" cried Poole, laughing. "It's a piece of impudence, isn't it, to want to interfere! But I say, Burnett, what father says sounds well, doesn't it—a hacienda at the mouth of a river, and a mountain-pass? That means going ashore and seeing something, if we are in luck. I do know that the country's glorious here, from the peep or two I once had. My word! People think because you go sailing about the world you must see all kinds of wonders, when all the time you get a peep or two of some dirty port without going ashore, and all your travels are up and down the deck of your ship—and nothing else but sea."

"I wish I could get landed at some big port," said Fitz bitterly. "I wouldn't call it dirty."

"My word, what a fellow you are!" said Poole. "Grumbling again!"

"Grumbling!" cried Fitz hotly. "Isn't it enough to make any one grumble, dragged off my ship a prisoner like this?"

"No," cried Poole. "Why, some chaps would call it grand. Now you've got about well again it's all a big lark for you. Every one's trying to make you comfortable. Look at the adventures you are going through! Look at last night! Why, it was all fine, now that we have got through it as we did. You can't say you didn't like that."

"Well, no," said Fitz; "it was exciting."

"So it is now. The gunboat's safe to be after us, and here we are, going to take refuge up a river in perhaps no end of a wild country at the Don's hacienda. Who knows what adventures we are going to have next!"

"Not likely to be many adventures at a muddy farm."

"How do you know?"

"Because I pretty well know what a farm is."

"Not a Central American one, my fine fellow. I dare say you will have to open your eyes wider than you think."

"Perhaps so," said Fitz, who was growing more good-humoured over his companion's frank, genial ways; "but I feel more disposed to shut my eyes up now, and to have a good sleep."

"Oh, don't do that! There will be plenty of time when it gets dark, and before then I hope we shall be off the river. We are slipping along pretty quickly now, and old Burgess is creeping closer in. That's his artfulness; it means looking out for creeks and islands, places where we could hide if the gunboat came into sight, or sneaking into shallows where she couldn't follow. The old man knows what he is about, and so does father too. Here, let's go and fetch a glass and get up aloft. I want to make out what the coast is like."

The binocular was fetched from the cabin, and the lads mounted the rigging as high as they could to get comfortably perched, and then shared the glass, turn and turn, to come to the conclusion that every knot they crept along through the shallow sea brought them more and more abreast of a district that looked wild and beautiful in the extreme: low mountain gorge and ravine, beautiful forest clothing the slopes, and parts where the country was green with the waving trees almost to the water's-edge.

And so the day slipped by, and the sun began to sink just as they glided into a narrow sheltered estuary, which, as far as they could make out, ran like a jagged gash inland; and an hour later the schooner was at anchor behind a headland which completely bid them from the open sea.

"There," cried Poole, turning to the middy, who was sweeping the forest-clad slopes on either hand, "what do you think of this?"

"Lovely!" cried Fitz enthusiastically, forgetting all his troubles in the wondrous tropic beauty of the golden shores.

"Come on, then. I don't know what Andy has got us for supper, but it smells uncommonly good."

"Supper!" said the middy, in tones of disgust. "Why, you can't leave a scene like this to go and eat?"

"Can't I?" cried Poole. "Do you mean to tell me that you are not hungry too?"

"Well, no," said Fitz, slowly, closing the glass; "I don't think I can. I didn't know how bad I was until you spoke."

Chapter Twenty Five
A tropic river

Strict watch was set, no lights were shown, and a quiet, uneventful night was passed, the boys sleeping so hard that it was with some difficulty that they were awakened, to start up wondering that it was day.

"Why," cried Fitz, "I feel as if I had only just lain down."

It proved, though, that they had each had nine hours' solid sleep, and after a hasty breakfast, preparations were made for ascending the river. The men were armed, the largest boat lowered, and Fitz hung about watching eagerly all that was going on; but, too proud to ask questions, he waited to see how matters would shape themselves.

As he expected, Poole came to him after a time, and in answer to the middy's questioning looks said eagerly—

"The Don's hacienda is right up this river somewhere, and the dad is going up in a boat with about half the lads, to see how the land lies, while old Burgess stops at home and takes care of the *Teal*. And I suppose he will have to take care of you too, you being a prisoner who don't take any interest in what we do. What do you think?"

"Think? That I shouldn't do any harm if I came with you, should I?"

"Well, I don't know," said Poole, with mock seriousness. "You wouldn't like to come too with me?" Fitz looked at him blankly.

"It's going to be quite an expedition. The lads are going to have rifles and plenty of ammunition; revolvers too. I am going to have the same, because there is no knowing what sort of fellows we may meet. But, as the dad says, if they see we are well-armed they won't meddle with us. In these revolutionary times, though, every one is on the rampage and spoiling for a fight. Pity you can't go with us." Fitz was silent.

"You see, I could have arranged it nicely. We might have had old Andy to carry a couple of bags, and you could have had the governor's double gun, and looked after the pot. We should have had you blazing away right and left as we went up the river at everything that the Camel said was good to eat. You would soon have filled both the bags, of course."

"Look here," said Fitz, "none of your sneers! I dare say if I tried I could shoot as well as you can."

"Sneers!" cried Poole, with mock solemnity. "Hark at him! Why should I sneer about your filling the bags when you are not going? Of course you wouldn't. You'd think it wouldn't be right. I thought of all that, and said so to father."

Fitz coughed, and then said huskily—

"What did he say?"

"What did he say? Well—"

"Why don't you speak?" cried Fitz angrily.

"You might give a fellow time. What did father say?"

"Yes, of course!"

"Oh, he said he didn't like much shooting, because he did not want the enemy to know we were up the river, but that if I saw anything in the shape of a deer or a big bird, or anything else good to eat, I was to fire."

"Hah!" sighed Fitz, as he saw himself spending a lonely day on board.

"Hah!" sighed Poole, in imitation. "I wish you had been going too."

Fitz looked at him searchingly.

"There!" he cried. "You are gammoning me."

Poole could not keep it in; his face expanded into a broad grin.

"I knew you were," cried Fitz.

"Yes, it's all right, old chap. The governor said that you were to come, for he didn't think that there would be any trouble, and it would be a pleasant change for you."

"Your father is a regular trump," cried Fitz excitedly. "I say, though; I should have liked to have a gun."

"Well, you are going to have his. I'll carry a rifle, so as to bring down all the bucks."

"How soon do we start?"

"Directly. Old Burgess is looking as blue as Butters' nose because he has got to stop at home, and Butters himself is doing nothing else but growl.

He didn't like it a bit when the dad said that he must be tired after the other night's work. But he's got to stop."

Half-an-hour later the well-manned boat was being pulled vigorously up the rapidly narrowing river, with the two boys in the bows, on the look-out for anything worthy of powder and shot which might appear on either bank; but there was nothing save beauty to recompense their watchful eyes.

Birds were plentiful enough, and of the loveliest plumage, while every now and then a loud splash followed the movement of what seemed to be a log of wood making the best of its way into deep water. And once high in a mighty tree which shot up its huge bole from the very mud of the bank, Poole pointed out a curious knot of purple, dull buff and brown, right in the fork where a large branch joined the bole. "Not a serpent, is it?" whispered Fitz. "It is, though," was the reply; and the middy raised his piece.

"No, no; don't shoot," said Poole softly. "It isn't good to eat, and we might be giving the alarm."

Fitz lowered the double gun with a sigh, and the boat glided on, sending the rushing water in a wave to go lapping amongst the bushes that overhung from the bank, and directly after the serpent knot was hidden by the leaves.

The rapid little river wound here and there, and they went on mile after mile, with the steamy heat growing at times almost unbearable. But the men did not murmur, tugging away at their oars and seeming to enjoy the beauty of the many scenes through which they passed, for every now and then the river widened out, to look like some shut-in lake. And so mile after mile was passed, no spot where they could land presenting itself in the dense jungle which covered the banks, and it was not till afternoon that at a sudden turn they came upon an opening which had evidently been produced by the axe, while a short distance farther on at a word from the skipper the progress of the boat was checked at a roughly-made pier of piles driven into the mud, to which were pinned huge sticks of timber, beyond which was a rough corduroy road leading evidently to something in the way of civilisation.

"It must be up here somewhere, boys," said the skipper. "Two of you stop as keepers, my lads, while we land and go and see. The hacienda must certainly be hereabouts from the description Don Ramon gave;" and as all stepped on to the rough timber pier, the skipper instructed the boat-keepers to get well under shelter out of the sun and to keep strict watch, before leading the way along the wooded road through the thick growth which had newly sprung up amongst the butts of the great trees that had been felled or burned off level with the soil.

It must not be judged from this, that it was any scene of desolation, for every stump and relic of fallen tree was ornamented with lovely orchids, or wreathed with tangling vines. Butterflies of the most vivid hues fluttered here and there in the glorious sunshine, while humming-birds literally flashed as they darted by.

The clearing had evidently been the work of many men, and it was plain to see what the place must have been before the axe was introduced, by the dense mass of giant trees that stood up untouched a couple of hundred yards on either side—the primaeval forest in its glory, untouched by man.

Chapter Twenty Six
A night watch

It was not many minutes later when, attracted by a group of the lovely insects playing about the shrubs that were in full bloom, Fitz had hung back, making them an excuse while he rested, standing mopping his face, streaming with perspiration, while Poole, no less willing to enjoy a few minutes' halt, stood looking back watching him.

Meanwhile the skipper had gone on, closely followed by the men, and passed out of sight. And then the few minutes became a few minutes more, neither of the lads noting the lapse of time, for everything around was so beautiful that they had no thought for the task in hand, nor fear of being interrupted by any of the enemy who might be near.

Everything was so dreamy and beautiful that Poole cast his eyes around in search of some fallen trunk, with the idea that nothing could be more delightful than to sit down there in the shade and drowse the time away.

Then he was awake again, for from somewhere ahead, but so far off that it sounded quite faint, there came a shout—

"Ahoy! Poole!"

The lad ran, rifle in hand, to answer his father's call, but only to stop short to look round sharply, feeling that he was leaving Fitz behind.

"Oh, there you are," he cried, as he caught sight of the lad following swiftly after. "I thought that you were not coming."

"I was obliged to. You don't suppose that I want to be left alone here by myself?"

"No, I suppose not. 'Tis a wild spot. It wouldn't be very pleasant if one of the enemy came upon you. You'd be rather safer along with us. Come on; we had better run. Mind how you come. These logs are rather slippery where the sun doesn't shine."

"Yes, and you had better mind, or some of this tangled stuff that's growing up between will trip you up. Rather awkward if your gun went off."

A few minutes later they came up to where the skipper was standing waiting for them.

"Found the place, father?"

"Yes; it's just over yonder in a clearing beyond those trees."

"Where are the men?"

"Inside the house."

"Has Don Ramon come?"

"No. There's not a soul in sight. I can't see any signs of a fight, but it looks to me as if the enemy had been destroying all they came across. I hope they didn't come upon him and take him prisoner, but it looks very bad."

"What shall you do, father?"

"What he told me, my boy: take possession, and hold it if the enemy come back. I have told the men to try and knock up a breastwork and close up the windows. To put it into a state of defence is not possible, but they can make it look stronger, and it will be better than the open jungle if those mongrel scoundrels do come on. Winks is there with half-a-dozen men; join them and superintend. Make them stick to it hard. I am afraid of their thinking that there is no danger, and taking it too coolly."

"All right, father," said Poole, giving Fitz a glance as he stood ready for starting off.

"Oh, by the way, Mr Burnett, I am sorry to have got you into this trouble. It doesn't seem the thing, does it? But I can't help myself. I daren't let you get into the hands of the enemy, for they are a shady lot. Only please mind this; you are a looker-on, and you are not to fight."

"Of course not, sir," cried Fitz.

"Well, don't forget it. Let's have none of your getting excited and joining in, if the row does begin. But it's hardly likely. If the scoundrels see a strong-looking place they will give it a wide berth. But if they do come, just bear this in mind; you are a spectator, and not to fire a shot."

"I shall not forget my position, sir," said Fitz quietly. "That's right. You can't be in a safer place than in the shelter of Ramon's farm. Off with you, Poole. I will join you soon."

The two lads trotted off, and as they ran on side by side, Fitz said rather testily—

"Your father needn't have talked to me like that. 'Tisn't likely that I should join in such a fight as this."

"Of course not," said Poole coolly; "only you look rather warlike carrying that double gun."

"Absurd! A sporting piece, loaded with small shot!" cried Fitz.

"Not so very small," said Poole, laughing. "I shouldn't like it to be loaded with them by any one firing at me. Oh, there's the hacienda yonder. I heard of this place when I was here before. It's a sort of summer-house near the river and sea, where Don Ramon used to come. My word, though, how it seems to have been knocked about! It looks as if there had been fighting here. The grounds have all been trampled down, and the porch has been torn away."

"What a pity!" cried Fitz, as he trotted up, with his gun at the trail. "It must have been a lovely place. Oh, there are some of our men."

"Yes," said Poole, smiling to himself and giving a little emphasis to one word which he repeated; "there are some of 'our' men. Look at old Chips scratching his head."

For the carpenter on hearing their approach had stepped out into the wrecked verandah, and two or three of the sailors appeared at the long low windows belonging to one of the principal rooms.

"Oh, here y'are, Mr Poole, sir!" cried the carpenter, waving his navy straw hat and giving it two or three vicious sweeps at the flies. "Just the very gent as I wanted to see. How are yer, Mr Burnett, sir? Warm, aren't it? Don't you wish you was a chips, sir?" he added sarcastically, as Fitz gave him a friendly nod.

"A chips? A carpenter, Winks?" said Fitz. "No; why should I?"

"Of course not, sir. Because if you was you would be every now and then having some nice little job chucked at your head by the skipper."

"Why, of course," cried Poole. "What are you on board the schooner for?"

"Oh, nothing at all, sir—only to stop leaks and recaulk, cut sticks out of the woods to make new spars and yards, build a new boat now and then, or a yard or two of bulwark or a new keel. Just a few little trifles of that sort. It's just like so much play. Here's the very last of them. Nice little job ashore by way of a change. Skipper's fresh idea. He didn't say so, but seems to me as if he means to retire from business, and this 'ere's going to be his country house."

"And a very nice place too," said Fitz, laughing. "It only wants doing up."

"That's right, sir," cried the carpenter; "only just wants doing up, and a bit of paint, and then all you'd have to do would be to order a 'technicum van or two of new furniture out of Totney Court Road, or elsewhere. And an other nice little job for me to lay down the carpets and hang the picturs, and it would be just lovely."

"Well, you seem in a nice temper, Chips," said Poole.

"Temper, Mr Poole! Why, I feel as soft and gentle as a baby. I arn't got nothing to grumble at."

"And if you had you are the very last person in the world to say a word; eh, Chips?"

"Hear that, Mr Burnett, sir? That's Mr Poole, that is! He's known me two years and a narf, which means ever since he come on his first voyage, when I teached him how to handle an adze without cutting off his pretty little toes. If ever I wanted my character, Mr Burnett, sir, I should refer captains and other such to Mr Poole Reed, as knows me from the top of my head down to the parts I put lowest in my shoes."

"Look here, Chips, I want you to get to work. Whatever is the matter now?"

"Oh, nothing at all, sir; nothing at all! Carn't you see how I am smiling all over my face?"

"Oh yes, I know your smile. Now then, speak out. What do you want? What is there wrong?"

"Oh, nothing worth speaking of, Mr Poole. I arn't the sort of fellow to grumble, Mr Burnett, sir; but now just look here, gentlemen.—Get out, will you! Bother the flies! I wish I could 'ford to keep a nigger with a whisk made out of a horse's tail. They are regular tarrifying me to-day. I wouldn't keer if I could kill one now and then; but I carn't. Either they're too fast or I'm too slow. But now just look here, both on you, gentlemen. Here's a pretty position for a fellow to be in! Nobody can't say even in this hot country as I arn't willing to work my spell, but here's the skipper says to me, he says, 'I want you to do everything you can,' he says; 'take what men you want, and make this 'ere aitch—he—hay—ender as strong as you can.' Now, I ask you, just give your eyes a quick turn round the place and tell me, as orficers as knows what's what, how am I to make a thing strong as arn't strong, and where there arn't a bit of stuff to do it with? For what's the good of a lot of bamboo-cane when what one wants is a load of good honest English oak, or I wouldn't say no to a bit of teak."

"Well, it is a ramshackle sort of place, certainly, Chips."

"Ramshackle, sir? Why, a ramshackle shed is a Tower of London to it. It's just a bandbox, that's what it is—just one of them chip and blue paper things the same as my old mother used to keep her Sunday bonnet in. Why, I could go to one end, shet my eyes, and walk through it anywhere. Why, it wouldn't even keep the wind out. Look at them windows—jalousies, as they calls them, in their ignorant foreign tongue. Look at 'em; just so many laths, like a Venetia blind. What's to be done to them? And then them doors. Why, they wouldn't keep a cat in, let alone a Spaniel out. I dunno what's to be done; and before I know where I am the skipper will be back asking me what I have been about. Do you know what I'm about? About off my head. A man can't make something out of nothing. Where's my tools? says you. Aboard the schooner. Where's the stuff to work with? Nowhere. Why, I aren't got so much as a tenpenny-nail. It's onreasonable; but I suppose it aren't no use to talk. Come on, my lads, and let's see. Axes here. Get one in between them two floor-boards and wedge one of them out—that's the style!" And as he spoke, *rip, rip, crack!* the board was wrenched out of its place, leaving a long opening and easy access to the boards on either side. "S'eady there, mates; don't lose a nail. They are very poor ones, and only rusty iron now, but just you handle them as if they was made of gold. That's your sort. We'll just nail them boards up across the lower parts of them windows, far enough apart for us to fire through, and when that's done they'll make a show if they don't do anything else. It'll satisfy the skipper; but as to keeping the bullets out, when the beggars begin to fire, why, Mr Poole, sir, I believe I could take half-a-dozen of them little sugar-loaf-shaped bits of lead in my mouth and stand outside and blow them through.—What do you say, Camel? Where's a hammer? There are dozens of them, mate, in High Street, Liverpool, at any price from one-and-six up to two bob. Did you leave your head aboard the schooner?"

"Did I leave my head aboard the schooner? What are you talking about?" growled the cook.

"Thought perhaps you had left it in the galley, stood up in one of the pots to keep it safe till you got back. Turn the axe round and use the head of that, stoopid. Chopper-heads was invented before hammers, I know."

"Well, you needn't be so nasty, mon," growled the cook.

"Make you nasty if you was set to cook a dinner without any fire, and no meat."

Andy grunted and began hammering away, helped by two of his messmates, who held the floor-boards in place while such nails as had come out of the joists were driven in.

Satisfied with this, the carpenter set to work at the end of one of the joists, using a sharp axe so deftly that the great wedge-like chips began to fly, and in a minute's time he had cut right through.

"That's your sort!" he cried. "Now, lads, two on you hoist up."

The men had hold of the freshly-cut end of the stout joist in an instant, raised it up, its length acting as a powerful lever, and it was wrenched out of its place, to be used beneath its fellows so dexterously that in a short time there was no longer any floor to the principal room of the hacienda, the joists being piled up on one side, and those who were in it stood now a couple of feet lower with the window-sills just on a level with their chests.

"Bravo! Splendid!" cried Fitz excitedly. "Why, that gives us a capital breastwork—bulwark, I mean—to fire over."

"Yes," cried Poole, "and plenty of stuff, Chips, for you to barricade the doors."

"Barricade the doors, sir? You mean stop 'em up, I suppose. But how? Arn't got a big cross-cut saw in your pocket, have you?"

"Go on, old chap, and don't chatter so," cried Poole. "Break them in half."

"Nice tradesman-like job that'll make, sir! It is all very fine to talk. Here, stand aside, some on you. I never was in a hurry but some thick-headed foremast-man was sure to get in the way. Let's see; where's my rule? Yah! No rule, no pencil, no square. Lay that there first one down, mates. What are they? About twelve foot. Might make three out of each of them."

One of the joists was laid on the earth close to a collection of dry leaves.

"Looks like an old rat's nest," said Fitz. "Like enough, sir, only we haven't no time to hunt 'em. Sure to be lots in a place like this."

"Yes, I can smell them," said Poole—"that nasty musky odour they have!"

The carpenter paced along beside the joist, dividing it into three, and made a notch in two places with his axe, to begin the next minute delivering a sharp blow or two where he intended to break the joist. But at the first stroke the violent jar made the far end of the joist leap and come heavily down upon the gathered-together nest of leaves.

"Wo-ho!" cried the carpenter. "Steady there!"

"Eh, mon! Look at that!" yelled the cook, as there was a scuffling rush, and a thickish snake, about seven feet long, dashed out from its nest and made for the door.

There was a yell of dismay, and the men rushed here and there for the windows, to escape, the boys as eager as their companions.

It was only the carpenter who stood firm, and he made a chop with his axe at the reptile's tail, but only to drive the blade into the dry earth a yard behind.

"After him, Camel!" he roared. "Don't lose him, lad! He'd do to cook like a big eel. Yah, butter-fingers! You let him go! Why didn't you try and catch him by the tail? Here, come back, all of you. Take hold of a joist or two and stir up them nest-like places in the corners. I dare say there's some more. We shall be hungry by and by. Don't let good dinners go begging like that. Here, Mr Burnett, sir, and you, Mr Poole, never you mind them cowardly lubbers; come inside and have a hunt. It'll be a regular bit of sport."

"Thanks, no," said Fitz, who was looking in through one of the windows, Poole following his example at another.

"You had better mind, Chips," said the latter. "I dare say there are several more there, and they may be poisonous."

"So am I, sir," said the carpenter, grinning. "Just you ketch hold of my axe."

"What are you going to do?" said Poole, as he took hold of the handle.

"You stand by a moment, sir," said the carpenter, picking up the joist upon which he had been operating, and holding it as if it were a lance. "I am going to poison them."

As he spoke he drove the end right into a heap of Indian corn-husks that lay in the first corner, the blow being followed by a violent rustling, and another snake made its appearance, not to dash for the door, but turning, wriggling, and lashing about as it fought hard till it wriggled itself free of the little beam which had pinned it into the corner, crushing its vertebra about a third of its length from the head, and ending by tying itself in a knot round the piece of wood and holding on.

"Below there!" shouted the carpenter. "Stand clear!"

He advanced towards Fitz with the joist, and as the boy leaped back he thrust out the piece of wood, resting the middle on the window-sill.

"Here you are, Camel," he cried; "fresh meat, all skewered for you like a bun on a toasting-fork. Look alive, old haggis, and take him off. He's a fine un, Master Poole. I can't abear to see waste."

Fitz and Poole both stepped back, and at that moment with one quick writhe the little serpent seemed to untie itself, dropping to the ground limply, writhed again as if to tie itself into a fresh knot, and then stretched itself out at full length.

"Take care, Mr Burnett, sir," cried the carpenter, hastily taking from Poole and holding out the axe he had been using. "Don't go too near. Them things can be precious vicious. Ketch hold of this and drop it on to him just behind his head."

"No, no, don't, Fitz!" cried Poole. "Look at its little fiery eyes. It may strike."

"Not it," cried Fitz. "Chips has spoiled all his fighting for good;" and taking a step or two forward with the axe he had snatched from the carpenter's hand, he made one quick cut and drove it into the earth, for the blade to be struck at once by the serpent's head, while the ugly coils were instantaneously knotted round the haft.

Fitz involuntarily started back, leaving the axe-handle with its ugly load standing out at an angle, and the two lads stood watching the serpent's head as the jaws parted once or twice and then became motionless, while the folds twisted round the stout ash-handle gradually grew lax and then dropped limply and loosely upon the earth, ending by heaving slightly as a shudder seemed to run from the bleeding neck right to the tail.

"He's as good as dead, gentlemen," said the carpenter. "He won't hunt no more rats under this place. Give me my chopper, please; I am thinking there are a few more here. Let's have 'em out, or they'll be in the way and get their tails trodden on when the fighting begins."

"Yes, let's have them out, Chips," cried Poole; "but be careful. They may be poisonous, and savage with being disturbed."

"Oh yes, I'll be careful enough," cried the carpenter; and raising the joist again he stepped back from the window and drove it into another corner of the room, the boys peering in through the nearest window and eagerly watching for the result.

"Nothing here," cried the carpenter, after giving two heavy thrusts. "Yes, there is. Here's a little baby one. Such a little wriggler! A pretty one too; seems a pity to kill him."

"No, no," cried Fitz, as he watched the active movements of the little snake that suddenly raised itself like a piece of spiral spring, its spade-shaped head playing about menacingly about a foot from the ground.

"Yes, take care," cried Poole. "I believe that's a viper."

"So's this," said the carpenter, letting one end of the joist rest upon the ground and the other fall heavily right across the threatening snake. "Hah! That's a wiper, and I wiped him out."

Next moment he lifted the joist again, and used it pitchfork-fashion to jerk the completely crushed dangerous reptile out of another window, before advancing to the third corner, where a larger heap of Indian corn-husks seemed to have been drawn together.

"Anything there, Chips?" cried Fitz.

"Oh yes, there's a big un here—two on 'em; and they're telling tales of it, too, for they've left 'em hanging outside. Now, whereabouts will their heads be?"

"Take care," cried Poole, "for you may cripple one and leave the other to dart at you."

"Yes, and that wouldn't be nice," said the carpenter thoughtfully. "I don't mind tackling one of them, but two at a time's coming it a bit too strong. 'Tarn't fair like."

"Look here," cried Fitz, "we'll come in, and each have a joist. We should be sure to kill them then."

"I dunno so much about that, gen'lemen. You might help, and you moten't. If they made a rush you might be in my way, and you know, as old Andy says, Too many cooks spoil the snake-soup. Here, I know; I can soon turn them out."

"How?" cried Poole, as the man stood the joist up against the wall.

"I'll soon show you," cried the carpenter, pulling out a match-box.

"You'll burn the place down."

"Nay," cried the man; "them corn-shucks will just flare up with a fizz; I can trample them out before they catch the wood. You two be on the look-out, for there's no knowing which window my gentlemen will make for as soon as they find as it aren't the sun as is warming them up."

He struck a match as he spoke, let the splint get well alight, and then stepping forward softly he stooped down to apply it to the pale, dry, creamy-looking corn-leaves.

"Look out!" cried Fitz excitedly.

"Oh, my fingers are too hard to burn," growled the carpenter, ignoring the notion of the danger being from the serpents; and he applied the burning match to three places, letting the flame drop in the last, before he stepped quickly back, watching the bright crackling flare which rose in each spot where he had applied the match and then began to run together to form one blaze.

"Why, there's nothing there," cried Poole.

"Oh, yes, there is, gen'lemen, and they're beginning to feel it. It's so nice and warm that—Look, they are pulling their tails in under the blanket to get their share. Now they says it's too hot. Look out; here they come."

The warning was not needed, for there was a sharp, fierce hissing heard plainly above the spluttering crackle of the burning husks, the pile was violently agitated, and then the burning heap was heaved up and scattered about in various directions, while, half-hidden by the smoke, it seemed as if a couple of pieces of stout Manilla cable were being furiously shaken upon the earthen floor.

"Murder!" shouted Poole, starting back from the window where he stood, his action being involuntarily imitated by Fitz, who just caught a glance of the snake that had startled his companion passing like a flash over the window-sill, and making at what seemed to be an impossible speed for a clump of bushes close at hand.

"That's one of them," cried Fitz breathlessly. "What about the other?"

Bang! Bang! Thud! Thud! came from inside the room, and then the answer in the carpenter's gruff voice—

"I got him at last," he said. "He was a lively one. Reg'lar dodger. Come and look here. It's all right; he's done. My! He is a whopper!"

The inclination to look in was not great, but the boys stepped back at once to the windows they had left, to see that the burning heap was well alight, but apparently all in motion, while the carpenter was standing near, half-hidden by smoke, pressing the end of the joist he had used down upon a writhing serpent which he was holding pinned against the earth in the middle of the flames.

"Take care! Take care!" cried Poole. "It'll be furious if it gets from underneath that piece of wood."

"He'd be clever if he did, sir. I got him too tight. It's all right, and I am making use of him at the same time."

"Nonsense! Come out, man; you will have the place on fire directly."

"Oh, no, I shan't, sir. Don't you see, I am letting him whack and scatter it all out. There won't be enough to do any mischief now.—Hah! He's quieting down; and he's the last on 'em. If there were any others they are smoked out."

As he spoke the lads could plainly see that the reptile's efforts to escape were growing weaker, while the rest of the party, who had been busy at the other end of the hacienda, had collected at window and door, attracted by the rising smoke.

"Just in time, mates! About another two minutes and he'll be done. Now then," the speaker added, "I don't want to spoil him," and raking out the heaving reptile, he forked it to the door and tossed it a few yards away into the clearing. "All together!" he shouted. "Fair play! Knives out. Who's for a cut of hot roast?"

Chips's pantomime was at an end, for, rifle in hand, the skipper came running up.

"What's the meaning of this?" he roared. "Why don't you put that fire out? Do you want to burn the place down? Who's been smoking here?"

"It's all right, father. There were snakes under the floor, but Chips has burned them out."

"Oh, that's it! Dangerous brutes! Here, Winks, how have you been getting on?"

"Oh, tidy, sir, tidy," said the carpenter, wiping his smarting eyes as he tried to check a cough and made it worse. "You see, there was no stuff, and I had to tear up the floor."

"Capital," said the skipper, as he examined the preparations. "Couldn't be better, my man. Here, if there's time you shall serve those other two rooms the same. Axes here, my lads. Cut down those bushes and pile them up under the windows. We mustn't leave them there for cover."

"Take care," cried Fitz. "There's a great snake in there. Here, Poole, let's each take a joist and beat him out."

"Hadn't we better try a match, sir? Them there bushes are that ily evergreen stuff as'll burn like fun."

"Yes," said the skipper. "We don't want the stuff for protection, and the enemy might throw a light in and burn us out. But look here, Chips, are there any sparks inside there, likely to set the wood-work alight?"

"Nay, sir; it was all fluffy touch-and-go stuff. There's nothing there now but smoke."

The man moved as he spoke towards the clump of ornamental shrubs in which the big snake had taken sanctuary, the two lads, each armed with a joist carried lance-fashion, following him up, while the skipper hurried into the building with one of the men, to satisfy himself that the carpenter's words were correct.

The remainder stood by to watch the firing of the clump of bushes, the news that they hid a serpent putting all upon the *qui vive*.

"Take care Chips," said Poole anxiously. "They are dangerous, treacherous things. We don't want to get you bitten."

"Of course you don't, my lad; but tchah! They aren't half so dangerous as I am with a box of matches in my hand. Here, wait a moment; which way's the wind? Oh, this 'ere. Blest if I know whether it's north south, or east west, for I've quite lost my bearings. Anyhow, it don't blow towards the house. Now then, I think I'll just have an armful of these 'ere plantain-leaves and them there bamboo. They're the things to burn."

He hastily collected as many dry great ragged banana-leaves as he could grasp, laid them in a heap to windward of the clump, and jumped back quickly, grinning hugely as he turned to the boys.

"He's there still," he said; "I heard him whisper like a sick goose as I popped that stuff down."

"We'd better look out, then, on the other side," cried Fitz, "or he'll make a bolt. Shall I get my gun?"

"No, no," said Poole; "we must have no firing now."

Fitz moved, joist in hand, towards the other side of the clump.

"Nay, you needn't do that, sir," cried the carpenter. "That's what we want him to do."

"Oh, I see; you don't want there to be any waste," said Poole.

"Ugh!" shuddered Fitz, and the carpenter grinned as he hurriedly snapped off as many dead bamboos as he could secure from a waving, feathery group, bore the bundle the next minute to the edge of the clump of shrubs, laid them on the heap of banana-leaves, and then rapidly applied a burning match to the dry growth, which still retained a sufficiency of inflammable oil to begin to flare at once, making the bamboos crackle and then explode with a series of little reports like those of a revolver.

"That's right," said the carpenter; "if we had only got a few dozen cocoanut-shells to help it on, we should have a bonfire as'd beat a Guy Foxer all to fits."

But there were no cocoanuts to be had without paying a visit to the seashore, so the fire was mended with the bushes that were cut down from here and there, blazing up so furiously that in a few minutes the clump was consumed, and the snake with it, for it was not seen again.

"Now then," said the skipper, "scatter those embers about, and put an end to that smoke, or it will attract the enemy and show them where we are."

These orders were carried out, and the next hour was spent in adding to the defences as far as was possible, in seeing to there being a supply of water, and examining what there was in the shape of provisions in store.

But other precautions were being taken at the same time, the skipper having sent out three of the men right and left along the forest-paths and towards the shore, so as to ensure them against surprise. Then the afternoon wore away, and the evening approached, without alarm, and before the night could fall in its rapid, tropical way, the scouts were recalled, sentries posted, and the defenders gathered-together in their little fortress for their evening meal, by the light of the great stars, which seemed to Fitz double the size that they were at home.

Every one had his arms ready for use at a moment's notice, and the two lads sat together nibbling the biscuit they had brought with them, and moistening it from time to time with a draught of the water from the big pannikin which they shared. That change from glowing sunset to darkness had been wonderfully swift, and as the beauty of the surrounding jungle, with its wondrous tints of green, changed into black gloom, the aspect of the place affected the two young adventurers at once, Fitz giving vent to a long-drawn sigh.

"What's the matter?" said Poole, in a low voice.

"Oh, I don't know," replied the middy. "It seems so strange and weird here in the darkness. It makes me feel quite low-spirited."

"Do you know why that is?" asked Poole.

"Of course I do. It is all dark and dangerous, and at any time we may have those mongrel Spaniels, as Chips calls them, rushing at us and firing as they come."

"Well, we should fire at them back again," said Poole coolly. "But it isn't that that makes you nervous and dull."

"Isn't it? Well, I suppose I am not so brave as you," whispered the middy.

"Fudge! It's nothing to do with being brave. I don't feel brave. I am just as low-spirited as you are. It's because we are tired and hungry."

"Why, we are keeping on eating."

"Yes; biscuit-and-water. But that only keeps you from starving; it doesn't do you good. Why, if old Andy had a good fire and was roasting a wild turkey, or grilling some fish, we shouldn't feel dull, but be all expectation, and sniffing at the cooking, impatient till it was done."

"Well, I suppose there is something in that," said Fitz, "for I feel as faint as can be. I seem to have been so ever since I began to get better. Always wanting something more to eat."

"Of course you do. That's right enough."

"What's that?" cried Fitz, catching his companion by the arm; for there was a loud slap, as if the water of the river had suddenly received a sharp blow with the blade of an oar.

"I d'know," said Poole. "Boat coming, I think. Did you hear that, father?" And the speaker looked in the direction where the skipper had last been seen.

"Oh yes," was the reply, coming from outside one of the windows of the room they had strengthened with a breastwork.

"It's a boat coming, isn't it, father?"

"No, my lad," said the skipper, in a deep-toned growl. "It's one of the crocodiles or alligators fishing for its supper."

"No, no, Mr Reed," cried Fitz; "we mean that sound like a heavy slap on the water. There it goes again! That!"

"Yes, that's the sound I meant," said the skipper. "Sounds queer, doesn't it, in the darkness? But that's right. It's one of the great alligator fellows thrashing the water to stun the fish. This makes them turn up, and then the great lizardly thing swallows them down."

Fitz uttered a little grunt as if he thought it was very queer, and then went on nibbling his biscuit.

"Poole," he whispered, "what stupids we were not to go and fish before it got dark."

"That's just what I was thinking," was the reply.

"Yes," continued Fitz; "we hadn't as much sense as an alligator. I wish we had a good fish or two here."

"To eat raw?" said Poole scornfully. "Raw? Nonsense! We'd set old Andy to work."

"No, we shouldn't. How could we have a fire here? It would be like setting ourselves up for the enemy to fire at. Why, they could creep in through the jungle till they were fifty or sixty yards away, and take pot-shots at us. But only let us get to-night over, and we will go shooting or fishing as soon as it's day."

"Hark at that," said Fitz, catching him by the arm. "Here they come at last!" And not only the boys, but every one present but the skipper, felt a strange fluttering about the heart, as a curious hollow cry rose from somewhere at the edge of the jungle.

And then from out of the darkness there was a sharp *click, click*! of the lock of a rifle, the force of example bringing out quite a series of the ominous little sounds, which came forth sharp and clear as every one prepared to use his piece.

"Steady there, my lads!" growled the skipper. "You don't think you can shoot that bird?"

"There, laddies; I kenned it was a bird—one of them long-legged, big-beaked chaps that stand out in the water spearing eels. Wish we had got him now."

"Was that a bird, father?" whispered Poole. "Why, you ought to have known it was, my lad. There goes another, and another. If you listen you can hear the cry dying right away in the distance—one of those great cranes."

"Fine bird to keep for singing," said the cook, "only I want everything for the pot or the spit. There he goes again. What a rich voice, laddies! Sounds as if he were fat."

The rifles were uncocked gently and carefully, and all sat listening again, thoroughly on the *qui vive*, for though fully expecting that the first warning of danger would be a shot from one of the sentries, all felt that there was a possibility of the enemy stealing up in the darkness and making a rush which would quite take them by surprise.

It was depressing work to the wakeful, and as the hours stole slowly on first one and then another, tired out with the exertions of the day, let his head sink upon his breast where he crouched and gave audible notice that he had forgotten everything in the way of danger, in sleep.

From time to time the boys kept up a desultory conversation, but at last this ceased, and Fitz suddenly lifted his head with a jerk and began to look wonderingly round at the great stars.

"What's the matter?" said Poole, in a startled way.

"I dunno," replied the middy. "It seemed to me that somebody got hold of me and gave me a jerk."

"That's just how I felt. Look out!"

Fitz did look out as far as the darkness would allow, and his hands began to turn moist against the stock of his gun; but there was nothing to be heard but the heavy breathing of the sleepers, and both lads were beginning to think that the start and jerk were caused by their having been asleep themselves, when there was a familiar voice close at hand.

"Well, lads, how are you getting on?"

"Not very well, father," replied Poole. "Is it all right?"

"Yes, my boy; I have heard nothing but the cries of the night birds, and the creeping of something now and then among the boughs."

"Think the enemy will come to-night, Mr Reed?" said Fitz.

"Can't say, my lad. They may, or they may not. If they knew how easily they could get the better of us they would make a rush. Tut, tut, tut! Kick that fellow, Poole. Can't he sleep without snoring like that? Who is it?"

"I think it's Winks, father."

"Rouse him up, then."

"Eh? Hullo! All right! My watch?"

"No, no," said Poole. "Be quiet; you are snoring away as if you were sawing wood."

"Was I, my lad?" whispered the man. "Well, I believe I dreamed I was at that game. Any fighting coming off?"

"No, not yet."

"All right; then I'll have another nap."

But at that moment from out of the darkness, at apparently the edge of the jungle beyond the hacienda clearing, there was a sudden crashing as of the breaking of wood, followed instantly by an exceedingly shrill and piercing shriek, the rustle and beating of leaves, two or three low piteous sobs, and then silence for a few moments, followed by a soft rustling which died away.

"Steady there!" whispered the skipper, as he heard the click of a lock. "Don't fire, my lad. It would only be wasting a charge."

"But the savage has killed somebody, Mr Reed," whispered Fitz, in a voice he did not know as his own; and he crouched rigidly there with the butt of his piece to his shoulder, aiming in the direction of the sounds, and with every nerve upon the strain.

"Yes," said the skipper coolly; "the savage has killed somebody and has carried him off. There, you can hear the faint rustling still."

"But a savage could not carry a man off like that," said Fitz wonderingly.

"No," replied the skipper, with a low chuckle. "But that savage has gone off with the body he seized. Don't you know what it was, my lad?"

"No," replied Fitz wonderingly.

"Then I'll tell you, as far as I know myself. I should say that was one of those great cats, the tigers, as they call them here, the jaguars. He was prowling along in one of those big trees till he could see a monkey roosting, and then it was a leap like a cat at a rat, and he carried him off."

"Ah!" said Fitz, with a sigh. "I thought it was something worse."

"Couldn't have been any worse for the monkey," said Poole, laughing.

"No," continued Fitz thoughtfully; "but I didn't know there were jaguars here."

"Didn't you, my lad?" said the skipper quietly. "Why, we are just at the edge of the impenetrable jungle. There is only this strip of land between it and the sea, and the only way into it is up that little river. If we were to row up there we should have right and left pretty well every wild creature that inhabits the South American jungles: tigers—you have had a taste of the snakes this afternoon—water-hogs, tapirs, pumas too, I dare say. There goes another of those great alligators slapping the water with his tail."

"Would there be any of the great serpents?" asked Fitz.

"Any number," replied the skipper, "if we could penetrate to where they are; the great tree-living ones, and those water-boas that live among the swamps and pools."

"They grow very big, don't they?" said Fitz, who began to find the conversation interesting.

"All sizes. Big as you or me round the thickest part, and as long as—"

"A hundred feet?" said Poole.

"Well, I don't know about that, my boy," said the skipper. "I shouldn't like to meet one that size. I saw the skin of one that was over thirty, and I have heard tell by people out here that they had seen them five-and-forty and fifty feet long. They may grow to that size in these hot, steamy jungles.

There is no reason why they shouldn't, when whales grow to seventy or eighty feet long in the sea; but I believe those monster anacondas of fifty feet long were only skins, and that either they or the stories had been very much stretched."

"What time do you think it is, father?"

"Well, by the feel of the night, my lad, I should say it's about three."

"As late as that, father? Time seems to have gone very quickly."

"Quickly, eh? That's proof positive, my boy, that you have had a nap or two. I have not, and I have found it slow."

Chapter Twenty Seven
A Junction

The skipper moved off into the darkness, and all was wonderfully still once more in the clearing. There was the dense jungle all round, but not a sound broke the silence, for it was the peculiar period between the going to rest of the myriad creatures who prey by night, and the waking up of those expectant of the sun.

Then there was a sound of about the most commonplace, matter-of-fact character that can be imagined. Fitz, as he lay half upon a heap of dry leaves and canes, opened his mouth very widely, yawned portentously and loudly, ending with, "Oh, dear me!" and a quickly-uttered correction of what seemed to him like bad manners: "I beg your pardon!"

"Ha, ha!" laughed Poole, "I was doing just the same. Here, you are a pretty sort of fellow," he continued, "to be on the watch, and kick up a shindy like that! Suppose the enemy had been sneaking in."

He had hardly finished speaking when Fitz caught him by the arm and sprang up, for there was a faint rustling, and the two lads felt more than saw that some one was approaching them. Relief came directly, for instead of a sudden attack, it was the skipper who spoke.

"Silence!" he said softly. "Here, if you two lads are as sleepy as that, lie down again till sunrise."

"No, no, father," said Poole; "I am all right now. You must be tired out. Burnett and I will go your rounds now."

"Thanks, my lad; but no, thank you."

"But you may trust me, father, and I will call you at daybreak."

"No, my boy; I couldn't sleep if I tried."

"No more could I now, father. Let me help you, then; and go round to see that the watch is all right." ·

"Very well. You go that way, and have a quiet chat with the man on duty. It will rouse him up. I am going round here."

The skipper moved off directly, and Poole, before starting off in the indicated direction, whispered to Fitz—

"You can have another snooze till I come back."

"Thank you; but I am going along with you."

Quite willing to accept his companionship, Poole led the way slowly and cautiously; but at the end of a few yards he stopped short.

"What's the matter?" whispered Fitz.

"Nothing yet; but I was just thinking. Is there any password?"

"I dunno," whispered Fitz.

"I didn't ask father, and it would be rather awkward if we were challenged and shot at."

"Oh, there's no fear of that. You'd know by the voice which of the men it was who spoke, and he'd know yours when you answered."

"To be sure. False alarm. Come on." It seemed darker than ever as they went forward on what seemed to be the track, but proved to be off it, for all at once as they were going cautiously on, literally feeling their way, Poole caught his foot against a stump and nearly fell headlong.

"Bother!" he ejaculated loudly, to add to the noise he made, and instantly a gruff voice from their right growled out, "Who goes there?" accompanying the question with a clicking of a rifle-lock. "Friends," cried Fitz sharply. "The word."

"*Teal*" cried Poole, as he scrambled up. "Aren't right," growled the same voice. "That you, Mr Poole?"

"Oh, it's you, Chips!" cried the lad, in a tone full of relief.

"Winks it is," was the reply; "but the skipper said I warn't to let anybody pass without he said Sponson."

"Sponson," cried Fitz, laughing.

"Ah, you know now," growled the carpenter, "because I told you; but it don't seem right somehow. But you aren't enemies, of course."

"Not much," said Poole. "Well, how are you getting on, Chips?"

"Oh, tidy, sir, tidy; only it's raither dull work, and precious damp. A bit wearisome like with nothing to do but chew. Thought when I heard you that there was going to be something to warm one up a bit. Wonderful how chilly it gets before the sun's up. I should just like to have a bit of timber here, and my saw."

"To let the enemy know exactly where we are?"

"Ah, of course; that wouldn't do. But I always feel when I haven't got another job on the way that it's a good thing to do to cut up a bit of timber into boards."

"Why?" asked Fitz, more for the sake of speaking than from any desire to know.

"Plaisters, my lad."

"Plaisters?"

"Ay; for sore hulls. A bit of thin board's always handy off a coast where there's rocks, and there's many a time when, if the carpenter had had plenty of sticking-plaister for a vessel's skin, a good ship could have been saved from going down. Nice place this. What a spot it would have been if it had been an island and the schooner had been wrecked!"

"What do you want the schooner wrecked for?" cried Poole.

"Me, sir? I don't want the schooner wrecked. I only said if it had been, and because you young gents was talking the other day about being on a desolate island to play Robinson Crusoe for a bit."

"Oh yes, I remember," said Fitz.

"So do I, sir. It set me thinking about that chap a good deal. Some men do get chances in life. Just think of him! Why, that fellow had everything a chap could wish for. Aren't talking too loud, are we, Mr Poole?"

"Oh no. No one could hear us whispering like this."

"That's right. I am glad you young gents come, for it was getting very unked and queer all alone. Quite cheers a fellow up. Set down, both on you."

"Thanks, no," said Fitz; "the ground's too wet."

"Nay, I don't mean on the ground. Feel just behind you. There aren't a arm-chair, but a big bit of timber as has been cut down.—There, that's better. May as well make one's miserable life happy, and I don't suppose we shall have anybody sneaking round now.—Ah, yes, that there Robinson Crusoe did have a fine time of it. Everything his own, including a ship safely docked ashore full of stores, and nothing to do but break her up and sort the bits. And there he'd got all the timbers, keel-knees, planks, tree-nails, ropes, spars and yards, and plenty of sheet-metal, I'll be bound, for copper bottoming. Why, with plenty of time on his hands, he might have built anything, from a yawl to a schooner. But he didn't seem to me to shine much in naval architecter. Why, at first he hadn't a soul much above a raft."

"It was very useful, though," said Fitz.

"Nay; more trouble, sir, than it was worth. Better have built himself some kind of a boat at once. Look at his raft! Always a-sinking, or fouling, or shooting off its cargo, or trying to navigate itself. I don't believe in rafts. They're no use unless you want to use one to get washed ashore. For my part—Pst!"

The boys sprang up at the man's whispered signal, Fitz the more actively from the fact that the carpenter's horny hand had suddenly gripped his knee so forcibly that he had hard work to restrain a cry of pain.

"Somebody coming," whispered Poole, quite unnecessarily, for a loud rustling through the bushes was announcing the approach of the expected enemy.

"Stand by!" roared the carpenter, and his rifle flashed a line of light through the darkness as he fired in the direction of the sounds. "Now, my lads," he whispered, "double back into the ship."

As the words passed his lips a voice from out of the darkness shouted in broken English, and with a very Spanish accent—

"Don't fire! Friends! Friends! Friends!"

The words checked the retreat on the hacienda, but they did not clear away the watch's doubts.

"Yes," growled the carpenter, "so you says, but it's too dark to see your faces." Then aloud, "Who are you? Give the word."

"Friends!" was shouted again.

"Well! Where's the word?—He don't say Sponson, Mr Poole," added the carpenter, in a whisper.

"Captain Reed! Captain Reed!" cried the same voice, from where all was perfectly still now, for the sounds of the advance had ceased.

"Who wants Captain Reed?" shouted Poole.

"Ah, yes, I know you," came excitedly. "Tell your father Don Ramon is here with his men."

Chapter Twenty Eight
Strange doings

All doubts as to the character of the new-comers were chased away by the coming up of the skipper to welcome the Don, who had nothing but bad news to communicate.

He had passed the night in full retreat with the remnant of his followers before the forces of the rival President.

"Everything has gone wrong," he said. "I have lost heavily, and thought that I should never have been able to join my friends. What about the hacienda? Have you done anything for its defence?"

"The best we could," replied the skipper. "I suppose you know that the enemy had been here, that there had been a fight, and that they had wrecked the place."

"I? No!" cried the Don, in a voice full of despair. "I sent a party of my friends here to meet you, and this was the *rendezvous*. Don't tell me that they have been attacked and beaten."

"I have as good as told you that," said the skipper dryly.

"Ah–h–h!" panted the Don.

"We have put the place in as good a state of defence as there was time for, but we have not seen a soul."

"It is terrible," groaned the Don. "My poor friends! prisoners, or driven off! But you! You have your brave men."

"I have about half my crew here, sir," said the skipper sternly; "but we haven't come to fight, only to bring what you know."

"Ah! The guns, the ammunition, the store of rifles!" cried the Don joyously. "Magnificent! Oh, you brave Englishmen! And you have them landed safe?"

"No," replied the skipper, as the middy's ears literally tingled at all he heard. "How could I land guns up here? And what could you do with them in these pathless tracts? Where are your horses and mules, even if there were roads?"

"True, true, true!" groaned the Don. "Fortune is against me now. But," he added sharply, "the rifles—cartridges?"

"Ah, as many of them as you like," cried the skipper, and Fitz Burnett's sense of duty began to awaken once again as he seemed in some undefined way to be getting hopelessly mixed up with people against whom it was his duty to war.

"Excellent; and you have them in the hacienda?"

"No, no; aboard my vessel."

"But where is this vessel? You could not get her up the river?"

"No; she is lying off the mouth. I came up here in a boat to meet you and get your instructions, after, as you know, being checked at San Cristobal and Velova, where your emissaries brought your despatches."

"Brave, true fellows! But the gunboat! Were you seen?"

"Seen? Yes, and nearly taken. I only escaped by the skin of my teeth."

"You were too clever," cried the Don enthusiastically. "But you should have sunk that gunboat. It would have meant life and success to me. Why did not you send her to the bottom?"

"Well," said the skipper quietly, "first, because I am not at war, and second, because she would have sent me to the bottom if I had tried."

"No, no," cried the Don enthusiastically. "You English are too clever and too brave. The captain of that gunboat is a fool. You could easily have done this thing. But you have the guns you brought all safe aboard?"

"Yes."

"And you have some of your brave men with you?"

"Yes; more than half my crew."

"Then I am saved, for you will fight upon my side, and every one of your brave Englishmen is worth a hundred of the miserable three parts Indian rabble bravos and cut-throats who follow Villarayo's flag."

"Well, I didn't come here to fight, Don Ramon, and I have no right to strengthen your force," said the skipper sternly. "My duty is to land the munitions of war consigned to you; and that duty I shall do."

"But your men! They are armed?"

"Oh yes. Every one has his rifle and revolver, and knows how to use them."

"And suppose you are attacked?" said the Don, catching him by the arm.

"Well," said the skipper dryly, "we English have a habit of hitting back if we are tackled, and if anybody interferes with us in what we have to do, I dare say we shall give a pretty good account of ourselves. But at the present moment it seems to me that it's my duty to get back to my ship and wait until you show me where I can land my cargo."

"Ah!" said the Don, and as he spoke Fitz had his first announcement that day was near at hand, for he began to dimly see the eager, animated countenance of the Spaniard, and to make out the figures of his well-armed followers clustering round.

"Well, sir, what is to be done?"

"One moment; let me think. It will be safest, perhaps, for you to return to the ship and wait."

"Where?" said the skipper. "That gunboat is hanging about the coast, waiting to capture us if she can."

"Yes, I know; I know. And ashore Villarayo's men are swarming. They have hunted us through the pass all night, and hundreds of them are coming along the coast to cut us off from reaching boats and escaping out to sea."

"Then it's time we were off," said the skipper sharply.

"Too late," replied the Don.

"But my schooner?"

"Will they capture that?" cried the Don.

"Well no," replied the skipper. "There's not much fear, sir; my mate will look out too sharply. No. That will be safe. Don Ramon, if you will take my advice, you and your party had better break up and take to flight for the present, while I will make for any port you like to name and wait your orders, ready for when you can gather your friends together and make another attempt."

"Ah, yes, Captain Reed, you mean well; but where shall I flee? This is my last place of refuge! Here, at my own home! It is best perhaps that you and your men should get back to your ship. I and my friends are pretty well surrounded, and have but two ways open to us. The one is to surrender to Villarayo's merciless cut-throats and die like dogs; the other, to stand at bay behind the walls of my poor home, fight to the last, and die for our wretched country like soldiers and like men. Shake hands, captain, in your brave English way. I and my friends thank you for all you have done, and for making, as you say you have, a little stronghold where we can hold on to the last. It is not your fault, neither is it mine. I could have won the day, and brought happiness and peace to my poor land; but it was not to be. Villarayo has been too strong. That war-vessel with its mighty gun holds us at its mercy. Whoever has that to back him up can rule this place; for any fort that we could raise, even with the guns you have brought, would be crumbled into the dust. There! Farewell! You have your boat. Save yourself and your true, brave men. Quickly, while there is time!"

"Yes, Don Ramon; that must be so," said the skipper, and Fitz Burnett's cheeks began to burn, heated with the spirit within him, as he listened to the speaker's words, almost in disgust, for in his excitement it seemed as cowardly as cruel to leave these brave Spaniards to such a fate.

But then came the change, and his heart gave a leap, and his eyes flashed with pride. He thought no more of his own position in the Royal Navy than he did of the complications that had placed him where he was. The British fighting spirit that has made our nation what it is was strong within him, and his fingers tingled to clasp the skipper's hand, and failing that, he tightly gripped Poole's arm, as the lad's father said—

"No, Don Ramon, I can't leave you in the lurch like this. You and your fellows must come with me."

"No," said the Don proudly; "my place is here," and he drew himself up, looking every inch in the broadening light the soldier and the man.

What more the skipper would have spoken remained unsaid, for *crack, crack, crack*! sounding smothered amongst the trees, came the reports of the rifles and the replies made by Don Ramon's vedettes as they were driven in, and the skipper's eyes flashed as he placed a little whistle to his lips and blew shrilly, bringing his own men together at the run.

Then taking in the position in one quick glance, he could see a puff of smoke arising from the direction of the river and the boat, telling only too plainly that even had he wished to escape with his men, the way to safety was cut off.

But in those moments no such idea entered his head, any more than it did that of Fitz or Poole. The way was open to the hacienda, and joining hands with the Spanish Don, he began to retire towards the defence he had prepared, and in a very few minutes the house had been reached, and the breastworks manned by the mingled force, consisting of Don Ramon's followers and the schooner's crew, whose shots began to tell in such a way that the enemy's advance was checked, and the bright sun rose above the distant jungle, lighting up the enemy at bay.

Chapter Twenty Nine
The non-combatant

"Here, you, Mr Burnett, you are a non-combatant," said the skipper, suddenly coming upon Fitz, after going round the walls of the hacienda with Don Ramon, and seeing that they were manned to the best advantage.

"Oh, yes, sir, I don't want to fight," replied the boy carelessly, and wincing rather with annoyance as he saw the Spaniard give him a peculiar look.

"But you look as if you do, fingering that double-barrelled gun."

"Do you wish me to give it up, sir?"

"No, certainly not. Keep it for your defence. You don't know how you will be situated, and it may keep one of the enemy from attacking you. The sight of it will be enough. You, Poole, keep well in shelter. I don't want you to be running risks."

"I shan't run risks, father, unless you do," replied Poole. "I shall keep close beside you all the time."

"No," said the skipper sharply, "you will stop with Mr Burnett. I leave him in your charge, and—Here! Who's that? Winks, you stop with my son and Mr Burnett there. Be ready to help them if they are in trouble."

"Ay, ay, sir," cried the carpenter, and he drew himself up with his rifle-butt resting on his bare toes.

"There, Fitz," said Poole, grinning with delight; "you can't go back to your old tea-kettle of a gunboat and say that we didn't take care of you."

"Such nonsense!" cried Fitz, flushing. "Any one would think that I was a child. I don't see anything to laugh at," and as he spoke the boy turned sharply from Poole's mirthful face to look searchingly at the carpenter, who was in the act of wiping a smile from his lips.

"Oh, no, sir, I warn't a-laughing," the man said, with his eyes twinkling. "What you see's a hecho like, or what you call a reflection from Mr Poole's physiomahogany. This 'ere's a nice game, aren't it! I'm sorry for those pore chaps aboard, and our two mates in the boat. They'll be missing all the fun."

"Why, Poole," cried Fitz suddenly, "I forgot all about them. I suppose they'll have gone back to the schooner."

"Not they!"

"Then you think the enemy's captured them?"

"That I don't," replied Poole. "They'll have run the boat in, according to orders, in amongst the shade, and be lying there as snug as can be, waiting till they're wanted."

"Well, I don't know so much about that, Mr Poole, sir," put in the carpenter. "Strikes me that as sure as nails don't hold as tight as screws unless they are well clinched, when we have driven off these here varmin, and go to look for them in that 'ere boat we shall find them gone."

"What do you mean?" cried Poole.

"Muskeeters will have eaten them up. They are just awful under the bushes and among the trees."

"Look there," said Fitz, interrupting the conversation. "Seem to be more coming on."

"That's just what I was thinking, Mr Burnett, sir. Reinforcement, don't you call it? My! How wild our lads will be, 'specially old Butters, when I come to tell 'em all about it. Makes me feel like being on board a man-o'-war again, all the more so for having a young officer at my elber."

"Don't you be insolent," said Fitz.

"Well!" cried the carpenter. "I say, Mr Poole, sir, I call that 'ard. I didn't mean cheek, sir, really."

"All right, Chips, I believe you," said Fitz excitedly. "Look, Poole; they're getting well round us. Look how they are swarming over yonder."

"Yes, it means the attack," replied Poole coolly.

"Yes," cried Fitz. "Oughtn't we to begin, and not let them get all the best places? There's nothing like getting first blow."

"Ha, ha!" laughed Poole, who did not seem in the slightest degree impressed by the serious nature of their position. "You're not a player, you know. This is our game."

Fitz reddened, and turned away with an impatient gesture, so that he did not see the carpenter give Poole a peculiar wink and his leg a silent slap, indicative of his enjoyment.

Every one's attention was fully taken up the next moment, for it was evident from the movements on the enemy's part that they were being divided into three bodies, each under a couple of leaders, who were getting their ragged, half Indian-looking followers into something like military form, prior to bringing them on to the attack in a rush.

Fitz watched all this from behind one of the breastworks he had seen put up by the carpenter, who was going about testing the nailing of the boards, and as he did so giving Don Ramon's followers a friendly nod from time to time, as much as to say, Only seeing as it had got a good hold, mate,—and then, once more forgetting Poole's reminder, the boy said excitedly—

"Well, I don't think much of Don Villarayo's tactics. He's exposing his men so that we might shoot half of them down before he got them up to the astack."

"Oh, they're no soldiers, nor sailors neither," replied Poole. "It's a sort of bounce. He thinks he's going to frighten us out of the place; and we are not going to be frightened, eh, Chips?"

"*We* are not, Mr Poole, sir; I'll answer for that. But I don't know how Mr Ramon's chaps will handle their tools."

"I should say well," cried Fitz, still warming up with the excitement, and speaking frankly and honestly. "They'll take the example of you old men-of-war's men, and fight like fun."

"Thankye, sir," said the carpenter, brightening up. "Hear him, Mr Poole? I call that handsome. That's your sort, sir! There's nothing like having one of your officers to give you a good word of encouragement before you start, and make the sawdust and shavings fly."

Just at that minute Don Ramon, who had been hurrying from side to side encouraging his followers, uttered a warning shout which was echoed by an order from the skipper to his men not to waste a single cartridge, and to aim low.

"Bring 'em down, my lads," he said. "Cripple 'em. We don't want to kill."

He had hardly spoken when the nearest body of the enemy uttered a wild yell, which was taken up by the others, and all advanced clear of the bushes at a run, firing wildly and without stopping to re-load, dashing on, long knife in hand.

But before they had accomplished half the distance, each party was met by a ragged volley from Don Ramon's men, whose instructions had been carefully carried out.

This staggered the enemy for the moment, but they came on, leaping over or avoiding their wounded comrades, and gaining confidence at the silence within the hacienda, they yelled again. So far not one of the Englishmen had fired a shot, but now at a word from the skipper, a slow, steady rifle fire began, with every shot carefully aimed, and seeming to tell, so that ere they got close up to the walls of the hacienda, nearly a score had dropped, the skipper having used his rifle and then stood with the barrel of his revolver resting on the edge of a plank and picking off man after man.

In the brief space of time occupied by the advance the enemy had had little time to think, but suddenly the fighting madness died out of one of the rough-looking bravos as he saw a companion at his side throw up his arms just in front of one of the windows and fall backwards. That started the panic, for the man turned with starting eyes, uttered a yell of dismay, and dashed back.

"Look at that," growled the carpenter. "Just like sheep. One goes for the gap in the hedge, and all the rest will follow. Ah, you may shout, old chap—Don whatever your name is. You'll have to holloa louder than that to stop 'em now."

For the whole of the attacking body was in retreat, racing for the shelter of the trees in a disorderly crowd whose paces were hastened by Don Ramon's men, now re-loaded, sending another ragged volley in their rear.

Their action was very different from that of the schooner's men, who contented themselves with re-loading and breaking out under the leadership of Winks into a hearty British cheer, in which Don Ramon's men now joined.

"Well," said Poole, taking out his pocket-handkerchief and carefully wiping the lock of his rifle, "what do you think of that?"

"Oh," cried Fitz excitedly, "I wouldn't have missed it for—eh? I don't know, though," he added, after breaking off short, his eyes having lit upon the fallen men who were crawling back into shelter. "It is very horrid, though, all the same."

"Yes," said Poole; "but we didn't ask them to come, and it would have been twenty times as horrid if we hadn't stood fast and they had got in here with those long knives."

Fitz looked at him fixedly.

"Think they'd have used them if they had got the day?"

"Think they'd have used them!" cried Poole scornfully. "Why, if they had been pure Spaniards I believe they would in the excitement; but fellows like those, nearly all of Indian blood, if they had got the upper hand, wounded or sound I don't believe they'd have left a man alive."

"I suppose not," said Fitz; "but it is very horrid, all the same. Where's your father? Oughtn't we to go and see to the wounded men?"

"We shall have to leave that to the enemy,"·replied Poole. "If we went out they'd begin firing from under cover. But here, I say—Here, you Chips, go and ask my governor whether we ought to do anything about those wounded men?"

"Ay, ay, sir," replied the carpenter; "but I know what he'll say."

"What?" said Fitz sharply.

"Same as Mr Poole did, sir, for sartin," and the man trotted away.

"You sent him off because you wanted to speak to me. What is it? Is there fresh danger?"

"Oh no; they'll think twice before they come again. But, I say, what have you been about?"

"Been—about? What do you mean?"

"Look at that gun! Why, Fitz Burnett, you've been firing too!"

The boy's jaw dropped, and he stared at the speaker, then at the lock of the double fowling-piece, and then back, before raising the cocks, opening the blackened breech, and withdrawing a couple of empty cartridges.

"I didn't know," he said softly. "Had it been fired before?"

"It's kept warm a long time if it had," said Poole, with his face wrinkling up with mirth. "Do you call this being a non-combatant?"

"Oh, but surely—" began Fitz. "I couldn't have fired without knowing, and—" He paused.

"It seems that you could," cried Poole mirthfully. "You've popped off two cartridges, for certain. Have you used any more?"

"Oh no! I am certain, quite certain; but I am afraid—in the excitement—hardly knowing what I was about—I must have done as the others did."

"Yes, and you said you didn't mean to fight. I say, nice behaviour this for an officer in your position. How many anti-revolutionists do you think you've killed?"

"Oh, Poole Reed, for goodness' sake don't say you think I've killed either of these poor wretches?"

"Any of these poor wretches," corrected Poole gravely, and looking as solemn as he could. Then reading his companion's horror in his face, he continued cheerily, "Nonsense, old chap! You couldn't have killed anybody with those cartridges of swan-shot unless they were close at hand."

"Ah!" gasped Fitz. "And I don't really think—"

"Oh, but you did. It was in the excitement. Every one about you was firing, and you did the same. It would have been rather curious if you had not. Oh, here's my governor coming along with Chips."

"I say," began Fitz excitedly.

"All right; I wasn't going to; but slip in two more cartridges and close the breech."

This was quickly done, and the skipper came up, talking to the carpenter the while.

"Yes, my lad," he was saying, "I'd give something if you had a hammer and a bag of spikes to strengthen all the wood-work here.—Well, Poole," he continued, "Don Ramon is in ecstasies. He says this is his first success, and I believe that if I were not here he'd go round and embrace all the lads.—But about those poor wretches lying out there. I'm not an unfeeling brute, my lads," he continued, taking in Fitz with a glance the while, "but all I can do I have done."

"But there are those two men moving out there, sir, that you can't have seen," cried Fitz imploringly, "and it seems so horrid—"

"Yes, my lad; war is horrid," said the skipper. "I saw them when they first went down, and"—he added to himself—"I am afraid I was answerable for one. But, as I was saying, I have done all I could, and that is, insisted upon Don Ramon ordering his men to leave them alone and not fire at every poor wretch who shows a sign of life."

"But," began Fitz, "Poole and I wouldn't mind going out and carrying them under shelter, one at a time."

"No, my lad," said the skipper, smiling sadly, "I know you would not; but I should, and very much indeed. You have both got mothers, and what would they say to me for letting two brave lads go to certain death?"

"Oh, but surely, sir," cried Fitz, "the enemy would not—"

"Those worthy of the name of enemy, my boy, certainly would not; but those fighting against us are most of them the bloodthirsty scum of a half-savage tropical city, let loose for a riot of murder, plunder, and destruction. Why, my dear boy, the moment you and Poole got outside the shelter of these walls, a hundred rifles would be aimed at you, with their owners burning to take revenge for the little defeat they have just now suffered."

"Are you sure you are right, Captain Reed?"

"Quite, my lad; as sure as I aim that it is not all ill that we have done this morning, for San Cristobal and Velova will both be the better for the absence of some of those who are lying dead out there."

He stood gazing out between two boards for some few minutes, before turning back, and glancing round the room he said a few words to the English defenders.

"Splendid, my lads," he said. "Nothing could have been cooler and better. We want no hurry at a time like this."

"Think they'll come again, father?" asked Poole.

"Sure to, my lad, and we shall drive them back again. After that, this Don Villarayo will have his work cut out to get them to come up again, and I don't believe he will succeed."

"Will they retreat then, sir?" asked Fitz.

The skipper smiled.

"I should like to give you a more encouraging reply," he said, "but— Oh, here's Don Ramon. Let's hear what he says."

"Ah, my friend," cried the Don, coming up to grasp the speaker's hands effusively. "And you too, my brave lads, as you English people say. It has been magnificent," and as he shook the boys' hands in turn, Fitz flushed vividly, feeling guilty in the extreme. "Oh, it has been magnificent—grand! Captain Reed, if I can only persuade you to join hands with me here with your men, and make me succeed, I would make you Admiral of my Fleet. Ah, yes, you smile. I know that it would only be a fleet of one, and not that till the gunboat was taken and become my own, but I would not be long before I made it two, and I would work until I made our republic one of which you would be proud."

"Don't let's talk about this, sir," said the skipper quietly, "until we have gained the day. Do you think that the enemy will come on again?"

"The wretches, yes! But Villarayo—the coward!—will keep watching from the rear. He seems to lead a charmed life."

"There, my lads; you hear. But we shall drive them back again, President?"

Don Ramon's eyes flashed at the compliment, and then he shrugged his shoulders and said sadly—

"President! Not yet, my brave captain. There is much yet to do, and fate has been bearing very hard upon me lately."

"It has, sir. But about the enemy; you think they will come on again?"

"Yes, for certain—and go back again like beaten curs. You and your men have done wonders here in strengthening this place."

Poole drove his elbow into the ribs of Chips, and winked at Fitz, who could hardly contain his countenance at the carpenter's peculiar looks, for the big rough sailor seemed as bashful as a girl, and nodded and gesticulated at the lads in turn, while the next moment he looked as if about to bolt, for the skipper suddenly clapped him on the shoulder and exclaimed as he turned him round—

"You must thank this man, President, not me, for he was my engineer-in-chief. Weren't you, Chips?"

"Ah, my friend," cried the Spaniard, "some day, when I get my own, believe me that I will pay you for all that you have done."

"Oh, it's all right, sir. Don't you worry about that. 'Course you see it warn't much of a job."

He took off his straw hat and wiped the great drops from his sun-browned brow with the back of his hand.

"You see, sir, it was like this 'ere. The skipper he puts me on the job, and 'Chips,' he says, 'make the best of it you can by way of offence.' 'Niver another word, sir,' and off he goes, and here was I when the young gents come up, all of a wax; warn't I, Mr Poole, sir? I put it to you, sir. 'Look here, sir,' I says, 'the skipper's put me on this 'ere job with my kit of tools left aboard the schooner, and not a bit of stuff.' Didn't I, sir? Speak out straight, sir. I only asks for the truth."

"You did, Chips," said Poole solemnly, and setting his teeth as he spoke; "didn't he, Burnett?"

"Oh yes," replied the middy, "he did say something like that," and then as he caught Poole's eye he had to turn his back, looking out through the slit in the window and biting his tongue hard the while, while he heard the carpenter maunder on to the President something more about not having a bit of stuff, and every nail to straighten before he could drive it in again.

"Yes, that's right. Winks," said the skipper, bringing the speech to an end, and not before it was time, for the carpenter was beginning to repeat himself again and again. "You did splendidly, and if we had a few hundred feet of battens and boards, we could hold this place for a month.—Well, President," he continued, turning his back on his man, who sighed with relief and whispered to Fitz that that was a good job done, "and after we've driven them back again?"

"Ah! After! Treachery, fire, powder to blow us up! The fighting of cowards. But with your help, my brave, as soon as they are cowering among the trees we must attack in turn."

"No, President," said the skipper, laying his hand upon the other's shoulders; "you are too brave and rash. This is your last stronghold, is it not?"

"Alas, yes!"

"Then you must hold it, sir, and tire the enemy out."

"Yes, yes; you are right. But food—water? What of them?"

"Ah! There we must see what strategy will do. There is the river not far away, and as soon as they grow thirsty, my lads will contrive that we have enough to drink."

"To drink—ah, yes. But the food?"

"Well, perhaps they will contrive that too. Sailors are splendid fellows to forage, sir."

"Yes. If I could only be a President of sailors!" cried the President warmly. "There seems to be nothing that the English sailor cannot do. But can they make powder-cartridges when their own is fired away?"

"Well, I don't say that," said the skipper; "but they know how to save them, and not fire good ammunition to waste; and that's what you must try to teach your men. But look out yonder; while we are talking there is something going on."

Don Ramon looked out keenly, ran into the next room to look out in another direction, and then came back.

"They are coming on again, captain," he said. "It may be an hour yet. But they mean attack, to leave more of their force behind."

"Now is your time, then, sir, to speak to your men. Tell them to use the cartridges as if each was the last he had and his life depended upon sending it home."

"Yes, yes," said the President. "I see; I see. But when my men are fighting and the blood is up they will not think; but we shall see."

Within half-an-hour another and a fiercer attack was made—one more ably sustained and better met too by the defence; for the President's words to his followers went home, the men grasping their position, and though the attack was more prolonged it ended by another panic and a roar of cheers.

"Now, President," said the skipper, "what of the next attack?"

"I don't know," was the reply. "If one is made it will be some treachery with fire; but you see they have retired farther back, and it is all their leaders can do to keep them from breaking up into retreat. Villarayo must be mad, and will be thinking how to scheme my downfall to the end. Captain, my heart is sick. What of the coming night? What of the darkness which will shroud them like a cloak?"

"It will not be dark for a couple of hours yet," replied the skipper. "We can rest now, and refresh our men. After that we must plant our outposts with those whom we can trust the most. They will warn us of any attack, and if one is made—well, we shall be stronger than we were this morning."

"Stronger! What do you mean? Do you see coming help?" replied Don Ramon.

"No, sir. We must help ourselves. But our men are more confident in their strength, while the enemy is weakened by defeat."

The hours went on and the darkness fell, with the men rested and refreshed; every avenue by which danger could advance was carefully commanded, and before half-an-hour of full darkness had passed one of the vedettes formed by Winks and Poole, with Fitz to keep him company, was alarmed by the approach of a stealthy figure, upon whom Winks pounced like a cat upon a mouse, and dragged him towards the hacienda, to be met directly after by the skipper, the prisoner protesting almost in a whisper that he was a friend, but covered by the barrel of a revolver the while.

Chapter Thirty
A cunning scheme

"Yes," said the skipper sternly, speaking in very fair Spanish, "you may say you are a friend, but a friend doesn't come crawling into a camp like a serpent. It seems to me you are a spy; and do you know what is the fate of a spy at a time like this?"

"Yes, yes, señor; a spy would be shot."

"Right—to save other people's lives. Where were you going?"

"I was coming here, señor, to the hacienda."

"So I supposed; but what for?"

The man seemed to hesitate, and tried to speak, but no words would come, for he was either suffering from agitation, exhaustion, or utter fear, and Fitz Burnett's hands turned wet and cold at the thought of the stern judgment that would be passed upon the trembling wretch if he could not prove his words.

"Do you hear what I say?" said the skipper, in a stern, fierce voice.

"Yes, yes, señor," gasped the man at last, just when the two lads had grasped hands, each to deliver a speaking pressure to the other.

"Tell me, then. Why were you coming here?"

"Because I believed that Don Ramon was here."

"Do you know Don Ramon?"

"Yes, señor; he is an old friend."

"We can soon prove that," said the skipper. "Here, Poole, the Don is lying down asleep, utterly worn out, but he must be awakened to see his friend," he added meaningly.

Poole gripped Fitz's hand tightly, as if to say, Come with me; and the two lads hurried off to where the Don was lying asleep, guarded by four of his men, under the shelter of a shed.

"I hope to goodness," whispered Poole, "that the poor fellow's told the truth."

"Your father wouldn't have him shot if he had not, surely?"

Poole was silent for a few moments.

"I don't know," he said evasively.—"Yes, friends," he said, in answer to a challenge in Spanish, "I want to speak to Don Ramon."

"He is asleep, señor, and must not be awakened," was the reply.

"I know he is asleep," said Poole sharply and authoritatively, "and he must be awakened. It is a case of life or death."

The awakening was already performed, for at the sound of the lad's half-angry voice the man he sought sprang up, revolver in hand, ready for action.

"Yes?" he said. "Are they coming on?"

"No," replied Poole. "We have taken a spy, as we think, but he professes to know you, sir, and asks to see you at once."

"I'll come," said the Don; and then turning to the lads with a smile: "Friends are very scarce; I mustn't slight this one."

In another minute he was where the prisoner was anxiously awaiting his coming, ready to utter a sigh of relief as the Don caught him in his arms with—

"Miguel, my friend! What brings you here?"

"I knew you were in danger," was the reply.

"And you came to tell me—"

"Yes, and it was a risky task. What with your enemies and your friends," he added meaningly, "I wonder that I am alive."

"Forgive me!" cried Don Ramon. "I had been looking upon you as one who had forsaken me in my distress. But yes, you are right; I am in danger, but still alive. Surely you have no worse news?"

"Yes, the worst."

"Well, tell me; I can bear anything now."

"You have beaten Villarayo off twice to-day."

"Yes, with the help of my friends," said the Don, turning in a courtly way towards the English party. "And you have come to warn me that they are just going to make another attack?"

"They are, but not yet. I have been with them at the risk of my life, and I know that the men were so horribly discouraged by their losses that they refused to attack again, and threatened to break up and return to their homes; but at last Villarayo has prevailed upon them to stay, and messengers went hours ago along the passes to Velova."

"Yes; what for?"

"With instructions that every fighting man from the fort and the earthworks facing the sea, is to be withdrawn, and come through the mountains to Villarayo's help. They will be here some time to-morrow, and you must be overwhelmed, or flee at once."

"It is impossible," said Ramon coldly. "We are shut in here, and my sun must rise or set to-morrow. This is my last stand."

"But your wife—your children! Think of them."

"I have thought of nothing else, waking and sleeping," said the Don coldly. "But my wife would not look upon me if I forsook my country, and my children shall not live with the knowledge that Ramon's is a coward's name."

"Is this your decision?" said the messenger of bad tidings.

"Yes. Captain Reed, my brave true friend, look at him. He is half-dead with hunger and exhaustion. Can you give him water and food?"

"He shall share what we have, sir, and I am sorry that we cannot give him better fare than biscuit and water; but the rations we brought with us were small, and they are nearly at an end. Don Miguel, I ask your pardon for me and mine. You will forgive us our rough treatment? We were fighting for your friend."

"I know," said the visitor faintly, and he took and grasped the captain's hand.

A few minutes later he was sharing Don Ramon's shelter, and struggling hard to recoup nature with the broken biscuit he was soaking in a pannikin of water, while Fitz and his companions returned to their old station to resume the watch.

They sat for some time thinking, for nobody seemed disposed to talk, even the carpenter, the most conversational of the trio, seeming to prefer the society of the piece of dirty-looking black tobacco which he kept within his teeth; but the silence became so irksome, for somehow the firing seemed to have driven every wild creature to a distance, that Fitz broke it at last.

"I don't know when I felt so nervous," he whispered. "I felt sure that something that would have seemed far more horrible than the fight was about to occur."

"What, my father ordering that poor fellow to be shot? Yes, it would have been horrible indeed."

"But would the skipper have ordered him to be shot, Mr Poole, sir?" said Winks thoughtfully.

"I'm afraid so, Chips."

"Humph! Don't seem like him. He bullies us chaps pretty sharp sometimes, and threatens, and sometimes the words he says don't smell of violets, nor look like precious stones; but I can't see him having a chap shot because he was a spy. Why, it'd be like having an execution without a judge."

"Yes, very horrible," said Fitz, "but it's time of war; as in the Duke of Wellington's time,—martial law."

"Who's him, sir? You mean Blucher—him as got into trouble over the Army boots?"

"No, no," said Poole. "Mr Burnett means the law that is used in fighting times when a Commander-in-chief acts as judge."

"Oh! All right, sir. But it sounds a bit harbitrary, as they calls it in the newspapers. I should have thought a hundred dozen would have been punishment enough, without putting a stinguisher on a man right out. I suppose it's all right, but I wouldn't have given it to him so hot as that. Well, I'm glad he come, because now we know what we've got to expect to-morrow. Do you know what I should like if I could have three wishes same as you reads of in the little story-books?"

"Camel to come up now with one of his hot steak-and-kidney puddings boiled in a basin?"

"*Tlat!*" ejaculated the carpenter, with a smack of the lips. "And the inions a-smelling looshus a hundred yards away. Nay, it warn't that."

"A carpenter's tools?" said Fitz.

"Nay, but you ain't far off, Mr Burnett. What I was wishing for was one of them barge-loads of neatly-cut timber as you see piled upon the Mersey, run right up this 'ere little river ready for all our chaps to unload. My word! Talk about a fortification! Why, I'd make a sixtification of it with them timbers, and so quickly that to-morrow when the enemy come they should find all our Spaniels sitting behind the little loop-holes like a row of monkeys cracking nuts, a-laughing and chaffing the enemy, and telling of them to come on."

"Oh, bother!" said Poole. "Don't talk so much. It's enough to tempt the enemy to sneak up and begin potting at us. I know what I should like to do." And he relapsed into silence.

"Well, what?" said Fitz, when he was tired of waiting.

"Get all the men together and make a sally."

"A what?" said the carpenter. "What for? Blest if ever I heard of such a dodge as that before. What'd be the good of a she-male at a time like this? I could make a guy, sir, if that would suit you."

"Will you hold your tongue, you chattering old glue-pot!"

"All right, sir! Go it! Stick it on thick! Glue-pot, eh? What will you call me next? But what would be the good of a Sally?"

"Sally! To issue forth all together, stupid, and surprise the enemy in their camp."

"Oh! Well, I suppose they would be surprised to have us drop upon them all at once; but if they heard us coming we should be surprised. No, sir; let them come to us, for they're about ten to one. We are safest where we are."

"Yes; Chips is right," said Fitz. "It would be very dangerous unless we could get them on the run. I wouldn't do that."

"What would you do, then?" said Poole.

"Well," said Fitz, "you told me I was not a player, and that it was your game."

"Yes, but that was before you began peppering the beggars with that double gun."

"Now, that's too bad," cried Fitz petulantly. "There, I've done now."

"No, you haven't. You have got something on your mind, and if it's a dodge to help us all out of this mess, you are not the fellow to keep it back. So come; out with it."

"Well, I'll tell you what I've been thinking," said Fitz, "almost ever since I heard what that Mr Miguel said about the reinforcements coming from Velova."

"What, to crush us up?" said Poole. "Enough to make any one think! But what about it?"

"Why, the fort and earthworks will be emptied and all the fighting men on the way to-morrow to come and fight us here."

"Of course, and they'll be here some time to-morrow afternoon, and if they don't beat us they will be going back with sore heads; but I am afraid that those of us who are left will be going back as prisoners. Is that what you meant?"

"No," said Fitz, and without heeding a faint rustling sound such as might have been made by some wild creature, or an enemy stealing up to listen to their words, he went on: "I was thinking that this is what we ought to do—I mean your father and the Don—steal off at once without making a sound, all of us, English and Spaniards too, down to that timber-wharf."

"But suppose the enemy have got scouts out there?"

"I don't believe they have. After that last thrashing they drew off ever so far, and that President is doing nothing but wait for the coming of his reinforcements."

"That sounds right, Mr Poole, sir," said the carpenter.

"Well, it's likely," said Poole, and the faint rustling went on unheard. "But what then?"

"Whistle up the boat. The men would know your signal."

"Yes?"

"Load her up till the water's above the streak, and let her drop down with the stream. I noticed that it ran pretty fast. Land the men at the mouth; leave them to signal for the schooner to come within reach—they could do that with the lantern, or a bit of fire on the shore, if they didn't hear the captain's pipe—and while they are doing that, four men with oars row back as hard as ever they could go, to fetch another boat-load."

"Boat-load?" said Poole. "Why, it would take about four journeys, if not more."

"Very likely," said Fitz. "But there would be hours to do it in."

"And what then?"

"Get everybody on board the schooner and make sail for the north. Get into Velova Bay, and you could take the town with ease."

"And what about the gunboat?" said Poole.

"Ah! That's the awkward point in my plan. But the gunboat is not obliged to be there, and even if she were you could take the town if you managed to get there in the dark; and once you've got the town you could hold it, even if she knocked the fort to pieces."

"Hum!" grunted the carpenter.

"It'd be a tight fit getting everybody here on board our schooner."

"Nonsense!" said Fitz. "I could get a hundred men on board easily; and besides, we should all be saved."

"And besides, we should all be saved," said Poole, half aloud. "Yes, that's true. It does seem possible, after all, for there would be no defenders hardly left at Velova, and we could fit up a defence of some kind to keep off the enemy when they found we had gone and old Villarayo came raging back; and that wouldn't be for another two days. Yes, there's something in it, if we could dodge the gunboat again."

"Humph!" grunted the carpenter once more. "No; there's a hole in your saucepan, and all the soup is tumbling out. The enemy is bound to have some fellows on the watch, and likely enough not a hundred yards from here, and they would soon find out that we were evacuating the place, come and take us at a disadvantage, and perhaps shoot the poor fellows crowded up in the boat. Oh no, my lad; it won't do at all."

"Humph!" grunted the carpenter again.

"Don't you be in such a hurry, Mr Son-of-the-skipper," said Fitz. "I'd thought of that, and I should keep the enemy from coming on."

"How?" said Poole, rather excitedly now.

"Light three or four watch-fires—quite little ones—and put up a stick or two amongst the bushes with blankets on them and the Spaniards' sombrero hats. They'd look at a distance like men keeping the fire, and we could make these fires so that they would glow till daylight and go on smoking then; and as long as smoke was rising from these fires, I believe not one of the enemy would come near until the reinforcements arrived. And by that time, if all went well, we should be off Velova Bay."

"Humph!" grunted the carpenter again.

"It won't do, Burnett," said Poole; "it's too risky. There's nothing in it."

"Humph!" grunted the carpenter once more.

"And hark at that! You've set old Chips off snoring with your plot."

"That he aren't!" growled the carpenter. "I've heared every precious word. It's fine, Mr Poole, sir—fine! There's only one thing wanted to put it right, and that's them Sallies sitting round the fire. I wouldn't have Sallies. I'd have guys. I could knock you up half-a-dozen with crossed bamboos, each on 'em looking like tatter-doolies looking after crows with a gun. I says the plan would do."

"And so do I, carpenter," said the skipper, in his quick short tones as he stepped out from among the trees, making the three start to their feet.

"And I, my friend," cried Don Ramon excitedly catching the middy by the hand.

"Poole, my lad," continued the skipper, "get one of the other men and go cautiously down to the landing-place with every care, and if you reach it unhindered, whistle up the boat at once. Carpenter, get others to help you, and start fires as quickly as you can. *Very* small. The others can do that, while you contrive your rough effigies.—Now, Don Ramon, you'll take the covering of our efforts with your men while mine work. Remember, it is for our lives, and our only chance."

Chapter Thirty One
Fitz shows pepper

"Here, Mr Burnett!" came out of the darkness, and Fitz stopped short. "Yes, sir."

"Do you know that you are a great nuisance?"

It was invisible, but Fitz flushed and felt, after his fashion, peppery.

"I don't understand you, sir," he said hotly.

"I spoke plainly, my lad. You are always in my way, and you never were more so than at this minute."

"Then why did you take me prisoner, sir?" said the boy angrily.

"Why, in the name of thunder, did you come and tumble down my hatchway instead of stopping on the gunboat? I didn't ask you to come. Here, you are as bad as having a girl on board, or something made of wax, that mustn't be spoiled. I can't stir without thinking of having to take care of you."

"Oh," cried Fitz angrily. "This is adding insult to injury, sir."

"Well, yes, it don't sound very pleasant, does it, my boy? But you are a young nuisance, you know. I mustn't have you hurt. You see, Poole's my own, and I can do what I like with him; but you— Now then, what were you going to do?"

"I was going with Poole, sir."

"Of course!" cried the skipper angrily. "Just like a middy. I never had anything to do with one before, but I've heard times enough from those who have, that if there's a bit of mischief afloat, the first nose that goes into it is a middy's."

"I don't know what I've done, sir, that you should keep on insulting me like this."

"Insult! Bah! Is it insulting you to stop you from going into the most dangerous bit of to-night's work?"

"Poole's going, sir."

"Yes; to do his duty as my son, in this emergency. But it's not your duty, and you will be in the way. It's very risky, my lad. For aught I know there may be half-a-dozen scouts between here and the landing-place, waiting to shoot down any one who tries to open up communication with the boats."

"I know that, sir."

"And yet you want to go?"

"Yes," said the boy warmly. "You are going to send poor Poole, and I want to share his danger with him. I might help him."

"I am going to send poor Poole? Yes, my boy, because I am obliged. That job has to be done, and I'd sooner trust him than any one here. I can't spare my men, and I can't send one of these Spanish chaps. It won't do to have it muffed. But *poor* Poole, eh? You seem to have grown mighty fond of him all at once."

"Oh no, I'm not," said the boy haughtily; "but he has been very kind to me, and I'm not ungrateful. I might be able to help him if he gets into danger."

"Oh," said the skipper; "and suppose you get into danger?"

"Oh, then he'd help me, sir, of course. I'm sorry for him. He can't help being a filibuster's son."

"Filibuster, eh? So I'm a filibuster, am I? Upon my word, you're about the most cheeky young gentleman I ever ran against in my life. Well, all right. You must chance it, I suppose."

"Yes, please," said Fitz eagerly.

"Yes, please, eh? Well, keep your eyes well skinned, my lad. You two sharp-eyed youngsters ought to be able to take care of yourselves; but look here, I don't want you to fight. This is our mess, not yours."

"Well, I don't want to fight," said Fitz. "I want to get back on board some English vessel."

"Same here. That's what I want to do: get you on board the schooner. That's an English vessel."

"But not the sort I want, sir."

"Beggars mustn't be choosers, my lad; but there, I've no more time to talk. Just one word, though: I don't want you to fight, but I see you've got my double gun, and I'll just say this. If you see Poole in difficulties with any of those murderous mongrels, nine parts Indian and one part Spaniard, don't you flinch about using it."

Fitz The Filibuster | 185

"I shouldn't, sir, then."

"All right; then be off."

The skipper turned away, and Poole hurried up.

"What's my governor been saying to you?"

"Bullied me for being here," replied Fitz; "but he said that I might go with you."

"He did!"

"Yes, and gave me orders to shoot all the niggers who attacked you."

"Hooray! Then come on."

The two lads hurried off together through the darkness, leaving the hacienda and its defenders behind as they began to retrace their steps along the rough track leading to the corduroy road.

"Here, we mustn't talk," whispered Poole. "There's pretty nearly sure to be a post of the enemy somewhere in front. We can't have such luck as to get down there to the river without something in our way. I'll go on first."

"That you don't," said Fitz. "If any one goes first I will."

"Now, no nonsense!" cried Poole angrily. "I'm boss of this job, and if you don't do as I tell you I'll leave you behind."

"I've got your father's orders to come and take care of you," retorted Fitz; "and if you come any of your bounce and cheek now there'll be a row, and it will end in my punching your head."

"Poof! Cock-a-doodle-do!" whispered Poole. "There: come on! Let's walk side by side. I'll settle all that with you when the work is done. I say, keep your eyes skinned, and both ears wide open. I'll look to the right, you look to the left. We'll get on that wooden road and follow it down to the wharf."

"Pretty wharf it is! I say, I hope those poor fellows haven't been murdered."

"Oh, don't talk like that. They've got the boat, and let's hope they're safe. But it's been hard lines for them, waiting there all this time, with nothing to do but nibble their biscuits and kill flies. — Pst!"

Fitz imitated his companion's act and stopped short, his eyes striving hard to pierce the gloom in front; but for nearly a minute both stood on the strain.

"Nothing," said Poole. "Come on. It was some little animal escaping through the bushes; but make ready."

The clicking of the locks of both pieces sounded painfully loud in the silence as they went cautiously on, stopping again and again to listen, each wishing they could hear some sound to relieve the painful tension from which they suffered; but everything living seemed to have been scared away, and they kept on without interruption, while the river instead of getting nearer seemed to grow farther off, till at last Poole slipped on one of the muddy logs which formed the road, and nearly went headlong, but was saved by his companion, who in his effort to hold him up, fetched him a sharp rap on the head with the barrel of his gun.

"Thank you," said Poole.

"Oh, I only tried to keep you up," said Fitz, breathing hard.

"I meant for that affectionate crack you fetched me on the head. I say, this arn't sporting, you know."

"What do you mean?" whispered Fitz.

"I mean, don't shoot me so as to fill the bag."

"Don't fool," cried Fitz angrily.

"All right; but don't hit me again like that. It hurts."

"Pish! It was an accident. I am afraid—"

"So am I," said Poole, taking him up sharply; "horribly."

"I mean, that we have got on the wrong road."

"I thought so; but we can't be. There is only this one, if you call it a road, leading straight down to the river—no, not straight; circumbendibus-y."

"No," said Fitz, "it must have branched off, or we should have been at the river long enough ago."

"No, we have come too slowly."

"Where is the river, then?" said Fitz.

Plash! Quenk!

At that moment some kind of waterfowl rose from its lair with a good deal of fluttering of its wings, and a plaintive cry of alarm.

"Ah!" sighed Fitz, with a deep expiration of his breath. "At last!"

"Yes, at last. Mind how you come. The wharf must be just here. Can you make out that bank of mist?"

"Yes; I can see the top of it cut off quite sharply, and with the stars above it. That must be the river, then."

"That's right," said Poole. "Here, look out; we are quite close to the edge of the wharf. I say, what luck! We've got here safely, after all. Ah–h! What are you about?"

"Slipped," said Fitz, with a gasp. "The wood's like ice."

"Precious hot ice. I'm dripping. Do take care. If you go overboard you'll be swept right away, and I'm bothered if I come after you."

"I don't believe you," said Fitz, with a little laugh. "But oh, I say!"

"What's the matter now? Smell crocs?"

"No, no. I was thinking about those poor fellows in the boat. It's so horribly silent. Surely they have escaped."

Poole was silent for a few moments, and it seemed to the middy that he was breathing unusually hard.

"Is anything the matter?" whispered Fitz, at last. "Oh, don't talk like that!" came in an excited whisper.

"Then why don't you give the signal? What is it?"

"I was listening, and fancied I heard some one coming behind us. Face round, and if any one tries to rush us let 'em have it—both barrels. Those big shot of yours may check them, and I'll hold my bullet in reserve."

Fitz made no answer, but breathed harder as he stood ready with his fingers on the triggers.

"Fancy," said Poole at last. "Now then."

"Are you going to shout?"

"No; I've got the dad's pipe," and applying the little silver whistle to his lips he made it give forth one little shrill chirrup, and then waited, while the stillness seemed to Fitz more awful than before, and his heart sank lower with the dread lest the men were dead, the boat gone, and his project completely at an end. *Chirrup!*

Another what seemed to be a painfully long pause, and then *Chirrup!* once again.

The pause seemed even longer than before to the listeners, but the interval was short indeed before from out of the mist in front came a low hoarse "What cheer, oh!" followed by a sneeze and a grunt. "Teals?" cried Poole.

"Ay, ay! Two on us," came back. "Shall we pull ashore?"

"Yes; come on."

"Right. That you, Mr Poole?"

"Yes! Look sharp!"

There was a loud rustling, apparently about a hundred yards away, followed by the scraping of an oar over the side of the boat, and then the sound of paddling coming nearer and nearer, till the dimly-seen forms appeared out of the mist, and the boat grated against the side of the rough pier. "How goes it, sir?" said one of the men. "All right so far," replied Poole. "But how is it with you two?"

"Offle, sir."

"What do you mean?"

"Heads so swelled up with skeeters that we can't wear our hats. We've finished the grub, and to-morrow morning we was a-going to toss whether I should eat him or him should eat I."

"No nonsense," said Poole.

"No, sir; there arn't been none," said the speaker, in a low growl. "This 'ere's been the roughest job I was ever on. We'd have given anything to come and jine our mates so as to get a shot. Anybody lost the number of his mess?"

"No," said Poole. "No one even hurt."

"'Cept us, sir, and we've each of us got ten hundred million wounds."

"Wounds?"

"Yes, sir; skeeters. Trunks as big as elephants. They'd have sucked poor Jem here quite dry, only he did as I did, made it up with water, and there was plenty of that.—But you've come to fetch us, haven't you?"

"No; only to set you on the alert."

"On the which, sir? What ship's that?"

"Nonsense!" cried Poole. "We are all coming down to get on board the schooner as quickly as we can."

"And a blessed good thing too," growled the other man. "But you'd better stop where y'are, for this 'ere's an awful place. Anybody might have my job for me."

"Yes," said Poole, "I know it must have been terribly bad, but we are off again directly with the news that you two are all right."

"That we are which, sir?" said the first speaker. "Oh, I say, Mr Poole, sir, don't go and tell the skipper a lie like that."

"No, no; of course I'll tell him about how you have suffered; but we haven't been lying in feather-beds up there. Here, I say, Fitz, don't laugh."

"I couldn't help it," cried Fitz.

"No, sir, you couldn't," said the first man. "We couldn't at first. I laughed at Jem to see him smacking his own face all over, and he laughed at me and said mine looked beastly. And we didn't either of us look nice when the sun rose this morning, not even when we'd had a good wash. But it's all over now, as you are coming down, and the first thing Jem and me's going to do as soon as we gets aboard the schooner is to go and hide our heads in the hold. Say, Jem, old lad, I wonder what Chips will say to you when he sees your mug!"

"Just the same as he will say to you, messmate, about yourn."

"Hush! Don't talk. Get back into hiding again, and be ready to pick up the first load as soon as they come down."

"What of, sir? Prisoners or plunder?"

"Spaniards, my lad. Come, be serious. We are in a queer fix up there, shut in by the enemy. Have you seen anything of them here?"

"Yes; about a couple of dozen ugly-looking beggars, sort of mahogany-brown, come and had a look; but they didn't see us, and went back. It was just afore that first firing began."

"That's right," cried Poole. "Back with you; but it won't be long before some one comes, and then you must drop down to the coast, signal the schooner, land your load, and come back; but keep two men to help you."

"Ay, ay, sir."

"One word; you haven't seen any of the Teals, I suppose?"

"Oh yes, sir. Old Butters rowed up with the dinghy this evening."

"Last evening, mate," growled the other.

"Yes, that's right, messmate. He just had a word with us. Mr Burgess sent him. He wanted news, but of course we had got none, only about the shooting. The bosun said that if the skipper didn't soon come back he was afraid accidents would happen to the schooner—catch fire, or something—for old Burgess was making it so hot for everybody that he was glad to get away in the little boat."

"Off with you!" said Poole, and he and his companion hurried back through the gathering mist.

Chapter Thirty Two
Winks's Sallys

The distance back to the hacienda seemed short enough, and in anticipation of his mission proving successful, the skipper had his first boat's load told off ready for their start.

"Well done! Splendid!" he said to the lads. "Off with you back. Take the command, Poole. Are you going again, Mr Burnett?"

"Yes, sir; of course."

Fitz turned sharply round when he was addressed, from where he was standing with the carpenter, after noting that here and there at a distance a tiny fire was burning, indicating the different posts between them and the enemy, and just before Winks had come hurriedly up to him and given him a nudge.

"I arn't got them set up yet, sir," he whispered, "but I've made four. Not much to look at, but they will be all right. Two crossed sticks, bamboos, blankets, and them Spanish hats. There's two Sallys and two Guys. The Sallys has got the blankets right over the tops with the hats down close. They looks just like old women a little way off.—Going back again, sir?"

"Yes," replied Fitz. "We shan't be very long this time."

"All right, sir. I shall have the traps set by the time you come again. My word! I should like to be there when the Span'ls finds they are nothing but a set of paddies. I should like to hear the words they said. It would be something pretty in bad Spanish, I'll be bound."

"Now, Mr Burnett," cried the skipper sharply, and somehow feeling as if he were one of the schooner's officers, the middy hurried off, helping to guide the party, consisting of Don Ramon's followers all but two, and succeeding in reaching the wharf without an adventure, the boat coming up at once on hearing their approach, and in a very short time loaded gunwale down, gliding off along the swift stream.

"That's one lot," said Poole excitedly, as the stern of the boat disappeared. "Well, we had no orders, but of course we've got to go back for another lot and bring them down. I suppose we shall have them here long before the empty boat returns from the schooner."

"It will be a stiff pull against the stream," said Fitz.

"Yes, but empty, and I made them fully understand that they were to start back after shipping the men and communicating with old Burgess. I think that will turn out all right."

It did, and in due time a second load was despatched to the schooner, forming half the human cargo she would have to bear.

They were anxious times during these journeys in the boat. All was going well, but at any moment the fiction of the watchers by the fires might have been discovered, and the enemy come on to the attack upon a force weakened first by one-fourth, then by half, and later on by three-fourths of its number, the danger increasing at a terrific ratio for those who were left. At last, still keeping manfully to their posts, the last portion—the last quarter of the little force—stood waiting, nearly all English, those of Spanish descent consisting of Don Ramon and his most staunch adherent.

The skipper had urged him to go with the third party, but he had scornfully refused.

"What!" he cried. "Provide for my safety, and leave you brave Englishmen to fight my battle all alone! Bah! You would never be able to call me friend again. But tell me this: why did you not go yourself and leave me to guard the hacienda till the boat came back?—Hah! You say nothing! You cannot. No, I shall stay, and we will escape together, ready to sail round, seize Velova, and meet mine enemies when they return."

The peril seemed to increase minute by minute, as the little party watched, straining their ears in the darkness to catch the slightest sound, while it seemed hours since the last party had left them, and they awaited the coming of the two lads to announce that the boat had returned.

It was weary work for these goers to and fro, but excitement and exertion kept them from feeling the agony of the Englishmen who, apparently calm, kept watch and ward at the hacienda, while from time to time the skipper and Winks went from fire to fire, mending them and arranging more fuel so that when they were left for good they might still keep burning.

They had been round for the last visit, and returned to the hacienda, walking very slowly, and pausing from time to time to listen for any movement in the enemy's lines, and at last they stopped short close to the spot where the carpenter had destroyed the snake, when after standing for some time listening to a faint murmur of voices close at hand, coming from the waiting crew, the carpenter uttered a peculiar husky cough. It was so strange and unnatural that the skipper put the right interpretation upon it at once.

"Yes?" he said. "You wanted to ask me something?"

"Yes, sir. It's this waiting makes me want to speak. I can't stand the doing nothing at a time like this. I'd ten times rather be on the fight."

"So would I, Winks, if you come to that. It's a cruel strain, my lad. Worse than being in the wildest storm. But go on; what did you want to say?"

"Oh, only this, sir. I want you to give me orders to go round again and give the fires a poke. You needn't come, sir. You are wanted here. You can trust me to do the lot."

"Yes, I know that," said the skipper sternly; "but that isn't all. You were thinking something else, and now it's come to the point you are afraid to speak."

"How did you know that, sir?" said the man huskily.

"By your manner and the tone of your voice. What is it you are thinking? Out with it at once."

"Well, sir, I dunno how you come to know, but it has come over me just lately like a skeer. Aren't the young gents been much longer this time?"

"Yes, much," replied the skipper; "or else it seems to be."

"I thought so, sir, and I've got so now that I feels as if I can't bear it. What are you going to do, sir? Follow 'em up and see what's wrong?"

"I shall give them ten minutes longer, Winks. I meant to stay here to the very last, ready to give the enemy a volley and a check if they should come on; but now the time has come to hurry on to the wharf and wait there in the hope that the boat may still come and take us off without further waste of time."

"But don't let me make you downhearted, sir," said the carpenter, trying to speak cheerily. "I'm a bit of an old woman in my ways sometimes. Maybe it's all right, after all."

"Maybe it is," said the skipper. "We are tired out and over-anxious now. It's quite possible that we shall have them back here soon."

"Pst!" whispered the carpenter. "There's some one coming."

It was from their rear, and the next moment they were joined by Don Ramon.

"Ah, you are here," he said. "Is it not time that the boys came back?"

"Nearly," said the skipper quietly.

"No, no," said Don Ramon; "they have been twice too long. Something must have happened, or they would have come by now."

"Pst! Look out!" whispered the carpenter, and he cocked his rifle. "No: all right," he continued. "It's not from the enemy's side."

He was quite right, for directly after the two boys trotted up.

"All right, father," cried Poole. "The boat's back."

"We thought she would never have come," added Fitz. "They have had a very hard pull up stream, for the water has risen, and they thought that they'd never get to the landing-place."

"But they are there!" cried the skipper eagerly. "What about the others? Have they got on board?"

"Everything was going right, father. I had a few words with Butters, and he was very eager to know how soon I could get you all down."

"And you couldn't tell him?"

"No, father.—I think that's all."

"Bravo! Magnificent!" cried Don Ramon. "You have both done wonders," and to the lads' disgust he caught them in turn to his breast and kissed them. "It is grand, and your fathers should be proud. My lads, it is the grandest thing in life to be a Spaniard of pure Castilian descent, but next to that the greatest thing in the world is to be an English boy."

"This is no time for compliments, Don Ramon," said the skipper sternly. "They have done their duty; that is all. Now then, will you lead on at once with half our party, and I with the rest will form the rear-guard. If even now the enemy come up we shall be able to hold them in check. We shall fire, and then double past you and your party, who will halt and fire, and then retire past us again. We are very few and they are many, but I think we can reach the boat in safety after all."

The Don made no reply, but put himself at the head of his little party at once, leaving the skipper, the two lads, and the remainder facing the enemy's camp and watching the flickering fires between, the hardest task of all when the way was open and they felt that with a good rush they might reach the boat in safety.

But discipline was master, and fighting down all desire to break away, the remnant of the little force stood waiting, while the carpenter made a last effort to find himself something to do, by suggesting that it would be best perhaps to give them there fires just another touch.

"No," said the skipper sternly. "In another two minutes we shall follow on."

"Thank goodness!" whispered Fitz excitedly. "I don't feel as if I could stand any more."

"Not even one of Don Ramon's speeches and a hug?"

"Oh, don't talk about it," whispered Fitz angrily.

"What! Isn't it grand to be an English boy?"

"Bosh!" cried Fitz, and like an echo of his ejaculation came the skipper's command—

"Forward!" And directly afterwards, "Poole—Mr Burnett—will you watch with me?"

The lads stepped to his side at once.

"The last to turn our backs, Fitz Burnett," whispered Poole. "The place of honour after all."

Chapter Thirty Three
Aboard again

The little party strained their ears as they tramped silently on towards the boat; but not a sound was heard suggesting that the enemy grasped the fact that the strategy had been cleverly carried out. The dull reflection of the fires had from time to time been faintly discernible upon the low-hanging mist; but this soon died out, and fortune seemed to be smiling kindly upon their efforts now.

"I'd give something to know what time it is," whispered Poole, and he took a step nearer to his father to ask him how long he thought it would be before day.

"I haven't the least idea, my boy," he replied. "The night has seemed far too short, but it must be nearly at an end. But if we can once get into the boat and reach the schooner I shall begin to hope that we may reach Velova before the enemy."

"We have got much farther to go than they have, though, father."

"Yes, and everything will depend upon how long it is before the reinforcements come and they make their advance. It may be hours yet, and it may be before the break of day. There, don't talk to me again, my lad; I want to think."

So it was in silence and darkness that the corduroy road was traversed, and the rear-guard reached the little wharf to find the advance gathered-together, waiting to fire or descend at once into the boat.

There was not a sound to be heard from the direction by which they had come, and the skipper giving the order to embark at once, the men stepped down carefully and well, till, dangerously packed, the order was given to push off, Poole and Fitz being together in the stern, where the skipper passed out an oar to steer, and they began rapidly to descend the flooded stream.

"There must have been rain in the mountains," he said quietly, and then aloud, "Sit fast, my lads, and keep her well in trim. Two oars out there, just to give me steering way, but you need hardly pull. Everything depends upon your keeping steady. There, boys," he said, to those at his side, "we are none too soon. It's lightening yonder in the east."

That morning the sun, as it rose high above the mist, shone down upon the crowded decks of the schooner, her white sails glistening as the land was left behind, with Poole and Fitz Burnett using the glass in turn to watch the mouth of the little river; but they watched in vain, for there was no sign of enemy hurrying to the bank, nothing to disturb the peace and beauty of the scene.

Poole scuffled up to the masthead, glass in hand, and Fitz Burnett followed him, to stand as near as he could, with the ratlines cutting into his feet and a crick coming in the back of his neck, as he held on tightly, and leaned back watching his companion's action, longing to get hold of the glass and use it himself. In fact, he was suffering from that impatience which often attacks us all and makes us feel as we watch another's action how much better we could do it ourselves, from the greatest matter down to such a trifle us untying a knot in a piece of string. Meanwhile, with the white sails swelling out above and below, and the double glass to his eye, the skipper's son was slowly sweeping the coast-line, letting nothing escape him, as he looked in vain for some sign of the enemy.

"See her, my boy?" came from the deck, and Fitz looked down, to see that the skipper and Don Ramon were watching them.

"No, father," cried Poole. "I wasn't looking out to sea."

"Then why don't you?" cried the skipper angrily. "Are you trying to see cocoanuts on the trees? Sweep the horizon, sir, and give us the first notice of that gunboat's masts."

"All right, father," said the lad quietly, and he wrenched himself round and made the lenses of the binocular slowly travel along the horizon-line, as he rocked gently here and there with the action of the schooner riding swiftly over the long smooth swell; for there was a pleasant breeze, all possible sail was set, and they were rapidly diminishing the distance between them and Velova Bay.

"See her?" said Fitz, as he noted that the skipper and his Spanish friend had walked together forward—Don Ramon's followers, who crowded the deck and sent up scores of tiny films of smoke from their cigarettes, politely making way and forming quite a lane for their leaders.

They were idling, chattering, and laughing together, the very types of a party of idlers out on a sea-trip, and their rifles were leaning against the bulwarks here and there, lying about the deck, or stuck in sheaves together with their barrels appearing above the sides of the boats swinging from the davits.

No one could have imagined from their careless indolent bearing that they were posing as patriots, men who a short time before had escaped from a deadly peril, and were now for aught they knew sailing straight away into one as great.

They formed a strong contrast to the old men-of-war's men, who retained their well-drilled bearing as the crew of the schooner, eager, alert, and ready at any moment to spring to sheet and brace at the mate's orders when they went upon another tack.

"No," replied Poole, after a long interval. "There's a shoal of fish out yonder, and something sprang out farther to the east and went in again with a splash, and there's a bad sign out yonder; cat's-paws on the surface."

"You don't mean to say that it looks like a calm coming?"

"Just like that," said Poole slowly, with the glass still at his eye.

"Well?" rose from the deck, as the two chiefs came slowly back.

"Nothing, father—not a sign," cried Poole. "Well, you needn't stop up there, my lad. Come down, and go up again in a quarter of an hour's time."

Poole slipped the glass into the case slung from his left shoulder, laid hold of a rope, and looked at his companion, who did the same, and they slid down together and dropped upon the deck, to begin walking forward.

"I shan't be sorry," said Poole quietly, "when all these fellows are ashore."

"Nor I neither," replied Fitz, and then he turned his head sharply, for a familiar head was thrust out of the galley, where the stove was black and cold.

"Weel, laddies," whispered the Camel, "I have had to put up the shutters and shut up shop, for I canna pretend to feed all this lot; but ah'm thenking ye'll feel a bit hungry now and then, and when ye do, joost go below into the cahbin when there's naebody looking, and open the little locker. I dinna mean to say another word, but—" He closed one ferrety-looking red eye, laid a finger alongside of his nose, showed his big teeth, and drew his head in again.

"A nod is as good as a wink to a blind horse," said Poole, laughing. "Well done, Camel! But that's all you, Fitz."

"Nonsense! It was a hint for both."

"No. He has taken a fancy to you. He told me himself he had, and that it was his doing that you got up your strength so quickly."

"Oh, gammon!" cried Fitz petulantly.

"No, it was what he calls his pheesic. He told me that when a man was in bad health—crenky, he called it—that the thing to pull him round was soup; and you know how he was always scheming something of the kind for you. I shouldn't like to analyse too strictly what he made it of."

"Why, meat, of course," cried the middy. "I don't know," said Poole dryly. "You see, it's not like being ashore; but you had soup pretty well every day, and you said yourself that it tasted all right. But it doesn't matter. It did you good."

"Don't you think we had better change the subject?" said Fitz sharply. "Yes; and we'll go up aloft again. Coming?"

"Of course," was the reply.

They turned back to go aft towards the mainmast-shrouds, Don Ramon's followers making room for them to pass; but as they reached the part of the deck where they were going to ascend, they came upon the boatswain looking as black as thunder.

"Hullo, Butters! Anything the matter?" said Poole. "Matter!" growled the copper-faced old fellow. "Look at my deck—I mean, as much of it as you can see. I am pretty nigh sick of this! A set of jabbering monkeys; that's about what they are."

"Up aloft again, Poole?" cried the skipper. "Just going," was the reply, and giving up his place by the starboard main-shrouds to Fitz, the lad ran across the deck to the port side, where he began to ascend, the pair meeting at the masthead upon equal terms. "Here, I'd give up the glass to you," cried Poole, "but father mightn't like it, though your eyes are as sharp or sharper than mine. I'll give one sweep round and report to the deck, and then you shall have a turn."

Poole passed his arm round a stay and raised the glass to his eyes, while Fitz took a turn round the rope with one leg, and waited, thinking.

"Isn't such a bad fellow," he said to himself, as he watched the captain's son, "but he's getting a little too familiar. He seems to forget sometimes that I'm an officer; but there, it doesn't much matter, and it won't last long."

"Well, my lad?" came from the deck.

"All clear, father," was the reply, and as Fitz glanced down he saw Don Ramon place the cigarette he was holding between his teeth and clap his hands, while from his crowd of followers who were looking on there ascended a loud *Viva!*

And the hot day glided on.

There was a fair breeze, and the schooner fairly danced over the laughing waters, sending shoals of flying-fish skimming out before them, with their wing-like fins glistening like those of gigantic dragon-flies, before they dropped back into the sea.

Rations were served out to the eager crowd, and a buzz of conversation was kept up, to ascend to the two lads, who spent most of their time aloft, watching, talking, and comparing notes about what a peaceful time it seemed and how strange a contrast to the excitement of the previous day and night.

"It's too good to be true, my lads," said the skipper quietly, as the afternoon glided by. "We have made such a splendid run that it isn't reasonable to expect fortune will favour us much farther."

"Ah, you think that?" said Don Ramon, who came up rolling a fresh cigarette.

"Yes, sir, I do. In another hour we shall be round that headland, and in sight of Velova if the mate keeps us clear of that long reef of rocks which guards the bay."

"Ah, and then you think Villarayo will be waiting for us with his men?"

"Oh no," said the skipper; "I can't say for certain, but I should doubt whether he has found out as yet that we are gone. I feel certain now that he would not stir till all his reinforcements had reached him."

"That is right," said the Don eagerly, "and even then—I know our people well—they will fight bravely twice, but it is very hard to move them again. But you spoke as if you *were* in doubt. What is it you expect?"

"I expect, sir, that as soon as we get round that headland we shall see the gunboat waiting for us, and ready to open fire. And once she gets well within range—"

Reed stopped. "Yes, what then?" cried Don Ramon eagerly. The skipper shrugged his shoulders. "What can we do, sir, with my schooner crowded up like this?"

"Fly," said the Don, with his eyes flashing. "Of course; there is nothing else to be done. But if they have decent men to work that gun, one well-placed shot or shell will wreck my rigging, and we shall lie like a wounded bird upon the water."

The Don looked fixedly in the skipper's face for some moments before giving him a short nod and turning away to light his cigarette.

Chapter Thirty Four
No Burgess aboard

But the skipper's forebodings were needless. As they sailed round the headland it was through a sea of golden light. There lay Velova with every window flashing in the late afternoon sunshine. Small coasting vessels were at anchor, boats were putting out to sea to reach the fishing-grounds; and, save that through the glass a few figures could be seen about the little fort with its flagstaff flying the national colours, and the rough earthworks could be made out mounting a few small guns, all was calm and peaceful.

"There, captain," cried Don Ramon triumphantly, "what do you say now?"

"It is for you to speak, sir. What do you say now?"

"Sail right in as close up to the wharf as you can get; you can lay your vessel alongside in these calm waters."

"And if they open fire?"

"They will not dare," cried the Don, his eyes flashing with excitement. "We must be first, and there will be scarcely any one there."

"But if they did, sir?"

"If they did, my men would crowd into your boats, we should row ashore and carry the fort and earthworks. We can do that with ease while you come right on to where we will meet you, and help to land the guns. Captain Reed, our young friend's plans have opened the way to triumph. You will see that all the people in Velova now will declare for me. I shall arm them with the rifles you have brought, strengthen the fort and earthworks, and plant three of the pieces upon the road leading to the mountain-pass by which the enemy are bound to come. Let them attack then if they dare. Do you see? Do you understand?" he added quickly.

"Yes. Excellent. Nothing could be better than your plan, sir; and if Villarayo should not arrive till morning the game would be your own."

"Would be! Will be," said the Spaniard fiercely. "What is to prevent it now?"

The skipper glanced round as they stood together aft, and saving the two lads there was no one to overhear his words, as he leaned a little nearer to the excited Spaniard and said, almost in a whisper—

"The gunboat."

There was a faint click. Don Ramon had closed his teeth sharply, and he turned half round to gaze out to sea. The next minute he turned back with his brow knit and his eyes half-closed.

"Yes, my good friend," he said quietly; "that is the great enemy. Ah! if you could show me how to get control of that it would mean all. Still I do not despair. She is not here now, and there is the land, the country all before me. Let her keep away till after Villarayo has returned, and I have scattered all his horde of ruffians, the sweepings of the place—as I shall, for once I have landed with my warlike supplies, all that is good and true in Velova will fight for me to the death—and then the march to San Cristobal will be an easy task. The news that Villarayo and his people are scattered will go before me, and the people there will crowd to me for arms, the arms that I shall send round by your vessel to meet me there. Oh, it will be all child's play now, and in another few days my flag will be flying at San Cristobal, as it will be flying here."

"If," said Fitz quietly to Poole, as the Spaniard walked forward to address his men, "he is not counting his chickens before they are hatched."

"Yes," said the skipper, who had heard his words; "and if the gunboat does not return."

"Well, father, there are some things in his favour," said Poole, "even about the gunboat."

"What?"

"This is a very rocky coast. That gunboat must draw a good deal of water."

"True, my boy; true."

"And, father," said Poole, with a smile, "they haven't got a Burgess on board."

Chapter Thirty Five
The contraband

The evening was coming on fast as the schooner sailed on towards the little port with her overburdened decks.

"Are we going to run right in, Poole?" asked Fitz, as he watched the excitement of the crowd on deck, where every one of Don Ramon's followers was busy polishing up his rifle, to the great amusement of the carpenter, who slouched up to where the lads were standing. "Just look at 'em," he said. "They thinks they're soldiers; that's what they have got in their heads. Rubbing up the outsides of them rifles! I've been watching of them this last half-hour. They're just like an old farmer I used to know. Always werry pertickler, he was, to whitewash the outsides of his pig-sties; but as to the insides—my!"

That last word sounded like a bad note on a clarionet, for, as he spoke, Winks was holding his nose tightly between his finger and thumb.

Fitz laughed, and asked the question that begins the second paragraph of this chapter.

"Seems like it," said Poole, "but I don't know whether it's going to be safe."

"Won't be safe for them," continued the carpenter, "if they don't run their loading-rods and a bit of rag through them barrels. Sore shoulders for some of them. My word, how they will kick! Soldiers!" he chuckled. "I say, Mr Burnett, have you ever seen them there recruiting-sergeants about Trafalgar Square, London?"

"Yes, often," said Fitz. "Why?"

"Nice smart-looking, well-built chaps, as looks as if their uniforms had growed on 'em like their skins."

"Yes, they are smart picked men of course," said Fitz.

"That's so, sir. What do you think they would say to these tan-leather-coloured ragged Jacks, if they went up and offered to take the shilling?"

"Well, they wouldn't take many of them, I think," replied the middy.

"Take many of them, sir? I seem to see one of the sergeants now. He'd hold that little walking-stick of his with both hands tight and close up under his left arm, stand werry stiff, and drop his head a little on one side as he looked down at them; and then he'd give a sniff, and that would be all."

But Don Ramon did not despise his followers. He was bustling about among them, addressing and exhorting and working them up to a tremendous pitch of excitement, making them shout and cheer till they were hoarse. Then they swarmed into the rigging and clustered in the shrouds, to wave their rifles and hats at the crowd gathering upon the shore and cheering shrilly in reply, the men's voices being mingled with those of women and children, who seemed to be welcoming them as their deliverers.

"Well, it's all right, Don Ramon," said the skipper, who was standing by Burgess busily conning the schooner as she glided in now towards the shore.

"Yes," cried the Don proudly; "it is what you call all right. You see there will be no fighting now."

Bang! went a gun from the fort, and the lads started as they gazed at the grey ball of smoke which began to turn golden as it rose in the air.

"They're reckoning without the fort," said Fitz excitedly, as he strained his eyes in vain for the ball which he expected to see come skipping over the smooth water.

"Yes," said Poole. — "No: it was a blank. Look, they are hauling down the flag. Oh, it's all right. A regular walk-over. Three cheers for Don Ramon!"

"Yes," shouted the skipper. "With a will, my lads! Three cheers for Don Ramon!" And they were given with such energy that the Don sprang up upon the cabin-light, to bow and press his hands to his breast.

He was down again the next instant, to run to the skipper and catch and wring his hands.

"You see," he cried, "the people are with me. But you will help me still?"

"As far as I can," was the reply; "but you must not call upon me to land my men and help you in your fight with Villarayo."

"No?" said the Don, in a questioning way.

"No," replied the skipper. "The fight at the hacienda was an exception. I was driven to that."

"But you will help me still? The arms—the ammunition?"

"Yes; it is our duty to land everything safely to your order."

"Then I want the rifles and cartridges now."

"Yes," said the skipper. "You feel satisfied that it will be safe to have them landed?"

"Quite. So as to arm my friends."

"Then as soon as your men are ashore I will have the cases got up from the hold."

"No," said Don Ramon; "you must do it now. Have them up on deck so that my people can bear them ashore as soon as we reach the wharf."

"It shall be done," said the skipper quietly. "All that I require is your authority, that you take them in charge."

"I give you my authority before all your witnesses," replied Don Ramon proudly; "and I take them in charge. Is that sufficient?"

"Quite, sir. Mr Burgess, you will lay the schooner alongside the wharf. Pass the word for the carpenter and eight or ten men. I want these tarpaulins and hatches off. Order your men back, Don Ramon. I want room for mine to work."

It was a busy scene that followed. Sails were lowered, for they were close in now; hammers were ringing; the way down into the hold was laid bare; tackle was rigged up; and by the time the schooner lay alongside a fairly-made wharf, a dozen long white cases bound with hoop-iron lay piled up upon the deck, while dozens more lay waiting to take their place. The excitement was tremendous; the wharf and its approaches were crowded by an enthusiastic mob, eager and clamouring for arms, which during the next hour were lavishly supplied, along with a sufficiency of ammunition, with the result that Don Ramon's little force had grown into a well-armed crowd, so full of enthusiasm that they gave promise, if not of victory, of making a desperate defence.

At last, with the help of those who seemed to be among the chief people of the place, the little army, well-armed, was marched away from the waterside to take up strategic positions under Don Ramon's instructions, after which he returned to where the skipper and his men had opened another hatch and were busily hoisting up the little battery of six-pounder field-guns, with their limbers, everything being of the newest and most finished kind. These, with their cases of ammunition, proving much heavier than they looked, were swung round from the deck with the tackle necessary and landed upon the wharf, where they were seized upon at once by the Don's roughly-selected artillery-men, and at last dragged off by teams of mules to the places of vantage where they were to be stationed; and all amidst a scene of the wildest enthusiasm.

As the last gun was landed, hastily put together, and seized and dragged away by a human team, Don Ramon came back from the shore, palpitating with emotion, and hurrying to where the skipper stood upon the deck with the lads, wiping his face after superintending every part of the delivery himself.

"There, Don Ramon," he cried, "my work's done, and you have got everything safe. I hope your fellows will be careful with the ammunition."

"Yes, yes," was the reply; "everything is being done. I have come back to thank you. If you do not see me again yet awhile, it is because I am over yonder—because I am wanted everywhere at once. Captain Reed, and you, my brave young friends, I want to tell you of the gratitude I feel, but—but— my heart is too full. I cannot speak. But one word; to-morrow the enemy will be here, a great battle will rage, for my people will fight now to the very death. If I fall—" He stopped short.

He truly could say no more, and waving his hands to them, he sprang back on to the wharf out of the light cast by the swinging lanterns, which had for some time past thrown their weird gleams upon the scene, and was gone.

Chapter Thirty Six
Real war

There was little sleep that night for those on board, for once his little cargo was discharged, the skipper had everything made snug and ready for putting to sea if necessary at a moment's notice.

Most of the men had been busy over the landing of the cases and guns, and Fitz had thoroughly enjoyed the looking on, feeling a strange longing the while to go ashore and superintend the unpacking and putting together of the gun-limbers, and the mounting of the pieces. Not that there was a great deal to do, for, in obedience to instructions, the British manufacturers had sent the little field-guns with everything so simplified that the rough artillery-men from the Central American fort had few difficulties with which to contend. He saw little of Poole in the darkness, but knew that he was busy over something with a couple of men at his beck, while a third had had a duty of his own where a bright light had gleamed out and a little chimney had roared in a way which made Poole anxiously consult his father, who was superintending the landing of cases, when in their brief conversation something was said about sparks, and then a couple of tarpaulins were rigged up with lines, in a way which entirely cut off the galley from the rest of the deck.

The result of all this was, that when the deck was clear and hatches replaced, the Camel stood smiling, with glistening face, for his work too was done, and the fresh provisions that had been abundantly brought on board by the women of the place were in a most welcome form for the half-starved, weary crew, and about midnight there was something as nearly like a banquet as could be expected under the circumstances, and to the delight of all.

There had been no form; the only ceremony had been for officers and men to sit down sailor or tailor fashion, cross-legged upon the deck, and eat as much as such men would.

"Hah!" said the boatswain, turning towards the two lads, after being very silent for quite half-an-hour. "I call this something like; but I do hope as the Camel's had time to pick a bit."

So busy had the party on board been, that they had thought little about the proceedings on shore, the less so that the excitement and noise of shouting orders, trampling feet, and the buzz of chattering women and children had drifted farther and farther away to the opposite side of the town, where beyond the low houses and hovels of the poorer part of the population the long low valley commenced which rapidly became a pass, the key, so to speak, of the little city.

Here Don Ramon had mustered his force, and here during the rest of the night his men worked by the light of the stars, making a wall of stones with openings for the field-pieces, and clearing the road behind between them and the earthwork nearer to the fort, to which in case of emergency they could be withdrawn ready for another stand.

He was no novice in such matters, having passed his life as he had amidst a volcanic people where revolutions came and went as if indigenous to the countries bordering upon the Mexican Gulf.

In his way he was no bad soldier, and in fact a better man than his rival the tyrant and oppressor, whom he had been urged by the superior part of his fellow-countrymen to supplant.

Hence it was that before morning, and without interruption, he made the most of the rough but enthusiastic and willing materials to his hand, so that at last he could breathe more freely and accept the congratulations of his friends over the knowledge they shared that Villarayo would find when he came up that not only had he a formidable nut to crack, but the probability before him that the nutcrackers would give way first.

All this was plain enough in the coming daylight, when the skipper and the two lads made their way ashore in one of the boats from the spot where the *Teal* was moored, floating more lightly now, and almost as gracefully in the pearly grey light as the beautiful little waterfowl after which she was named.

"Why, it looks almost like an anthill," said Fitz, as they approached the mouth of the pass, whose sides were dotted with men, most of whom were carrying rifles, while each displayed a formidable knife in his belt. "But there doesn't seem to be any sign of the enemy as yet."

"No," said Poole; "but I say, father, do you think that they will be able to manage those guns?"

"Yes," said the skipper gravely. "The men who had the gumption to plant them like that will be pretty sure to find out the way to use them with effect. Besides, they have had some experience, of course, with the old-fashioned pieces in the fort."

"There go their colours up!" cried Fitz excitedly, as the national flag was run up to the head of the flagstaff that had been raised during the night. "I hope they'll win, Captain Reed, for the Don's been very plucky, and I suppose he is in the right."

"If he hadn't been in the right I wouldn't have helped him as I have," said the skipper gruffly.

"No," said Poole firmly, as if to endorse his father's words. "But don't you think, father, that if you brought all our chaps ashore to set these men by the guns at liberty and leave our lads to work them, they'd manage them much better—fire more regularly and twice as fast?"

"Yes, that they would," cried Fitz excitedly. "There's hardly one of them who doesn't know his gun-drill."

"How do you know that?" said the skipper grimly.

"Oh, I asked them," replied the lad, flushing. "They all talk to me about their old life on board different Queen's ships. It was because I was a midshipman, I suppose. Why," he continued, growing more excited by what he saw, "our Chips—I mean, your Chips," he said, hastily correcting himself—"would make a splendid captain for one of the guns; Mr Butters another, of course; and the Camel, though he's cook now. Oh, I could man all those guns easily."

"Like to do it, perhaps," said the skipper dryly, "and fancy that battery was the broadside of a ship?"

"Yes, of course," said the lad; "I mean—" he stammered—"that is— Oh, it's nothing to do with me."

"No," said the skipper quietly, as he stood looking critically at the preparations Don Ramon had made, while the scene around seemed to have had the same peculiar exciting effect upon his son as it had upon the midshipman, for Poole said suddenly—

"Why, father, if you were to do that it would make all the difference, and be like turning the scale to Don Ramon's side."

"Yes, my boy," said the skipper, "and here he is;" for the Don suddenly appeared, mounted upon a sturdy mule, cantering towards them, with his steed making very light of the rugged stony ground, and stopping short close up to the group in response to a touch upon its rein, when its rider sprang lightly to the ground, looking as wiry and fresh as the beast he rode, in spite of the labours of the night.

"Ah, my friend! Welcome!" he cried. "And you too, my braves. Now," he added joyously, his eyes sparkling with excitement, "have not my brave fellows worked? Are we not ready for the enemy when he comes? What have you to say? There are the guns! Tell me, are they well-placed? You who have brought them know so much. If they are not right, tell me what to do, and it shall be done."

"I would not alter anything now," said the skipper gravely.

"Why not, if they, are wrong? There is time, and plenty, for my scouts are far enough away, and the enemy is not in sight."

The skipper was silent, but his eyes were not idle, and he seemed to be examining every disposition closely.

"He does not speak," continued Don Ramon. "Then you, my young English officer; you come from a ship with guns, what have you to say?"

"I was wondering," said Fitz, flushing, "not about the guns, for they seem well-placed, but whether the enemy could come down that little valley up yonder or get round by the rear."

"No, no, no," cried the Don exultantly. "Velova can only be reached by this pass, which my guns command. There is no other way—by land—but there is the sea."

"And the gunboat?" said Fitz.

"Ah–h, yes, the gunboat!" cried the Don, with his face convulsed, as he clenched his hands. "The gunboat—yes. It is the key to the Presidency."

"No," said the skipper suddenly, "I would change nothing, Don Ramon. As far as I know, your position is magnificent."

"Hah!" cried the Don, with his face smoothing once more, and his eyes lighting up with pleasure. "But you think my grand, my beautiful and perfect little guns that you have brought me are well-placed?"

"Capitally," said the skipper sincerely. "But they are not perfcct," said the Don, with a peculiar smile, as he keenly watched the skipper the while. "There is one thing wanting."

"Surely not," cried the skipper angrily. "I saw them packed myself, and I can answer for it that nothing was left out, unless it was in the hurry of the unpacking last night. Quick, while there is time! What has been left behind? Do you mean there is something still on board?"

"Yes, my good friend," said the Don softly; "the crew. Captain Reed," he continued excitedly, "with your brave fellows to man that battery the day must be my own. Villarayo's sun would set in blood and dust; my poor oppressed country would rise in pride to happiness and peace; and I should be President indeed—my people's father—he who has saved them from slavery and chains."

The skipper shook his head.

"No, no," continued the Don softly. "Listen. This country is rich in mines; there are precious stones; there is no reward you could ask me afterwards that I would not give. I care for nothing of these things, for I am fighting for my country and my people's homes. Captain Reed, you have always been my friend, my trusted friend, who brought me all these in answer to my prayer. There is this one thing more. I ask it of my trusted friend."

Poole glanced at his father's stern face, which seemed to turn colder and harder than he had ever seen it before, and then turned quickly to look at Fitz, who was watching him with questioning eyes which seemed to say, What will he reply?

But reply there was none, apparently for minutes, though the space of time that elapsed could have been numbered in moments, before he spoke, and then it was in a low, softened and pained voice.

"No, Don Ramon," he said. "You ask me for what I cannot give."

"Give!" cried the Don passionately. "I offer to pay you!"

"Yes, sir," said the captain, without changing his tone, "and that makes it worse. I tell you my heart is with you in your project, and that I wish you success, but I am answerable to those men, their friends, and I suppose to my country's laws for their lives. I have no right to enter into such an enterprise as this."

"Why?" cried the Don passionately. "You fought with me before!"

"Yes—to save their lives and yours. It was in an emergency. This is a different thing. I cannot do it."

"Then you forsake me?" cried the Don angrily. "That is neither true nor fair," replied the skipper sternly. "I have helped you truly and well, and run great risks in bringing you those munitions of war. With that you must be content. As for forsaking you, you know in your heart, through my help and the counsel you have received from my young companion here, you never stood in a better position for dealing a death-blow at your rival's position. Is that the truth, or is it not?"

"Ah!" cried the Don passionately, evading the question. "When your help means so much you give me empty words."

"That is no answer, sir," replied the skipper. "Is what I have said the truth, or is it not?"

Don Ramon turned upon him furiously, his eyes flashing and his hands clenched; but as he met the Englishman's stern questioning eyes he stopped short, fixed by them, as it were, and then tossing his open hands in the air with a gesture which seemed to say, There, I surrender! his angry countenance softened, and he supported himself by taking hold of the pommel of his saddle.

"Yes," he said wearily, "of course it is the truth. You always were the man in whom I could trust, and I suppose you are right. Forgive me for being so exacting. But, captain, I have so much at stake."

"Then trust to the strength of your cause, your position, and the bravery of your people. But I am not going to forsake you, Ramon," continued the skipper, in a graver and softer tone, "and I will tell you this; if the day goes against you, the schooner will be lying a few hundred yards from shore with her boats ready to take off you and as many of your friends as you wish to bring. I will do that at any risk, but I can do no more."

Don Ramon was silent for a few moments, before repeating the captain's last words slowly. Then, after a pause—

"It may be different," he said, "but if matters are as bad as that, it will be because I have fired my last shot, and Villarayo has found that another lover of his country is in his way no more. No, Captain Reed, I shall not have to put your hospitality to the test. I could not escape, and leave those who have been fighting for me to the death. There," he added quickly, completely changing his tone, "I do not mean to die; I mean to win. Forgive me once again. You will after your fashion shake hands?"

"With all my heart," cried the skipper, stretching out both his, which were eagerly caught and raised quickly to the Spaniard's lips.

"Thank you," he cried, "I am a man once more. Just now I talked like a disappointed woman who could not have her way.—What does that mean?" he said sharply as there was a shout from the distance.

"People coming down the pass," cried Fitz excitedly, and there was the report of a rifle which ran reverberating with many echoes along the rocks.

Before the sounds had ceased Don Ramon had sprung upon his mule, to turn smiling with a comprehensive wave of his hand to the trio, and then cantered off amongst the rugged stones, while they watched him till he reached the battery of field-pieces and sprang off to throw the rein to one of his men.

"That shot was the opening of the ball," said the skipper. "Now, my lads, back aboard the schooner, to make our arrangements, Poole, for keeping my word with the Don if he and his people have to run."

"No!" burst out both the boys in a breath.

"No?" cried the skipper good-humouredly. "What do you mean? This isn't going to be a show. You don't want to stop and see the fight?"

"Not want to stop and see it?" cried Fitz excitedly.

"Well, I am not fond of fighting, father," said Poole, "but I do. I want to see Don Ramon win."

"Humph!" grunted the skipper. "Well, you must be disappointed. As for you, Mr Burnett, the sooner you are out of reach of bullets the better."

"Well," cried Fitz, "I like that—coming from the skipper of a trading schooner! Do you know what I am?"

"Of course," was the answer, with a smile.

"It doesn't seem like it," cried Fitz. "I know I am almost a boy still— Don't laugh, Poole!" he added sharply, with a stamp of the foot—"Well, quite a boy; but young as I am, I am a naval officer, and I was never taught that it was my duty to run away if ever I came under fire."

"It's the safest way," said the skipper mockingly. "'He who fights and runs away, will live to fight another day.' That's it, isn't it?"

"I suppose so," said Fitz, getting on his stilts—"to be laughed at for a coward as long as he lives. Look here, Captain Reed, I am your prisoner, but you are not my captain, and I mean to stop and see this fight. Why, I must. I shall have to tell. Captain Glossop all about this some day, and I should look well if I owned that I had run away.—But you don't mean it, sir. It's all nonsense to talk of being in danger up here, all this distance off. Yes, he is joking, isn't he, Poole?"

"Well, there's not much joke about it, my lad," said the skipper gravely. "I must own that I don't want to go away myself. Seems to me that what we ought to do is to hurry back to where the women are, get a good supply of linen and bandages from them, and muster some bearers for— Yes, the firing is going on, and I don't suppose that it will be long before some poor fellows will be falling out and crawling back to the rear."

"Yes," said Fitz eagerly; "I never thought of that. Come on, then, and let's make haste so as to get back in time."

The skipper nodded, and they hurried away, but had very little distance to go, for the sound of the firing was bringing the curious from out of the town, and it was not long before they had been furnished with the material for binding up wounds, and better still, with a doctor, who joined hands with them at once in making the rough ambulance arrangements.

Within half-an-hour they were back at the spot where the interview with Don Ramon had taken place, to find that which their ears had prepared them for, the rattle of musketry going steadily on as the enemy advanced, while they were just in time for the sharp dull thud and echoing roar of the first field-piece, whose shell was seen to burst and send up its puff of smoke far along the rugged valley.

This checked the advance for some minutes, scattering the enemy in all directions, but it was plain to the lookers-on from their post of observation, that they were being rallied, and the speaking out of the second gun from the battery plainly told that this was the case.

What followed in the next two hours was a scene of confusion and excitement far up the valley, and of quiet steady firing from the battery, whose shells left little for Don Ramon's advance posts to do.

They lay low in their shelters, and built up rifle-screens, hastily made, firing as they had a chance, but their work only helped to keep the enemy back. It was to the guns that Don Ramon owed his success. There was no lack of bravery on the part of the enemy's officers, for they exposed themselves recklessly, rallying their men again and again, and gradually getting them nearer and nearer to those who served the guns.

But the rifle-firing was wild, and not a man among the gunners went down, or was startled from his task of loading and laying the sheltered pieces. All the same the enemy advanced, the rugged pass affording them plenty of places that they could hold, and at the end of three hours they had made such progress that matters were beginning to look serious for the defenders of Velova, and the time had come when it was evident to the watchers that Don Ramon was making ready to retire his guns to his next defence, for the teams of mules were hurried up and placed in a hollow beyond the reach of the enemy's rifles; and now too it was seen plainly enough that Villarayo or his captains were preparing for a rush to capture the guns, and in the excitement the skipper forgot about all risks to him and his, and proposed that they should hurry to a spot higher up one side of the pass and fifty yards nearer to the battery.

This proved to be an admirable point of vantage, and enlightened the lookers-on to far more than they had been before, for they were startled to see how much greater was the number of the attacking force than they had believed.

The enemy were in two bodies, gathered-together and lying down on the opposite sides of the pass, and the lads had hardly raised their heads above the shelter of some stones when they saw that the order had been given for the advance, and the men were springing to their feet.

"I must go and warn him," cried the skipper, beneath his breath, "or he will lose his guns; and then—"

He said no more, but stood spellbound like his young companions at what was taking place, for Don Ramon was better supplied with information than he had believed, and as the attacking forces of the enemy sprang up, he found that the direction of the battery's fire had been altered to left and right, and the attacking forces had barely commenced their crowded charge when the six pieces burst forth almost together with such a hurricane of grape that a way was torn through each rough column and the fight was over, the smoke from the discharge as it rose showing the enemy scattered and in full flight, the steep sides of the little valley littered with the wounded, and more and more faltering behind and dropping as their comrades fled.

"*Viva!*" shouted the skipper, with all his might; but it was a feeble sound compared with the roar of voices which rose from the battery and beyond, while it only needed the rifle-shots of those lying in the shelters higher up the pass, and a shell dropped here and there till the full range of the field-pieces had been reached, to complete Villarayo's discomfiture for that day at least.

"Now," said the skipper quietly, "we must leave the succour of the wounded to Ramon's own people. I am sick of all this. Let's get back on board the schooner."

It was about an hour afterwards that Poole went to his father on the deck of the *Teal*.

"Oughtn't we to have stopped a little longer," he said, "and tried to be of some help?"

"I should have liked to, my boy," said the skipper sadly, "but I didn't want you and young Burnett to see what was bound to follow. The rougher portion of Don Ramon's followers have not the same ideas of mercy to a fallen enemy that belong to a European mind, and so I came away."

Chapter Thirty Seven
Political questions

Happily for them, the boys saw little more of the horrors of the petty war. Aboard the schooner what met their eyes were the triumphs of peace. The next day flags were flying, bells ringing, guns firing, and the whole of the inhabitants of the town were marching in procession and shouting *Vivas*.

Crowds gathered upon the shore nearest to where the schooner was moored, to shout themselves hoarse; and not content with this, they crowded into boats to row out round the little English vessel and shout themselves hoarser there, many of the boats containing women, who threw flowers which floated round.

"I am getting rather tired of this," said Fitz, at last. "I suppose it's very nice to them, and they feel very grateful to your father for bringing the guns and ammunition to beat off this other President fellow; but keeping on with all this seems so babyish and silly. Why can't they say, 'Thank Heaven!' and have done with it?"

"Because they are what they are," said Poole, half contemptuously. "Why, they must have been spoiling their gardens to bring all these flowers. They are no use to us. I should call that boat alongside—that big one with the flag up and all those well-dressed women on board."

"No, don't!" cried Fitz excitedly. "Why, they'd come and shout more than ever, and begin singing again. What's the good of doing that?"

"I'll tell you," said Poole; "and I should tell them that it would be a deal more sensible to go back and fetch us a boat-load of fruit and vegetables, and fowls and eggs."

"Ah, to be sure," cried Fitz. "It would please old Andy too; but—but look there; they are more sensible than you think for."

"Well done!" cried Poole, "Why, they couldn't have heard what I said."

"No," said Fitz, "and if they had there wouldn't have been time. You must have telegraphed your thoughts. Why, there are two boat-loads."

"Three," said Poole.

And he was right, and a few minutes later that number of good-sized market-boats were close alongside, their owners apparently bent upon doing a good stroke of trade in the edibles most welcome to a ship's crew after a long voyage.

"Well, boys," said the skipper, joining them, "who's going to do the marketing? You, Poole, or I?"

"Oh, you had better do it, father. I should be too extravagant."

"No," said the skipper quietly. "The owners of the *Teal* and I don't wish to be stingy. The lads have done their work well, and I should like them to have a bit of a feast and a holiday now. Here, boatswain, pass the word for the cook and get half-a-dozen men to help. We must store up all that will keep. Here, Burgess, we may as well fill a chicken-coop or two."

"Humph!" grunted the mate surlily. "Want to turn my deck into a shop?"

"No," said the skipper good-humouredly, "but I want to have the cabin-table with something better on it to eat than we have had lately. I am afraid we shall be having Mr Burnett here so disgusted with the prog that he will be wanting to go ashore, and won't come back."

"All right," growled the mate, and he walked away with the skipper, to follow out the orders he had received.

"I say," said Fitz, "I wonder your father puts up with so much of the mate's insolence. Any one would think that Burgess was the skipper; he puts on such airs."

"Oh, the dad knows him by heart. It is only his way. He always seems surly like that, but he'd do anything for father; and see what a seaman he is. Here, I say, let's have some of those bananas. They do look prime."

"Yes," said Fitz; "I like bananas. I should like that big golden bunch."

"Why, there must be a quarter of a hundredweight," said Poole.

"Do you think they'll take my English money?"

"Trust them!" said Poole. "I never met anybody yet who wouldn't."

They made a sign to a swarthy-looking fellow in the stern of the nearest boat, and Fitz pointed to the great golden bunch.

"How much?" he said.

The man grinned, seized the bunch with his boat-hook, passed it over the bulwark, and let it fall upon the deck, hooked up another quickly, treated that the same, and was repeating the process, when Poole shouted at him to stop.

"Hold hard!" he cried. "I am not going to pay for all these."

But the man paid no heed, but went on tossing in fruit, calling to the lads in Spanish to catch, and *feeding* them, as we say, in a game, with great golden balls in the shape of delicious-looking melons.

"Here, is the fellow mad?" cried Fitz, who, a regular boy once more, enjoyed the fun of catching the beautiful gourds. "We shall have to throw all these back."

"Try one now," said Poole.

"Right," cried Fitz. "Catch, stupid!" And he sent one of the biggest melons back.

The man caught it deftly, and returned it, shouting—

"No, no, no! Don Ramon—Don Ramon!"

Something similar was going on upon the other side of the schooner, where, grinning with delight, the Camel was seizing the poultry handed in, and setting them at liberty upon the deck, while now an explanation followed.

The three boat-loads of provisions were gifts from Don Ramon and his people to those who had helped them in their time of need, while the Don's messengers seemed wild with delight, eagerly pointing out the good qualities of all they had brought, and chattering away as hard as ever they could, or laughing with delight when some active chicken escaped from the hands that held it or took flight when pitched aboard and made its way back to the shore. It was not only the men in the provision-barges that kept up an excited chorus, for they were joined by those in the boats that crowded round, the delivery being accompanied by cheers and the waving of hats and veils, the women's voices rising shrilly in what seemed to be quite a paean of welcome and praise.

"What time would you like dinner, laddies?" came from behind just then, in a familiar voice, and the boys turned sharply round to face the Camel, who seemed to be showing nearly all his teeth after the fashion of one of his namesakes in a good temper. "Ma word, isn't it grand! Joost look! Roast and boiled cheecan and curry; and look at the garden-stuff. I suppose it's all good to eat, but they're throwing in things I never washed nor boiled before. It's grand, laddies—it's grand! Why, ma word! Hark at 'em! Here's another big boat coming, and the skipper will have to give a great dinner, or we shall never get it all eaten."

"No," cried Poole, "it's a big boat with armed men, and—I say, Fitz, this doesn't mean treachery? No, all right; that's Don Ramon coming on board."

The tremendous burst of cheering from every boat endorsed the lad's words, every one standing up shouting and cheering as the President's craft came nearer, threading its way through the crowd of boats, whose occupants seemed to consider that there was not the slightest risk of a capsize into a bay that swarmed with sharks. But thanks to the management of Don Ramon's crew, his barge reached the side of the schooner without causing mishap, and he sprang aboard, a gay-looking object in gold-laced uniform, not to grasp the skipper's extended hand, but to fall upon his neck in silence and with tears in his eyes, while directly afterwards the two lads had to submit to a similar embrace.

"Oh, I say," whispered Fitz, as soon as the President had gone below with the skipper; "isn't it horrid!"

"Yes," said Poole; "I often grumble at what I am, only a sort of apprentice aboard a schooner, though I am better off through the dad being one of the owners than most chaps would be; but one is English, after all."

"Yes," said Fitz, with a sigh of content; "there is no getting over that."

Further conversation was ended by the approach of Burgess, the mate, who at a word from the captain had followed him and the President below, and who now came up to them with a peculiar grim smile about his lips, and the upper part of his face in the clouds, as Poole afterwards expressed it, probably meaning that the mate's brow was wrinkled up into one of his fiercest frowns.

"Here," he growled, "you two young fellows have got to go below."

"Who said so?" cried Fitz. "The skipper?"

"No, the President."

"But what for?" cried the middy.

"Oh, I dunno," replied the mate grimly, and with the smile expanding as he recalled something of which he had been a witness. "I thinks he wants to kiss you both again."

"Then I'll be hanged if I go," cried Fitz; "and that's flat!"

"Haw haw!" came from the mate's lips, evidently meant for a laugh, which made the middy turn upon him fiercely; but there was no vestige of even a smile now as he said gruffly, "Yes, you must both come at once. The Don's waiting to speak, and he said that he wouldn't begin till you were there to hear it too."

"Come on, Burnett," said Poole seriously, and then with his eyes twinkling he added, "You can have a good wash afterwards if he does."

"Oh," cried Fitz, with his face scarlet, "I do hate these people's ways;" and then, in spite of his previous remark about suspension, he followed the skipper's son down into the cabin, with Burgess close behind, to find the President facing the door ready to rise with a dignified smile and point to the locker for the boys to take their seats.

This done, he resumed his own, and proceeded to relate to the skipper as much as he could recall of what had been taking place, the main thing being that Villarayo's large force had completely scattered on its way back through the mountains *en route* to San Cristobal, while Velova and the country round was entirely declaring for the victor, whose position was but for one thing quite safe.

"Then," said the skipper, as the President ceased, "you feel that if you marched for San Cristobal you would gain an easy victory there?"

"I know my people so well, sir," replied the President proudly, "that I can say there will be no victory and no fight. Villarayo would not get fifty men to stand by him, and he would either make for the mountains or come to meet me, and throw himself upon my mercy. And all this is through you. How great—how great the English people are!"

Poole jumped and clapped his right hand upon his left arm, while Fitz turned scarlet as he looked an apology, for as the middy heard the President's last words and saw him rise, a thrill of horror had run through him, and he had thrown out one hand, to give his companion a most painful pinch.

But the President resumed his seat, and feeling that there was for the moment nothing to mind, the boy grew calm.

"Ah," said the skipper gravely. "Then but for one thing, Don Ramon, you feel now that you can hold your own."

"Yes," was the reply bitterly. "But I shall not feel secure while that gunboat commands these seas. It seems absurd, ridiculous, that that small armour-plated vessel with its one great gun should have such power; but yet after all it is not absurd. It is to this little State what your grand navy is to your empire and the world. While that gunboat commands our bays I cannot feel safe."

"But you don't know yet," said the skipper quietly. "How will it be when her captain hears of Villarayo's defeat? He may declare for you."

"No," said the President. "That is what all my friends say. He is Villarayo's cousin, and has always been my greatest enemy. He knows too that my first act would be to deprive him of his command."

"Then why do so?" said the skipper. "He need be your enemy no longer. Make him your friend."

"Impossible! I know him of old as a man I could not trust. The moment he hears of the defeat he will be sending messages to Villarayo bidding him fortify San Cristobal and gather his people there, while at any hour we may expect to see him steaming into this bay. That is the main reason of my coming to tell you now to be on your guard, and that I have been having the guns you brought mounted in a new earthwork on the point yonder, close to the sea."

"Well done!" cried the captain enthusiastically. "That was brave and thoughtful of you, Don Ramon," and he held out his hand. "Why, you are quite an engineer. Then you did not mean to forsake your friend?"

"Forsake him!" said the Don reproachfully, and he frowned. But it was for a moment only. "Ah," he continued, "if you had only brought me over such a gunboat as that which holds me down, commanded by such a man as you, how changed my position would be!"

"Yes," said the skipper quietly. "But I did not; and I had hard work to bring you what I did, eh, Mr Burnett? The British Government did not much approve of what it called my filibustering expedition, Don."

"The British Government does not know Villarayo, sir, and it does not know me."

"That's the evil of it, sir," replied the captain. "Unfortunately the British Government recognises Villarayo as the President of the State, and you only as the head of a revolution; but once you are the accepted head of the people, the leader of what is good and right, Master Villarayo's star will set; and that is bound to come."

"Yes," said Don Ramon proudly; "that is bound to come in the future, if I live. For all that is good and right in this little State is on my side. But there is the gunboat, captain."

"Yes," was the reply; "there is the gunboat, and as to my schooner, if I ventured everything on your side at sea, with her steaming power she would have me completely at her mercy, and with one shot send me to the bottom like a stone."

"Yes, I know," said the Don, "as far as strength goes you would be like an infant fighting against a giant. But you English are clever. It was due to the bright thought of this young officer here that I was able to turn the tables upon Villarayo."

The blood flushed to Fitz's forehead again—for he was, as Poole afterwards told him, a beggar to blush—and he gave a sudden start which made Poole move a little farther off to avoid a pinch.

"What say you, Don Burnett?"

If possible Fitz's face grew a deeper scarlet.

"Have you another such lightning stroke of genius to propose?"

"No, sir," said the boy sharply; "and if I had I must recollect that I am a neutral, a prisoner here, and it is my duty to hold my tongue."

"Ah, yes," said the Don, frowning a little; "I had forgotten. You are in the Government's service, and my good friend Captain Reed has told me how you happen to be here. But if the British Government knew exactly how things were, they would honour you for the way in which you have helped me on towards success."

"Yes, sir, no doubt," said the lad frankly; "but the British Government doesn't know what you say, and it doesn't know me; but Captain Glossop does. He's my government, sir, and it will be bad enough when I meet him, as it is. What will he say when he knows I've been fighting for the people in the schooner I came to take?"

"Hah!" said the President thoughtfully, and he was silent for a few moments. Then rising he turned to the skipper. "I must go back, Captain Reed," he said, "for there is much to do. But I have warned you of the peril in which you stand. You will help me, I know, if you can; but you must not have your brave little schooner sunk, and I know you will do what is best. Fate may favour us still more, and I shall go on in that hope."

Then without another word he strode out of the cabin, and went down into his barge amidst a storm of cheers and wavings of scarves and flags, while those on deck watched him threading his way towards the little fort.

"He's the best Spaniard I ever met, Burgess," said the skipper.

"Yes," said the mate. "He isn't a bad sort for his kind. If it was not for the poor beggars on board, who naturally enough all want to live, I should like to go some night and put a keg of powder aboard that gunboat, and send her to the bottom."

"Ah, but then you'd be doing wrong," said the skipper.

"Well, I said so, didn't I? I shouldn't like to have it on my conscience that I'd killed a couple of score fellow-creatures like that."

"Of course not; but that isn't what I mean. That gunboat's too valuable to sink, and, as you heard the Don say, the man who holds command of that vessel has the two cities at his mercy."

"Yes, I heard," said Burgess; "and t'other side's got it."

"That's right," said the skipper; "and if we could make the change—"

"Yes," said Burgess; "but it seems to me we can't."

"It seems to me we can't. It seems to me we can't," said Poole, repeating the mate's words, as the two lads stood alone watching the cheering people in the boats.

"Well," cried Fitz pettishly, "what's the good of keeping on saying that?"

"None at all. But don't you wish we could?"

"No, I don't, and I'd thank you not to talk to me like that. It's like playing at trying to tempt a fellow situated as I am. Bother the gunboat and both the Dons! I wish I were back in the old *Tonans* again."

"I don't believe you," said Poole, laughing. "You're having ten times as much fun and excitement out here. I say," he added, with a sniff, "I can smell something good."

And strangely enough the next minute the Camel came smiling up to them.

"I say, laddies," he said, "joost come for'ard as far as the galley. I don't ask ye to come in, for, ma wud, she is hot! But just come and take a sniff as ye gang by. There's a dinner cooking as would have satisfied the Don. I thot he meant to stay, but, puir chiel, I suppose he dinna ken what's good."

Chapter Thirty Eight
A night's excitement

Every one seemed bent on celebrating that day as a festival. The fight was a victory, and all were rejoicing in a noisy holiday, while for some hours the crew of the schooner had their turn.

Not all, for after a few words with the skipper, the two lads went aloft with the binocular to keep a sharp look-out seaward, and more especially at the two headlands at the entrance to the bay, which they watched in the full expectation of seeing the grim grey nose of the gunboat peering round, prior to her showing her whole length and her swarthy plume of smoke.

Arrangements had been made below as well, and the schooner was swinging to a big buoy—head to sea, the sails ready for running up or dropping down from her thin yards.

"A nice land wind," the skipper had said, "and if she came it would not be long before we were on equal terms with her."

"But it won't last," said Burgess gruffly. "It'll either drop to a dead calm at sundown, or swing round and be dead ahead."

"Well, I don't mind the last," replied the captain, "but a dead calm would be dangerous, and sets me thinking whether it wouldn't be better to be off at once."

"Well, that depends on you," said the mate. "If it was me I should stop till night and chance it. But where do you mean to go? Right away home?"

"I don't know yet," was the reply. "For some reasons I should like to stop and see Don Ramon right out of his difficulties. Besides, I have a little business to transact with him that may take days. No, I shan't go off yet. I may stay here for months, working for Don Ramon. It all depends."

"Very well," said the mate coolly, as if it did not matter in the slightest degree to him so long as he was at sea.

From time to time the skipper in his walk up and down the deck paused to look up inquiringly, but always to be met with a quiet shake of the head, and go on again.

But about half-an-hour before sundown, just when festivities were at their height on shore, and the men were for the most part idling about, leaning over the bulwarks and watching as much of the proceedings as they could see, the two lads, after an hour's rest below, having returned to their look-out, Fitz suddenly exclaimed—

"There she is! But she doesn't look grey."

"No," replied Poole eagerly. "What there is of her looks as if turned to gold." Then loudly, "Sail ho!" though there was not a sail in sight, only the steamer's funnel slowly coming into sight from behind one headland and beginning to show her smoke.

All was activity now, the men starting to their different places at the bulwarks, and eagerly listening to the skipper's "Where away?"

"Coming round the south headland," replied Poole.

"That's right," said the skipper. "I can see her now."

"Well?" said Burgess.

"I shan't move yet. It will be pitch-dark in less than an hour. We can see her plainly enough with the open sea beyond her, but like as not they can't see us, lying close up here under the land. The chances are that they won't see us at all, and then we can run out in the darkness; and I suppose you will have no difficulty in avoiding the rocks?"

"Oh, I don't know," said the mate coolly. "Like as not I may run spang on to them in the dark. I shan't, of course, if I can help it."

"No," said the skipper dryly; "I suppose not."

Their task ended, the boys slid down to the deck once more, and somehow the thought of his anomalous position on board the schooner did not trouble the middy for the time being, for he was seaman enough to be intensely interested in their position, and as eager as Poole for their escape.

"Do you think the sun's going down as quickly as usual?" he said suddenly; and his companion laughed.

"What's that for?" said Fitz. "Did I say something comic?"

"Comic or stupid, whichever you like."

"Bah!" ejaculated Fitz angrily, feeling more annoyed with himself than with Poole.

"Why of course she is going down at her usual rate."

"Sun's a he," said Fitz. "It isn't the moon."

"Thankye. You have grown wise," replied Poole sarcastically. "Do you know, I should have almost known that myself. But bother all this! I want to see the canvas shaken out ready for making a start."

"Very stupid too," said Fitz.

"Why?"

"Because the people on board the gunboat mayn't see us now, with our bare poles; and even if they could make us out they wouldn't be able to distinguish us from the other craft lying close in shore."

"Right," said Poole sharply. "I was getting impatient. I suppose we are going to run out through the darkness, same as we did before."

"I hope not," said Fitz meaningly. "Once was enough for a scrape like that."

Poole grunted, with agreement in his cones, and then they leaned over the bulwarks together forward, following the example of most of the men, who were just as keenly on the look-out, and growing as excited in the expectation of the coming adventure, all but two, who, in obedience to a growl from the mate, lowered down the dinghy and then pulled her hand-over-hand by the mooring-cable to where it was made fast to the big ring in the buoy; and there they held on, ready to slip the minute the order was given from the deck.

Meanwhile the rejoicings were going on ashore, no one so far having become aware of the approach of the enemy, till she was well clear of the headland, with her smoke floating out like an orange-plume upon a golden sky.

"There's the signal," cried Fitz suddenly, as a ball of smoke darted out from the front of the fort, followed by a dull thud.

"Hah!" said Poole. "That's like the snap of a mongrel pup. By and by perhaps we shall hear the gunboat speak with a big bark like a mastiff. I wonder whether they will make us out."

"So do I," said Fitz.

"It will be easy enough to sneak off if they don't."

"Don't say sneak," said Fitz.

"Why?"

"It sounds so cowardly."

"Well, this isn't the *Tonans*. The *Teal* was made to sail, not to fight."

"Yes, of course," said Fitz; "but I don't like it all the same."

"All right, then, I won't say it again. I wonder where the dad will make for."

"Well, that will depend on whether the gunboat sights us. I say, does it make you feel excited?"

"Yes, awfully. I seem to want to be doing something."

"So do I," said Fitz, "instead of watching the sun go down so slowly."

"Look at the gunboat, then. She's not moving slowly. My word, she is slipping through the water! Why, she's bound to see us if it don't soon get dark."

The boys lapsed into silence, and as they ceased speaking they were almost startled by the change that had taken place on shore.

The shouting and singing had ceased; there was no sound of music, and the bells had left off their clangour; while in place there came a low, dull, murmurous roar as of surf beating upon some rocky coast, a strange mingling of voices, hurrying foot-steps, indescribable, indistinct, and yet apparently expressive of excitement and the change from joy to fear.

"It has upset them pretty well," said Poole. "Why, I did hear that they were going in for fireworks as soon as it was dark, and they fired that gun like a challenge. I shouldn't wonder if they have fireworks of a different kind to what they expect."

"Yes," said Fitz excitedly. "The gunboat will begin firing shells perhaps, and set fire to the town."

"Bad luck to them if they do," cried Poole earnestly, "for it's a beautiful old place with its groves and gardens. Here, I say, Burnett, I wish this wretched little schooner were your *Tonans*, and we were going to fight for poor old Don Ramon. Don't you?"

"There's the sun beginning to go down behind the mountain," said Fitz, evading the question. "I say, how long will it be before it's dark?"

"Oh, you know as near as I do. Very soon, and the sooner the better. Oh, I say, she must see us. She's heading round and coming straight in."

"For us or the fort?"

"Both," said Poole emphatically.

And then they waited, fancying as the last gleam of the orange sun sank out of sight that they could hear the men breathing hard with suppressed excitement, as they stood there with their sleeves rolled up, waiting for the first order which should mean hauling away at ropes and the schooner beginning to glide towards the great buoy, slackening the cable for the men in the dinghy to cast-off.

"Here, look at that!" cried Fitz excitedly, unconsciously identifying himself more and more with the crew.

"What's the matter?" said Poole.

"Wet your hand, and hold it up."

"Right," said Poole; "and so was old Burgess. I don't believe there's a man at sea knows more about the wind than he does. Half-an-hour ago, dead to sea; now right ashore."

"Stand by, my lads," growled the boatswain in response to a word from the mate; and a deep low sigh seemed to run all across the deck, as to a man the crew drew in a deep long breath, while with the light rapidly dying out, and the golden tips of the mountains turning purple and then grey, the first order was given, a couple of staysails ran with jigging motion up to their full length, and a chirruping, creaking sound was heard as the men began to haul upon the yard of the mainsail.

"Ah!" sighed Fitz. "We are beginning to move."

As he spoke the man at the wheel began to run the spokes quickly through his hands, with the result that to all appearance the men in the dinghy, and the buoy, appeared to be coming close under their quarter. Then there was a splash, the dinghy grated against the side, and one of its occupants climbed aboard with the painter, closely followed by the other, the first man running aft with the rope, to make it fast to the ring-bolt astern, while the stops of the capstan rattled as the cast-off cable began to come inboard.

"Oh, it will be dark directly," said Poole excitedly, "and I don't believe they can see us now."

The enemy would have required keen eyes and good glasses on board the gunboat to have made them out, for as the sails filled, the schooner careened over and began to glide slowly along the shore as if making for the fort, which she passed and left about a quarter of a mile behind, before she was thrown up into the wind to go upon the other tack, spreading more and more canvas and increasing her speed, as the gunboat, now invisible save for a couple of lights which were hoisted up, came dead on for the town, nearing them fast, and calling for all the mate's seamanship to get the schooner during one of her tacks well out of the heavy craft's course, and leaving her to glide by; though as the darkness increased and they were evidently unseen, this became comparatively easy, for the war-vessel's two lights shone out brighter and brighter at every one of the schooner's tacks.

But they were anxious times, and Fitz's heart beat fast during the most vital reach, when it seemed to him as they were gliding by the gunboat's bows that they must be seen, even as he could now make out a few sparks rising from time to time from the great funnel, to be smothered in the rolling smoke.

But the next minute they were far away, and as they tacked it was this time so that they passed well abaft under the enemy's stern.

"Ah," said a voice close to them; and as they looked round sharply it was to see the skipper close at hand. "There, boys," he said, "that was running it pretty close. They can't have been keeping a very good look-out aboard that craft. It was much nearer than I liked. — Ah, I wonder how poor Don Ramon will get on."

That finished the excitement for the night, for the next hours were passed in a monotonous tacking to and fro, making longer and longer reaches as they got farther out to sea; but they looked shoreward in vain for the flashes of guns and the deep thunderous roar of the big breech-loading cannon. But the sighing of the wind in the rigging and the lapping of water against the schooner's bows were the only sounds that greeted them in the soft tropic night.

Chapter Thirty Nine
"Never say die!"

As long as the excitement kept up, Fitz paced the deck with Poole, but for two or three nights past regular sleep and his eyelids had been at odds. The consequence was that all at once in the silence and darkness, when there was nothing to take his attention, he became very silent, walking up and down the deck mechanically with his companion to keep himself awake, and a short time afterwards for no reason at all that he was aware of, but because one leg went before the other automatically, his will having ceased to convey its desires to these his supporters, and long after Poole had ceased talking to him, he suddenly gave a violent lurch, driving Poole, who was in a similar condition, sideways, and if it had not been for the bulwark close at hand they would both have gone down like skittles. For they were both fast asleep, sound as a top, fast as a church, but on the instant wide-awake and angry.

"What did you do that for?" cried Fitz fiercely. "I didn't," cried Poole angrily. "You threw yourself at me."

"That I didn't! How could I?"

"How should I know? But you've made a great bruise on my elbow; I know that."

"Quiet! quiet!" said the mate, in a deep low growl. "Do you want to bring the gunboat down on us, shouting like that?" And he seemed to loom up upon them out of the darkness.

"Well, but he—" began Fitz.

"Quiet, I tell you! I have been watching you lads these last ten minutes. You've both been rolling about all over the deck, and I expected to see you go down on your noses every moment. Snoring too, one of you was."

"Well, that wasn't I, I'm sure," cried Fitz shortly.

"Oh, are you?" said the mate. "Well, I'm not. There, you are no use up here, either of you. Go down and tumble into your bunks at once."

"But—" began Poole.

"You heard what I said, my lad. Go and have a good long snooze, and don't make a stupid of yourself, bandying words like that. The watch have all been laughing at you both. Now then, clear the deck. I am going to keep things quiet."

The officer in charge of a deck is "monarch of all he surveys," like Robinson Crusoe of old, according to the poem, and as "his right there is none to dispute," both lads yielded to Burgesses sway, went down to their berths, rolled in just as they were, and the next minute were fast asleep, breathing more loudly than would have been pleasant to any neighbour. But there was none.

Their sleep was very short but very solid all the same, and they were ready to spring up wide-awake and hurry on deck just before sunrise, upon hearing the trampling overhead of the watch going through the manoeuvres known as 'bout ship, and then proceeding to obey orders angrily shouted at them by the mate, whose loud voice betokened that he was in an unusual state of excitement, for his words were emphatic in the extreme as he addressed the men after the cry of "all hands on deck," in a way which suggested to one who overheard that they were a gang of the laziest, slowest slovens that ever handled a rope.

"Here, rouse up!" cried Poole. "Hear him?"

"Hear him? Yes. What's the matter?"

"I dunno. Any one would think that we were going to run the gunboat down."

The lads ran up on deck, and stared in wonder, for instead of the catastrophe that Poole had verbally portrayed, the reverse seemed the probability. In fact, instead of their tacking against the adverse wind having carried them well out to sea, the progress they had made in a direct line was comparatively small, and to the dismay of both the sleepers as they looked over the stern, there was the gunboat not three miles away, foaming down after them under a full pressure of steam.

"How do you account for this?" said Fitz.

"I dunno, unless they went right in, got to know that we had just left, and came after us full chase."

It was the idea of the moment, and to use the familiar saying, Poole had hit the right nail on the head. It was morning, and Nature's signals were in the east, announcing that the sun was coming up full speed, while the former tactics of tacking against the freshening wind had to be set aside at once, for it was evidently only a question of an hour before the gunboat would be within easy range, and what she might do in the interim was simply doubtful. But the skipper and his mate were hard at work; the course had been altered for another run southward, close along the coast; studding-sail booms were being run out from the yards ready for the white sails to be hoisted; and a trial of speed was being prepared between canvas and steam, proof of which was given from the gunboat by the dense clouds of black smoke rolling out of the funnel and showing how hard the stokers were at work.

It was a busy time then; sail after sail filled out till the schooner showed as a cloud of canvas gilded by the rising sun, while she literally skimmed through the water dangerously near to a rocky coast.

But as the sun rose higher that danger passed away, for as if by magic the wind dropped, leaving the sails flapping, the graceful vessel no longer dipping her cut-water low-down into the surface and covering the deck with spray.

Poole looked at his father and drew his breath hard, for he saw too plainly the peril in which they stood. They were still gliding gently through the water, but more slowly each minute, and riding now upon an even keel, while the gunboat astern was tearing along, literally ploughing her way, and sending a diverging foam-covered wave to starboard and port.

"Pretty well all over, Burgess," he said, in a low hoarse voice, and Fitz stole out his hand to grip Poole's wrist and give a warm sympathetic pressure; and he did not draw it back, but stood holding on, listening the while to the mate's slow, thoughtful reply.

"I don't know yet," said the latter, half closing his eyes and looking towards the west. "The winds play rum games here sometimes, and you hardly know where you are. They may go through one of their manoeuvres now. This is just about the time, and I shouldn't wonder if we had a sharp breeze from the west again, same as we did yesterday and the day before."

"No such luck," said the skipper bitterly. "It won't be the wind off shore; it will be the *Teal* on. You'll have to make for the first opening you see as soon as there's wind enough, and run her right in. Don't hesitate a moment, Burgess; run her right ashore, and then we must do the best we can with the boats, or swim for it."

"Run her right ashore!" said the mate grimly.

"Yes—so that she's a hopeless wreck, impossible to get off."

"Seems a pity," growled the mate; and his words found an echo in Fitz Burnett's breast.

"Yes, but it would be a greater pity for my beautiful little schooner to fall a prize to that wretched tea-kettle there; and I won't have my lads treated as prisoners. I'd sooner we all had to take to the woods."

"All right, sir. You're skipper; I'm mate. It's you to give orders, me to carry them out. But I'm beginning to think that they'll have us before we get the wind. You see, it's nearly calm."

"Yes," said the skipper, "I see; and I wonder they haven't begun firing before."

He walked right aft with the mate, leaving the lads alone, with Poole looking five years older, so blank and drawn was his face. But it brightened directly, as he felt the warm grip of the young middy's hand, and heard his words.

"Oh, Poole, old chap," Fitz half whispered, after a glance round to see if they were likely to be overheard, but only to find that every seaman was either intent upon his duty or watching the enemy in expectation of a first shell or ball from the heavy gun. "Oh, Poole, old chap," he said again, "I am sorry—I am indeed!"

"Sorry?" said Poole quietly. "Yes; for you've all been very kind to me."

"Well, I am glad to hear you say so, for I tried to be, and the dad liked you because you were such a cocky, plucky little chap. But there: it's no use to cry over spilt milk. I suppose it isn't spilt yet, though," he added, with a little laugh; "but the jug will be cracked directly, and away it will all go into the sea. But I say, can you swim?"

"Oh yes, I can swim. I learnt when I was a cadet."

"That's right; and if we can't get off in one of the boats you keep close alongside of me—I know the dad will like me to stick with you—and I'll get a life-belt, or one of the buoys, and we will share it together, one to rest in it while the other swims and tows. We'll get to shore somehow, never fear—the whole lot of us, I expect, for the lads will stand by, I am sure."

"Yes, yes," said Fitz, glancing round over the sunlit sea. "But what about the sharks?"

"Oh!" ejaculated Poole involuntarily, and he changed colour.

It was just as the skipper and mate came walking sharply forward again.

"There!" cried the latter triumphantly. "What did I say?"

"Splendid!" cried the skipper. "But will it last?"

"It did yesterday. Why not to-day?" cried the mate fiercely.

For the wind had suddenly come in a sharp gust which filled the sails, making several of them snap with a loud report, laid the schooner on her beam-ends, and sent her rushing through the water for some hundred yards, making it come foaming up through the scuppers in fountains, to flood the deck, before she was eased off by the man at the wheel and rose again.

But directly after the calm asserted itself once more; the greater part of the sea was like a mirror, with only cat's-paws here and there; and the gunboat came pounding on as stern as fate.

"All right," said the mate cheerily; "it's coming again," and he ran to the man at the wheel.

"Stand by, my lads," cried the skipper, "ready to let go those stuns'ls. We mustn't be taken again like that."

The men rushed to the sheets, and when the wind came again, it came to stay, striking the heavily-canvassed schooner a tremendous blow, to which she only careened over, and not a drop of water came on board, for the light studding-sails were let go to begin flapping and snapping like whip-thongs until the violence of the gust had passed; and by that time the men were busy reducing the canvas, and the schooner was flying through the water like the winning yacht in a race.

"Never say die!" cried Poole, with a laugh. "We are going faster than the gunboat now."

"Yes," replied Fitz thoughtfully; "but she has the command of the sea, and can cut us off."

"As long as her coals last," said Poole, "and they're burning them pretty fast over this. I'd give something to guess what old Burgess means to do. He's got something in his head that I don't believe my father knows."

"Oh, he'd be sure to know," said Fitz, whose hopes were rising fast, his sympathies being entirely now with those who had proved such friends.

"Oh, no, he wouldn't. Old Burgess can be as mute as a fish when he likes, and there's nothing pleases him better than taking people by surprise."

"But what can he do more than race right away?"

"Well, I'll tell you, Burnett, old chap. It's no use for him to think of racing right away. What he'll do is this. I have said something of the kind to you before. He knows this coast just like his ABC, the bays and rivers and backwaters and crannies all amongst the rocks. He's spent days and days out in a boat sounding and making rough charts; and what he'll do, I feel certain, is this—make for some passage in amongst the rocks where he can take the little *Teal*, run right in where the gunboat dare not come, and stay there till she's tired out."

"But then they'll sink us with their gun."

"Oh no; he'll get her right into shelter where she can't be seen."

"Then the gunboat captain will send after us with his armed boats and board us where we lie."

"Let him," said Poole grimly. "That's just what old Burgess and all the lads would like. Mr Don what's-his-name and his men would find they had such a hedgehog to tackle that they'd soon go back again faster than they came."

"Do you think your father would do that?" said Fitz, after a glance aft, to note that they were leaving the gunboat steadily behind.

"Why, of course," cried Poole. "But it's resisting a man-of-war."

"Well, what of that? We didn't boggle about doing it with one of the Queen's ships, so you don't suppose that dad would make much bones about refusing to strike to a mongrel Spaniard like that?"

Fitz was silent, and somehow then in a whirl of exciting thoughts it did not seem so very serious a thing, but brought up passages he had read in old naval books of cutting-out expeditions and brave fightings against heavy odds. And then as they went flying through the water the exhilaration of the chase took up all his attention, and the conversation dropped out of his mental sight, for it lasted hours, and during all that time the *Teal* skimmed along, following out her old tactics close to a lovely surf-beaten shore, passing bluff and valley openings where there were evidently streams pouring out from the mountains to discolour the silver sea, and offering, as the middy thought, endless havens of refuge, till about the hottest part of the day, when the pitch seemed to be seething in the seams. All at once the captain, after a short conversation with his mate, went forward with a couple of men, and Burgess went himself to take the wheel. "Now then," said Poole, "what did I tell you?"

"Do you think we are going to turn in here?"

"That's just what I do think. Here, do you want a job?"

"Yes—no—of course—What do you want me to do?"

"Go and tell the Camel to get the oiliest breakfast he can all ready, for we are half-starved."

"Don't talk nonsense!" cried Fitz angrily. "What do you mean?"

"Mean? Why, look! Old Grumbo's running us right in for the line of surf below that bluff. There's an opening there, I'll be bound. Look at the coloured water too. There must be a good-sized river coming down from somewhere. Oh, the old fox! He knows what he's about. There's one of his holes in there, and the hunt is nearly up. I mean, the little *Teal* is going in to find her nest."

"Well, I hope you are right," said Fitz quietly; and then he stood watching while the little schooner seemed as if being steered to certain destruction, but only to glide by the threatened danger into a wide opening hidden heretofore, and where the rocks ran up, jungle-covered, forming the sides of a lovely valley whose limits were hidden from the deck.

At that moment the middy became aware of the fact that one of the men was busy with the skipper heaving the lead and shouting the soundings loud enough for the mate to hear, while with educated ear Fitz listened and grasped the fact how dangerously the water shoaled, till it seemed at last that the next minute they must run aground.

For a few minutes it was as though something was clutching at the boy's throat, making his breath come hot and fast; and he glanced back to see where the gunboat was, but looked in vain, for a side of the valley rose like a towering wall between, and on glancing in the other direction there was another stupendous wall running up to mountain height, and all of gorgeous greens.

The next minute, when he looked forward, feeling that at any moment he might have to swim, the voice of the man with the lead-line seemed to ring out louder and more clear, announcing fathoms, as a short time before he had shouted feet.

There was a curious stillness too reigning around. The roar of surf upon the rocky shore was gone; the wind had dropped; and the *Teal* was gliding slowly up the grand natural sanctuary into which she had been steered, while the lad awakened to the fact that they had entered a rushing stream, and as the feeling gained ground of all this being unreal, their safety being, as it were, a dream, he was brought back to the bare matter-of-fact by hearing an order given, the anchor descending with a splash, and Poole bringing his hand down sharply upon his shoulder, to cry exultantly—

"There, old chap; what did I say!"

Chapter Forty
"Defence, not defiance"

"What did you say? Oh yes, I remember. It has come out all right; but we shall have them in here directly, after us."

"What's that?" said the skipper, who overheard his words. "I hope not, and I doubt of their getting within shot. Here, Burgess."

"Hallo!" growled the mate, and he came slowly up, looking, as Poole afterwards said, like the proverbial bear with a sore head.

"Here's Mr Burnett prophesying all kinds of evil things about us."

"Ah!" growled the mate. "He didn't know any better. I never prophesy till after the thing has taken place. What did he say?"

"That we shall have the gunboat in here after us directly. What do you say to that?"

The mate's sour countenance expanded into a broad smile, and he came close up to the middy and clapped him on the shoulder.

"Good lad," he said. "I hope you are right."

"Hope I'm right!" said Fitz, staring. "Why, if she steams in within shot they'll make such practice with that gun that we shall be knocked all to pieces."

"You mean they would if they got well within sight; but look for yourself. Where could they lay her to get a shot? I can't see."

"No," said Fitz thoughtfully, as he looked anxiously back and saw that they were thoroughly sheltered by projecting cliff and headland. "I suppose they couldn't get within shot."

"No. That's right, my lad; and they couldn't come in anything like near enough if it were all open water from here to where they are now."

"What, is the water so shoal?" asked Fitz.

"Shoal? Yes," growled the mate, his face growing sour again. "We've nearly scraped the bottom over and over again. I only wish they'd try it. They'd be fast on some of those jags and splinters, and most likely with a hole in the bottom. My opinion, Captain Reed, is that if the skipper of that gunboat does venture in he'll never get out again; and that would suit us down to the ground. Bah—bah! He knows this coast too well, and he won't be such a fool as to try."

"No," said the skipper confidently; "you are quite right, Burgess. He won't be such a fool as to try. But we must have a boat out at once to go back and watch, for I'm pretty sure that Don what's-his-name will be lowering a couple of his with armed crews to come in and scuttle us if they can't tow us out."

"Ah, well, they can't do that," said the mate coolly. "They'd be meeting us on equal terms then, and you won't let them."

"No," said the skipper, smiling, as he turned to Fitz; "I don't think we shall let them do that, Mr Burnett. My lads will be only too glad to receive the gunboat's crew on equal terms and send them back with a flea in their ears."

"Ay," said the mate, with a grunt; "and quite right too. I think it is our turn to give them a bit of our mind, after the way in which they have been scuffling us about lately. Shall I go with the boat?"

"Yes, you'd better. Take the gig, and four men to row."

"I can go, father?" cried Poole eagerly.

"Well, I don't know," said the skipper. "If you go, Mr Burnett here will want to be with you, and I know how particular he is as a young officer not to be seen having anything to do with our filibustering, as he calls it."

Fitz frowned with annoyance, and seemed to give himself a regular snatch.

"You'd rather not go, of course?" continued the skipper dryly.

"I can't help wanting to go, Mr Reed," replied the lad sharply; "and if I went just as a spectator I don't see how I should be favouring any of your designs."

"Well, no," said the skipper dryly, "if you put it like that. I don't see after all how you could be accused of turning buccaneer. But would you really like to go?"

"Why, of course," said Fitz. "It's all experience."

"Off with you then," said the skipper; "only don't get within shot. I don't want to have to turn amateur doctor again on your behalf. I am clever enough at cuts and bruises, and I dare say if I were hard put to it I could manage to mend a broken leg or arm, but I wouldn't undertake to be hunting you all over to find where a rifle-bullet had gone. Accidents are my line, not wounds received in war; and, by the way, while we are talking of such subjects, if we have to lie up here in this river for any time, you had better let me give you a dose or two of quinine."

"Oh, but I am quite well now," cried Fitz.

"Yes, and I want you to keep so, my lad. That's a very good old proverb that says, 'Prevention is better than cure.'"

A very short time afterwards the schooner's gig, with her little well-armed crew, was allowed to glide down with the stream, with the mate, boat-hook in hand, standing in the bows, Poole astern with the rudder-lines, and Fitz a spectator, thoroughly enjoying the beauty of the vast cliffs that arose on either side as they descended towards the river's mouth.

It was all zigzag and winding, the stream carrying them along slowly, for a sharp sea-breeze was dead against them, explaining how it was that the schooner had sailed up so easily as she had.

Fitz had ample proof, without Poole's drawing his attention to the fact, that there was no possibility of the gunboat making practice with her heavy piece, for everywhere the schooner was sheltered, the course of the river being all zigzag and wind, till all at once, as the men were dipping their oars gently, the gig passed round a bend, and there was the enemy about three miles off shore, lying-to, with her great black plume of smoke floating towards them, spreading out like a haze and making her look strange and indistinct.

"Did you bring a glass, Poole, my lad?" growled the mate.

"No; I never thought of that."

"Humph! Never mind. I think I can manage. Both of you lads give a sharp look-out and tell me what you can see."

"Why, there's something between us and her hull," said Poole, "but I can't quite make out what it is. Surely she isn't on a rock?"

"No," cried Fitz; "I can see. She has lowered a boat."

"Two," said the mate, in his deep hoarse voice. "I can make 'em out now. I thought that was it at first. Pull away, my lads, for all you're worth. Pull your port line, my lad, and let's run back. Hug the shore as much as you can, so as to keep out of the stream. Hah! If we had thought to bring a mast and sail and one of the other boats we could have been back in no time with this wind astern."

The gig swung round as the men bent in their quick steady pull, and they began to ascend the stream once more, while Fitz rose in his place, to look back watching the half-obscured gunboat till they had swept round the bend once more and she was out of sight, when he re-seated himself and noticed that the mate was still standing, intent upon cautiously taking cartridges from his pouch and thrusting them into the chambers of the revolver which he had drawn from the holster of his belt.

This looked like business, and Fitz turned to dart an inquiring look at his companion, who answered it with a nod.

"Well," thought Fitz, "if he thinks we are going to have a fight before we get back, why doesn't he order his men to load?"

But it proved that the mate did not anticipate a fight before they got back. He had other thoughts in his head, and when at last, after a long and anxious row against the sharp current, with the lads constantly looking back to see if the gunboat's men were within sight, they reached the final zigzag, and caught sight of the schooner, old Burgess raised his hand and fired three shots at the face of the towering cliff.

These three were echoed back as about a score, when there was an interval, and three tiny puffs of grey smoke darted from the schooner's deck, and echoed in their turn.

"Signal answered," said Poole quietly, and the men made their ash-blades bend again in their eagerness to get back aboard.

"Why, what have they been about?" whispered Fitz.

"Looks like going fishing," said Poole, with a grin. "Don't chaff at a time like this," cried Fitz pettishly. "I didn't know that you had got boarding-netting like a man-of-war."

"What, don't you remember the night you came aboard?"

"Not likely, with everything knocked out of my head as it was."

"Oh yes, we've got all these little necessaries. Father goes on the Volunteer system: 'Defence, not Defiance.'"

"Well, that's defiant enough," said Fitz. "It's like saying, 'You're not coming aboard here,' in string."

"Of course. You don't suppose we want a set of half Indian, half Spanish mongrel sailors taking possession of the *Teal*? You wait till we get aboard, and you'll see all our lads busy with the fleas."

"Busy with the fleas?" said Fitz. "What do you mean?"

"Those father talked about, to put in the Don's ears before we send them back."

"How can you go on making poor jokes at a time like this?" said the middy, in a tone of annoyance. "Why, it looks as if we are in for a serious fight."

"As if *we* are!" said Poole, emphasising the "we."

"How many more times am I to tell you that it is our game and not yours?"

"But look here," said Fitz excitedly. "Your father really does mean to fight?"

"My father does, and so does every one else," replied Poole. "In oars, my lads," and the next moment the mate hooked on close to the gangway. "I suppose," continued Poole, "you will stop on deck till the row begins? You will want to see all you can."

"Of course," said Fitz, whose face was once more growing flushed.

"Well, I wouldn't stop up too long. The enemy may fire, and you will be safer down below."

"Yes, I suppose so," said the middy coolly; "and of course you are coming too?"

"Coming too? That's likely, isn't it?" said Poole contemptuously.

"Just as likely as that I should go and hide."

"But it's no business of yours. You are not going to fight."

"No," said Fitz, "but I want to see."

Chapter Forty One
Fitz forgets

The boarding-netting was partially drawn aside, and Fitz noted that more than ever the crew of the schooner looked like well-trained man-of-war's men, each with his cutlass belted on, waiting for the next order, given in the skipper's voice, when the gig's falls were hooked on and she was run up to the davits and swung inboard, as were the other boats, and when the lad sprang on deck he saw that the netting was being lowered down and secured over the gangway.

It was plain enough that from the moment the gig had pushed off, all hands had been at work preparing to resist attack if an attempt at capture were made; and once more the middy forgot his own identity as a naval officer in his eagerness and interest in all that was going on.

"Oh, one word, Mr Burnett," said the skipper, as he passed where the lad was standing. "Hadn't you better go below? You've got to think about who you are if the Spaniards take us," and then with a good-humoured smile as he read the vexation in the boy's countenance, "Hadn't I better lock you up in the cabin?"

"I say, Captain Reed," cried the boy, in a voice full of protest, "I do wish you wouldn't do this. I can't help having a nasty temper, and this puts me all of a tingle. It seems so hard that men should always laugh at boys and think they are cowards. We can't help being young."

"Of course you can't, my lad," said the skipper, patting him on the back. "There, I will never tease you again. In all probability there won't be anything serious, but if there is, take care of yourself, my boy, for I shouldn't like you to be hurt."

He gave his listener a pleasant nod, and hurried on towards the mate, while Fitz joined Poole, who had nothing now to do, and they occupied themselves in keeping watch for the expected boats and going about amongst the men, whose general appearance seemed to Fitz to be that they were going to some entertainment by way of a treat.

But the treat promised to be serious, for rifles were here and there placed ready for use, and close to every man there was a capstan-bar, evidently intended to use as a club, a most effective weapon whose injuries would not prove of a very dangerous type.

Fitz whispered as much to his companion, who nodded and then replied—

"Well, that depends on what the lads call the spaniel dogs. The dad doesn't want it to be too serious, of course, but we can't help it if these fellows make our lads savage. You see, we've got cutlasses and rifles, and fellows forget to be gentle if they are hurt."

"But we are not at war with Don Villarayo's State."

"No," said Poole, "and Villarayo is not at war with our schooner and the men, but if he begins giving us Olivers he must expect to get Rolands back. Those who play at bowls, you know, must expect rubbers, and when Englishmen rub, they rub hard."

Fitz half turned away to look astern. "I say," he said, "aren't they a long time coming?"

"No; they had a long way to row."

"Seems a long time. Perhaps they have thought better of it and gone back."

"Think so? Well, I don't. They are sure to come. But I dare say it will be a good quarter of an hour yet—perhaps half."

"Well," said Fitz, "for my part, I—" He stopped short, and Poole looked at him curiously.

"Well?" he said. "You what? What were you going to say?"

"Nothing. You'd only think that I was afraid."

"Oh, I know," said Poole. "You were going to say that you hope it won't turn out serious. I shouldn't think that you were afraid. I feel just the same. But you may make up your mind for one thing. We are in the strongest position, and Villarayo's sailors won't be allowed to take the *Teal*. If it comes to bloodshed, it's their doing, mind, and not ours. Now, don't let's talk any more."

"Why not?" said Fitz. "I feel as if I must. Perhaps I shouldn't if I were one of your crew, and like that."

He pointed quickly to his companion's belt, from which hung a sword, and then quickly touched the flap of the little holster buttoned over the brass stud. "You won't use that, will you?" he said. "Not if I can help it," was the reply. "Help it! Why, of course you needn't unless you like."

"Well, I shouldn't like to, of course. But if you were I, and you saw one of these fellows aiming at one of your men, say at old Butters or Chips, setting aside the dad, wouldn't you try and whip it out to have first shot?"

Fitz nodded shortly, and for the time being the conversation ceased, while the lads' attention was taken up by the sight of the Camel, who after making a rattling noise as if stoking his fire in the galley, shut the door with a bang, and came out red-faced and hot, wiping his hands prior to buckling on a belt with its cutlass and then helping himself to a capstan-bar.

It was only a few minutes later that the bows of a large cutter came in sight, followed by the regularly dipping oars of the crew of swarthy sailors who were pulling hard.

The next moment the uniforms of two officers could be made out in the stern-sheets, where they sat surrounded by what answered to marines, and before the cutter had come many yards the bows of its consort appeared.

As they came within sight of the schooner a cheer arose, a sort of imitation British cheer, which had a curious effect upon the schooner's crew, for to them it seemed so comic that they laughed; but a growl from the mate made every one intent for the serious work in hand, as at the next order they divided in two parties, each taking one side of the schooner for the defence under command of the skipper and his chief officer.

"You understand, Burgess?" said the former sternly. "You will keep a sharp eye on us, and I'll keep one on you. It must be a case of the one helping the other who is pressed."

The mate grunted, and the skipper spoke out to his men.

"Look here, my lads," he said; "we are not at war, and I want no bloodshed. Use your capstan-bars as hard as you like, and tumble them back into their boats, or overboard. No cutlass, edge or point, unless I give the word."

The answer was a cheer, and then all eyes were directed to the boats, which were coming faster through the water now, till, at a command from the foremost stern-sheets, the men slackened and waited for their consort to come up abreast.

Another command was given, when the oars dipped faster all together, the boats dividing so as to take the schooner starboard and port.

"Not going to summon us to surrender?" said the skipper sharply. "Very well; but I think we shall make them speak."

The two boys stood together in the stern, close to the wheel, seeing the boats divide and pass them on either hand; and then with hearts throbbing they waited for what was to come—and not for long.

Matters moved quickly now, till the boats bumped and grazed against the schooner's sides, two sharp orders rang out as their coxswains hooked on, and then with a strange snarling roar their crews began to scramble up to the bulwarks, and with very bad success. They had not far to go, for the schooner's bulwarks were very low for a sea-going vessel, but here was the main defence, the nets fully ten feet high and very strong—a defence suggestive of the old gladiatorial fight between the Retiarius, or net and trident-bearer, and the Secutor, or sword and shield-carrying man-at-arms.

Catching the Spaniard in the chest and sending him backwards into the boat.
Frontispiece.]

There was no firing then; the Spaniards seized the net and began to climb, some becoming entangled, as in their hurry a leg or an arm slipped through, while the defenders dashed at them and brought their capstan-bars into use, crack and thud resounding, sending some back upon their companions, others into the boats, while three or four splashes announced the fall of unfortunates into the water.

Loud shouts came from the boats as the officers urged the men on, and from each an officer in uniform began to climb now and lead, followed by quite a crowd on either side, some of them hacking at the stout cord with their cutlasses, but doing little mischief, crippled as they were by the sharp blows which were hailed down by the schooner's crew, upon hand, foot, and now and then upon some unlucky head.

Chips the carpenter, who was nothing without making some improvement upon the acts of his fellows, made a dash at the officer leading the attacking boat on the starboard side, delivering a thrust with the bar he carried, which passed right through the large mesh of the net, catching the Spaniard in the chest and sending him backwards into the boat.

"That's what I calls a Canterbury poke, dear boys," he cried. "Let 'em have it, my lads. The beggars look like so many flies in a spider's web; and we are the spiders."

The shouting, yelling, and struggling did not last five minutes. Man after man succeeded the fallen, and then it was all over, the boats floating back with the current until they were checked by those in command, who ordered the oars out and the men to row. But it was some little time before the confusion on board each could be mastered, and the disabled portions of the crew drawn aside.

"Well done, my lads!" cried the skipper. "Couldn't be better!"

"Here," shouted the mate, "a couple of you up aloft and tighten that net up to the stay. Two more of you get a bit of signal-line and lace up those holes."

"Ay, ay, sir!" came readily enough, and the men rushed to their duty.

"Think that they have had enough of it?" said Fitz huskily.

"Not they," replied Poole. "We shall hear directly what they have got to say."

He had scarcely spoken before there was a fierce hail from one of the boats, whose commander shouted in Spanish to the skipper to surrender; and upon receiving a defiant reply in his own tongue, the officer roared—

"Surrender, you scum, or I'll order my men to fire; and as soon as you are my prisoners I'll hang you all, like the dogs you are."

"Back with you to your ship, you idiot, before you get worse off," cried the captain sternly. "Dogs can bite, and when English dogs do, they hold on."

"Surrender!" roared the officer again, "or I fire."

"At the first shot from your boat," cried the skipper, "I'll give the order too; and my men from shelter can pick off yours much faster than yours from the open boat."

"Insolent dog!" roared the officer, and raising a revolver he fired at the skipper, the bullet whistling just above his head.

In an instant Poole's revolver was out, and without aiming he fired too in the direction of the boat. He fired again and again over the attacking party's heads, until the whole of the six chambers were empty, and with the effect of making the Republican sailors cease rowing, while their boats drifted with the current, rapidly increasing the distance.

The order to fire from the boats did not come, but the second boat closed up to the first, and a loud and excited colloquy arose, there being evidently a difference of opinion between the leaders, one officer being for another attack; the second—so the skipper interpreted it from such of the words as he could catch—being for giving up and going back to the gunboat for advice.

And all the time, both boats still in confusion drifted farther and farther away; but at last the fiery leader of the first gained the day; his fellow gave up, and when the order was given to advance once more in the first boat he supplemented it in the second, and a low deep murmur rose up.

"Why, Fitz," whispered Poole, "they have had enough of it. The mongrels won't come on."

"Think so?" whispered back Fitz, gazing excitedly over the stern, while Poole's fingers were busy thrusting in fresh cartridges till his revolver chambers were full.

"Yes, it's plain enough," cried Poole, for the voices of the officers could be heard angrily threatening and abusing their men; but all in vain.

There was the appearance of struggles going on, and in one boat the sun flashed two or three times from the blade of a sword as it was raised in the air and used as a weapon of correction, its owner striking viciously at his mutinous men.

"Ah!" ejaculated Fitz. "That's done it. They are more afraid of him than they are of us—of you, I mean. They are coming on again."

For the oars were dipping, making the water foam once more, as the crews in both the boats began to pull with all their might. But only half; the others backed water, and directly after the boats' heads had been turned and they were being rowed back as hard as they would go, till they disappeared round the first bend to the tune of a triumphant cheer given in strong chorus by every man upon the *Teal*.

Just at that moment Fitz clapped one hand to his cheek, for it felt hot, consequent upon the thought having struck him, that in his excitement he had been cheering too. That burning sensation was the result of a hint from his conscience that such conduct was not creditable to a young officer in the Royal Navy.

Chapter Forty Two
The Camel's demand

The nets were soon mended and the slack places hauled up taut, while the *Teal's* crew sauntered about the deck, waiting patiently for the next attack, and compared notes about the slight injuries they had received.

Meanwhile the skipper and mate were anxiously on the alert for what might happen next.

"I want to know what they mean, Burgess," the lads heard the skipper say. "They'll never put up with such a rebuff as this."

"Oh, I don't know," growled Burgess. "The officers wouldn't, of course, but they'll never get those swabs to face us for another bout."

"What do you think, then? That they will go back for fresh boats' crews?"

"That's somewhere about it, or some stinkpots to heave aboard, or maybe, if they have got one, for a barge or pinnace with a boat's gun."

"Possibly," said the skipper, and Poole gave Fitz a nudge with his elbow as if to ask, Did you hear that?—a quite unnecessary performance, for Fitz had drunk in every word.

"Yes," continued the skipper; "they'll be after something or another. Don Cousin is bound to take us by some means, and we must be on the look-out for a surprise. Can we wait till dark and slip out to sea again?"

"No," said the mate abruptly; "I want broad daylight for anything like that. I couldn't take the schooner a quarter of a mile in the dark without getting her on the rocks."

"I suppose not," said the skipper; "and I suppose it's no use to try and get higher up the stream?"

"Not a bit," replied the mate. "The boats would follow us anywhere. I am very sorry. I've brought you into a regular trap, and there's only one way out, and the gunboat's sitting on it. But under the circumstances there was nothing else to be done. How I do hate these tea-kettles! But one must look the plain truth in the face. They can go anywhere, and we, who depend upon our sails, can't."

"That's all true enough," said the skipper, "but it doesn't better our position. What I want to know is, how things are going on lower down. Now, if you lads, or one of you," he continued, turning to the boys, "could shin up that high cliff yonder you could see the boats and the gunboat too, and make signals to us so that we might know what to expect."

"All right, father," said Poole sharply, and he glanced at Fitz as he spoke; "have me landed in the dinghy, and I'll go up and see."

Fitz looked at the speaker, and his eyes said, "All right, I'll come with you;" but the skipper made no answer for a time, but stood shading his eyes and sweeping the face of the cliff, before dropping his hand and saying—

"How would you do it, my lad?"

"Oh, by climbing up, father, a bit at a time, getting hold of the bushes and hauling oneself up sometimes."

"Ah," said the skipper quietly. "You would be very clever if you did. It might be managed for a little way up, but all that upper part isn't perpendicular; it hangs right over towards us. Impossible, my lad. Nothing could get up there but a bird or a fly. We must give up that idea. Burgess, you will have to lower a boat and let her drift down to the headland there, stern on, and with the men ready to pull for their lives, as you may be fired at. When you get to the head you must let her slide along close under the bushes till you get a sight of the boats and see what they're doing."

"Right," said the mate. "Now?"

"Yes; the sooner the better."

Poole glanced at Fitz, and then started to speak to his father; but before he could open his lips there was an emphatic—

"No! You would only be in the way, my lads. I want four strong men to row, and one in the stern to look out; and that one is Mr Burgess."

"Very well, father," said the lad quietly, but he looked his disappointment at Fitz, whose vexation was plainly marked on his countenance, as he mentally said, "Oh, bother! He might have let us go."

Things were done promptly on board the *Teal*, and in a few moments the cutter was lowered down with its little crew after the netting had been cast loose and raised; and then they watched her glide down with the stream, stern on, with the rowers balancing their oars, the stroke dipping his now and then to keep her head to stream, and the mate standing with his back to them till the headland was reached, when he knelt down, caught at the overhanging bushes and water-plants, and let the boat drift close in and on and on without making a sign, till she disappeared.

Just then Fitz heaved a sigh.

"What's the matter, old chap?" said Poole.

"Oh, we shall have nothing to do but wait now, perhaps for hours, for I expect the enemy has gone right back to the gunboat, and waiting is a thing I do thoroughly hate. Eh? Is that you, Camel?"

"Andy Cawmell it is, sir. A'm thenking that it would be joost a good time for a wee bit food. Ah've been watching Mr Burnett here, and the puir laddie looks quite white and faint. Would you mind telling the skipper that I've got a wee bit hot dinner a' ready? and if he will gi'e the word I'll have it in the cabin in less time than Duncan Made-Hose took his pinch of sneeshin."

"Well done, Camel!" cried Poole, who darted to his father, leaving the cook blinking and smiling at Fitz, who looked at him in admiration.

"Why, Camel," he said, "you are a deal too clever for a ship's cook, and I don't know what I owe you for all you have done for me."

"Oh, joost naething at all, laddie."

"Nothing! I want to make you a big present when I can."

"You do, laddie? Vairy weel, and I'll tell you what I'd like. Ye'll just gi'e me one of them quarter-poond tins of Glasgie sneeshin."

"Snuff!" said Poole contemptuously. "Ay, laddie; snuff, as ye call it. Nay, don't turn your nose up at sneeshin. Ye should turn it down. Thenk of what it is to a man condemned to get naething but a bit of dirty black pigtail tobaccy that he has to chew like the lads do in their barbarous way. Ye'll mind that: a four-ounce tin of the rale Glasgie."

"Oh, but—"

"Nay, nay, laddie. That'll make us square. Now then, what's the young skipper got to say?"

"The sooner the better, Camel, for he's half-starved; but you are to keep a bit hot for Mr Burgess."

"Ou, ay," said the Camel, smiling. "I never forget the mate. He wadna let me if I would."

The two lads watched anxiously for the return of the boat, but in vain, and then, in answer to the summons, went reluctantly below as far as their minds were concerned, but with wondrous willingness on the part of their bodies, to join the skipper over a capital meal, which was hastily discussed, and then the trio went on deck to where the men were keeping watch, and ordered them to go below.

"Get your dinner, lads, as quickly as you can, and then come up again. We'll keep watch until you do."

They took their places aft at once, and the watch began, lasting till, headed by the boatswain, the men hurried up again, looking inquiringly in the faces of those they relieved; but they looked in vain, for nothing had been seen of the cutter, and quite an hour had passed when she came round the bend, being rowed swiftly, for the mate to hail the skipper and make the announcement—

"They have gone right back to the gunboat, and I waited till they were run up to the davits, and then came back. Is there anything we can have to eat?"

Chapter Forty Three
Winks's Plans

The mate and the boat's crew went below, and the skipper took a turn or so up and down the deck, thinking deeply, while the two lads went and settled themselves down aft to keep a keen look-out for any danger that might approach, and naturally dropped into conversation, first about the fight, a subject which they thoroughly exhausted before they began a debate upon their position.

"What's to be done, eh?" said Poole, in response to a question. "I don't know. We are regularly boxed up—trapped. You heard what was said, and here we are. We can't attempt to sail out in the daylight because Don Cousin would sink us as sure as his great gun, and we can't sneak out in the dark because, even if we got a favourable wind, old Burgess couldn't find the way."

"We might take to the boats, and slip off as soon as it was dark, and row along close in shore. We should be out of sight long before daybreak, and join Don Ramon at Velova."

"Exactly," said Poole sarcastically; "and leave a note on the binnacle, 'With father's compliments to Don Cousin, and he begged to make him a present of the smartest little schooner, just as she stands, that ever crossed the Atlantic.' Likely, isn't it?"

"Oh no," said Fitz hurriedly. "Of course that wouldn't do."

"Oh, I don't know," said Poole, in the same mocking vein. "It doesn't do to be in too much of a hurry over a good idea. There, you wait till the dad turns and is coming back this way, and then you go and propose it to him."

"Likely, as you say," said Fitz, with a laugh. "But look here, what is to be done?"

"I only know of one thing," replied Poole; "keep a strict watch for the next prank they will play, and beat them off again till they get tired and give it up as a bad job."

"That they will never do," said Fitz decidedly. "Think they could land and get up on one of these cliffs from the shore side, and pick us off by degrees with their rifles?"

"No," said Poole, leaning back and gazing upwards. "I think that would be impossible."

"Well," said Fitz, "what do you say to this? Man the boats after dark, row out to the gunboat, board her, and take her. Now, I think that would be grand."

"Oh yes, grand enough; but she's a man-of-war with small guns as well as the big one, and a large, well-drilled crew. No, no, they would be too keenly on the watch. I don't believe we could do that. I've a good mind to mention it, though, to father. No, I won't. He'd have thought of that, and he'd only look upon it as so much impudence, coming from me."

"I dunno," said Fitz. "Here he comes. Try."

"Here, you two," said the skipper, coming close up to them; "I have a nice little job for you. Take four men, Poole, and drop down in a boat cautiously. Don't be seen, and get down to where you can watch the gunboat till dark, and then come back here and report what you have made out. Of course if they make any movement you come back directly and let me know."

These orders put all farther scheming out of the lads' heads, and a very short time afterwards Poole had selected Chips and three other men, and the boat was gliding down with the current, each bend being cautiously rounded in the expectation of the enemy being seen once more ascending the river. But the last headland was passed with the boat kept well under shelter of the overhanging growth, and the open sea lay before them; and there, about two miles away, and exactly opposite the mouth of the river, lay the gunboat with a film of smoke rising from her funnel, indicating that steam was being kept up, while by means of the glass that this time had not been left behind, they could plainly make out that she was lying at anchor, keeping watch upon the shore.

"There," said Poole, "I'll be bound to say she's just at the mouth of the channel by which we came in, and as close as she dare come. We should look nice sailing down nearer and nearer to her. Bah! We should never get half-way there."

"Well, what's to be done?" said Fitz.

"What we were told. Make ourselves comfortable till the sun's just beginning to go down, and then get back as quickly as we can.—Make her fast, my lads, with the painter—there, to that branch, only so that we can slip off in a minute, for we may have to go in a hurry at any time."

This was done, and they watched and waited in silence, keeping well out of sight behind the shrubby growth, from the knowledge that the mouth of the river was certain to be carefully scanned by those on board the gunboat with their glasses.

"Looks to me," observed Poole, "as if they mean to tire us out."

"Oh yes, sir, that's it," said Chips. "I wish I had brought my tools with me."

"Why?" said Poole, who was glad to break the monotony of their watch by a chat with the men.

"Oh, it's as well to make the most use of your time, sir. Looks to me as if the Don Captain had taken a lease of that pitch and meant to stay; and under the suckumstances I couldn't do better than land here and get up to that sort of shelf yonder. Beautiful situation too, freehold if you held tight. Raither lonely perhaps, but with my axe and these 'ere three stoopids to help me, I could knock the skipper up a nice eligible marine villa, as they calls it, where we could all live comfortable for a year or two; and you young gents could have nice little gardens of your own. Then I could make you a little harbour where you could keep your boat and go fishing and shooting and having a high old time. I don't think you'd get such a chance again."

"And what about the schooner?" said Fitz, laughing.

"Oh, we should have to dismantle her, and work up the stuff, bulkheads and such-like, to line the new house. I've got an idea that I could work in all the hatches and tarpaulins for a roof; for though you get plenty of sunshine out here, my word, when it do rain, it do! What do you say, sir?"

"Nothing," said Poole. "It won't do, Chips."

"Well, no, sir; I thought it wouldn't when I first began to speak."

"Try again."

"Don't think I have got any more stuff, sir. But lookye here; why don't the skipper take us all down in the boats when it's dark, and let us board the enemy and take her? We could, couldn't we, messmates?"

"Yes, of course," came in a growl.

"There, sir! You 'ear?"

"Yes, I hear," said Poole, "and I dare say we could, but only at the expense of half the lads killed and wounded; and that would be paying too dear. Now, look here, my lad; here's an idea rather in your way. Couldn't we make a plan to scuttle and sink the gunboat where she lies? What do you say to that?"

"Can't be did, sir. I could creep alongside the schooner and do it to her; but that there gunboat's got heavy steel plates right round her, going ever so deep, and they'd be rather too much for my tools. They'd spoil every auger I've got. The skipper hasn't got a torpedo aboard, has he? One of them new 'uns that you winds up and sets a-going with a little screw-propeller somewheres astern, and a head full of nitro—what-d'ye-call-it, which goes off when it hits?"

"No," said Poole, as he lay back gazing at the gunboat through his half-closed eyes, and in imagination saw the little thread-like appearance formed by the disturbed water as a fish-torpedo ploughed its way along; "we didn't bring anything of the kind."

"No, sir; I thought you wouldn't. But what about a big bag of powder stuck alongside her rudder? You see, you might tie the bag up with a bit of spun-yarn rubbed with wet powder, and leave a long end hanging down as far as the boat in which you rowed out."

"And set a light to it?" said Fitz.

"That's right, sir. You see," cried Chips, "and it would go fizzling and sparkling till we rowed right away out of reach, and up she'd go, bang."

"And while you were striking matches to light the touch-string, the enemy would be shooting at you or dropping cold shot or pig-ballast into us to sink the boat," said Poole.

"Bah!" said Fitz. "They keep such a strict watch that they would never let a row-boat come near."

"No, sir," said Chips; "that's just what I think. Them Spaniels aren't very clever, but they all seem to have got eyes in their heads. Now, this 'ere's a better idee. Say you are the skipper, and you says to half-a-dozen of us, 'Now, my lads, them there Span'ls is making themselves a regular noosance with that there big gun. Don't you think you could take the gig to-night, drop down under their bows, hook on by the fore-chains, and then swarm up on the quiet like, catch hold of the big gun, carry her to the side, and drop her over into deep water!'"

"Ha! ha! Capital!" cried Fitz. "Splendid! Yes, I don't believe she weighs more than two or three tons. Why, Poole, we ought to go to-night. They wouldn't be able to get her up again without a lighter and divers from New York. But it's a capital idea."

"Don't you mind what he says," growled the carpenter. "He's a-quizzing on us, my lads. Well, I gives that up. That job would be a bit too stiff."

"Yes," said Poole, laughing. "Try again."

"I dunno what they wants a great clumsy lumbering thing like that aboard a ship for. Bower-anchors is bad enough, banging against your craft; but you can lower them down to the bottom when your ship gets tired, and give her a bit of a rest."

"Yes," said one of the other sailors; "you'll have to think of something better than that, Shavings."

"Ay, but that was a fine idea, my lad, if the gun had been a bit lighter. The Span'ls would have been so flabbergasted when they heard the splash, that we should have had lots of time to get away. Now, let me see; let me see. What we wants is a big hole in that gunboat's bottom, so that they would be obliged to take to their boats. What do you say to this? I've got a bottle of stain aboard as I used to do over the wood at the top of the locker in the skipper's cabin, and made it look like hoggermy. Now, suppose I undressed a bit, say to my flannel-shirt, tied an old red comforter that I've got round my waist, to keep my trowges up, and then touches my hands and arms and phiz over with some of that stain. Then I swims off to the gunboat, asks civil like for the Don skipper, and says I'm a Spanish AB and a volunteer come on the job."

"And what then?" said Fitz, laughing.

"Ah, you may laugh, sir. But you can't expect a common sailor like me, who's a bit handy with his hammer and saw, to be up to all the dodges of an educated young gent like you as has sarved his time aboard the *Brytannia* in Dartmouth Harbour. But of course there's a 'what then' to all I said. I shouldn't want to dress myself up like a play-hactor in a penny show, with a red pocket-hankerchy tied to a mop-stick, big boots, and a petticut instead of trowges, pretending he's a black pirate, with a blood-red flag, one of your penny plain and twopence coloured kind, you know. I did lots of them when I was a young 'un, and had a box of paints. Not me. There's a 'what then' to all this 'ere, a sting to it, same as there is in a wopse's tail."

"Let's have it then," said Fitz. "I want to hear what you'd do when Don Cousin there shakes hands with you and says, 'You're the very man I've been waiting for all through this voyage.'"

"Yes, sir; that's it. You've got it to rights. That's just what he says, only it'd be in his Spanish liquorice lingo; and then the very first time I takes my trick at the wheel I looks out for one of them ugly sharp-pinted rocks like a fang just sticking out of the water, runs the gunboat right a-top of it, makes a big hole in her bottom; down she goes, great gun and all, and there you are. Now, Mr Poole, sir, what have you got to say to that?"

"Nothing," said Poole. "It's too big for me. When do you mean to start?"

"Well, I haven't quite made up my mind as to that yet, sir," said Chips quietly. "There's the skipper's consent to get, and the painting to do; and then I aren't quite sure about that there red comforter. I am afraid it's in my old chest, the one that's at home, and I shouldn't look so Span'l-like without a bit of colour. But it's a good idea, isn't it, sir, although Mr Fitz don't seem to think much of it? What do you make of them now on board the gunboat?"

"There's somebody on the bridge, and he's got a glass, and I saw the light flash off the lens just now."

"Then they must be a-watching of us, sir, taking stock of the place. I shouldn't wonder if we had a visit from them soon after dark, to try and take us by surprise."

"Well, they won't do that," said Poole. "We shall keep too good a watch; but I shouldn't wonder if they tried." The time glided by, and the sun began to sink, to disappear quite early to the watchers, shut in by high cliffs; and as soon as it was out of sight the boat was dragged up stream, well hidden behind the overhanging boughs that dipped their tips to the edge of the river, till the first bend had been passed, when the men took to their oars and pulled hard till the schooner was reached.

There was scarcely anything to report, the only thing that took the skipper's attention being Fitz's statement that he had seen somebody on the gunboat's bridge using a glass, and this was sufficient to start the skipper making preparations for the night, for after a short consultation with Burgess, they came to the conclusion that they would be attacked before long; and about an hour after darkness had set in, a whisper from one of the watch told that he had heard the faint creakings of oars on rowlocks.

A minute later a faint spark lit up what appeared to be a scale hanging from its chains and being lowered down from the schooner's side into the water; but as it touched the surface it grew and grew, and went gliding down the stream, developing as it went into a tin dish containing some combustible which grew brighter and brighter as it went on, till it flashed out into a dazzling blue light which lit up the sides of the cliffs and glistened like moonlight in the water, till at about a hundred yards from the schooner's stern it threw up into clear relief the shapes of three boats crowded with men, the spray thrown up by their oars glittering in the blue flare, and then ceasing.

For all at once a few softly-uttered words were heard upon the schooner's deck, followed by a bright flash, and the roar of a volley echoed like thunder from the cliff-sides, for the skipper's preparations had been well made, so that about a score of rifle-bullets were sent whizzing and hissing over the enemy's heads, while those who looked on over the schooner's bulwarks saw the blue light begin to sink and grow pale as it went on down stream, throwing up the boats in less bold relief as they too went down towards the mouth in company with their illuminator.

Five minutes later all was dark and still again.

"Showed them we were pretty well prepared for them," said Poole, at last.

"Yes," replied Fitz. "Think they'll come again?"

"No," said the skipper, who was standing by in the darkness. "We shall keep watch, of course, but I don't think we shall see any more of them to-night. There, you two go below and sleep as hard as ever you can. I'll have you roused if anything occurs."

"Honour bright, father?"

"Yes, and extra polished too," replied the skipper.

"Come on, then, Burnett," whispered Poole, gripping his companion by the arm. "I don't think that I ever felt so sleepy in my life."

Chapter Forty Four
Fitz has a dream

The middy did not say much, but a very short time later he proved that he shared his companion's feelings, both lads sleeping with all their might, and trying to make up for a great deal of exertion connected with their disturbed existence of the past few days.

It is generally conceded by the thoughtful over such matters, that dreams come after the more solid portion of a person's sleep, that they are connected with a time when the rested brain is preparing to become active once again, and set to work in its daily routine of thought.

This may be the rule, but it is said that there is no rule without an exception. Fitz Burnett's slumber in his hot, stuffy berth was one of these exceptions, and rather a remarkable one too, for almost directly after dropping off he began to dream in the most outrageous manner, that proving for him a sort of Arabian Night which had somehow been blown across on the equatorial winds to Central America. The whole of his dream was vivid in the extreme while it was in progress, and if it could have been transcribed then, no doubt it would have proved to be of the most intense interest; but unfortunately it had to be recalled the next morning when its clearness was muddled, the sharpness of its features blurred.

Two or three times over he tried to dismiss it from his mind altogether, for it worried him; but it absolutely refused to be got rid of, and kept coming back with the utmost persistency, making him feel bound to drag it back and try to set it in order, though this proved very difficult. It was some time before he could get hold of the thread at all, and at the first pull he found that he drew up several threads, tangled and knotted up in the most inextricable confusion, while they were all in some way connected with Chips the carpenter's plans.

He did not want the task: it bothered him, for in the broad sunshine of the morning Chips's notions seemed to him to be ludicrously absurd; but somehow he felt bound to go on disentangling them, because he was, as it were, in some way mixed up with them, and had been during the night helping him to carry them out.

"Makes my head feel quite hot," he said to himself, as he leaned over the bulwark looking down at the water hurrying past the schooner. "I haven't got a fever coming on, have I? If it doesn't all soon go off I'll ask Captain Reed to give me some of his quinine. Ugh! Horribly bitter stuff! I have had enough physic this voyage to last me for a year."

And then he lapsed into a sort of dreamy state in which he dragged out of his sleeping adventures that he had been acting as a sort of carpenter's boy, carrying the bag, which weighed him down, while all the time he had to keep handing gigantic augers to Chips, and wiping his forehead every now and then with handfuls of shavings, while his master kept on turning away, trying to bore holes through the steel plates of the gunboat, and never making so much as a scratch. Then came a rest, and he and Chips were lying down together in a beautiful summer-house built upon a shelf of the cliff, with lovely vines running all over it covered with brilliant flowers, and growing higher and higher, with the upper parts laden with fruit which somehow seemed to be like beans. He did not know why it was, but his rest in this beautiful vine-shaded place, whose coverings seemed to grow right up into the skies, was disturbed by the carpenter's banter, for Chips kept calling him Jack, and laughing at him for selling his mother's cow for a handful of beans, and asking why he didn't begin to climb right up to the top of the great stalk into the giant land. Before he could answer they were back again by the side of the gunboat, seated in the dinghy, and Chips was turning away at his cross-handled auger, which now seemed to go through the steel as easily as if it were cheese-rind, while when the dreamer took hold of a handful of the shavings that were turned out, they were of bright steel, and so hard and sharp that they made the carpenter angry because they did not remove the perspiration and only scratched his face. But he kept on turning all the time, till the auger had gone in about six inches, when he left off and asked for another, driving this in at a tremendous rate and again asking for another and another, until he had driven in a whole series of them which extended from the level of the dinghy's gunwale right up the gunboat's side.

Then it seemed to the sleeper that the dinghy was passed along to the war-vessel's stern, where Chips made her fast to the rudder-chains, and then held out his hand for the powder-bag, which was so big that it filled up all the bottom of the little boat and swelled right over the side. It was very heavy, but Fitz felt that it must be done, though it was not proper work for a young officer in Her Majesty's Navy.

But Chips was sitting astride the rudder, holding out his hands, and the bag was obliged to be passed up. Directly afterwards it was made fast, and Chips came back holding a black string moistened with gunpowder, and holding out the end to him to light with a match. This he did, after striking many which would not go off because his hands were wet; and then he sat back watching the powder sparkle as it gradually burned along the string towards the neck of the bag full of black powder, which somehow seemed to be the soot from one of the chimneys at home, while Chips the carpenter was only the sweep.

Fitz remembered his sensations of horror as he sat expecting to see the explosion which would blow him into the water; and his dread was agonising; but just then the dinghy began to glide along till it was underneath the augers extending upwards like a ladder, and up these the carpenter climbed, beckoning him to follow, to the gunboat's deck, where all the Spanish sailors were lying fast asleep.

Here he seemed to know that he must step cautiously for fear of treading on and waking the crew; but Chips did not seem to mind at all, going straight in one stride right to where the big breech-loader lay amidships on its carriage, waiting to be lifted out and dropped overboard.

And here the confused muddle of dreams became condensed into a good solid nightmare that would not go, for Fitz felt himself obliged to step to the heaviest part of the huge gun and lift, while Chips took the light end and grinned at him in his efforts to raise it, while as he lifted, and they got the gun poised between them, each with his clasped hands underneath, it kept going down again as if to crush his toes. But he felt no pain, and kept on lifting again and again, till somehow it seemed that they were doing this not upon the gunboat's planks, and that they could not get it overboard because the deck was that shown in the tinselled picture of the Red Rover hanging upon the wall of the gardener's cottage at home, while the sea beyond was only paper painted blue. All the same, though, and in spite of his holding one end of the gun, Chips was there, wearing a scarlet sash and waving a black flag upon which was a grinning skull and cross-bones.

When he got as far as that, Fitz could get no farther, for things grew rather too much entangled; so much so that it seemed to him that he awoke just then with his brain seething and confusion worse confounded, telling himself that he must have had the nightmare very badly indeed, and wondering whether it was due to fever coming on, or something indigestible he had had to eat.

But he said nothing about his dream for some hours, long after he had been on deck, to find that there had been no alarm during the night, had been refreshed by breakfast, and had heard that the gunboat was at anchor where she had been the previous night, and this from Mr Burgess's lips, for he had been down stream with the boat himself.

It was getting towards mid-day, when the sun was shining with full power, and the opinion was strong on deck that if the gunboat people intended to make another attack they would defer it till the day was not quite so hot.

Just then Fitz Burnett seemed to come all at once to a conclusion about his confused dream. Perhaps it was due to the heat in that valley, having ripened his thoughts. Whatever it might have been, he hurried to Poole, got hold of his arm, and told him to come forward into the bows.

"What for?" asked Poole.

"Because there's no one there, and we can talk."

"All right," said the lad. Leading the way he perched himself astride upon the bowsprit and signified that his companion should follow his example; and there they sat, with the loose jib-sail flapping gently to and fro and forming an awning half the time.

"Now then," said Poole, "what is it? You look as if you had found something, or heard some news. Is the gunboat going away?"

"I wish it were," was the reply. "I wanted to tell you that I had last night such a dream."

"Had you? Well, are you going to tell it to me?"

"No; impossible, for I can't recollect it all myself, only the stupid and muddled part of it. But I have been trying to puzzle it out this morning, and that set me thinking about other things as well, till at last, all of a sudden, I got the very idea we want."

"You have! What is it?" cried Poole excitedly. "Tell me gently, for perhaps I could not bear it all at once."

"It's the way to disable the gunboat."

"Do you mean it?"

"Yes."

"A good sensible, possible way, that could be done?"

"Yes, and by one person too, if he had the pluck."

Chapter Forty Five
Too good to be true

It was rather a queer position occupied by the two lads, seated astride the bowsprit like children playing at horses—sea- or river-horses, in this case, for the swift current was running beneath them.

Poole looked hard at Fitz, his sharp eyes seeming to plunge into those of his companion as if he read his very thoughts, while as Fitz returned the gaze his look became timid and shrinking; a curious feeling of nervousness and regret attacked him, and the next minute he was wishing that instead of planning out a suggestion by which he would help these filibusters, he had kept silence and not begun a proposal which he felt to be beneath his dignity as a young officer of the Queen.

"Well," said Poole at last, in a tone of voice which added to Fitz's chill; "what is it?" Fitz remained silent.

"Well, out with it! What's the scheme?" Still Fitz did not speak, and Poole went on—"It ought to be something good to make you so cocksure. I have gone over it all again and again, turned it upside down and downside up, and I can't get at anything one-half so good as old Chips's cock-and-bull notions. I suppose you are cleverer than I am, and if you are, so much the better, for it's horrible to be shut up like this, and I feel as if I'd rather wait for a good wind, clap on all sail, and make a dash for it, going right ahead for the gunboat as if you meant to run her down, and when we got very close, give the wheel a spin and shoot by her. They'd think we were coming right on to her, and it might scare the crew so that they wouldn't be able to shoot straight till we got right by. And then—"

"Yes," said Fitz; "and then perhaps when they had got over the scare they'd shoot straight enough. And suppose they did before they were frightened. What about the first big shell that came aboard?"

"Ah, yes, I didn't think of that," said Poole. "But anyhow, that's the best I can do. I've thought till my head is all in a buzz, and I shan't try to think any more. I suppose, then, that yours is a better idea than that."

"Ye–es. Rather."

"Well, let's have it."

Fitz was silent, and more full of bitter regret that he had spoken.

"I say, you are a precious long time about it."

"Well, I don't know," stammered Fitz. "I don't think I ought to; perhaps it wouldn't be a good one, after all."

"Well, you are a rum fellow, Burnett! I began to believe in you, and you quite made my mouth water, while now you snatch the idea away. What's the matter?"

Fitz cleared his throat, and pulled himself together.

"Well," he said; "you see, it's like this. I've no business as your prisoner to take part with you against a State which is recognised by the British Government, and to which your father has surreptitiously been bringing arms and ammunition that are contraband of war."

"*Phee-ew!*" whistled Poole, grinning. "What big words! What a splendid speech!"

"Look here, if you are beginning to banter," replied Fitz hotly, "I'm off."

"Yes, you've just let yourself off—bang. We had got to be such friends that I thought you had dropped all that and were going to make the best of things. You know well enough that Villarayo was a bully and a brute, a regular tyrant, and that Don Ramon is a grand fellow and a regular patriot, fighting for his country and for everything that is good."

"Yes, yes, I know all that," said Fitz; "but that doesn't alter my position until he has quite got the upper hand and is acknowledged by England. I feel that it is my duty to be—to be—what do they call it?—neutral."

"Oh, you are a punctilious chap. Then you would be neutral, as you call it, and let Villarayo smash up and murder everybody, because Don Ramon has not been acknowledged by England?"

"Yes, I suppose so," said Fitz; "but these are all diplomatic things with which I have nothing to do."

"And you have got a good idea, then, that might save us out of this position?"

"Ye–es; I think so."

"And you won't speak?"

"I feel now that I can't."

"Humph!" grunted Poole. "It seems too bad, and not half fair to the governor."

"It is not fair to me to make me a prisoner," retorted Fitz.

"He didn't make you one. You came and tumbled down into our hold, and we did the best we could for you. But don't let's begin arguing about all that again. Perhaps you are right from your point of view, and I can't think the same, only of helping to get the *Teal* out of this scrape."

"I wish I could help you and do my duty too," said Fitz.

"I wish you could," replied Poole. "But I don't think much of your notion. You said it was all a dream."

"No, not all. It came from my dreaming and getting into a muddle over what Chips the carpenter said."

"I thought so," said Poole coolly; "all a muddle, after all. Dreams are precious poor thin stuff."

"This isn't a dream," cried Fitz sharply.

"And this isn't a dream," cried Poole, flushing up. "I have been thinking about it, and I can't help seeing that as sure as we two are sitting here, those mongrel brutes that swarm in the gunboat will sooner or later get the better of us. Our lads are plucky enough, but the enemy is about six to one, and they'll hang about there till they surprise us or starve us out; and how will it be then?"

"Why, you will all be prisoners of war, of course."

"Prisoners of war!" cried Poole contemptuously. "What, of Villarayo's men, the sweepings and scum of the place, every one of them armed with a long knife stuck in his scarf that he likes to whip out and use! Hot-blooded savage wretches! Prisoners of war! Once they get the upper hand, there will be a regular massacre. They'll make the schooner a prisoner of war if I don't contrive to get below and fire two or three shots into the little magazine; and that I will do sooner than fall alive into their hands. Do you think you would escape because you are an English officer? Not you! Whether you are fighting on our side or only looking on, it will be all the same to them. I know them, Burnett; you don't; and I am telling you the honest truth. There! We'll take our chance," continued the lad coldly. "I don't want to know anything about your dreams now."

Poole was in the act of throwing one leg over the bowsprit, and half turned away; but Fitz caught him tightly by the arm.

"I can't help it," he cried excitedly, "even if it's wrong. Sit still, Poole, old chap. I've been thinking this. You see, when I went aboard the *Tonans* everything was so fresh and interesting to me about the gun-drill and our great breech-loader.—Did you ever see one?"

"Not close to," said Poole coldly. "Ah, well, I have, and you have no idea what it's like. Big as it is, it's all beautifully made. The breech opens and shuts, and parts of it move on hinges that are finished as neatly as the lock of a gun; and it is wonderful how easily everything moves. There are great screws which you turn as quietly as if everything were silk, and then there's a great piece that they call the breech-block, which is lifted out, and then you can stand and look right through the great polished barrel as if it were a telescope, while all inside is grooves, screwed as you may say, so that the great bolt or shell when it is fired is made to spin round, which makes it go perfectly straight."

"Well, yes, I think I knew a good deal of that," said Poole, almost grudgingly.

"Well, you know," continued Fitz excitedly, "perhaps you don't know that when they are going to fire, the gun is unscrewed and the breech-block is lifted out. Then you can look through her; the shell or bolt and the cartridge are pushed in, the solid breech-block is dropped in behind them, and the breech screwed up all tightly once again."

"Yes, I understand; and there's no ramming in from the muzzle as with the old-fashioned guns."

"Exactly," said Fitz, growing more and more excited as he spoke. "And you know now what a tremendously dangerous weapon a great gun like that is."

"Yes, my lad," said Poole carelessly; "of course I do. But it's no good."

"What's no good?" said Fitz sharply.

"You are as bad as Chips. If we got on board we couldn't disable that gun, or get her to the side. She'd be far too heavy to move."

"Yes," said Fitz, with his eyes brightening, and he gripped his companion more tightly than ever. "But what's the most important part of a gun like that?"

"Why, the charge, of course."

"No," cried Fitz; "the breech-block. Suppose I, or you and I, got on board some night in the dark, unscrewed the breech, lifted out the block, and dropped it overboard. What then?"

Poole started, and gripped his companion in turn.

"Why," he said, in a hoarse whisper, "they couldn't fire the gun. The charge would come out at both ends."

"To be sure it would."

"Well— Oh, I don't know," said Poole, trembling with excitement; "I should muddle it. I don't understand a gun like that."

"No," cried Fitz; "but I do."

"Here," panted Poole; "come along aft."

"What are you going to do?"

"Do! Why, tell my governor, of course! Oh, Burnett, old fellow, you'll be the saving of us all!"

The lad's emotion communicated itself to the proposer of the plan, and neither of them could speak as they climbed back on to the deck, and, seeing nothing before their eyes but breech-loaders, hurried off, to meet Mr Burgess just coming out of the cabin-hatch.

"Is father below there?" cried Poole huskily. "Yes; just left him," grunted the mate, as he stared hard at the excited countenances of the two lads. "Anything the matter?"

"Yes. Quick!" cried Poole. "Come on down below." The skipper looked up from the log he was writing as his son flung open the cabin-door, paused for the others to enter, and then shut it after them with a bang which made the skipper frown.

"Here, what's this, sir?" he said sternly, as he glanced from one to the other. "Oh, I see; you two boys have been quarrelling, and want to fight. Well, wait a little, and you'll have enough of that. Now, Mr Burnett, speak out. What is it? Have you and my son been having words?"

"Yes, father," half shouted Poole, interposing—"such words as will make you stare. Tell him, Burnett, all that you have said."

The skipper and the mate listened in silence, while Poole watched the play of emotion their faces displayed, before the skipper spoke.

"Splendid, my lad!" he cried. "But it sounds too good to be true. You say you understand these guns?"

"Yes, sir; I have often stood by to watch the drill, and seen blank cartridge fired again and again."

"But the breech-block? Could it be lifted out?"

"It could aboard the *Tonans*, sir, and I should say that this would be about the same."

"Hah!" ejaculated the skipper. "But it could only be done by one who understands the working of the piece, and we should be all worse than children over such a job."

Poole's eyes were directed searchingly at the middy, who met them without a wink.

"As I understand," continued the captain, "it would be done by one who crept aboard in the dark, unscrewed the gun, took out the block, and carried it to the side. I repeat, it could only be done by one who understands the task. Who could do this?"

"I could, sir," said Fitz quietly.

"And you would?"

"If I were strong enough. But I am sure that I could do it if Poole would help."

"Then if it's possible to do, father," said the lad quietly, "the job is done."

"But look here," interposed the mate, in his gruff way; "what about Don Ramon? What will he say? He wouldn't have that great breech-loader spoiled for the world."

"How would it be spoiled?" cried Fitz sharply.

"Aren't you going to disable it by chucking the breech-block over the side?"

"Pooh!" cried Fitz contemptuously. "These parts are all numbered, and you can send over to England and get as many new ones as you like."

Chapter Forty Six
To cut and run

The mate's face lit up in a way that those who knew him had not seen for months.

"Well done, youngster!" he said, in quite a musical growl. "Splendid! Here, Poole Reed, you ought to have thought of that."

"How could I?" said the lad. "I never learnt anything about breech-loading cannon."

"No more you did, my boy," said the skipper; "and we don't want to take the honour from Mr Burnett. We shall have to do this, sir, but it will be risky work, and I don't know what to say about letting you go."

"Oh, I don't think that there will be much risk, Captain Reed," said Fitz nonchalantly. "It only means going very quietly in the dark. It would be done best from the dinghy, because it's so small."

"And how would you go to work?" said the skipper.

"Oh," said Fitz, "I should arrange to go about two bells, let the dinghy drift close in under her bows after studying the gunboat well with a glass, and I think one ought to be able to mount by climbing up the anchor on the starboard side. If not, by the fore-chains."

"And what about the watch?"

"I've thought about that, sir, and I don't believe that they keep a good one at all. It won't be like trying to board a gunboat in the British Navy. Like as not those on deck will be asleep."

"Yes, I think so too," said Poole.

"Well," said the skipper, "I have something of the same sort of idea. They'd never believe that any one from the schooner would do such a daring thing. What do you say, Burgess?"

"Same as you do, sir," said the mate gruffly.

"But what do you think would be the great advantage of doing this, Mr Burnett?" said the skipper.

"The advantage, sir?" replied the middy, staring. "Why, it would be like drawing a snake's fangs! You wouldn't be afraid of the gunboat without her gun."

"No," said the skipper thoughtfully, "I don't think I should; and for certain she'd be spoiled for doing any mischief to Don Ramon's forts."

"Oh yes, father," cried Poole excitedly. "It would turn the tables completely. You remember what Don Ramon said?"

"What, about the power going with the party who held the gunboat? Well, it's a pity we can't capture her too."

"Or run her ashore, father."

"What, wreck her? That would be a pity."

"I meant get her ashore so that she'd be helpless for a time."

"Well, now's your time, my boy. It has come to a pretty pass, though, Burgess, for these young chaps to be taking the wind out of our sails."

"Oh, I don't mind," growled the mate. "Here, let's have it, Poole. Look at him! He's got something bottled up as big as young Mr Burnett, I dare say."

"Eh? Is that so, my boy? Have you been planning some scheme as well?"

"Well, father, I had some sort of an idea. It came all of a jump after Burnett had proposed disabling the gun."

"Well done!" whispered Fitz excitedly.

"What is it, my lad?" said the skipper.

"Oh, I feel rather nervous about it, father, and I don't know that it would answer; but I should like to try."

"Go on, then; let's hear what it is."

"You see, I noticed that they have always got steam up ready to come in chase at any time if we try to slip out."

"That's right," growled the mate.

"Well, I was thinking, father, how would it be if we could foul the screw?"

"Why, a job, my lad, for them to clear it again."

"But wouldn't it be very risky work lying waiting while they tried to clear the screw? You know what tremendous currents there are running along the coast."

"But they wouldn't affect a craft lying at anchor, my lad," growled the mate.

"No," said Poole excitedly; "but I should expect to foul the screw just when they had given orders to up with the anchor to come in chase of us or to resist attack."

"And how would you do it, my lad?" said the skipper.

"Well, father, I was thinking—But I don't profess for a moment that it would succeed."

"Let's have what you thought, and don't talk so much," cried the skipper. "How could you foul the screw?"

"Well, the dinghy wouldn't do, father; it would be too small. We should have to go in the gig, with four men to row. I should like to take the big coil of Manilla cable aboard, with one end loose and handy, and a good rope ready. Then I should get astern and make the end fast to one of the fans of the screw, and give the cable a hitch round as well so as to give a good hold with the loop before we lowered it overboard to sink."

"Good," said Burgess. "Capital! And then if the fans didn't cut it when they began to revolve, they'd wind the whole of that cable round and round, and most likely regularly foul the screw badly before they found out what was wrong."

"Yes," said the skipper quietly. "The idea is excellent if it answered, but means the loss of a good new cable that I can't spare if things went wrong; and that's what they'd be pretty sure to do."

Poole drew a deep breath, and his face grew cloudy.

"The idea is too good, my lad. It is asking too much of luck, and we couldn't expect two such plans to succeed. What do you say, Burgess?"

"Same as you do," said the mate roughly. "But if we got one of our shots to go off right we ought to be satisfied, and if it was me I should have a try at both."

"Yes," said the skipper, "and we will. But it seems to me, Burgess, that you and I are going to be out of it all."

"Oh yes. They've planned it; let 'em do it, I say."

"Yes," said the skipper; "they shall. But look here, do you lads propose to do all this in one visit to the gunboat?"

"Poole's idea, sir, is all fresh to me," cried Fitz. "I knew nothing of it till he began to speak, but it seems to me that it must all be done in one visit. They'd never give us a chance to go twice."

"No," said the mate laconically, and as he uttered the word he shut his teeth with a snap.

"When's it to be, then?"

"To-night, sir," said Fitz, "while it's all red-hot."

"Yes, father; it ought to be done to-night. It's not likely to be darker than it is just now."

"Very well," said the skipper; "then I give you both authority to make your plans before night. But the dinghy is out of the question. With the current running off the coast here you'd never get back in that. You must take the gig, and five men. Pick out who you like, Poole: the men you would rather trust. You'd better let him choose, Mr Burnett; he knows the men so much better than you, and besides, it would be better that they should be under his orders than under yours. There, I have no more to say, except this—whether they succeed or not, your plans are both excellent; but you cannot expect to do anything by force. This is a case for scheme and cunning. Under the darkness it may be done. What I should like best would be for you to get that breech-block overboard. If you can do the other too, so much the better, but I shall be perfectly satisfied if you can do one, and get back safely into the river. There, Poole; make what arrangements you like. I shall not interfere in the least."

"Nor I," said the mate. "Good luck to you both! But I shouldn't worry much about preparing for a fight. What you have got to do is to act, cut, and run."

Chapter Forty Seven
'Cause why

"Now we know," said Poole joyously, as they left the cabin and went forward to their old place to discuss their plans: "what we have got to do is to cut and run. Come on; let's go and sit on the bowsprit again. It will soon be dinner-time. I wonder what the Camel has got?"

"Oh, don't talk about eating now," cried Fitz, as they reached the big spar, upon which he scrambled out, to sit swinging his legs, and closely followed by Poole. "What's the first thing?"

"Who's to man the gig," said Poole; "and I've got to pick the crew."

"I should like to pick one," cried Fitz.

"All right, go on; only don't choose the Camel, nor Bob Jackson."

"No, no; neither of them," cried Fitz. "I say, we ought to have old Butters."

"One," said Poole sharply. "Now it's my turn; Chips."

"Yes, I should like to have him," cried the middy. "But I don't know," he continued seriously. "He's a splendid fellow, and so handy; but he might want to turn it all into a lark."

"Not he," cried Poole. "He likes his bit of fun sometimes, but for a good man and true to have at my back in a job like this, he's the pick of the whole crew."

"Chips it is, then," said Fitz. "That's two."

"Dick Boulter, then."

"Three!" cried Fitz.

"Harry Smith."

"Four," said Fitz.

"Four, four, four, four," said Poole thoughtfully. "Who shall we have for number five? Here, we'll have the Camel, after all."

"Oh," cried Fitz; "there'll be nothing to cook."

"Yes, there will; the big gun and the propeller. He's cook, of course, but he's nearly as good a seaman as there is on board the schooner, and he'll row all right and never utter a word. There, we've got a splendid boat's crew, and I vote we go and tell father what we've done."

"I wouldn't," said Fitz. "It'll make him think that we hadn't confidence in ourselves. Unless he asks us, I wouldn't say a word."

"You are right," said Poole; "right as right. Now then, what's next? I know: we'll go and make the lads get up the Manilla rope and lay it down again in rings as close as they'll go."

"On the deck here?" said Fitz.

"No, no; right along the bottom of the gig. And we must have her lowered down first with two men in her, ready to coil the cable as the others pass it down. Now then, let's get inboard again and find old Butters."

"But he'll be wanting to know what we want with that rope."

"Sure to," said Poole; "but he'll have to wait. Oh, here he comes. Here, bosun!" he cried. "I want you to get up that new Manilla cable, lower down the gig, and coil it in the bottom so that it will take up as little room as possible, and not be in the men's way."

"What men's way?" said the boatswain. "Chips, Harry Smith, the Camel, and Dick Boulter," said Poole.

"Ho!" grunted the boatswain, and he took off his cap and began to scratch his head, staring at both in turn. "Whose orders?" he grunted, at last. "I just seen Mr Burgess, and he never said a word."

"The skipper's orders," cried Poole.

"Ho!" said the boatswain again. "Well, that's good enough for me," and he stood staring at them.

"Well, get the men together and see about the rope," cried Poole.

"What's your game? Going to take the end out to a steam-tug, or is the gunboat going to tow us out to sea?"

"Don't ask questions, please. It's private business of the skipper's, under the orders of Mr Burnett and me."

"Ho! All right, my lad; only oughtn't I to know what we are going to do? You are going off somewhere in the boat, eh?"

"Yes, that's right."

"And I'm not to come?"

"Oh, but you are," cried Poole, "and I've told you the men I've picked for the job. Don't you think it's a good crew?"

"Middling," said the boatswain grudgingly. "Might be better; might be wuss. But look here, young fellow; I don't like working in the dark."

"I am sorry for you," said Fitz, "for this will be an all-night job."

"Then I'd better take my nightcap," said the boatswain quietly. "But what's up? Are you going to make fast to the gunboat and tow her in?"

"You know we are not," replied Poole.

"Well, I did think it was rather an unpossible sort of job. But hadn't you better be open and above-board with a man, and say what it all means?"

"It means that you and the other men are under the orders of Mr Burnett and me, and that we look to you to do your best over what's going to be a particular venture. You'll know soon enough. Till then, please wait."

"All right," said the boatswain. "I'm your man. For the skipper wouldn't have given you these orders if it wasn't square;" saying which the man walked off to rouse up the little crew, all but the Camel, whom he left to his regular work in the galley. "We shan't want him yet," said Butters, as the boys followed him. "Had he better get us some rations to take with us?"

"Oh no," said Poole. "We oughtn't to be away more than three or four hours if we are lucky."

"Why, this 'ere gets mysteriouser and mysteriouser," grumbled the boatswain. "But I suppose it's going to be all right," and he proceeded to give his orders to the men.

"Now we shall begin to have them full of questions," said Poole. "I begin to wish we were making it all open and above-aboard."

"I don't," said Fitz; "I like it as it is. If we told everybody it would spoil half the fun."

"Fun!" cried Poole, screwing up his face into a quaint smile. "Fun, do you call it? Do you know that this is going to be a very risky job?"

"Well, I suppose there'll be some risk in it," replied the middy; "but it will be all in the dark, and we ought to get it done without a shot being fired. I say, though, I have been thinking that you and I must keep together, for I am afraid to trust myself over getting out that block. I should have liked to have done that first, but the splash it would make is bound to give the alarm, and there would be no chance afterwards to get that cable fast, without you let old Butters and the men do that while we were busy with the gun."

"No," said Poole decisively; "everything depends upon our doing these things ourselves. The cable can be made fast without a sound, and as soon as it is passed over the side of the boat, the men must lay the gig alongside the bows for us to swarm up, do our part, and then get to them the best way we can. I expect it will mean a jump overboard and a swim till they pick us up."

"Yes," said Fitz; "that's right. Ah, there comes the end of the cable. It's nice and soft to handle."

"Yes," said Poole, "and needn't make any noise."

The lads sauntered up to where the men were at work, three of them lowering down the gig, while the carpenter and boatswain were bringing up the cable out of the tier, the former on deck, the boatswain down below.

"So you're going to have a night's fishing, my lad?" said the carpenter. "Well, you'll find this 'ere a splendid line. But what about a hook?"

"Oh, we shan't want that yet, Chips," said Poole coolly.

"Nay, I know that, my lad; but you've got to think about it all the same, and you'll want a pretty tidy one for a line like this. I didn't know the fish run so big along this coast. Any one would think you'd got whales in your heads. I never 'eard, though, as there was any harpoons on board."

"Oh no, we are not going whale-fishing," said Poole quietly.

"What's it to be then, sir? Bottom fishing or top?"

"Top," said Poole.

"Then you'll be wanting me to make you a float. What's it to be? One of them big water-barrels with the topsail-yard run through? And you'll want a sinker. And what about a bait?"

"We haven't thought about that yet, Chips."

"Ah, you aren't like what I was when I was a boy, Mr Poole, sir. I used to think about it the whole day before, and go to the butcher's for my maggits, and down the garden for my wums. Of course I never fished in a big way like this 'ere; but I am thinking about a bait. I should like you to have good sport. Means hard work for the Camel to-morrow, I suppose."

"And to-night too, Chips, I hope," said Poole.

"That's right, sir," said the man cheerily, as he hauled upon the cable. "But what about that bait? I know what would be the right thing; perhaps the skipper mightn't approve, and not being used to it Mr Burnett here mightn't like to use such a bait."

"Oh, I don't suppose I should mind, Chips," said Fitz, laughing. "What should you recommend?"

"Well, sir, I should say, have the dinghy and go up the river a mile or two till we could land and catch a nice lively little nigger—one of them very shiny ones. That would be the sort."

The two lads forgot the seriousness of the mission they had in view, exchanged glances, and began to laugh, with the result that the man turned upon them quite an injured look.

"Oh, it's quite right, gentlemen; fishes have their fancies and likings for a tasty bit, same as crocodiles has. I arn't sailed all round the world without picking up a few odds and ends to pack up in my knowledge-box. Why, look at sharks. They don't care for nigger; it's too plentiful. But let them catch sight of a leg or a wing of a nice smart white sailor, they're after it directly. Them crocs too! Only think of a big ugly lizardy-looking creetur boxed up in a skin half rhinoceros, half cow-horn—just fancy him having his fads and fancies! Do you know what the crocodile as lives in the river Nile thinks is the choicest tit-bit he can get hold of?"

"Not I," said Poole. "Giraffe perhaps."

"No, sir; what he says is dog, and if he only hears a dog running along the bank yelping and snapping and chy-iking, he's after him directly, finishes him up, and then goes and lies down in the hot sun with his mouth wide open, and goes to sleep. Ah, you may laugh, sir; but I've been up there in one of them barges as they calls darbyers, though how they got hold of such an Irish name as that I don't know. It was along with a orficer as went up there shooting crocs and pottomhouses. Oh, I've seen the crocs there often—lots of them. Do you know what they opens their mouths for when they goes to sleep, Mr Burnett, sir?"

"To yawn, I suppose," said Fitz. "Haul away there, my lad! Look alive!" came in a deep growl from below; and Chips winked and made the great muscles stand out in his brown arms as he hauled, but kept on talking all the same.

"Yawn, sir! Nay, that isn't it. It's a curiosity in nat'ral history, and this 'ere's fact. You young gents may believe it or not, just as you like."

"Thank you," said Fitz dryly; "I'll take my choice."

"Ah, I expect you won't believe it, sir. But this 'ere's what it's for. He leaves his front-door wide open like that, and there's a little bird with a long beak as has been waiting comes along, hippity-hop, and settles on the top of Mr Croc's head, and looks at first one eye and then at the other to see if he's really asleep, and that there is no gammon. He aren't a-going to run no risks, knowing as he does that a croc's about one of the artfullest beggars as ever lived. I suppose that's why they calls 'em amphibious. Oh, they're rum 'uns, they are! They can sham being dead, and make theirselves look like logs of wood with the rough bark on, and play at being in great trouble and cry, so as to get people to come nigh them to help, and then snip, snap, they has 'em by the leg, takes them under water to drown, and then goes and puts 'em away in the cupboard under the bank."

"What for?" said Poole.

"What for, sir? Why, to keep till they gets tender. Them there Errubs of the desert gets so sun-tanned that they are as tough as string; so hard, you know, that they wouldn't even agree with a croc. Yo-hoy! Haul oh, and here she comes!" added the man, in a low musical bass voice to himself, as he kept on dragging at the soft Manilla rope.

"I say, Burnett," said Poole seriously, "don't you think we'd better get pencil and paper and put all this down—Natural History Notes by Peter Winks, Head Carpenter of the Schooner *Teal*?"

"Nay, nay, sir, don't you do that. Stick to fact. That's what I don't like in people as writes books about travel. They do paint it up so, and lay it on so thick that the stuff cracks, comes off, and don't look nat'ral."

"Then you wouldn't put down about that little bird that comes hippity-hop and looks at the crocodile's eyes?"

"What, sir! Why, that's the best part of it. That's the crumb of the whole business."

"Oh, I see," said Fitz. "Then that's a fact?"

"To be sure, sir. He's larnt it from old experience. I dare say he's seen lots go down through the croc turning them big jaws of his into a bird-trap and shutting them up sudden, when of course there aren't no more bird. But that's been going on for hundreds of thousands of years, and the birds know better now, and wait till it's quite safe before they begin."

"Begin what?" said Fitz sharply.

"Well, sir," said the carpenter, as he hauled away, "that's what I want to tell you, only you keep on interrupting me so."

Fitz closed his teeth with a snap.

"Go on, Chips," he said. "I'll be mute as a fish."

"Well, sir, as I said afore, you young gents can believe it or you can let it alone: that there little bird, or them little birds, for there's thousands of them, just the same as there is crocodiles, and they are all friendly together, I suppose because crocs is like birds in one thing—they makes nests and lays eggs, and the birds, as I'm telling of you, does this as reg'lar as clockwork. When the croc's had his dinner and gone to sleep with his front-door wide open, the little chap comes hopping and peeping along close round the edge, and then gets his own living by picking the crocodile's teeth."

"Ha-ha!" laughed Fitz. "'Pon my word, Poole, I should like to put this down."

"Oh, it don't want no putting down, sir; it's a fact; a cracker turns mouldy and drops off."

"Well, won't this go bad?" cried Fitz, laughing.

"Not it, sir. You don't believe it, I see, but it's all natur'. It's a-using up of the good food as the croc don't want, and which would all be wasted, for he ain't a clean-feeding sort of beast. He takes his food in chops and chunks, and swallows it indecent-like all in lumps. A croc ain't like a cow as sits down with her eyes half shut and chews and chews away, sentimental-like, turning herself into a dairy and making a good supply of beautiful milk such as we poor sailors never hardly gets a taste on in our tea. A croc is as bad as a shark, a nasty sort of feeder, and if I was you young gents I'd have a study when I got ashore again, and look in some of your big books, and you'd find what I says is all there."

"Did you find what you've been telling us all there?" said Poole.

"Nay, my lad; I heard best part of it from my officer that I used to go with. Restless sort of chap he was—plenty of money, and he liked spending it in what he called exhibitions—No, that aren't right—expeditions—that's it; and he used to take me. What he wanted to find was what he called the Nile Sauce; but he never found it, and we never wanted it. My word, the annymiles as he used to shoot when we was hungry, and that was always. My word, the fires I used to make, and the way I used to cook! Why, I could have given the Camel fifty out of a hundred and beat him. We didn't want any sauce. Did either of you gents ever taste heland steak? No, I suppose not. Fresh cut, frizzled brown, sprinkled with salt, made hotter with a dash of pepper, and then talk about juice and gravy! Lovely! Wish we'd got some now. Why, in some of our journeys up there in what you may call the land of nowhere and nobody, we was weeks sometimes without seeing a soul, only annymiles—ah, and miles and miles of them. I never see such droves and never shall again. They tell me that no end of them has got shot.—Beautiful creatures they were too! Such coats; and such long thin legs and arms, and the way they'd go over the sandy ground was wonderful. They never seemed to get tired. I've seen a drove of them go along like a hurricane, and when they have pulled up short to stare at us, and you'd think that they hadn't got a bit of breath left in their bodies, they set-to larking, hip, snip, jumping over one another's backs like a lot of school-boys at leap-frog, only ten times as high."

"Did you ever see any lions?" said Fitz, growing more serious as he began to realise that there was very little fiction and a great deal of fact in the sailor's yarn.

"Lots, sir. There have been times when you could hear them roaring all round our camp. Here, I want to speak the truth. My governor used to call it camp, but it was only a wagging, and we used to sleep on the sand among the wheels. Why, I've lain there with my hand making my gun rusty, it got so hot and wet with listening to them pretty pussy-cats come creeping round us, and one of them every now and then putting up his head and roaring till you could almost feel the ground shake. Ah, you may chuckle, Mr Poole, but that's a fact too; I've felt it, and I know. And do you know why they roared?"

"Because they were hungry?"

"Partly, sir; but most of it's artfulness. It's because they know that it will make the bullocks break away—stampede, as they calls it—and rush off from where there's people to take care of them with rifles, and then they can pick off just what they like. But they don't care much about big bullock. They've got tasty ideas of their own, same as crocs have. What they likes is horse, and the horses knows it too, poor beggars! It's been hard work to hold them sometimes—my governor's horse, you know, as he hunted on; and I've heard them sigh and groan as if with satisfaction when the governor's fired with his big double breech-loader and sent the lions off with their tails trailing behind and leaving a channel among their footprints in the sand. I've seen it, Mr Burnett, next morning, and I know."

"All right, Chips," cried Poole. "We won't laugh at you and your yarns. But now look here; there must be no more chaff. This is serious work."

"All right, sir," said the man good-humouredly, as he wiped his dripping face. "No one can't say as I aren't working—not even old Butters."

"No, no," said Poole hastily. "You are working well."

"And no one can't say, sir, as I've got my grumbling stop out, which I do have sometimes," he added, with a broad grin, "and lets go a bit."

"You do, Chips; but I want you to understand that this is a very serious bit of business we are on."

"O!"

A very large, round, thoughtful O, and the man hauled steadily away, nodding his head the while.

"Serous, eh? Then you aren't going fishing?"

"Fishing, no!"

"Then it's something to do with the gunboat?"

"Don't ask questions," cried Poole. "Be satisfied that we are going on a very serious expedition, and we want you to help us all you can."

"Of course, my lads. Shall I want my tools?"

"No."

The man was silent for a few moments, looking keenly from one to the other, and then at the rope, before giving his leg a sharp slap, and whispering with his face full of animation—

"Why, you're going to steal aboard the gunboat in the dark, and make fast one end of this 'ere rope to that there big pocket-pistol, so as we can haul her overboard. But no, lads, it can't be done. But even if it could it would only stick fast among them coral rocks that lie off yonder."

"And what would that matter, so long as we got it overboard?"

"Ah, I never thought of that. But no, my lad; you may give that up. It couldn't be done."

"Well, it isn't going to be done," said Fitz sharply; "and now let's have no more talk. But mind this—Mr Poole and I don't want you to say anything to the other men. It's a serious business, and we want you to wait."

"That's right, sir. I'll wait and help you all I can; and I'll make half-a-davy, as the lawyers calls it, that I won't tell the other lads anything. 'Cause why—I don't know."

Chapter Forty Eight
Very wrong

Very little more was said, and the preparations were soon finished, with the rest of the crew looking on in silence. It seemed to be an understood thing, after a few words had passed with the selected men, that there was to be no palaver, as they termed it.

As for Fitz and Poole, they had nothing to do but think, and naturally they thought a great deal, especially when the night came on, with the watching party who had been sent below to the mouth of the river back with the announcement that the gunboat was in its old place, the boats all up to the davits, and not a sign of anything going on. But far from taking this as a token of safety, the skipper and mate made their arrangements to give the enemy a warm welcome if they should attack, and also despatched a couple of men in the dinghy to make fast just off the edge of the first bend and keep watch there, trusting well to their ears for the first warning of any boat that might be coming up.

The two lads stole away into their favourite place for consultations as soon as it was dark, to have what they called a quiet chat over their plans.

"I don't see that we could do any more," said Fitz, "but we must keep talking about it. The time goes so horribly slowly. Generally speaking when you are expecting anything it goes so fast; now it crawls as if the time would never be here."

"Well, that's queer," said Poole. "Ever since I knew that we were going it has seemed to gallop."

"Well, whether it gallops or whether it crawls it can't be very long before it's time to start. I say, how do you feel?"

"Horrible," said Poole. "It makes me think that I must be a bit of a coward, for I want to shirk the responsibility and be under somebody's command. My part seems to be too much for a fellow like me to undertake. You don't feel like that, of course."

Fitz sat there in the darkness for a few minutes without speaking. Then after heaving a deep sigh—

"I say," he whispered, "shall you think me a coward if I say I feel just like that?"

"No. Feeling as I do, of course I can't."

"Well, that's just how I am," said Fitz. "Sometimes I feel as if I were quite a man, but now it's as if I was never so young before, and that it is too much for chaps like us to understand such a thing."

"Then if we are both like that," said Poole sadly, "I suppose we ought to be honest and go straight to the dad and tell him that we don't feel up to it. What do you say?"

"What!" cried Fitz. "Go and tell him coolly that we are a pair of cowardly boys, for him and Mr Burgess to laugh at, and the men—for they'd be sure to hear—to think of us always afterwards as a pair of curs? I'd go and be killed first! And so would you; so don't tell me you wouldn't."

"Not going to," said Poole. "I'll only own up that I'm afraid of the job; but as we've proposed it, and it would be doing so much good if we were to succeed, I mean to go splash at it and carry it through to the end. You will too, won't you?"

"Yes, of course."

There was a slight rustling sound then, caused by the two lads reaching towards one another and joining hands in a long firm grip.

"Hah!" exclaimed Fitz, with a long-drawn expiration of the breath. "I'm glad I've got that off my mind. I feel better now."

"Same here. Now, what shall we do next? Go and talk to old Butters and tell him what we want him to do?"

"No," cried Fitz excitedly. "You forget that we are in command. We've no business to do anything till the time comes, and then give the men their orders sharp and short, as if we were two skippers."

"Ah, yes," said Poole, "that's right. That's what I want to do, only it seems all so new."

"I tell you what, though," said Fitz. "We shall be going for hours and hours without getting anything, and that'll make us done up and weak. I vote that as we are to do as we like, we go and stir up the Camel and tell him to send us in a nice meal to the cabin."

"But it isn't long since we had something," suggested Poole.

"Yes, but neither of us could eat nor enjoy it. I couldn't, and I was watching you; but I feel that I could eat now, so come on. It'll help to pass the time, and make us fit to do anything."

"All right," said Poole, and they fetched Andy from where he was sitting forward talking in whispers with his messmates, told him what they wanted, and ordered him to prepare a sort of tea-supper for the little crew of the gig.

The Camel was ready enough, and within half-an-hour the two lads were doing what Poole termed stowing cargo, the said cargo consisting of rashers of prime fried ham, cold bread-cake, hot coffee and preserved milk.

They did good justice to the meal too, and before they had ended the skipper came down to them, looked on for a minute or two, and then nodded his satisfaction.

"That looks well, my lads," he said. "It's business-like, and as if your hearts were so much in your work that you didn't feel disposed to shirk it. It makes me comfortable, for I was getting a little nervous about you, I must own."

The boys exchanged glances, but said nothing.

"Here, don't mind me," continued the skipper. "Make a good hearty meal, and I'll talk to you as you eat."

"About our going and what we are about to do, father?" said Poole.

"Well, my boy, yes, of course."

"I wish you wouldn't, father. It's too late now to be planning and altering, and that sort of thing."

"Yes, please, Captain Reed," cried Fitz excitedly. "It's like lessons at school. We ought to know what we've got to do by now, and learning at the last minute won't do a bit of good. If we succeed we succeed, and if we fail we fail."

"Do you know what a big writer said, my boy, when one of his characters was going off upon an expedition?"

"No, sir," said Fitz.

"Good luck to you, perhaps," said Poole, laughing, though the laugh was not cheery.

"No, my lad," said the skipper. "I have not been much of a reader, and I'm not very good at remembering wise people's sayings, but he said to the young fellow when he talked as you did about failing, 'In the bright lexicon of youth there is no such word as fail,' which I suppose was a fine way of saying, Go and do what you have got to do, and never think of not succeeding. You're not going to fail. You mustn't. There's too much hanging to it, my boys; and now I quite agree with you that we'll let things go as they are."

Chapter Forty Nine
Chips sniffs

The silence and darkness made the lads' start for their venturesome expedition doubly impressive, the more so that the men were looking on in silence and wonder, and no light was shown on board the schooner. The gig with its load of cable had been swinging for hours by the painter, and midnight was near at hand, when the little crew, each armed with cutlass and revolver, stood waiting for their orders to slip down into their seats.

This order came at last, accompanied by one command from the skipper, and it was this—

"Perfect silence, my lads. Obey orders, and do your best.—Now, my boys," he continued, as soon as the men were in the boat, "do not fire a shot unless you are absolutely obliged. Mr Burgess will follow in the large boat with a dozen men, to lie off the mouth of the river ready to help you if you are in trouble; so make for there. If you want to signal to them to come to you, strike a couple of matches one after the other, and throw them into the water at once. Last night the gunboat did not show a light. I expect that it will be the same to-night, as they will think they are safer; but I fancy amongst you, you will have eyes sharp enough to make her out, and the darkness will be your best friend, so I hope the sea will not brime. There, your hand, Mr Burnett. Now yours, Poole, my boy. Over with you at once."

The next minute the boys had slid down into the boat, to seat themselves in the stern-sheets with the boatswain; the carpenter pulled the stroke oar, so that he was within reach if they wished to speak, and with the boatswain taking the rudder-lines they glided slowly down the stream.

"Tell them just to dip their oars to keep her head straight, boatswain," said Poole quietly. "We have plenty of time, and we had better keep out in mid-stream. A sharp look-out for anything coming up."

"Ay, ay, my lad," was the reply, and they seemed to slip on into the black darkness which rose before them like a wall, while overhead, like a deep purple band studded with gold, the sky stretched from cliff to cliff of the deep ravine through which the river ran.

"Now, Poole," said Fitz suddenly, speaking in a low voice, almost a whisper, "you had better say a word or two to Mr Butters about the work we are on."

"No," replied Poole; "it was your idea, and you're accustomed to take command of a boat, so you had better speak, for the boatswain and the carpenter ought to know. The other men will have nothing to do but manage the gig—"

"Hah!" ejaculated the boatswain, in a deep sigh, while Chips, who had heard every word, only gave vent to a sniff.

Fitz coughed slightly, as if troubled with something that checked his breath.

"Then look here, Mr Butters," he said quickly; "we're off to disable the gunboat yonder, and do two things."

"Good!" came like a croak.

"First thing is to foul the screw."

There was another croak, followed by—

"Lay that there cable so that she tangles herself up first time she turns. That's one."

Fitz coughed again slightly.

"You will run the boat up in silence, the men will hold on, while you and Chips make fast the end to one of the fans, and then let the cable glide out into the water as we pass round to the bows. It must all be done without a sound. All the rope must be run out, to sink, and then I propose that you hold on again under the starboard anchor."

"Suppose starboard anchor's down?" growled the boatswain.

"Pass the boat round to the port; either will do; but if we are seen or heard, all is over."

"Won't be seen," growled the boatswain. "It's black enough to puzzle a cat."

"Very well, then—heard," continued Fitz.

"Right, sir. What next?"

"There are no more orders. You will hold on while Mr Poole and I get aboard. We shall do the rest."

"Hah!" sighed the boatswain; and like an echo came a similar sound from the carpenter.

Then *pat, pat, pat* came the kissing of the water against the bows of the gig, and the sides of the ravine seemed as weird and strange as ever, while the darkness if anything grew more profound.

At this point, with the boat gliding swiftly down stream, Poole leaned sideways to run his hand down Fitz's sleeve, feel for his hand, and give it a warm pressure, which was returned.

Then they went on round bend after bend, the current keeping them pretty well in the centre, till at last the final curve was reached, the starry band overhead seemed to have suddenly grown wider and the air less oppressive, both hints that they were getting out to sea, and that the time for the performance of the daring enterprise was close at hand.

Most fortunately the sea did not "brime," as the West-countrymen say, when the very meshes of their nets turn into threads of gold through the presence of the myriad phosphorescent creatures that swarm so thickly at times that the surface of the sea looks as if it could be skimmed to clear it of so much lambent liquid gold.

This was what was wanted, for with a phosphorescent sea, every dip of the oar, every wavelet which broke against the boat, would have served as signal to warn the watch on board the gunboat that enemies were near.

But unfortunately, on the other hand, there was the darkness profound, and not the scintillation of a riding light to show where the gunboat lay. They knew that she was about two miles from shore, and as nearly as could be made out just at the mouth of the channel along which the *Teal* had been piloted to enable her to reach the sanctuary in which she lay.

But where was she now? The answer did not come to the watchers who with straining eyes strove to make out the long, low, dark hull, the one mast, and the dwarfed and massive funnel, but strove in vain.

Fitz's heart sank, for the successful issue of his exploit seemed to be fading away, and minute by minute it grew more evident that there was not the slightest likelihood of their discovering the object of their search; so that in a voice tinged by the despair he felt, he whispered his orders to the boatswain to tell the men to cease rowing.

Then for what seemed to be quite a long space of time, they lay rising and falling upon the heaving sea, listening, straining their eyes, but all in vain; and at last, warned by the feeling that unless something was done they were bound to lose touch of their position when they wanted to make back for the mouth of the little river, Fitz whispered an order to the boatswain to keep the gig's head straight off shore, and then turned to lay his hand on Poole's shoulder and, with his lips close to his ear, whisper —

"What's to be done?"

"Don't know," came back. "This is a regular floorer."

The boy's heart sank lower still at this, but feeling that he was in command, he made an effort to pull himself together.

"In the bright lexicon of youth there is no such word as fail," seemed to begin ringing as if at a great distance into his ears, and he rose up in his place, steadied himself by a hand on his companion's shoulder, and slowly swept the horizon; that is to say, the lower portion of the sky, to which the stars did not descend.

In vain!

There was no sign of gunboat funnel, nothing to help them in the least, and coming to the conclusion that their only chance of finding her was by quartering the sea as a sporting dog does a field, and at the same time telling himself that the task was hopeless, he bent down to try if he could get a hint from the boatswain, when he muttered to himself the words that had now ceased to ring, and his heart gave quite a jump. For apparently about a hundred yards away there appeared a faint speck of light which burned brightly for a few moments before with a sudden dart it described a curve, descending towards the level of the sea; and then all was black again.

For a moment or two the darkness upon the sea seemed to lie there thicker and heavier than ever, till, faint, so dim that it was hardly visible, the lad was conscious of a tiny light which brightened slightly, grew dim, brightened again, and then the boatswain uttered a low "Hah!" and Chips sniffed softly, this time for a reason, for he was inhaling the aroma of a cigar, borne towards them upon the soft damp night air.

The lads joined hands again, and in the warm pressure a thrill of exultation seemed to run from their fingers right up their arms and into their breasts, to set their hearts pumping with a heavy throb.

Neither dared venture upon a whisper to inform his comrade of that which he already knew—that some one on board the gunboat was smoking, probably the officer of the watch, and that they must wait in the hope that he might go below after a look round, when there was still a possibility that the crew might sleep, or at least be sufficiently lax in their duty to enable the adventurers to carry out their plans. They could do nothing else, only wait; but as they waited, with Fitz still grasping his companion's hand, they both became conscious of the fact that by slow degrees the glowing end of that cigar grew brighter; and the reason became patent—that the current running outward from the river, even at that distance from the shore, was bearing them almost imperceptibly nearer to where the gunboat lay.

The idea was quite right, for fortune was after all favouring them, more than they dared to have hoped. All at once, as they were watching the glowing light, whose power rose and fell, those on board the gig were conscious of a slight jerk, accompanied by a grating sound. This was followed by a faint rustle from the fore part of the boat. What caused this, for a few moments no one in the after part could tell.

They knew that they had run upon something, and by degrees Fitz worked out the mental problem in his mind, as with his heart beating fast he watched the glowing light, in expectation of some sign that the smoker had heard the sound as well.

But he still smoked on, and nothing happened to the boat, which had careened over at first and threatened to capsize, but only resumed her level trim and completely reversed her position, head taking the place of stern, so that to continue to watch the light the middy had to wrench himself completely round; and then he grasped the fact that the current had carried them right on to the anchor-chain where it dipped beneath the surface, before bearing them onward, still to swing at ease.

The man who acted as coxswain—the Camel to wit—having leaned over, grasped the chain-cable and almost without a sound made fast the painter to one of the links.

Chapter Fifty
A daring deed

The brains of the other occupants of the boat had been as active as those of Fitz, and their owners had come to pretty well the same conclusion, as they all involuntarily lowered their heads and sat perfectly still listening, and hardly able to believe that the man who was smoking was not watching them and about to give the alarm.

But the moments glided by and became minutes, while the silence on board the gunboat seemed painful. The perspiration stood upon Fitz's brow, forming drops which gradually ran together and then began to trickle down the sides of his nose, tickling horribly; but he dared not even raise his hand to wipe them away.

By degrees, though, all became convinced that they could not be seen, and something in the way of relief came at the end of about a quarter of an hour, when all at once the cigar in the man's mouth glowed more brightly, and then brighter still as it made a rush through the air, describing a curve and falling into the sea, when the silence was broken by a hiss so faint that it was hardly heard, and by something else which was heard plainly.

Some one, evidently the smoker, gave vent to a yawn, a Spanish yawn, no doubt, but as much like an English one as it could be. Then, just audible in the silence, there was the faint sound of feet, as of some one pacing up and down the deck, another yawn, and then utter silence once again.

No one stirred in the gig; no one seemed to breathe; till at last Poole raised his hand to Fitz's shoulder, leaned closer till he could place his lips close to his companion's ear, and whispered softly—

"I think they've let the fires out. I've been watching where the funnel must be, and I haven't seen a spark come out."

Fitz changed his position a little so as to follow his companion's example, and whispered in turn—

"Nor I neither, but I fancy I can see a quivering glow, and I've smelt the sulphur quite plainly."

There was another pause, and Poole whispered—

"Think there's anybody on deck?"

The answer came—

"If there is he must be asleep."

"What about that chap who was smoking?"

"I think after that last yawn he went below."

"Then isn't it time we began?"

Fitz whispered back—

"Yes, if we are going to do anything; but our plans seem turned topsy-turvy. We are close to the bows, where we ought to get up for me to tackle the gun."

"Yes," whispered Poole, "but if we do that there'll be no chance afterwards to foul the screw; and that ought to be done, so that we can get rid of this cable. It will be horribly in the way if we have to row for our lives."

Fitz pressed his companion's arm sharply, for at that moment there was another yawn from the gunboat's deck, followed by a muttering grumbling sound as of two men talking, suggesting that one had woke the other, who was finding fault. But all sound died out, and then there was the deep silence once again.

The lads waited till they thought all was safe, while their crew never stirred, and Poole whispered once more—"Well, what is to be done?"

The next moment Fitz's lips were sending tickling words into the lad's ear, as he said sharply—

"Mustn't change—stick to our plans. I am going to tell Butters to work the boat alongside, and then pass her to the stern."

"Hah!" breathed Poole, as he listened for the faint rustle made by his companion in leaning towards the boatswain and whispering his commands.

The next minute the boat was in motion, being paddled slowly towards the gunboat in a way the boys did not know till afterwards, for it was as if the gig as it lay there in the black darkness was some kind of fish, which had suddenly put its fins in motion, the five men having leaned sideways, each to lower a hand into the water and paddle the boat along without a sound.

The darkness seemed to be as black as it could possibly be, but all at once, paradoxical as it may seem, it grew thicker, for a great black wall had suddenly appeared looming over the boat, and Poole put out his hand, to feel the cold armour-plating gliding by his fingers, as the men, to his astonishment, kept the craft in motion till they had passed right along and their progress was checked by the gig being laid bow-on beside the gunboat's rudder; and as soon as the lads could fully realise their position they grasped the fact that the propeller must be just beneath the water the boat's length in front of where they sat.

Then silence once again, every one's heart beating slowly, but with a dull heavy throb that seemed to send the blood rushing through the arteries and veins, producing in the case of the lads a sensation of dizziness that was some moments before it passed off, driven away as it was by the tension and the acute desire to grasp the slightest sound where there was none to grasp.

Every one was waiting now—as all felt sure that so far they had not been heard—for the middy's order to commence, while he felt as if he dared not give it, sitting there and letting the time glide by, convinced as he was now that the end of the Manilla cable could not be attached to one of the fans without their being heard, and in imagination he fancied the alarm spread, and saw his chance of ascending to the deck and reaching the gun, die away.

Then he started, for Poole pinched his arm, sending a thrill through him, and as it were setting the whole of his human machine in action.

"Now or never," he said to himself, and leaning forward to the boatswain he whispered a few words in the man's ear, with the result that a very faint rustling began, a sound so slight that it was almost inaudible to him who gave the order; but he could feel the boat move slightly, as it was held fast beside the rudder, and the next minute when the young captain of the adventure raised his hand—as he could not see—to feel how the boatswain was getting on, he touched nothing, for the big sturdy fellow was already half-way to the bows of the gig.

Fitz breathed hard again, and listened trembling now lest they should fail; but all was perfectly still save that the boat rocked slightly, which rocking ceased and gave place to a quivering pulsation, as if the slight craft had been endowed with life. This went on while the two lads gazed forward and with their minds' eyes saw the boatswain reach the bows and join the Camel, while two of the men who had not stirred from their places held on by the rudder and stern-post, one of them having felt about till his hand encountered a ring-bolt, into which he had thrust a finger to form a living hook.

And as the lads watched they saw in imagination all that went on. They did not hear a sound, either in the bows or from above upon the gunboat's deck, while the two handy men were hard at work laying out the rope that was already securely attached to the cable; and then came the first sound, just after the boat moved sharply, as if it had given a slight jump.

The slight sound was the faintest of splashes, such as might have been caused by a small fish, and it was due to the end of the rope slipping down into the water, while the jump on the part of the boat was caused by its having been lightened of Chips's weight, for he had drawn himself upwards by grasping the rudder, across which he now sat astride, to grip it with his knees. The man wanted no telling what to do. He had rehearsed it all mentally again and again, and quick and clever of finger, he passed the rope through the opening between rudder and stern-post, and drew upon it softly and steadily till he had it taut, and was dragging upon the cable. Old Burgess was working with him as if one mind animated the two bodies.

He knew what would come, and waited as the spiral strands of the rope passed through his hand; and when it began to grow taut he was ready to raise up the end of the big soft cable, pass it upwards, and hold it in place, so that it gradually assumed the form of a loop some ten feet long, and it was the head of that loop that jammed as it was drawn tight against the opening between stern-post and rudder, and very slowly laced tightly in position by means of the rope.

But this took time, and twice over Chips ceased working, as if he had failed; but it was only for a rest and a renewal of his strength, before he ceased for the third time and made a longer wait. But no one made a sign; no one stirred, though the two lads sat in agony, building up in imagination a very mountain of horror and despair branded failure in their minds, for they could hardly conceive that their plans were being carried out so silently and so well.

At last Fitz gripped Poole's arm again so as to whisper to him; but the whisper did not pass, for at that moment, after being perfectly still for some time, the boat began to pulsate again, for the carpenter was hard at work once more, his hands acting in combination with those of the boatswain, for, still very slowly, working like a piece of machinery, they began to haul upon the cable in the boat. At the first tightening that cable now seemed to begin to live like some huge serpent, and creep towards them, the life with which it was infused coming, however, from the Camel's hands, as, feeling that it was wanted, he began to pass it along, raising each coil so that it should not touch against the gunwale of the boat, or scrape upon a thwart.

He too knew what was going on, as between them, the boatswain in the bows, the carpenter still astride the upper portion of the rudder, they got up enough of the cable to form another loop, whose head was softly plunged down into the water, passed under one fan of the great screw and over another, and then, its elasticity permitting, drawn as tight as the men could work it.

This feat was performed again, and as final security the boatswain formed a bight, which he thrust down and passed over the fan whose edge was almost level with the surface.

Then as the boys sat breathing hard, and fancying that the daylight must be close at hand, the boat gave another jerk, careening over sideways towards the rudder, for the carpenter had slowly descended into the bows, to crouch down and rest.

But the boatswain was still at work, with the Camel now for mate, and between them they two were keeping up the quivering motion of the gig, as, slowly and silently, they went on passing the thick soft Manilla cable over the side, to sink down into the sea until the last of the long snaky coils had gone.

The announcement of this fact was conveyed to the two lads by the motion of the boat, Fitz learning it first by feeling his right hand as it hung over the side begin to pass steadily through the water, which rippled between his fingers; and as he snatched it out to stretch it forth as far as he could reach, he for a few moments touched nothing. Then it came in contact with the sides of the gunboat, and his heart gave a jump and his nerves thrilled, for he knew that the first act of their desperate venture was at an end, that the gig was gliding forward, paddled by the sailors' hands, towards the gunboat's bows, so as to reach one or other of the hanging anchors, up which he had engaged to scramble and get on board to do his part, which, now that the other had been achieved, seemed to be the most desperate of all.

"I shall never be able to go through with it," he seemed to groan to himself in his despair; but at that moment, as if by way of encouragement, he felt Poole's hand grip his arm, and at the touch the remembrance of the skipper's words thrilled through his nerves, to give him strength.

The next moment he was sitting up firmly and bravely in his place, tucking up his cuffs as if for the fight, as he softly muttered—

"There is no such word as fail."

Chapter Fifty One
Is the deed done?

The boat had stopped, and Fitz had heard the faintest of faint clicks as of iron against iron, for the hook in the carpenter's hands had lightly come in contact with the port anchor, which was hanging in its place, teaching them that it was the starboard that was down; and as Fitz looked up sharply, he fully expected to see a row of faces peering over the bulwark and looking down into the boat as the watchers gave the alarm, which would result in a shower of missiles being hurled upon their heads, the precursors of a heavy shot that would go crashing through the bottom of the boat. But he was only gazing up at a black edge and the stars beyond, and just above his head something rugged and curved which he knew were the anchor's flukes.

Fitz knew that to hesitate was to give place to doubts as to his success, and that the longer he waited the more likely they were to be discovered. That no watch was being kept was certain, and rising in the boat he took hold of the anchor as far up as he could reach, its ponderous nature rendering it immovable; and drawing himself steadily upward he began to climb.

It was easy enough to an active lad, and once started there was no time for shrinking. Quickly enough he was standing first upon the flukes, then upon the stock, while the next minute he was grasping the port-rail and trying to look down on to the deck, where he fancied he made out the figures of three or four men. But everything was so indistinct that he could not be sure, and he prepared to climb over, when he felt a touch upon his arm and started violently, for he had forgotten their arrangement that Poole should bear a part in the disabling of the gun.

He dared not speak, but just gave his companion's arm a grip, slipped silently over the bulwark, and went down at once on all-fours like a dog. Poole was by his side directly, and as they knelt, both tried to make out the exact position of the gun, and both failed, till Fitz lowered himself a little more, and then repeating his investigation managed to bring the muzzle of the great piece between him and the stars, towards which it was pointed, slightly raised.

All was so still, and the deck apparently so deserted, that his task now seemed to be ridiculously easy; and beginning to creep aft towards the great carriage, which was planted a little forward of 'midships, one hand suddenly came into contact with something soft and warm, with the result that there was an angry snarl, a snap, and a hand was brought down with a heavy slap upon the deck.

In an instant there was a start, and a low growling voice asked what was apparently a question as to what was the matter. The response came from the man who had struck the blow; but what he said was unintelligible to the listeners, who had immediately shrunk flat upon the deck, conscious as they were that two of the crew had been sleeping within touch, while for aught they knew others might be all around.

All notion now of the task being ridiculously easy was swept away, and the two adventurous lads lay hardly daring to breathe for what seemed a quarter of an hour, before a deep stertorous breathing told that the danger was for the moment passed and the time for action come.

It was Fitz who this time set the example of beginning, and he did it by thrusting softly with one foot till he could feel where Poole lay ready to seize him by the ankle and give it a warm pressure which the lad took to mean—Go on.

Raising himself a little, he began to creep aft once more, bearing to his left towards where he believed the carriage and turn-table of the great gun to be, and reaching them without further interruption, and so easily that his task seemed to become once more simple in the extreme.

Reaching carefully out, he satisfied himself as to his position, took a step upward, and found directly after that he was about the middle of the gun, whose breech lay a little to the right and was reached with ease.

"Oh, if I could only whisper to Poole," he thought. "Come on, quick, old fellow, and then together we can get it to the side, drop it overboard, and follow so quickly that we need only make one splash, for it would be impossible to go back as we came."

"Yes, that will be the way," thought Fitz; "and our fellows will row towards the splash at once, and pick us up. Why didn't I think to tell them? Never mind. That's what they are sure to do."

Directly after he was running his hand along the pleasantly cool surface of the gun; but he paused for a moment to listen, and begin to wonder in the darkness why it was that Poole had not made some sign of being near.

He reached back, giving a sweep with his hand; but Poole was not there, and he took a step forward to repeat the movement—still in vain.

"Oh, I am wasting time," thought Fitz, as he stepped back to his former position. "He's waiting for me to reconnoitre and fetch him if I want him."

In this spirit he felt the gun again, guiding himself by his hands to its huge butt, his fingers coming in contact first with the sight and then with the two massive ball-ended levers which turned the great screw.

He could barely see at all, but his finger-tips told him that it was just such a piece as they had on board the *Tonans*, but not so large.

Forgetting Poole for the moment, he passed right round to the breech, thrust in his hand, which came in contact with the solid block, and then withdrawing his hand he seized hold of the great balls, gave them a wrench, and in perfect silence the heavy mass of forged and polished steel began to turn, the well-oiled grooves and worm gliding together without a sound, and, after the first tug, with the greatest ease.

It was all simple enough till he came to the final part of his task, and attempted to lift out the breech-block, the quoin that when the breech was screwed up held all fast.

He took hold and tried to lift, but tried in vain, for it seemed beyond his strength. His teeth gritted together as he set them fast in his exasperation against Poole for not being at hand to help and make what now seemed an impossibility an easy task.

Perspiring at every pore, he tried again and again, the more eagerly now, for a low growling voice was heard from the direction whence he had crawled.

But the piece of steel was immovable, and in his despair he felt that all was over and that he had failed.

Then came light—not light to make the gun visible, but mental light, with the question, Had he turned the levers far enough?

Uttering a low gasp in his despair, for the growling talk grew louder, he seized the great balls again, gave them another turn or two, and once more tried to stir the block, when his heart seemed to give a great jump, for it came right out as he exerted himself, with comparative ease, and directly after he had it hugged to his chest and was staggering and nearly falling headlong as he stepped down from the iron platform, making for the side. But he recovered himself, tottering on, and then in the darkness kicking against something soft—a sleeper—the encounter sending him, top-heavy as he was, crash against the bulwark, but doing all that he wanted, for the breech-block struck against the rail, glanced off, and went overboard, to fall with a tremendous splash, followed by another, which the middy made himself, as he half flung himself over, half rolled from the rail, to go down with the water thundering in his ears.

The heaviness of his plunge naturally sent him below for some distance, but it was not long before he was rising again.

It was long enough, though, for thought—and thoughts come quickly at a time like this. Fitz's first flash was a brilliant one, connected with his success, for the breech-block was gone beyond recovery; his next was one of horror, and connected with the sharks that haunted those waters; his third was full of despair; where was Poole, whom he seemed to have left to his fate?

Hah! The surface again, and he could breathe; but which way to swim for the boat? There was none needed, for his shoulders were barely clear of the water when his arm was seized in a tremendous grip, another hand was thrust under his arm-pit, and he was literally jumped, dripping, into a boat, to pant out his first audible utterance for the past hour. It was only a word, and that was—

"Poole!"

"I'm all right," came from out of the darkness close at hand.

"Then give way, my lads, for your lives!" panted Fitz, and the oars began to splash.

It was quite time, for there was no sleeping on board the gunboat now. All was rush and confusion; voices in Spanish were shouting orders, men hurrying here and there, a few shots were fired in their direction, evidently from revolvers, and then a steam-whistle was heard to blow, followed by a hissing, clanking sound, and the man who had hauled Fitz in over the bows put his face close to him and whispered—

"Steam-capstan. They're getting up their anchor. But there was three splashes, sir. What was that there first?"

"The breech-block, Chips."

"Hooroar!"

It was some little time before another word was spoken, during which period the men had been rowing hard, and the boatswain, who had got hold of the rudder-lines, was steering almost at random for the shore, taking his bearings as well as he could from the gunboat, out of whose funnel sparks kept flying, and a lurid glare appeared upon the cloud of smoke which floated out, pointing to the fact that the stokers were hard at work.

"Mr Burnett—Mr Poole, sir," said Butters, at last, "I aren't at all satisfied about the way we are going. I suppose we may speak out now?"

"Oh yes," cried Fitz; "I don't suppose they can hear us, and if they did they couldn't do us any harm, for it must be impossible for them to make us out."

"Oh yes, sir," cried the boatswain. "No fear of that."

"But what do you mean about not being satisfied?"

"Well, sir, my eyes is pretty good, and if you give me a fair start I can take my bearings pretty easy from the stars when I knows what time it is. But you see, it's quite another thing to hit the mouth of that little river in the dark. I know the land's right in front, but whether we are south'ard or north'ard of where the schooner lays is more than I can tell, and there's some awkward surf upon some of the rocks of this 'ere coast. Will you give your orders, please."

"Well, I don't know that I can," replied Fitz. "I think the best thing is to lie-to till daylight. What do you say, Poole?" he continued, from his position to where Poole was, right forward.

"Same as you do," was the reply. "It's impossible to make for the river now. We may be only getting farther away."

"Just keep her head on to the swell, my lads."

The next minute the gig began riding gently over the long smooth waves, while her occupants sat watching the gunboat, the only light from which now was the glow from the funnel.

"Bit wet, aren't you, Mr Burnett, sir?" said Chips. "What do you say to taking off two or three things and letting me give them a wring?"

"Ah, it would be as well," replied Fitz, beginning at once to slip off his jacket, and as if instinctively to take off attention from what he was doing he began to question Poole.

"You had better do the same, hadn't you?" he cried.

"Doing it," was the reply. "I say, are you all right?"

"No; I am so horribly wet. What about you?"

"Just the same, of course."

"But I say," said Fitz, who was calming down after the excitement; "why didn't you come on and help?"

"How could I? One of those fellows lying on the deck threw a leg and an arm over me in his sleep. I just brushed against him, and he started as if I had touched a spring, and held me fast. I tried to get away, but it was of no use, and if I had shouted it would have only given the alarm. I didn't get loose till the row began, and then there was nothing to do but come overboard and be picked up. I was in a way about you."

"Same here about you," cried fitz. "I didn't know what had happened, and when I tumbled over the rail—I didn't jump—I felt as if I had left you in the lurch."

"Well, but that's what I felt," said Poole. "It was queer."

"It made us all feel pretty tidy queer, young gentlemen," said the boatswain; "but if I may speak, the fust question is, are either of you hurt?"

"I am not," cried Fitz.

"Nor I," said Poole.

"That's right, then," said the boatswain gruffly. "Now then, what about that there block of iron? Was it that as come over plosh, only about a yard from the boat's nose?"

"Yes," cried Fitz excitedly.

"Then all I can say is, that it's a precious good job that Mr Burnett didn't chuck it a little further, for if he had it would have come right down on Chips and drove him through the bottom, and we couldn't have stopped a leak like that."

"But I should have come up again," said the carpenter, "just where I went down, and as the hole I made would have been just the same size as me, I should have fitted in quite proper."

"Yah!" growled the boatswain. "What's the use of trying to cut jokes at a time like this? Look here, gentlemen, have we done our job to rights?"

"As far as the gun's concerned," replied Fitz, "it's completely disabled, and of no use again until they get another block."

"Then that's done, sir."

"And about my job," said Poole. "I am afraid the screw's not fouled, for I fancy the gunboat is slowly steaming out to sea."

"Well, I don't see as how we can tell that, Mr Poole, sir," said the boatswain. "I can't say as she's moving, for we are both in a sharp current, and she may be only drifting; but seeing the way as you made fast the end of that there cable, and then looped over bight after bight round them there fans, and twistened it all up tight, it seems to me that the screw must be fouled, and that every turn made it wuss and wuss. I say that you made a fine job of that there, Mr Poole. What do you say, Chips, my lad?"

"Splendid!" cried the carpenter.

"Why, it was you two did it," said Fitz.

"Well, that's what I thought, sir," said the carpenter; "but it was so dark, I couldn't see a bit."

"Zackly," said the boatswain; "and you said it was your job, sir."

"Oh, nonsense!" cried Poole. "I meant yours."

"Well," said Fitz, "all I can say is that I hope your knots were good."

"I'll answer for mine," said the boatswain, "but I won't say nothing for Chips here. He aren't much account unless it's hammers and spikes, or a job at caulking or using his adze."

"That's right," said Chips, "but you might tell the young gents that I'm handiest with a pot o' glue."

There was silence for a few moments, and then Fitz said—

"It's almost too much to expect that both things have turned out all right; but I can't help believing they have."

"Well, sir," said the boatswain, "I do hope as that there cable is not all twisted up in a bunch about them fans—reg'lar wound up tight—and if it is there's no knowing where that there gunboat will drift during the night; for I don't care how big a crew they've got aboard, they can't free that there propeller till daylight, if they do then. But it do seem a pity to spoil a beautiful new soft bit of stuff like that, for it'll never be no good again."

"Fine tackle for caulking," said the carpenter, "or making ships' fenders."

"Yah!" cried the boatswain. "We should never get it again. It's gone, and it give me quite a heartache to use up new ship's stores like that. But what I was going to say was, that the skipper will be saddersfied enough when we get back and tell him that Mr Burnett's crippled the big gun."

"Oh, but that was the easy job," said Fitz. "It was just play, lifting out that block and dropping it overboard."

"And a very pretty game too, Mr Burnett, sir," said the boatswain, chuckling. "But I say, seems quite to freshen a man up to be able to open his mouth and speak. While you two young gents was swarming up that anchor, and all the time you was aboard till you come back plish, plosh, I felt as if I couldn't breathe. I say, Mr Poole, would you like to take these 'ere lines?"

"No," said Poole shortly; "I want to get dry. But why do you want me to take the lines?"

"To get shut of the 'sponsibility, sir. I can't see which way to steer."

"Oh, never mind the steering," cried Fitz. "Just keep her head to the swell, and let's all rest, my lads. I feel so done up that I could go to sleep. We can't do anything till daylight. Here, I say, Camel, did you bring anything to eat?"

"The orders were to bring the rations stowed inside, sir," replied the cook; "but a'm thinking I did slip a wee bit something into the locker for'ard there, juist ahind where ye are sitting, sir. Would you mind feeling? Hech! I never thought of that!"

"Thought of what?" said Fitz.

"Ye've got the ship's carpenter there, and he's got a nose like a cat for feesh. Awm skeart that he smelt it oot in the dairk and it's all gone."

"Haw, haw!" chuckled the carpenter. "You are wrong this time, Andy. I got my smelling tackle all choked up with the stuff the bearings of that gunboat's fan was oiled with—nasty rank stuff like Scotch oil. I don't believe I shall smell anything else for a week."

Rap! went the lid of the little locker.

"It's all right, my lads," cried Fitz. "Here, Andy, man, those who hide can find. Come over here and serve out the rations; but I wish we'd got some of your hot prime soup."

"Ay, laddie," said the cook softly, as he obeyed his orders; "it would ha' been juist the thing for such a wetting as you got with your joomp. Mr Poole, will ye come here too? I got one little tin with enough for you and Mr Poole, and a big one for the lads and mysen. But I'm vairy sorry to say I forgot the saut."

"He needn't have troubled himself about the salt," said Poole softly. "I should never have missed it. You and I have taken in enough to-night through our pores."

"Yes," said Fitz.—"Splendid, Andy."

"Ah," said the Camel; "I never haud wi' going upon a journey, however short, wi'out something in the way of food."

Chapter Fifty Two
Fitz's conscience pricks

Daybreak brought a blank look of amazement into the lads' countenances. The soft, sweet, bracing air of morning floated from the glorious shore, all cliff and indentation looking of a pearly grey, almost the same tint as the surf that curled over upon the rocks distant about two miles.

A mere glance was directed at the dangerous coast, for every eye was turned seaward, east, north, and south, in search of the gunboat; but she was not to be seen.

"Surely she's not gone down!" cried Fitz.

"Oh, hardly," said Poole; "but it's very puzzling. What do you make of it, Butters?"

"Well, sir," said the boatswain, "I'm thinking that like enough she's got upon a rock and stuck fast, while the sharp current has carried us along miles and miles, and quite out of sight."

"But they may have got the screw all right, and gone straight out to sea."

"Nay, sir. Not in the dark. We got them fans too fast; and besides, I don't see no smoke on the sea-line. The steamer leaves a mark that you can see her by many miles away. No, sir, I think I'm right; it's us as has drifted."

"Which way?" said Poole. "North or south?"

"Can't say yet, sir. May be either. South," he added emphatically the next moment.

"How do you know?" cried Fitz.

The boatswain smiled.

"By the colour of the sea, sir," replied the man, screwing up his eyes. "Look at the water. It isn't bright and clear. It's got the mark of the river in it. Not much, but just enough to show that the current hugs the shore, bringing the river water with it; and there it all is plain enough. Look at them little rocks just showing above the surface. You watch them a minute, and you'll see we are floating by southward, and we may think ourselves precious lucky that we haven't run upon any of them in the night and been capsized.

You see, we have come by two headlands, and we have only got to row back to the north to come sooner or later in sight of landmarks that we know."

"Then give way, my lads," said Fitz; "a fair long steady stroke, for the skipper must be getting terribly uncomfortable about us, Poole, eh?"

"Yes. Pull your best, boys. What do you say, Fitz, to taking an oar each for a bit? I'm chilly, and a good way from being dry."

"Good idea," said Fitz, changing places with one of the men. "You'll keep a sharp look-out, boatswain. The enemy may come into sight at any moment as we round these points, and even if she daren't come close in, she may send after us with her boats."

"Trust me for that, sir," said the boatswain, and the oars began to dip, with the sun soon beginning to show tokens of its coming appearance, and sending hope and light into every breast.

It was a glorious row, the chill of the night giving place to a pleasant glow which set the lads talking merrily, discussing the darkness through which they had passed, the events of the night, and their triumphant success.

"If we could only see that gunboat ashore, Burnett!" cried Poole.

"Ah," said Fitz, rather gravely; "if we only could!" And then he relapsed into silence, for thoughts began to come fast, and he found himself wondering what Commander Glossop would say if he could see him then and know all that he had done in the night attack.

"I couldn't help it," the boy said to himself, as he pulled away. "I shouldn't wonder if he would have done precisely the same if he had been in my place. I feel a bit sorry now; but that's no good. What's done can't be undone, and I shan't bother about it any more."

"Now, Mr Burnett, sir," said the boatswain, in a tone full of remonstrance, "don't keep that there oar all day. Seems to me quite time you took your trick at the wheel."

"Yes," said the lad cheerily; "I am beginning to feel precious stiff," and he rose to exchange seats with the speaker, Poole rising directly afterwards for the carpenter to take his place.

"I'd keep a sharp look-out for'ard along the coast, Mr Burnett, sir," said the boatswain, with a peculiar smile, as the lad lifted the lines.

"Oh yes, of course," cried Fitz, gazing forward now, and then uttering an ejaculation: "Here, Poole! Look! Why didn't you speak before, Butters?"

"Because I thought you'd like to see it fust, sir. Yes, there she lies, just beyond that headland."

"At anchor?" cried Poole.

"Can't say yet, sir, till we've cleared that point; but she's upon an even keel, and seems to be about her old distance from the shore. That must be the southernmost of them two great cliffs, and we are nearer the river than I thought."

"Lay your backs into it, my lads," cried Poole.

The gig travelled faster as the two strong men took the place of the tired lads; and as they rowed on it was plain to see that the gunboat was much farther from the point and shore than had been at first imagined.

"It would be awkward," said Fitz, "if they sent out boats to try and take us, for they must see us by now."

But the occupants of the gunboat made no sign, and when at last the *Teal's* gig was rowed round the headland which formed the southern side of the entrance to the river, all on board could hardly realise how greatly they had been deceived by the clear morning light, for the gunboat was still some three or four miles away, and apparently fast upon one of the reefs of rocks, while from her lowered boats, crowded with men, it was evident that they were either busy over something astern, or preparing to leave.

"They must be hard at work trying to clear the screw," cried Fitz excitedly.

"Can't make out, for my part, sir," replied the boatswain, while Poole carefully kept silence; "but it looks as much like that as ever it can, and we have nothing to mind now, for we can get right in and up the river long before their boats could row to the mouth."

Poole steered close in to the right bank of the river, so as to avoid the swift rush of the stream, this taking them close under the perpendicular cliff; and they had not gone far before there was a loud "Ahoy!" from high overhead. Looking up they made out the face of Burgess the mate projecting from the bushes as, high upon a shelf, he held on by a bough and leaned outwards so as to watch the motions of the boat.

"Ahoy!" came from the men, in answer to his hail.

"All right aboard?" shouted the mate.

"Yes. All right!" roared the boatswain. "What are they doing out yonder to the Spaniel?"

"Trying to get her off, I suppose. She went ashore in the night. I came up here with a glass to look out for you, and there she was, and hasn't moved since. What about that gun?"

"Burnett has drawn its tooth," shouted Poole. "Father all right?"

"No. Got the grumps about you. Thinks you are lost. You didn't foul the screw, did you?"

"Yes," shouted Poole.

"Then that's what they're about; trying to clear her again; and when they do they've got to get their vessel off the rocks. I'm going to stop and see; but you had better row up stream as hard as you can, so as to let the skipper see that you have not all gone to the bottom. He told me he was sure you had."

The men's oars dipped again, and they rowed with all their might, passing the dinghy with the man in charge moored at the foot of the cliff, while soon after they had turned one of the bends and came in sight of the schooner a loud hail welcomed them from those who were on board. Then Poole stood up in the stern, after handing the rudder-lines to his companion, and began waving his hat to the skipper, who made a slight recognition and then stood watching them till they came within hail.

"Well," he said, through his speaking-trumpet, "what luck?"

"The gun's done for, father, and the gunboat's ashore," shouted Poole, through his hands.

"Oh. I heard that the enemy had gone on the rocks. And what about the propeller?"

"Oh, we fouled it, father," said Poole coolly. "That's right," said the skipper, in the most unconcerned way. "I thought you would. There, look sharp and come aboard. There's some breakfast ready, but I began to think you didn't mean to come. What made you so long?"

He did not wait to hear the answer, but began giving orders for the lowering of another boat which he was about to send down to communicate with the mate.

"I say," said Fitz, grinning, "your dad seems in a nice temper. He's quite rusty."

"Yes," said Poole, returning the laugh. "I suppose it's because we stopped out all night. There, get out! He's as pleased as can be, only he won't make a fuss. It's his way."

The day glided on till the sun was beginning to go down. Messages had passed to and fro from the watchers, who had kept an eye upon the gunboat, which was still fast.

Fitz, after a hearty meal, being regularly fagged out, had had three or four hours' rest in his bunk, to get up none the worse for his night's adventure, when he joined Poole, who had just preceded him on deck.

He came upon the skipper directly afterwards, who gave him a searching look and a short nod, and said abruptly—

"All right?"

"Yes, quite right, thank you, sir."

"Hah!" said the skipper, and walked on, taking no notice of Poole, who was coming up, and leaving the lads together.

"I say," said Fitz sarcastically, "I can bear a good deal, but your father goes too far."

"What do you mean?" asked Poole.

"He makes such a dreadful fuss over one, just for doing a trifling thing like that. Almost too much to bear."

"Well, he didn't make much fuss over me," said Poole, in rather an ill-used tone. "I felt as if we had done nothing, instead of disabling a man-of-war.—Hullo! what does this mean?"

For just then the boat came swiftly round the bend, with the mate sitting in the stern-sheets, the dinghy towed by its painter behind.

A shout from the man on the watch astern brought up the skipper and the rest of the crew, including those who had been making up for their last night's labours in their bunks, all expectant of some fresh news; and they were not disappointed, nearly every one hearing it as the boat came alongside and the mate spoke out to the captain on the deck.

"Found a way right up to the top of the cliff," he said, "and from there I could regularly look down on the gunboat's deck."

"Well?" said the skipper sharply.

"No, ill—for them; she's completely fast ashore in the midst of a regular wilderness of rocks that hardly peep above the surface; and as far as I could make out with my spyglass, they are not likely to get off again. They seem to know it too, for when I began to come down they had got three boats manned on the other side, and I left them putting off as if they were coming up here."

"Again?" said the skipper thoughtfully.

"Yes; to take it out of us, I suppose, for what we've done. How would it be to turn the tables on them and make a counter attack?"

"Granting that we should win," said the skipper, "it would mean half our men wounded; perhaps three or four dead. I can't afford that, Burgess."

"No," said the mate abruptly. "Better stop here and give them what they seem to want. I think we can do that."

"Yes," said the skipper. "All aboard; and look sharp, Burgess. Let's be as ready for them as we can. The fight will be more desperate this time, I'm afraid."

"Not you," said the mate, with a chuckle, as he sprang on deck. "Well, my lads, you did wonders last night. How did you like your job?"

"Not at all," cried Fitz, laughing. "It was too wet."

The mate smiled, and the next minute he was hard at work helping the skipper to prepare to give the Spaniards a warm reception, taking it for granted that it would not be long before they arrived, burning for revenge.

The preparations were much the same as were made before, but with this addition, that the carpenter, looking as fresh as if he had passed the night in his bunk, was hard at work with four men, lashing spare spars to the shrouds, so as to form a stout rail about eighteen inches above the bulwarks, to which the netting was firmly attached.

There was no question this time about arming the crew with rifles, for every one felt that success on the part of Villarayo's men would mean no quarter.

"Then you mean this to be a regular fight?" Fitz whispered to Poole, after watching what was going on for some time.

"Why, of course! Why not?"

"Oh, I don't like the idea of killing people," said Fitz, wrinkling up his forehead.

"Well, I don't," said Poole, laughing. "I don't like killing anything. I should never have done for a butcher, but I would a great deal rather kill one of Villarayo's black-looking ruffians than let him kill me."

"But do you think they really would massacre us?" said Fitz. "They can't help looking ruffianly."

"No, but they have got a most horribly bad character. Father and I have heard of some very ugly things that they have done in some of their fights. They are supposed to be civilised, and I dare say the officers are all right; but if you let loose a lot of half-savage fellows armed with knives and get their blood up, I don't think you need expect much mercy. They needn't come and interfere with us unless they like, but if they come shouting and striking at us they must take the consequences."

"Yes, I suppose so," said Fitz; "but it seems a pity."

"Awful," replied Poole; "but there always has been war, and people take a deal of civilising before they give it up. And they don't seem to then," said the lad, with a dry smile.

"No," said Fitz; and the little discussion came to an end.

Chapter Fifty Three
Worse than ever

"This is bad, my lads," said the skipper, joining the boys.

"What's wrong, father?" said Poole. "Why, it's close upon sundown, and it begins to look as if they are going to steal upon us in the dark, which will give them a lot of advantage. I would rather have been able to see what we are about. What an evening, though, for a fight! I have journeyed about the islands and Central America a good deal, and it is nearly all beautiful, but this river and its cliffs, seen in the warm glow, is just my idea of a perfect paradise. Look at the sky, with those gorgeous clouds! Look at the river, reflecting all their beauties! And the trees and shrubs, looking darker in the shades, and in the light as if they had suddenly burst forth into bloom with dazzling golden flowers. And here we are going to spoil everything with savage bloodshed."

"We are not, Captain Reed," said Fitz sharply; "you would not fire a shot if you were not obliged."

"Not even a blank cartridge, my boy," said the skipper, laying his hand upon the middy's shoulder. "I loathe it, and I feel all of a shiver at the thought of my brave lads being drilled with bullets or hacked with knives. If it comes to it—and I am afraid it will—"

"I say, father, don't talk of trembling and being afraid!" said Poole reproachfully.

"Why not, my boy?"

"Because I don't know what Fitz Burnett will think."

"Whatever he thinks he'll know that I am speaking the truth. But I say, lad," continued the skipper, gripping the middy's shoulder tightly; "you'll help me, won't you?"

"Haven't I forgotten myself enough, sir?" said Fitz, in a tone as full of reproach as that of Poole.

"No, my boy. I think you have behaved very bravely; and I don't think, if your superior officer knew all, that he would have much to say. But I don't want you to fight. I mean, help me after the trouble's over; I mean, turn assistant-surgeon when I take off my jacket."

"Yes, that I will," cried Fitz. "I ought to be getting ready some bandages and things now."

"Oh, I think I've got preparations enough of that sort made," said the skipper; "and there is still a chance that we may not want them. Hah! That hope's gone. Ahoy! bosun! Let them have the pipe."

Old Butters's silver whistle rang out shrill and clear, but only called one man to his duty, and that was the Camel, who came tumbling out of the galley and gave the door a bang.

Every one else was on the alert, watching a boat coming round the bend, followed by two more, crowded with armed men whose oars sent the water splashing up like so much liquid gold. The fight began at once, for the skipper had given his instructions.

These he supplemented now with a sharp order which was followed by the crack of a rifle echoing from cliff to cliff, and Fitz, who had run towards the stern to look over, was in time to see that the skipper's comment, "Good shot, my lad!" was well deserved, for one of the officers in the stern-sheets of the first boat sprang up and would have gone overboard but for the efforts of his men, who caught and lowered him back amidst a little scene of confusion and a cessation of the rowing.

Another shot rang out and there was more confusion, the way of the leading boat being stopped; but the orders issued in the other boats were plainly heard on board the schooner; oars splashed more rapidly, and once more all three boats were coming on fast.

"Fire!" cried the skipper, and with slow regularity shot after shot rang out, to be followed by a ragged volley from the enemy, the bullets whizzing overhead and pattering amongst the rigging of the well-moored vessel, but doing no real harm.

"Keep it up steadily, my lads," shouted the skipper. "No hurry. One hit is worth five hundred misses. We mustn't let them board if we can keep them back. Go on firing till they are close up, and then cutlasses and bars."

But in spite of the steady defence the enemy came on, showing no sign of shrinking, firing rapidly and responding to their officers' orders with savage defiant yells, while shots came thick and fast, the two lads growing so excited as they watched the fray that they forgot the danger and the nearness of the enemy coming on.

"They are showing more pluck this time, Burgess," said the skipper, taking out his revolver and unconsciously turning the chambers to see that all was right.

"Yes," growled the mate. "It's a horrible nuisance, for I don't want to fight. But we've made rather a mess of it, after all."

"What do you mean?" said the skipper. "Ought to have dropped that other anchor."

"Why?" said the skipper sharply. "Because they may row right up and cut us adrift."

"Yes," said the skipper quietly; "it would have been as well. Take a rifle and go forward if they try to pass us, and pick off every man who attempts to cut the cable."

"All right," replied the mate; "I will if there is time. But in five minutes we shall be busy driving these chaps back into their boats, and they will be swarming up the sides like so many monkeys."

"Yes," said the skipper. "But you must do it if there *is* time. They don't seem to mind our firing a bit."

"No," Fitz heard the chief officer growl angrily. "Their blood's up, and they are too stupid, I suppose."

"Cease firing!" shouted the skipper. "Here they come!" The order came too late to check six of the men, who in their excitement finished off their regular shots with a ragged volley directed at the foremost boat, and with such terrible effect that in the midst of a scene of confusion the oars were dropped and the boat swung round broadside to the stream, which carried it on to the next boat, fouling it so that the two hung together and confusion became worse confounded as they crashed on to the third boat, putting a stop to the firing as well as the rowing. The commands of the officer in the last boat were of no effect, and the defenders of the schooner, who had sprung to their positions where their efforts would have been of most avail, burst forth with a wild cheer, and then turned to the skipper for orders to fire again.

But these orders did not come, for their captain had turned to the mate with—

"Why, Burgess, that's done it! I believe we've given them enough." Then heartily, "Well done, boys! Give 'em another cheer."

In their wild excitement and delight the schooner's crew gave two; and they had good cause for their exultation, for the firing from the boats had quite ceased, the efforts of their commanders being directed towards disentangling themselves from their sorry plight, many minutes elapsing before the boats were clear and the men able to row, while by this time several hundred yards had been placed between them and the object of their attack.

Then the Spanish officers gave their orders to advance almost simultaneously; but they were not obeyed.

They raged and roared at their men, but in vain—the boats were still drifting down stream towards the bend, and as the darkness was giving its first sign of closing in, the last one disappeared, the skipper saying quietly—

"Thank you, my lads. It was bravely done."

A murmur rose from among the men, only one speaking out loudly; and that was the carpenter, who, as he took off his cap and wiped his streaming forehead, gave Fitz a comic look and said—

"Well, yes; I think we made a neat job of that."

Some of the men chuckled, but their attention was taken off directly by the boatswain, who shouted—

"Here, you Camel, don't wait for orders, but get the lads something to peck at and drink. I feel as if I hadn't had anything to eat for a week."

"Yes, and be quick," cried the skipper. "It's all right, my lads; I don't think we shall see the enemy again."

Chapter Fifty Four
"Of course we will"

The next morning reconnoitring began once more, prior to the skipper giving his orders, and the schooner dropping down slowly towards the mouth of the river; for the mate had been up on the cliff soon after daybreak, busy with his glass, and had returned to report that the spot where the gunboat lay still fast on the rocks was so distant from the Channel through which the schooner had sailed, that it was doubtful whether, if they attempted to sail out, she could be reached by the small pieces that the enemy had on board.

"Then we won't give them the chance to attack again," was the skipper's comment, and the wind favouring, the channel was soon reached, and with the mate conning the craft, they sailed outward along the clear water, with the men armed and ready for any attack that might be attempted by the man-of-war's boats.

It was not very long before the boys, who had mounted aloft with their glass to watch the deck of the foe, were able to announce that boats were being manned for lowering, and the tortuous nature of the channel now began to lead the schooner ominously near; but both the skipper and the mate were of opinion that at the rate they were sailing they would be able to evade an attack.

"And if they are not very careful," growled the latter, "it strikes me I shall be running one if not two of them down. They'd be much safer if they stopped aboard."

But still the dangerous nature of the rocks forced them nearer and nearer to the enemy.

"Not much doubt about the big gun being disabled," Poole remarked to his companion, as they noted how busily the crew were preparing to lower the boats. "We should have had a shot long before this."

"And there's no doubt either about the screw being fouled," said Fitz. "I say, take the glass. They're doing something which I can't make out. You try."

Poole re-focussed the binocular, but it was some moments before he spoke.

"Can't you?" cried Fitz excitedly.

"Yes, but I'm not quite sure. Yes, now I am. Right!"

For at that moment a white ball of smoke shot out from the gunboat's deck, followed by a dull thud, and something came skipping over the heaving sea, before there was another sharp crack and a shell burst about a hundred yards from the schooner's stern.

"I wonder whether we shall have to go any nearer," said Poole excitedly. "They'd be able to do us a deal of mischief like that. I believe she's got four of those small guns on board."

"Judging from their gunnery," said Fitz coolly, "they are not likely to hit us, even if we go much more near."

"Well, I hope not," said Poole. "Those are nasty waspish things, those shells. There she goes again. I wonder whether we could do anything with rifles at this range."

The skipper proved to be of opinion that they could, but he preferred to devote all his attention to the navigation of the schooner, and in fact there was plenty to do, for every now and then they found themselves dangerously near the spots where a little creamy foam showed upon the surface of the sea, insidious, beautiful patches that would have meant destruction to the slight timbers of the yacht-like craft.

But the mate was perched up on high, and between him and the steersman the skipper stood ready to transmit the keen chief officer's signals to the man at the wheel, so that they rode in safety through the watery maze, paying no heed whatever to the shells which came at intervals from the gunboat's deck, the small modern guns having a terribly long range. The boats filled with men still hung from the davits, ready for the order to start, which was never given, the captain of the gunboat evidently being of opinion that his rowing men would not be able to compete with the schooner's sails, and waiting as he was for the bursting of some shell overhead bringing down one of the important spars by the run, while it was always possible that the schooner's fate might be the same as his, to wit, running stem on to some rock, to sink or remain fast.

Under these circumstances the boats would have been of avail, and another attempt might have been made to board and take the little schooner.

But the Spaniards' gunnery was not good enough; the shells were startling, but their segments did no worse than speckle the surface of the sea, and at last involuntarily cheers rang out, for the *Teal* was running swiftly away from the danger, and the shells that came dropping were far astern. About half-an-hour later, and long after the firing had ceased to be dangerous, the mate came down from his eyrie, to seat himself and begin wiping his dripping face.

"You look tired, Mr Burgess," said Fitz, going up to him, "Shall I get you a tin of water?"

"Thank you, my lad," said the rugged fellow huskily. "I am nearly choked with thirst."

Fitz ran to the breaker, took the tin that stood ready, dipped it, and bore it to the mate, who drained it to the last drop.

"Thank you, my lad. That's the sweetest drop I ever tasted in my life. Hard work for the body will make a man thirsty, but work like that I have just been doing is ten times as bad. Hah! It's horrid!—horrid! I believed I knew that channel pretty well, but for the last hour, and every minute of it, I have been waiting to hear the little schooner go scrunch on to some hidden rock; and now I feel quite done."

"It must have been horrible," said the middy, looking his sympathy. "Of course we all knew it was dangerous, but none of us could have felt like that."

"No, my lad," said the mate, holding out his rough hand. "I don't believe anybody felt like that," and he gripped the boy's hand firmly. "But I say, between ourselves, I didn't mean to speak. It's made me feel a little soft like, and I shouldn't like anybody to know what I said."

"You may trust me, Mr Burgess," said the lad warmly.

"I do, my lad; I do, for I know what a gentleman you are. But to nobody, please, not even to young Poole."

The rough mate nodded his satisfaction as he met the middy's eyes, and somehow from that minute it seemed to Fitz that they had become great friends.

"Now, that's what I call the prettiest view we've seen of that gunboat yet, Mr Burnett, sir," said the carpenter a short time later, as the lad strolled up to where he was leaning over the bulwarks shading his eyes from the sun. "I don't profess to be a artist, sir; nighest I ever come to making a picter was putting a frame round it and a bit of glass in front, as I kep' in tight with brads. But I've seen a deal of natur' in my time, hot and cold, and I say that's the prettiest bit of a sea-view I ever set eyes on. She's a fine-built boat—nice shape. Looks like about half-way between a flat-iron and one of them as the laundresses use with a red-hot thing in their insides. But it ain't only her shape as takes my fancy. It's her position, and that's one that everybody on board must admire, as she lies there nice and distant with the coast behind, sea in front, and a lovely bit of foam and breakers both sides. Ah! she makes a lovely pictur'. She don't want no frame, and the beauty of her is that she's one of them what they used to call dissolving views. You see, we shan't see her no more, and don't want to, and that's the beauty of it."

"Yes, you're right, Chips," said Poole, laughing. "We've seen rather too much of her as it is. But you are a bit wrong. I dare say we shall see her again. Don Ramon will be for trying to get her off the rocks when he hears how she lies. Why, Chips, that's in your way. What a job it would be for you!"

"Job for me, sir?" said the man, staring.

"Yes. That gunboat and her fittings must have cost a tremendous sum of money. It would be the making of you if you could get her off."

The carpenter stared, and then gave his thigh a slap which sounded like the crack of a revolver.

"Yuss!" he cried. "I never thought of that. My word, shouldn't I like the job!"

"Think you could do it, Chips?" cried Fitz.

"I'd try, sir. Only let 'em give me the job. But the skipper wouldn't let me go."

"Well, you don't want to go, Winks," said Poole.

"That's a true word, sir. I don't want to go. The *Teal's* good enough for me. But I should like to have the getting of that gunboat off all the same. Let's see; that there Don Ramon wants it, doesn't he?"

"Yes," cried Poole.

"I say, look out!" cried Fitz. "Here's Chips's dissolving view dissolving away."

The declaration was quite true, for the gunboat was slowly disappearing, as the *Teal* sailed on, to reach Velova Bay without further adventure or mishap.

All seemed well as they sighted the port, and Don Ramon's flag was fluttering out jauntily; but to the astonishment of all on board, as they drew nearer the fort there was a white puff of smoke, and then another and another.

The British colours were run up, but the firing went on, and the skipper grew uneasy.

"Villarayo must have captured the place," he said, as he looked through his double glass.

"Here, I don't see any shot striking up the water, father," cried Poole.

"No; I tell you what it is," cried Fitz. "They are glad to see us back. They are firing a salute."

Fitz was right, and before long a barge was coming off, with the national colours trailing behind, Don Ramon being made out seated in the stern-sheets in uniform, and surrounded by his officers. He looked ceremonious and grand enough in his State barge, but there was no ceremony in his acts. He sprang up the side as soon as the coxswain hooked on, and embraced the skipper with the tears in his eyes, the two lads having to suffer the same greeting in turn, so as not to hurt the feelings of one whose warmth was very genuine.

"Oh, my friend the captain," he cried, "I have been wasting tears on your behalf. You did not *come* back, and the news was brought by three different fishing-boats that the enemy had driven you ashore and wrecked and burned your beautiful schooner, while there had been a desperate fight, they said, and they had heard the firing, so that I could only guess what must have been the result. I believed my brave true friend and all on board had been slain, while now I have you all safely back again, and my heart is very glad."

"And so am I, Don Ramon," said the skipper warmly, for he felt how genuine the greeting was. "But things are much better than you thought."

"Yes, better far," cried the Don. "But make haste. Let us get ashore. My people are getting up a banquet in your honour and that of every *one* on board."

"Oh, I'm not a banqueting man," said the skipper, laughing.

"Ha, ha! We shall see," said the Don, laughing in his turn. "How came they, though, to tell me such false news? I believed the men who brought it could be trusted."

"Well, I dare say they can be," said the skipper. "But they didn't stay long enough. We had almost to run ashore, and there were two or three fights; that was true enough. But if they had stayed long enough they could have brought you the best news that you have had for months."

"Best news!" cried the Don excitedly.

"Yes; the gunboat, with her big breech-loader and propeller disabled, is fast upon the rocks."

"Captain Reed!" cried the Don, seizing him by both hands. "Is this true?"

"As true as that I am telling you."

"But the captain and his men?"

"They're standing by her. But they will never get her off."

"Oh!" shouted Fitz, giving a sudden jump and turning sharply round, to see the carpenter backing away confused and shamefaced, for he had been listening eagerly to the conversation, and at the critical point alluding to the gunboat being got off, he had in his excitement given Fitz a vigorous pinch.

"Here, what are you thinking of doing?" said the skipper.

"Doing?" said the Don excitedly. "There will be no banquet to-night. I must gather together my men, and make for the gunboat at once."

"What for?" cried the skipper.

"To strike the last blow for victory," cried the Don. "We must surround and take the gunboat's crew, and then at any cost that gunboat must be floated. I don't quite see yet how it is to be done, but the attempt must be made before there is another gale. That gunboat must be saved. No," he continued thoughtfully, "I don't see yet how it can be done."

"I do, sir," cried Winks, dashing forward. "I'll take the job, sir, and do it cheap. Say a word for me, skipper. You know me. It's fust come fust served at times like this. Say a word for me, sir, afore some other lubber steps in and gets the job as won't do it half so well. Mr Burnett, sir—Mr Poole, you will put a word in too, won't you?"

"I do not want any words put in," said the new President gravely. "I know you, my man, and what you can do. I know you too as one of the friends who have fought for me so bravely and so well. You shall get the gunboat off the rocks."

In his excitement Chips did the first steps of the sailor's hornpipe, but suddenly awakening to a sense of his great responsibility, he pulled himself up short with a sharp stamp upon the deck, thrust his right fore-finger into his cheek, and brought it out again *plop*.

"Stand by there, sir! Steady it is. I like things right and square. I never did a job like this afore; but you trust me, and I'll do my best."

"I do trust you," said Don Ramon, smiling and holding out his hand, "and I know such a British seaman as you will do his best."

The carpenter flushed like a girl and raised his hand to grasp the President's, but snatched his own back again to give it three or four rubs up and down, back and front, upon the leg of his trousers, like a barber's finishing-touch to a razor, and then gave the much smaller Spanish hand such a grip as brought tears not of emotion but of pain into the President's eyes.

"Now then, for the shore!" cried the Don. "But, Captain Reed, my friend, I am never satisfied. You will help me once again?"

"You know," replied the skipper, "as far as I can."

"Oh, you will not refuse this," said the President, laughingly. "It is only to transport as many of my people as the schooner will bear. I shall have to trust to fishing-boats and the two small trading vessels that are in the port to bear the rest, I must take a strong force, and make many prisoners, for not one of the gunboat's crew must escape."

"Oh, you won't have much trouble with that," said the skipper. "Once you have the full upper hand—"

"I have it now," said the Spaniard haughtily.

"Then they will all come over to your side."

"You will come with me ashore?" said the Don.

"Yes; but when shall you want to sail? To-morrow—the next day?"

"Within an hour," cried the Spaniard, "or as soon after as I can. I must strike, as you English say, while the iron is in the fire."

"Well, that's quick enough for anything," whispered Fitz.

The two lads stood watching the departing barge, with the skipper by the President's side, and then turned to go aft to the cabin.

"This is rather a bother," said Fitz. "I should have liked to have gone ashore and seen the banquet, and gone up the country. I am getting rather sick of being a prisoner, and always set to work. But—hullo, Chips!"

"Just one moment, sir; and you too, Mr Poole."

"Yes; what is it?"

"That's rather a large order, gentlemen, aren't it? That there Don will be wanting to make me his chief naval constructor, perhaps. But that wouldn't do. I say, though, Mr Burnett, sir, can you give a poor fellow a tip or two?"

"What about?" said Fitz.

"What about, sir? Oh, I say, come! I like that! How am I going to get off that there gunboat? She's a harmoured vessel, you know."

"Oh, you'll do it, Chips. You could always do anything, even when you hadn't got any stuff. What about pulling up the hacienda floor?"

"To make fortifications, sir? Yes, we did work that to rights. But iron's iron, and wood's wood. You can drive one into t'other, but you can't drive t'other into one."

"No, Chips," said Fitz, laughing. "But there are more ways of killing a cat than hanging."

"So there are, sir; toe be sure. Making up your mind to do a thing is half the battle. I should like to have the help of you two young gents, though, all the same. A word from a young officer as knows how to disable a Armstrong gun, and from another who thinks nothing of tying a screw-propeller up in a knot, is worth having."

"Oh, I'll help you," said Fitz. "But I am afraid my help won't be of much use."

"The same here," said Poole. "Ditto and ditto."

"Then I shall do it, sir," cried the carpenter confidently. "Of course," cried Fitz. "But that gunboat must be very heavy. How shall you go to work?"

The carpenter gave a sharp look round, and then said in a low confidential tone—

"A deal too heavy, sir, for us to lift her. The only way to do is to make her lift herself."

"How?"

"Taking out of her everything that can be moved; guns first, then shot and shell, and laying them overboard outside upon the rocks, ready for hoisting in again at low water when she's afloat. Next thing I should do would be to find out whether she's got any holes in her, and if she hasn't— and I don't believe she has, for there's been no storm to bump her on the rocks—then I shall pump her dry, have her fires got up, and at high water full steam ahead, and if she don't come off then I'm a double Dutchman."

"But what about the screw?"

"Them as hides can find, sir, which means them as tie can untie. I think we can get her off, sir, if we put our backs into it. What say you?"

"Get her off?" cried Fitz. "Of course we will!"

Chapter Fifty Five
Boarding the gunboat

That evening, followed by a heterogeneous fleet of about twenty small vessels crammed with fighting men, the *Teal* sailed again, and their time of arrival was so contrived that dawn of the next morning but one found the little fleet in delightfully calm weather forming a semi-circle from one point of the shore to the other, the focus of its radius being formed by the gunboat on the rocks.

The plans had been made on the voyage, and as there was plenty of water for every vessel but the schooner, the latter's boats, well filled with men, alone accompanied the rest.

It was an attack, but no defence, for as soon as the crew of the gunboat realised the formidable nature and numbers of the expedition, they took to the boats to try and escape to the shore. But the cliffs forbade this, and after another attempt or two to get away, all surrendered and gave up their arms, ready, as had been predicted, to begin cheering Don Ramon, the officers as they gave up their swords humbly asking to be allowed to retain their positions under the new Government, for there seemed to be a general acceptation of the fact now that the petty war was at an end.

Don Ramon's answer to this was to accept the services of the officers and the best of the men. The rest were boated off to the mouth of the river and set ashore.

"Ornamental, I call it," said Chips, as he sat forward in one of the schooner's boats commanded by Poole, in which, as a matter of course, Fitz had taken his place.

"What is, Chips?" said Poole. "Do you mean your head?"

"My head, sir," said the carpenter, staring. "Well, no, sir, I didn't mean my head. 'Tain't a bad one as it goes, but I never set myself up for a good-looking chap, one of your handsome sort. I allus left that to the Camel here."

The men, who were resting on their oars, burst into a roar of laughter, and the cook laughing as heartily as the rest and displaying his great teeth, but his mirth was silent.

"Hark at him," he said. "Chips is a wonderful man for a joke."

"Nay, and I never set up as a joker either," said the carpenter; "but about this 'ere head of mine, I allus reckoned it was more useful than ornamental. What did you mean was the matter with it, Mr Poole?"

"Oh, only that it was swelled out so since you've been head contractor and engineer-in-chief for the getting the gunboat off the rocks. Doesn't your hat feel very tight?"

"Nay, sir, and you are all wrong, for there's such a breeze here coming off the sea, hitting slap agin the rocks and coming back right in your face, that I have been longing for a piece of paper to fold up and put inside the band of my hat to make it tight. Why I nearly lost it twice."

"Oh," said Poole, "I thought it must be swelled. You've grown so important ever since you took the job."

"Never mind what he says, Chips," cried Fitz, "he's only chaffing you."

"Bless your 'eart, sir," cried the carpenter, "I know: this aren't the first voyage I've had with Master Poole."

"But what do you mean about being ornamental?" said Poole.

"Oh, us Teals, sir, and our boats. Here have we been figuring about holding up our rifles in the sun, and with these here cutlashes getting in the men's way wherever we rowed. Regular ornamental I calls us, never so much as fired a shot or hit any one on the nose with one's fist. We have done a bit of shouting though. I've hooroared till if I had tried to do any more, I should roar like a sick bull in a cow-yard shut up to eat straw, while all the cows were in the next field getting fat on grass. I want to know what's the use of our coming at all!"

"As supporters of the Don," said Fitz; "for prestige."

"For what, sir?"

"Prestige," said Fitz, laughing.

"Oh! that's it, was it, sir? Well, I'm glad you told me. Where does that come in?"

"Why, all through. Shows how English men-of-war's-men have helped to frighten these mongrels into surrender. Haven't you?"

"Well, I dunno about me, sir. I dare say the sight of the Camel there has scared them a bit. Wherever he showed his teeth, they must have said to themselves, 'What a beggar that would be to bite!' And I suppose that made them a bit the readier to chuck it up as they did. But it's just what I said. We Teals have been ornamental all through this job, and I should have liked to have had just one more go in by way of putting a neat finish."

"Oh, you've got job enough coming off," said Poole. "There's your work," and he pointed to the gunboat lying about a quarter of a mile away.

The carpenter became serious directly, frowned severely, laid his coxswain's boat-hook across his knees, and took off his straw hat to give his dewy forehead a couple of wipes with his bare mahogany-brown arms.

"Yes, gentlemen," he said, "that's a big handful for one man, and I feel a bit staggered, and get thinking every now and then that it was the biggest bit of cheek I ever showed in my life."

"What was?" said Fitz.

"What was, sir? Why, to say that I would get that there vessel off them rocks. There are times when I feel skeered, and ready to tuck my tail between my legs and run away like a frightened dog."

"You!" cried Fitz, and the two lads laughed heartily.

"Ah, it's all very fine, gentlemen, you are on the right side. You aren't got it to do. I have, and if I was to try and laugh now it would be on the other side of my mouth."

"Get out," said Poole, "you'll do it right enough. Won't he, Fitz?"

"Of course."

"Think so, gentlemen?"

"To be sure we do," cried Fitz. "You'll do it, Chips. Go in and win."

"Thank you, sir," said the man, rather sadly. "I did say I'd do it, didn't I?"

"To be sure you did."

"Well then, of course I must try."

"To be sure you must," cried Fitz. "Why, you'll be able to do it in broad daylight with nobody to interrupt you."

"So I shall, Mr Burnett, sir. It won't be like swarming up her side in the dark, expecting a couple of dozen of them half-bred niggers to come at you with their long knives ready to pitch you overboard. Here: I am glad you talked. I was getting all in the downs like over that job, when it aren't half so 'ard as for a young gent like you to swarm up that anker, that very *one* yonder as is hanging from the cat-head now, and then taking out that breech-block and—"

"There, that will do," cried Fitz, turning scarlet; "I don't want to hear any more about that. I say, Chips, how do you mean to begin?"

The carpenter screwed his face up into a very cunning smile.

"Like me to tell you, sir?"

"Of course," cried the boys in a breath.

"Well," said the carpenter, "you are both very pleasant young gents as has allus been good friends to me, and I'd tell you in a minute but for one reason."

"You don't want your messmates to know your plans?" said Fitz quickly.

"Oh no, sir, it's a bigger reason than that. You see, it's just like this 'ere. I'll tell you, only don't let 'em know in the other boat. You see there's Mr Burgess yonder, and old Butters."

"Well, don't make such a rigmarole of it all, Chips," cried Poole. "What's your big reason?"

"Well, sir, it's just this 'ere," said the carpenter solemnly. "I'll be blessed if I know it myself."

"Bah!" cried Poole angrily.

"What I want is clean decks, with all them there trash cleared away, and time for me and the bosun having the craft to ourselves just to go round and smell it all over before we begin."

"Of course," cried Poole.

"You see, it's a big job, gentlemen, and it's no use for us to roosh it. What I want is for us to be able to lay this 'ere boat aboard, and leave to begin. I want room, sir, and to see what tools I want, and—"

"Ahoy there, Mr Poole!" came from the next boat. "Let your men give way and follow me. I am going to board the gunboat now, and put a prize crew on board."

"Ay, ay, sir," cried Poole; and then to the carpenter, who sat moistening his hands prior to giving them a rub on his knees, "There you are, Chips. Give way, my lads. We are going to make fast a tow-rope to the gunboat's stern. Keep your eyes open, and you will see how Chips will haul her off."

There was another laugh as the men bent to their oars, rowing so vigorously that several of the small craft full of Don Ramon's followers, hanging round the ponderous-looking craft upon the rocks, hurriedly made way as if half expecting to be run down, and a few minutes later the schooner's boats, headed by Mr Burgess, were alongside their late dangerous enemy, to spring on board, the Spanish crew drawing back to the other side to crowd together and look carelessly on, all idea of resistance being at an end.

Chapter Fifty Six
Winks's luck

Neither Fitz nor Poole had felt any desire to pose as the heroes of the little night attack, which had resulted in the disabling of the armoured man-of-war, but it was with a strange feeling of exultation that they climbed on board in the full sunshine, eager as they were to stand once more upon the decks, and see in the broad daylight what the vessel was like into which they had climbed in the darkness of the night.

Fitz's first thought as he passed through the gangway was to make for the great gun that stood amidships upon its iron platform and revolving carriage, the huge muzzle elevated, and looking ready to hurl its great shells far and wide; but he had to wait and stand with the schooner's men drawn up while the prisoners and volunteers who had joined the winning side filed down into the boats that swarmed around, till with one exception the crew had all left the deck, the exception being the firemen, who willy nilly were retained on board for service in connection with the engine under the new President.

All this took time, but at last Don Ramon's dread had become his joy, and he showed his feeling of triumph as he paced the gunboat's deck rubbing his hands, and every now and then giving vent to a satisfied "Hah!" as he stopped to converse with Burgess, or to say a kindly word to one or other of the prize crew, not least to the two boys.

"Hah!" cried the carpenter at last. "Now then, gentlemen, I think we must say going to begin. Here's Mr Burgess as hungry as I am. You would like to come round with us, wouldn't you, Mr Poole? Mr Burgess says we can get to work as soon as ever we like."

"Of course we should," said Poole. "Come on, Fitz;" for just then Don Ramon came up to the mate to make a flowery speech, telling him that he left him in perfect confidence to hold the prize while he went to see to the disposal of the rest of the prisoners who were left, so that no attempt might be made to regain the upper hand.

Poole turned to Fitz expecting to see him eager to follow the carpenter, but it was to find him standing with one foot upon the platform of the great gun, looking at the muzzle, as it sloped toward the sky, evidently deep in thought, and he did not stir until Poole laid a hand upon his arm with the query—

"What are you thinking about?"

"That night," was the reply.

"So was I just now," said Poole. "Look there, that's where I lay with one of the Spaniards holding me down, and afraid to make a sound, or to struggle. It was horrid, and I couldn't tell what sort of a position you were in. It was ticklish work and no mistake."

"Yes," said Fitz, thoughtfully, "horrible for you, but I believe it was worse for me, because something seemed to be tagging at me all the time and telling me that I had no business there."

Poole looked at his companion curiously.

"But you felt that you must do it, didn't you?" he said.

"Oh, yes," cried Fitz, "I was desperate; but I never want to go through such a five minutes again. Let's see, I stepped along there," he continued, pointing and following the steps his memory taught him that he must have taken to get round to the back of the great gun. "Yes, this is exactly where I stood to swing round those great balls and open the breech, but only to be disappointed, finding as I did that the block was fast. Oh, Poole, how I did tug and strain at it, feeling all the while that I had been boasting and bragging to your father, and that after all I was only a poor miserable impostor who had been professing to know a great deal, when I was as ignorant as could be, and that I was being deservedly punished in that terrible failure that was taking place."

"Ah, I remember," cried Poole; "you said the block stuck fast?"

"Yes, till the idea came that I had not turned the great screw far enough."

"But you ought to have made sure of that at first."

"Of course I ought," cried Fitz sharply, "and I ought to have been as cool and calm as possible when doing such a venturesome thing—in the pitch-darkness, with perhaps ten or a dozen of the Spanish sailors—the watch—"

"The watch!" cried Poole, laughing. "Come, I like that."

"Well, then, men lying about all round us. You were perfectly cool of course?"

"I!" replied Poole. "Why I was in a state of high fever. I didn't know whether I was on my head or my heels. I believe, old fellow, that I was half mad with excitement."

"I'm sure I was," cried Fitz, "till the thought came that perhaps I had not turned the screw far enough. That thought made me quite jump. Then there was the feeling the screw move. I felt as if I could see the great thread all shining as it glided along, while I must have seen the block when I lifted it out."

"But that was all fancy of course. It was the darkest, blackest night I ever saw."

"I know, but I certainly seemed to see the block as I held it hugged to my breast."

"I should have liked to see you when you were making for the side all top-heavy, and went flying over after the great quoin as you called it. My word, Fitz, that was a flying leap overboard."

"Ugh!" ejaculated the latter with a shudder. "As I go over the task again, it seems as if it is all part of a queer dream."

"A very lively one though," said Poole, laughing. "I say, I wonder how deep you went down."

"Oh, don't talk about it! Ever so far. It seemed a terribly long time all going down and down, feeling all that time as if I should never come up again, and thinking about sharks too. Why, it couldn't have been half-a-minute from the time I touched the water till I was at the top again swimming, and yet it seemed to be an hour at least."

"It does seem long at a time like that. But I say, what a narrow escape that was."

"Of being caught, yes."

"No, no," cried Poole; "I mean when the breech-block went over the side."

"It just was," said the carpenter, coming up. "I know somebody, gentlemen, who thinks as he had a very narrow squeak of being took down to the bottom with that bit o' steel and kept there. But that would ha' been better than floating up again to be pulled to pieces by the sharks. I don't suppose that they stops much about the bottom o' the sea; they generally seem to be too busy up at top, drying their back-fins in the open air. Trying your little bit o' performance over again, gentlemen?"

"Yes, Chips," said Fitz, as the man stood smiling at him. "It was a horrible night's work."

"Well, no, sir, not horrid. We came out to do something and we did it fine. The on'y awkward bit on it is the risk you ran a-popping that there breech-block on somebody's head, for which miss he's very much obliged — very much indeed. But I came to see if you gents wouldn't like to come down below with us to sound the well, for I expect there's a precious lot o' water there, and a big hole to let it in. Mr Burgess have gone down with Butters."

The two lads hurriedly followed the carpenter below, to encounter the mate and boatswain fresh from their task.

"Deal more water than I like to see, my lads," said the boatswain, "but we shall know better where we stand after that steam-pump has been going for a couple of hours."

"Job for that engineer and his fireman," said the carpenter coolly; and very soon after the panting of the donkey-engine, the rattle of the pump, and the vigorous splashing down of clear water betokened the relieving of the gunboat's lower parts of some portion of their burden, as Poole said, but only to be met by a damping remark from Fitz.

"Not much good," he said, "if the water runs in as fast as it runs out."

As time could be the only test for this, the little party of examiners descended now into one of the schooner's boats, the carpenter standing up in her bows and passing her along to make fast by one of the ringbolts of the stern-post, and giving the two lads a peculiar look as he proceeded to examine the propeller.

"Well, how does it seem?" said the mate.

"Seem, Mr Burgess, sir?" said the carpenter dryly, "don't seem at all, sir. There's nothing here but the biggest ball o' string I ever see. Would you mind coming forard, Mr Butters, sir, and seeing what you can make of it?"

The boatswain passed over the thwarts and joined his comrade of the past night's work, stood looking down for a few moments, and then took off his cap and scratched one ear.

"You young gents had better come and have a look," he said; "you had the designing on it."

The boys did not wait for a second invitation, but hurriedly went forward, to find that their scheme had acted far beyond their expectations, for the fans of the propeller had wound up the thick soft cable so tightly that the opening in which the fish-tail mechanism turned was completely filled with the tightly-compressed strands of rope, so that Poole suggested that all that needed was to get hold of one end, and then as soon as the steam was well on to reverse and wind the cable off in a similar way to that in which it had been wound on.

Freeing of the propeller.

"Hah, to be sure," said the boatswain, giving his leg a sailor's slap, "there's nothing like a bit o' sense, Mr Poole, sir; that nice noo Manilla cable's been twisted round my heart, sir, ever since it was used, and made me feel quite sore. Nothing I hates worse than waste."

"It wasn't waste," said Fitz, impatiently. "You might just as well say the bait was wasted when you have been fishing. Don't you get something good in return?"

"Ah, but that's fishing, young gentlemen, and this aren't," said Butters, with a very knowing smile.

"Not fishing!" cried Fitz. "I think it was fishing. You used the cable, and you've caught a gunboat."

"But s'pose we've got the gunboat and the bait back as well, how then?" cried the boatswain. "Look ye here, my lad, I'm going to have that there end of the cable taken a turn round the steam-capstan, and as soon as the chaps have got full steam on, the screw shall be turned, and we'll wind it off fine and good as noo."

Fitz shook his head as he gazed down through the clear water at the mass of rope, and exclaimed—

"I know it won't do."

"What, aren't you saddasfied now?" said the boatswain, while Chips wrinkled up his face and looked uneasy.

"Aren't never seen a screw fouled like that afore, along of a coir cable, Mr Fitz, sir, have you?"

"No," replied the middy. "But I've seen a Manilla cable after it's been down with a heavy anchor in a rocky sea off the Channel Islands."

"And how was that, sir?"

"Frayed in half-a-dozen places by the rocks, so that the anchor parted before we'd got it weighed, and the captain was obliged to send for a diver to get the anchor up."

"But there aren't no rocks here, Mr Fitz, sir, to fray this here one, because it has never been down."

"No, but it has been ground against the iron stern-post till it's nearly through in ever so many places. Look there, and there, and there."

"Hah, look at that, bosun," cried the carpenter triumphantly. "Just cast your eye along there and there. Our side's right and the Manilla cable's all wrong. I'm afeard too as we're going to find out a good many other things is wrong, and the gunboat aren't afloat yet."

"No, but you've undertaken to float her, Chips," said Poole. "I wouldn't reckon on being Don Ramon's head naval architect and engineer just yet."

"No, sir, I don't," said the carpenter seriously. "But anyhow we'll set the screw free before we trouble any more about that leakage;" and in a very business-like way he carried out the boatswain's plans, connecting the cable with the capstan, and winding it off; but it was so damaged by grinding against the edges of the opening that it parted five different times before it was all off, to the boatswain's great disgust.

"What have you got to say about the leakage, Mr Burnett, sir?" whispered the carpenter after the cable task was ended, and the fans of the propeller showed clearly in the water just below the surface, and had been set whirling round in both directions to churn up the water, and prove that the shaft had not been wrenched or dragged from its bearings.

"Nothing at present, Chips," replied the middy.

"Because I'd take it kindly, sir, if you'd drop a fellow a hint or two. This is a big job, sir, and means my making or my breaking, sir."

"But you shouldn't ask me, my man," replied the middy. "You are old and experienced, while I'm only a boy."

"Yes, sir, I knows that," said the man; "but you're come out of a gunboat, sir, and you've got your head screwed on the right way, sir. I never see a young gent with such a head as yours, nor yet one as was screwed on so tight."

"Oh, nonsense, Chips," cried the boy, flushing. "It's your job, not mine."

"Nay, sir, it aren't nonsense, it's sound sense. I like a bit of the first as well as any man when larking helps to make hard work go easy. Often enough a bit o' fun acts like ile to a hard job, but it won't ile this one. And as I said afore, sir, I'd take it kindly if you'd put in a word now and then over the rest o' the job same as you did over the cable."

"But you ought to consult with Mr Burgess or the captain, my man," said Fitz, uneasily.

"Nay, I oughtn't, sir. I'd a deal rayther have a word or two from you when you see things going wrong."

"Why?" said Fitz quickly.

"I've told you, sir. Doesn't all you say come right? I've kinder got a sort o' confidence in you, Mr Burnett, sir, as makes me feel as if I should like to be under you in some ship or another, and I aren't the on'y one aboard as feels that, I'm sure."

"Well, it's very kind of you to put so much faith in me," said the middy; "but don't say any more, please, and don't believe in me too much for fear I should make some horrible blunder, and disappoint you after all."

"Ah, you won't do that, sir," said the carpenter confidently.

"Of course I shall be only too glad to help you if I can, for I should be very glad to see you float the vessel."

"And you will keep an eye on what I do, sir, and put in a word if you think I'm going wrong?"

"If you wish it, yes," replied Fitz.

"Thanky, sir," whispered the man earnestly. "It may be the making of me, sir, and anyhow, as I have took up this job, I don't want these Spaniel chaps to see an Englishman fail."

"They shall not, Chips, if I can help it," cried Fitz, warmly. "There now, let's see whether the donkey-engine is able to keep the water down, or whether she's lower in the water than she was."

"There, sir," whispered the man, "hark at you! Call yourself a boy! why you couldn't ha' spoken better if you'd been a hold man of a 'undered. You made me want to give you a shout, only I had to keep quiet, and let the Spaniels think I'm doing it all to rights. I don't mind about our lads. They all know me, and what I can do and what I can't. I don't want to try anything and chuck dust in their eyes—not me; but I do want to show off a bit and let these Spanish Mullotter chaps see what an Englishman can do, for the sake of the old country and the British flag."

"Then let's go below, Chips," said Fitz, "and see what the pumping has done."

Poole, who had been aft with the mate during this conversation, rejoined them now, and together they went below to sound the well.

"Good luck to us, gentlemen," said the carpenter, rubbing his hands.

"Good luck," cried Poole eagerly. "You don't mean to say she's making less water?"

"Nay, sir, but I do say that the engine's lowering it. There's a foot less in her now than when we began pumping, and that means we win."

A few hours later, after the donkey-engine had kept on its steady pumping, Chips made another inspection, and came up to where Fitz and Poole were together, pulling a very long face.

"Why, what's the matter, Chips?" cried Fitz anxiously. "You don't mean to say that anything is wrong?"

"Horribly, gentlemen," cried the man. "It's always my luck! Chucking away my chances! Why, she's as good as new!"

"Well, what more do you want? Isn't that good enough for you?"

"Yes, sir, it's good enough; but Mr Butters here and me, we was half asleep. We ought to have formed ourselves into a company—Winks and Co., or Butters and Co., or Butters and Winks, or Winks and Butters, or Co. and Co."

"Why not Cocoa and Cocoa?" said Fitz, laughing.

"Anyhow you like, gentlemen, only we ought to have done it. Bought the gunboat cheap, and there was a fortune for us."

"Never mind that," said Poole. "You'll be all right, Chips. Don Ramon wiil be presenting you with a brass tobacco-box, or something else, if you get her off."

"Go and ast him to order it at once, so as to have it ready, for we shall have her off to-morrow as soon as them 'hogany lubbers have got the steam up."

"You don't mean that?" cried Poole.

"Ask Mr Butters here, and see what he says."

"Yes," said the boatswain coolly; "and I thought we should have to lighten her by a couple of hundred tons or so. But it makes a man feel very proud of being an English sailor. These half-breeds here give up at once. Why, if she'd had an English crew aboard, that cable wouldn't have stopped round the screw, and the lads wouldn't have sat down to smoke cigarettes and holloa. Why, they might have had her off a score of times."

"But what about getting her safely into the channel again?" said Poole.

"What about getting old Burgess aboard to con her; she going slow with a couple of fellows at work with the lead in the chains? Why, it's all as easy as buttering a bit of biscuit."

Not quite, but the next evening the gunboat was well out in deep water, comparatively undamaged, and flying Don Ramon's colours, making her way towards Velova Bay, towing a whole regiment of boats, the *Teal* proudly leading under easy sail.

Chapter Fifty Seven
A Startler

"Ah," said Don Ramon to the skipper, the morning after their arrival, "if only that gun were perfect!"

"Well, it ought to be in two months' time. You'll have to get command of the telegraph at San Cristobal."

"To get command?" cried the Don. "I have full command. Resistance to my rule is dead, and I have only to wait to be acknowledged by the Powers. But go on with what you were saying."

"Oh, it was only this. You can wire to the makers of the gun to send you out a new breech-block by the first steamer. They will honour your order, I'll be bound."

"It shall be done," said Don Ramon eagerly.

This took place in the principal building of the little port, where the Don was entertaining the skipper and the two lads; and he seemed quite disturbed when, after a short communication had passed, Fitz and Poole got up and asked their host to excuse them.

"You wish to go so soon?" he said. "Why, I have friends coming to whom I wish to introduce you as the brave young heroes who helped me to success."

"Oh, there's no need for that sir," said Fitz. "We don't want to be made a fuss over."

"But I take it that you would be willing to gratify your host," replied the Don loftily, "and it would please me much if you would stay."

"But we must get back on board, sir," said Fitz anxiously. Then noticing the air of displeasure in the President's countenance, the middy added hastily, "There, sir, we will come back at once."

They hurried down to the shore, where the schooner's gig was lying with her crew on board.

"Well, I don't understand whatever you want," said Poole, "unless you have suddenly found out that because ladies are coming you ought to put on a clean shirt."

"Get out!" cried Fitz; and then, assuming command of the boat, to Poole's great amusement, though he said nothing, Fitz gave orders to the men to give way and row them out to the gunboat.

"Why, I thought you wanted to go to the *Teal*! Oh, I see. Well, it's very nice of you. You want us to go and take charge of the prize crew so as to let old Burgess go and have some tucker with the Don."

"Nothing of the kind," said Fitz shortly.

"What is it then?" said Poole. "What's the good of keeping things so close?"

"Wait and see. I don't know yet myself."

"Dear me!" said Poole. "I suppose his lordship has found out that he left his purse in the cabin."

"Wrong," said Fitz. "It was only an old leather one if he had, with nothing in it. Can't you wait a few minutes till I see if I am right?"

"Oh, yes, I'll wait; only too glad to get away while the other people come. I say, Fitz, old chap, let's be as long as we can. I do hate all that fuss. It makes me feel so weak."

"Yes; I don't like it. That's the worst of foreigners. They are so fond of show. I say, Poole, old chap, I've got such a grand idea."

"What is it?"

"Wait and see."

"Now, just you look here," said Poole; "you can't say but what I'm a good-tempered sort of fellow, but if there's much more of this you'll put me out. I'm not a little child, and you are not playing at bob-cherry, so leave off dangling nothing before my lips and then snatching it away."

"Ah, you wait and see," said Fitz.

Just then, as Poole turned upon him irritably, the gig touched the gunboat's side, and the boys sprang on board, to be greeted by the mate and the members of the prize crew, who had moored her well under the guns of the little fort.

"Hullo, young fellows! I know what you want," cried the mate.

"Then you are cleverer than I am," said Poole, laughing, "for I don't."

"Then why have you come?"

"Ask Burnett here. He seems to be Grand Panjandrum now."

"You've come," said the mate, "by the President's orders, to bring me ashore to drink wine and eat cake, or some nonsense of that kind, and you may go back and tell him I can't leave my post."

"Wrong," said Fitz; and he hurried away forward, to come into sight again waving his hand to Poole to join him.

"Whatever's the matter with the fellow?" said Poole to himself, as he followed the middy.

Fitz met him half-way, caught him by the collar, and with his face flushed and eyes flashing, whispered something in his ear.

"No!" cried Poole. "You don't mean it!"

"I do," said Fitz, and he whispered a few more words that made his companion stare.

"Shall we?" cried Fitz excitedly.

"Oh, I don't know," replied Poole. "It would make such a scare."

"I don't care," said Fitz. "It will make Don Ramon ready to jump out of his skin. I don't know what he won't say when he gets the news; and besides, I feel as if I had a right."

Meanwhile the people were beginning to arrive to crowd the *salle* where the President and the skipper were ready to receive them, and the President had risen at once, and amidst a tremendous burst of applause, to begin a speech in which he intended to congratulate his hearers upon the end of the war and the commencement of what he hoped would be a long term of peace, when he and all present were startled by a terrific roar as of thunder close at hand, followed by what seemed like a minute's silence, when the echoes began to speak, carrying on the sound along the valley and up into the mountains, where it rolled and died out, rose again, and was eddied on and on, to finally fade away in a dull whisper.

For the time no one spoke, no one stirred, but stood as if turned to stone, as so many statues where but a few minutes before all was animation and suppressed excitement consequent upon what was looked upon as the successful determination of the revolution.

Upon every face horror was now depicted, cheeks were pale, eyes dilated and staring, and fear with all its horrors seemed to have enchained the crowded *salle*.

There was one pale face though that seemed to stand out the central figure of the gaily-dressed and uniformed crowd. It was that of the President, who slowly stretched out his hands on high, his fists clenching and his features convulsed. There was no horror there in his looks, but one great reflex of the despair within his heart.

"Oh," he groaned, "and at a time like this, when I have fought so hard, when I would have given up my very life for my unhappy country. Gentlemen, we have a new enemy to contend with, and that is Fate. Am I to own that all is lost, or appeal to you, my faithful friends, to begin again to fight the deadly battle to the very last?"

"But what is it?" cried one of the officials.

"Yes," shouted another, "what does this mean?"

The President smiled bitterly, and stood for a few moments gazing back sadly at his questioners as the crowd began to sway to and fro, some of those present beginning to make for the door, but in an undecided way, and swaying back to press once more upon their leader, as if feeling that he was their only hope.

He seemed to read this in their faces, and suddenly the blood began to flush like a cloud across his pallid brow, nerving him as it were to action.

Throwing his right hand across his breast he sought for the hilt of his sword, which his left raised ready, and he snatched the blade from its scabbard, whirled it on high, and then held it pointed towards the nearest open window, through which a thin dank odoured cloud of smoke was beginning to float, telling its own tale of what the explosion was.

For a few moments the President was silent, rigid and statuesque in his attitude, while his eyes flashed defiance and determination.

"Gentlemen," he cried, "you ask me what this means," and he seemed to flash his glance around the room to take in everybody before letting his eyes rest at last upon the skipper. "It means that the scotched snake has raised its poisoned head once more, how I know not, nor yet what following he hab. But the enemy still lives, and we must fight again to the very death if needs be."

A murmur of excitement ran through the *salle*, and once more the weak amongst those assembled raised a murmur, and glances were directed towards the door, as if the next moment panic was about to set in and a rush was imminent. At that moment, as if in response to the President's appealing look, the big bronzed skipper, Poole's father, British to the backbone, took a step or two forward, and the President's face lit up with a smile as he uttered a loud "Hah!" full of the satisfaction he felt.

"Silence there," he shouted, directing his words at his wavering followers, whose spirits seemed to have been completely dashed. "Silence, and let our brave captain speak."

"I have only this to say," cried the skipper. "Be calm, gentlemen, be calm. Are we who have carried all before us to be frightened by a noise? It is an explosion. Whatever has happened you must be cool, and act like the brave men you are. This is either some accident, or the cunning enemy has sent in some emissary to lay a train. It is all plain enough. Some of the powder collected in the magazine of the fort has gone. There was a great flash, I saw it myself, and it evidently came from there. Now, President, take the lead. Out with your swords, gentlemen. I don't believe you will need them. Some pounds of gunpowder have been destroyed. Had the enemy been there we should have heard their burst of cheering, and the noise of their coming on, for this place would have been the first they would have attacked."

The skipper's sensible words were greeted with a groan of despair, for at that moment that of which he had spoken came floating in turn through the open window.

"Ah," cried the President, catching at the skipper's arm and gripping it fast as he pointed to the open window with his sword. "Brave words, my friend, but you hear— you hear—" and another murmur of despair ran through the crowd.

"Oh yes," said the skipper, "I can hear."

"The cries," said the President, "of the savage enemy."

"No," roared the skipper with a mocking laugh. "Your enemies, man, can't cheer like that," and he rushed to the window. "There they go again. Why, Don, that's not a Spanish but good old English shout. Yes, there they go again. I don't know what it means, but I can hear, far off as they are, those were the voices of some of my crew."

"What?" cried the President.

"Come here, all of you," cried the captain, "and look out. There's nothing to fear. Follow my lead and give another cheer back. That shouting came from the gunboat deck. Look, Don Ramon, you can see my fellows waving their caps, and those two boys are busy on the bridge doing something, I can't make out what. Yes, I can, they're bending on a flag. There: up it goes. Why, gentlemen, we have been scaring ourselves at a puff of powder smoke. Why, by all that's wonderful—" He stopped short and held up his hand.

"Silence, please," he cried after a pause, and a dead stillness reigned once more as every one who could get a glimpse of the gunboat strained his neck to stare.

"I am stunned, confused," whispered the President. "What is it, captain? For pity's sake speak."

"No, sir, I'll let your best friend do that."

"My best friend? You speak in riddles."

"Yes, wait a minute, and the answer, a big one, to this great riddle will come," cried the captain. "Can't you see, man? the lads are busy there getting ready for your friend to speak. Another moment or two and you will hear what he says—that Don Ramon is President of this Republic, and his seat in the chair is safe against any enemy that may come. Ah, all together. Hooray! Hooray! Hooray!"

The skipper's cheer was loud, but it was stifled before it was half-uttered, for once more that terrific roar arose, making the Presidential building quiver and the glass in several of the windows come tinkling down into the stone-paved court.

Most of those present had this time seen the flash—the roar had set the ears of all ringing once again, as a great puff of smoke dashed out like a ball and then rose slowly in the sunshine, forming itself into a great grey ring, quivering as another burst of cheering arose from the gunboat's deck.

For it was neither attack from the cunning enemy nor the catastrophe caused by explosion, as the fresh burst of cheering from the gunboat fully explained, for they were British cheers from the prize crew, echoed by those on board the schooner.

There was nothing the matter, only a happy thought had occurred to the middy, and he wondered that it had not come before, as he hurried to the proper spot, made a little search, and found that he was right—that there was a spare breech-block on board which enabled him and Poole, after gaining access to the magazine, to thrust a blank cartridge into the great gun and announce the fact in what was literally a *feu de joie*.

Chapter Fifty Eight
A regular young Filibuster

"Oh, pray don't say any more to me about it, sir," cried Fitz, the next day. "It was only just an idea."

"An idea, my dear young friend!" cried the President.

"Yes, sir; a mere trifle."

"A trifle!" said the President. "Oh, how lightly you English boys do take such things. Your trifle, as you call it, has made me fast in the Governmental chair. I shall always think that I owe you my success."

"What, because I thought there was another breech-block, sir?"

"Oh, not merely that. There was your first idea about getting away from the hacienda and coming round here by sea. They may seem trifles to your young elastic spirit, but their effect has been great."

"Once more, sir; please don't say any more. My only wonder is now, that somebody else on board the gunboat did not think about the spare block and get it into use."

"Ah, yes; one of the officers has been talking to me about it. He said he was the only man on board who knew of its existence, and—simply because it had not been wanted—he had almost forgotten, or, as he put it, it was for the time driven out of his head by the great trouble they were in, caused by the fouling of the screw, and the current carrying them on to the rocks."

"Oh, I am glad of that," said Fitz. "Glad? Why?" said the President, looking at him wonderingly.

"Because it makes Poole Reed stand out so much better than I do. It was entirely his notion to foul the screw."

"Oh, come, come, come!" cried Don Ramon. "I am not going to weigh you both in the balance to see which was the better. I shall always look upon you as a pair of young heroes."

"Oh, I say," cried Poole, "please don't!"

"Very well," said the Spaniard, laughing; "I'll say no more, but I shall think."

"I don't mind his thinking," said Fitz, a short time later when he was talking to his companion about what had been said. "But I hope next time he wants to go into ecstasies about what we did, he'll let them all off at you."

"Thankye," said Poole; "much obliged." The lads had something else to think of the next day, for in the midst of the rejoicings over Don Ramon's success, and when the gunboat was dressed with colours from head to stern, the new President's flag predominant, and her old officers accepting the alteration in the state of affairs with the greatest nonchalance, and in fact on the whole pleased with the change of rulers, signals were shown from the high look-out at the entrance of the harbour indicating that a vessel was in sight. In the midst of the excitement that this caused, steam was hastily got up on board the gunboat, and the decks cleared for action ready for an engagement if necessary in Don Ramon's cause.

The excitement soon ceased to be alarming, for in due course the stranger's flag was made out, her signal for a pilot answered, and in the course of the afternoon a United States cruiser steamed in, answering the salute from the fort and gunboat, and taking up her position close under their guns.

The rest of the customary civilities were interchanged, and the captain of the Yankee came ashore to visit the new President, laughingly saying that he had come to see Don Villarayo, but as he was in the mountains and a new President governed in his stead, and as he supposed it was only a matter of form before Don Ramon would be acknowledged by the American Government, he had nothing to do but wait for instructions after he had communicated with Washington.

The captain made himself very agreeable, chatting with Don Ramon's notabilities, and the schooner's skipper; but several times he glanced searchingly in the direction of Fitz Burnett, who had been awaiting his opportunity either to be introduced or to go up and speak.

His turn came at last, for the captain fixed his eyes upon him with a look of invitation to which Fitz instantly responded by closing up, colouring slightly the while with consciousness, as it seemed to him that the American captain, all spick and span in his neat naval uniform, was looking askant at the well-worn garments the lad was wearing.

"How do, youngster?" he said. "I didn't know one of your cruisers was in these waters. Has she left you here as a hostage, or something of the kind? You English chaps are everywhere."

For long enough Fitz Burnett had been waiting for this moment, ready to pour out his troubles and adventures to somebody who would give him help; and now that the time had come he could hardly speak.

The American captain noticed it, and raised his eyebrows a little.

"Why was it?" he said kindly, as he saw how thoroughly agitated the boy was. "In trouble?"

"Yes, sir," cried Fitz.

"You don't mean to tell me you've done such a stupid school-boy act as to desert your ship?"

"Oh, no, no, no!" cried Fitz excitedly; and out it all came, the captain listening eagerly and questioning him wherever the boy hesitated, till he had finished his adventurous tale.

"Well, this is something fresh, my lad," cried the American captain. "But I reckon that the time will come when you'll think you've been in luck. For you've done nothing wrong. You were regularly taken prisoner while doing your duty, and your skipper can't blame you."

"Think not, sir?" cried Fitz, warming up in the gratitude he felt for the captain's sympathy.

"Think not? Of course! If he does, and won't have you back, I'll find you a berth on my ship, and be glad to have you. What do you say? Will you come?"

Fitz looked at him searchingly, and shook his head.

"I am in the Queen's service, sir," he said.

"And a fine service too, my lad. But how has this skipper behaved to you since you've been with him?"

"Oh, as if I had been his own son, sir," cried Fitz warmly; "and his boy and I have been the best of friends."

"But I say, you've been a regular young filibuster all the time, breaking the laws and helping in a revolution. Why, you've been carrying on high jinks, and no mistake! But you don't mean to tell me you want to stay with them?"

"Oh no, of course not. I want to rejoin the *Tonans*."

"Where do you say—in the Channel Service? Well, I can't take you there."

"I thought, sir, that perhaps you would put me on board some English cruiser," cried Fitz.

"And I will, of course. But it may be a month first."

"I don't mind that, sir," said Fitz, "so long as I can send a message home, for they must think I'm—"

He broke down here, for he could bear no more.

What he had thought would be all joy proved to be pain, and as he was turning away, it was with the knowledge that the American captain had read him through and through, giving him a warm pressure of the hand, and saying, just loud enough for him to hear—

"Directly I can get at the wires I'll send a message to New York, telling our people to communicate with your Admiralty, that you are alive and well."

The next minute the captain was talking with both the Reeds, and to Fitz's great satisfaction he saw that they were chatting, evidently on the most friendly terms.

As the American captain had suggested, it was nearly a month before he sailed away with Fitz on board, after a parting that made the hearts of the two lads ache, while the pressure of the skipper's hand lingered long.

But after the fashion of most boys under such circumstances they hid their emotions like men.

"I suppose," said the skipper, "I shall never have the chance to give you such a cruise again."

"No," said Fitz, laughing; "never, I should say. Good-bye, sir! Good-bye, Poole, old chap, till next time."

"Yes," said Poole merrily. "So long!"